The Auroral Entanglement

The Auroral Entanglement

James Nabi Michael

James Nabi Michael
Sept, 2022

iUniverse, Inc.
Bloomington

The Auroral Entanglement

iUniverse books may be ordered through booksellers or by contacting:

iUniverse
1663 Liberty Drive
Bloomington, IN 47403
www.iuniverse.com
1-800-Authors (1-800-288-4677)

ISBN: 978-1-4759-4466-2 (sc)
ISBN: 978-1-4759-4467-9 (hc)
ISBN: 978-1-4759-4468-6 (e)

Library of Congress Control Number: 2012914916

Printed in the United States of America

iUniverse rev. date: 09/24/2012

To Joni and Mary

Special thanks to Sebastian Voltmer and Wim Houquet for the cover photographs, and to my brother David for his help and insight.

Chapter 1

Jack walked out to his plane. The sun was just rising, and a light mist covered the ground. A low fog floated over the water of the bay, located only a stone's throw away from the airport runway. The trees on the other side of the small airport were quiet that October morning since many of the birds native to the area had already migrated south for the winter. It was getting colder and darker in the morning now. Jack had done well that year; he'd had quite a few tourists, so he was happy that things were starting to slow down a bit. He had a de Havilland Canada Beaver bush plane that sat six comfortably, and he chartered it out to people in Alaska. He loved flying and enjoyed taking tourists up to see Alaska from the sky. It was fun to see the awe in people's faces when he flew them over the rugged wilderness of Alaska's terrain.

Jack was cold, and he zipped up his faded leather jacket and pulled up the collar to try and keep his ears warm. He did his preflight inspection, slowly walking around the plane checking for anything unusual. He climbed up on the wing and checked the fuel tanks to make sure they were full. He walked around the back of the plane and checked the rudder and hinges and the vertical tail. These were things he did every day, but he always did them diligently—it was the safest way to fly. He had a few people he was taking up that day; they wanted to see McKinley, which was one of the more popular landmarks tourists liked to fly to. He loved what he was doing—beautiful area, maybe a little lonely but not that bad really. He had lots of friends, and in fact, he was meeting up with a few that

1

evening to just hang out, relax, and have a few beers after work. After he completed his preflight inspection, he walked back inside the hangar. Four people, two women and two men, were waiting there in a small office.

"All right, folks, we're ready to roll," Jack said, smiling broadly to his customers. "Hope you're not too squeamish, because it can get a little bumpy up there but … uh … you'll enjoy the ride. It's a beautiful view. Who's flown here before?"

One guy raised his hand.

"Okay, well, we've got mostly newcomers. Don't worry—it will be fun. So where are you from?"

One lady exclaimed, "I'm from New Jersey!"

"New Jersey!" Jack replied. "Well, it's quite a change of scenery for you, ma'am."

The woman smiled and nodded, then replied, "It sure is, and I'm loving it!"

Jack smiled again and then looked at his watch. "Well, it's seven thirty now, just about time to head out. The sun is just rising, and the fog will clear in the next ten minutes or so. It looks like some clear skies, so we should have a good ride."

They were flying out of Birchwood Airport that morning, an airport twenty minutes north of downtown Anchorage just off the main highway near the town of Chugiak. Jack, in fact, stored his plane there and tried to schedule most of his charter flights to McKinley from Birchwood. The airport was small but had a well-kept commercial runway and was located next to the water along the Knik Arm Bay. This made it an ideal airport for not just land but also water takeoffs and landings, and on many occasions, Jack had mounted floats to his plane for charter flights to the Aleutian Islands southwest of Anchorage.

All four of the passengers seemed to enjoy the flight that day as far as Jack could tell. It took them about an hour to get up to McKinley. He spent well over an hour flying around the mountain. He flew his plane toward the top of it and then did some nice circles closer to the base of the mountain as he pointed out scenic areas and landmarks for those who asked. It was an enjoyable trip, and the people were very pleasant and friendly. He enjoyed talking to them and getting to know a little about their backgrounds.

They made a short stopover at a small airport near the mountain. This gave the people some time to relax, check out the scenery from the ground, and get a snack. They did a little more flying near the mountain before they headed back. He landed the plane just after three o'clock that afternoon. He said good-bye to everyone, gave them a few brochures about his charter service, and thanked them all for flying with him that day.

He was going to meet up with his friends at seven o'clock. He had a few hours to burn so he ran some errands, picked up a couple things he needed for his apartment, and then headed over to meet his friends.

★★★★★

"Hey, Jack!" a deep voice called out as soon as Jack stepped into the dim, wooden-walled pub. "What's up, man?"

Jack looked toward the voice and saw his friend Bob, balding and a little overweight, leaning on the bar.

"Hi, Bob, what's going on? How are you doing? Where are you guys at?"

"Oh, we're just over there at that corner table." Bob gestured with his hand to the backside of the bar.

"Well, good, I'm just going to grab a beer at the bar and then I'll meet up with you."

"Sounds good, man."

Jack ordered his favorite micro-brewed pale ale, but the bar was busy that night and he had to wait several minutes as the bartender served up drinks to the patrons ahead of him. As he stood there at the bar waiting for his beer, it started to happen. It was the strangest thing, but it had been happening sporadically now for several years, especially at places where food was served. His mouth was filled with the tastes of food, almost as if he were tasting the food off the plates of the people around him. He looked to his left and saw a young woman taking a bite of her cheeseburger. At that moment, Jack felt his mouth fill with the taste of well-done hamburger meat and cheese. Then a few seconds later, he tasted salmon in his mouth. He looked to his right and spotted another patron sitting at the bar a few stools down eating fresh-cooked salmon. At first when this started happening several years back, he thought he must just have an oversensitive nose, but the tastes were so strong he had a hard time believing that it was just his nose. The odd thing was it didn't occur all the time, only every once in a while, and it didn't seem to follow any kind of set pattern, other than it occurred more often at bars and diners. He hadn't given it much thought; it was unusual and quite strange, but it didn't bother him too much; in fact, it was quite fun having these tastes appear in his mouth. When the bartender brought him his beer, his mind shifted, and he simply dismissed what had just happened, focusing instead on the pale ale in his hand and how all of a sudden he was quite thirsty. He took a big gulp of the beer before the bartender spoke to him.

"That'll be three fifty, Jack. Do you want to start a tab?"

"No, that's okay, Joe, I'm probably just up for a few tonight."

Jack handed Joe a five dollar bill and then headed over and sat down with his buddies.

Jack, Bob, Bryan, Darrell, and George sat around a smooth wood table, each man with a beer in front of him, with peanuts and pretzels on the table. Jack and his friends tried to meet up at least once a month. Jack had known most of these guys for several years, so they were good friends; it was a nice way to relax.

"So what have you been up to, Jack?" Bob asked as he chewed on some peanuts and took a gulp of his beer.

"Oh, not too much, just hanging. Did some flying today, took a group up to Mount McKinley, you know. Things are starting to die down a little bit now. I'm thinking about flying out of Fairbanks, probably in another couple of weeks. Things usually start picking up there by the end of October, sometimes earlier. I'll start getting some people up there who want to see the aurora borealis. It's kind of neat—I really enjoy those evening flights and all those colors in the sky."

"Wow, that's cool. Sounds pretty awesome," Bryan said as he peeled the label off his beer bottle. "What else have you been up to?"

"Oh, not too much. Just hanging out, drinking a couple of beers with my buddies."

Everyone laughed a little bit.

"So what have you guys been doing?"

"Oh, been pretty busy, pretty busy," George said as he leaned back in his chair, putting it on two legs. "Been busy out at the oil rigs. We hit a big pocket last week, got pretty hectic. We've had a few new babes come into work the other day, been trying to find out a little about them. So how's your love life, Jack?"

"Oh, I've been doing some dating. Playing the field a little bit. No one real serious, but I've been dating a couple of different women trying to get to know them better. I'll see how things pan out." Jack actually had been seeing one woman now off and on for seven months, but he didn't like to discuss the details of his love life in this type of setting.

"Cool," George said as he stroked his deep red beard.

★★★★★

They were just sitting, not saying too much, when George spoke up.

"Yeah, man, I was out at that oil rig the other day. You should have seen how much oil we pumped out of that well. We had a huge rupture in one of those oil lines, and I busted my butt trying to get that thing wrapped up. There was oil spilling out all over the place, but I got that thing fixed up; they didn't even have to shut down that pump! I must have worked fifteen hours that day, you know!"

Oh boy, Jack thought, *here he goes again.* Old George had a reputation for blowing his horn. When there was nothing to talk about, it could be somewhat fun to humor him, but sometimes it got old listening to him drone on about how great he was. At least for now, Jack sat and listened.

"Yeah, I tell you, my boss gave me a pat on the back. He said to me, 'George, I've never seen anyone bust his butt as hard as you did today. You're one of my best workers out here, you know that.' That's what he said to me, you know that, guys! That's what he said. And I tell you, know how much oil we pumped out of that well that day? You know we pumped twice as much as what they normally do, maybe three times as much."

Yeah, right, George, Jack thought, *probably more like five percent more than normal, but eh, who's counting? Let him go on,* he said to himself. *He seems to get a kick out of it.*

"Yeah, and you know these other guys I work with, they're a bunch of wimps compared to me. I'm so good, I'm the best guy out there."

Oh man, Jack thought, *I better think of something to shut him up because this is getting old.* Jack didn't mind so much when George was blowing his horn, but when he started putting down the other people he worked with, well, that was too much.

"Yeah, you know I work out so much—look at my muscles. These guys I work with can't hold a candle to me. They just go to the oil rig, work, and then go home, watch TV, and drink beer. They're not nearly as tough as I am."

Okay, Jack thought, *this is too much; I'm going to have to intervene here. He's going overboard—I don't want to hear another word. I want to talk about something else.*

"You know, George, you are just the most amazing human being. I just wish I could experience it firsthand. What do you say I become you for just a few moments. What do you think, buddy? Can we do a swap for just a few seconds, or even just a split-second?"

Everyone laughed, including George.

"Right, Jack, you couldn't handle being me even if you wanted to be."

There was another round of laughter, but it did get George to stop talking about himself so much. During the next few hours, they chatted about normal stuff—women, their jobs, the weather, their families, their plans for the winter. It was a good time.

Eventually it was starting to get late, and Jack had to get up early the next morning.

"It's about ten thirty, guys. I'm heading out. Don't want to get up too late tomorrow morning." Jack said good-bye to his friends and headed back to his apartment.

*****

Jack rented a small apartment in Anchorage. He spent a good portion of the year in Anchorage because that was where the work was. He liked Anchorage, but it was a little too much of a big city atmosphere for him. He also owned an older house up in Fairbanks, where he felt more at home. He didn't get to spend much time there, but during the off-season, he lived there and spent most of his time renovating the house. It was difficult working on the house in the winter, but before complete darkness set in, he would work on his outside projects even with the few hours of daylight. He had a huge flood lamp, as well, if he needed to do some work on the outside of the house after the sky turned dark. In the evenings, he would work inside, renovating the rooms.

Fairbanks was more secluded than Anchorage, and he felt more like an explorer or adventurer living there. For his Fairbanks tours, he usually flew out of Fairbanks International Airport from a hangar on the north side of the runway, but there was a small private airport located only a few minutes from his house in a rural neighborhood. When Jack was in Fairbanks but not doing tours, he would park his plane there and make the short walk to his home. Even this late in the season, he could still pull together a trip out of Anchorage, but Fairbanks started picking up in the fall and winter. In Fairbanks, you could see the aurora borealis more clearly and vividly, and he got a fair share of business from aurora hunters who wanted to see the phenomenon from the sky. The aurora borealis was fascinating; in fact, sometimes when there was a really spectacular one, Jack would fly up into the night sky on his own.

The aurora borealis exists in the earth's upper atmosphere, in the range of two hundred to three hundred thousand feet. Jack's plane could only climb to about eighteen thousand feet on a good day, but even then, it seemed so close that you could reach out and touch it. Sometimes he'd take off when it was vivid in the sky and he'd fly straight toward it. His plane could climb better than most, and he'd point the nose straight up, facing right toward the aurora borealis, and he'd imagine he was flying right through it, like flying through a rainbow. He would not do this with the tourists—it would probably scare them a bit—but every so often he would do it himself. With the tourists, he would first spend some time on the ground letting them absorb its beauty, and then they would board the plane and gently climb, while Jack turned the plane to capture the full panorama of the spectacle. As they climbed up and up, he would do figure eights, so that the passengers on both sides of the plane could get a good view.

It was difficult to schedule his flights since there was no set time the aurora borealis would appear, but he would scan all the forecasts, particularly from one station that kept track of the sun's activity twenty-four hours a day and could predict with relatively fine accuracy when an aurora borealis would occur. The aurora borealis is most spectacular when an unusually large number of light photons from the sun strike and excite tiny particles in the earth's upper atmosphere. Since the aurora is most pronounced within a twelve- to seventy-two-hour period after major sun activity, with an accurate account of prominent sunbursts, the forecast was fairly reliable. He advertised his services around many of the local hotels in Fairbanks and gave a number that people could call to get an update on aurora borealis activity and when Jack had flights scheduled. It worked quite well; many visitors to Alaska were there for a week or two, which gave them time to schedule something in advance. During peak season, Jack could usually get four or five people to go up with him to see the aurora from his plane; but in early October, he was lucky to get one or two at a time. It was quite fun, but sometimes the passengers would be a bit disappointed if the aurora borealis were faint. Usually, though, it worked out well, and people were satisfied with what they saw.

When Jack got home that evening from the bar, he checked with his forecaster to see the level of sunburst activity. Sure enough, within the next day, an exceptionally vivid aurora borealis was expected. *Shoot*, Jack thought, *it's a little early in the season, isn't it?* Usually the best sightings were toward the end of October or the beginning of November when the nights were longer; this one was unusual, since it was only the first day of October. *Well*, Jack thought to himself, *I should have checked in earlier; I could have lined up a good tour. If I hadn't headed to the bar to sit and listen to George go on about his escapades, I could have pulled something together.*

Usually people would check his recording and book a seat the day before the scheduled flight. Sometimes people would book the day of the flight, but this was rare, especially this early in the season. *Oh well, there's a missed opportunity,* he thought. *If I can get up there tomorrow, maybe I can get a few people to go up.* He didn't have anything scheduled out of Anchorage for four days, so it was worth a try. It was almost midnight, but Jack called his message service and changed his recording with the new information.

★★★★★

He got up at six o'clock the next morning, headed down to the airport, and took off for Fairbanks.

It was doubtful he would be able to line up a group for the anticipated aurora, but he had some time to kill *so what the heck,* he thought. It was a beautifully clear, crisp morning. It was mornings like these that he loved about living in Alaska. His mind started wandering during the flight; he couldn't seem to focus very well, but since it was so clear and calm, it was an easy flight. It took him just over two hours at a leisurely one-hundred-and-twenty-knot pace.

On his way, he contacted his friend Rich, who was stationed at the airport. "Hey, Rich, how are you doing?"

"Jack! What's up—did you have fun down in Anchorage?"

"Yeah, you know, same old same old. So how's the report looking on the aurora borealis?"

"Oh, Jack, you should have been up here a few days earlier—you could have lined up a good trip. It's looking like it's going to be a pretty major one, quite an unusual coronal mass ejection yesterday and it's continuing. By tonight, we'll see the effect in the sky, especially north of Fairbanks."

"Great," Jack replied. "So what have you been up to, Rich?"

"Oh, been doing a little ice fishing, getting ready for the winter. The wife's doing well, and the little baby is just learning how to walk. We're going to put some snowshoes on her pretty quick. Get her on some cross-country skis soon or something."

"Sounds like fun," Jack replied. "It must be pretty neat having a little baby."

"Oh yeah, you know, she can be a pain sometimes, but usually she's a lot of fun."

"That's great," Jack said. "Well, thanks for the info, Rich. Talk to you soon."

"Sure thing, Jack," Rich replied.

★★★★★

When Jack got in later that morning, about ten o'clock, he checked his messages. One guy had called asking about going up, but he wasn't sure if he could arrange it since he wanted to bring his wife along but she was feeling a bit ill. *Hmm,* Jack thought, *maybe an opportunity here. I should get an update for tonight.*

He checked back with Rich to see. "So, Rich, how's it looking?"

"This one just keeps getting better," Rich replied. "It's going to be quite spectacular tonight, although it looks like it will dissipate by tomorrow. If you're going to jump on it, Jack, tonight is the night. The forecast is for crystal clear skies too. It's unusual to have such a good one this early, and I don't think we'll have anything exceptional for at least four weeks, closer to normal season."

"All right, Rich, thanks for the update. Have fun with the little one, okay?"

"Sure, Jack, swing by when you have the chance—you're always welcome. Talk to you later."

"Talk to you later, Rich," Jack replied.

Jack replaced the message on his recording machine with more detailed information about the aurora borealis in case others called in. Then he called back the guy who had phoned earlier. He was staying at the White Sand Hotel, but he was not there when Jack called. Jack left a message confirming availability and told him to expect a spectacular one.

By now it was eleven thirty, and he went out and grabbed something to eat. He checked his messages when he got back, but no one had called.

Hmm, Jack thought, *well, I have a few things to do on the plane—might as well get out there and attend to them.*

He went out and cleaned up the interior of the plane and then checked the oil and tire pressures. He played around with the radios a little bit to make sure he had them set with the right transponder frequencies and the weather stations tuned in for Fairbanks.

I might as well go ahead and file a flight plan, he thought. *I might not even go up tonight, but it can't hurt to have it ready in case the guy calls me.* He went back inside about three o'clock into the small makeshift office located in the middle of the hangar. The office was located there to better protect it from the weather outside. It had two large airplane bays on either side of it. He checked his recordings, and sure enough, the guy had called and had left a message.

"Yes, Jack, I got your message. Yes, I'm definitely interested, but I'm not sure if I can get my wife to go up. I wanted to take her along, but she's been a little under the weather so it's iffy. Give me a couple of hours, if you could, and I'll let you know."

Jack called him back, and luckily he was still in his room.

"Hi, Stan, this is Jack from the charter service. Yes, I just wanted to let you know that this is an unusual one so early in the season, and it will most likely dissipate by tomorrow night. We probably won't have another good one for three or four weeks, so it's a good opportunity."

"Yeah, well, I've seen several from the ground, but to get in a plane and fly toward it, now that's got to be a sight. We're leaving next week, so I really want to go."

"You won't regret it, Stan. It's a different experience from watching on the ground. When you're sixteen thousand feet up, it's almost like you could put out your hand and touch it. Nothing quite like it," Jack replied.

"All right, Jack, I'm going to give it my best shot. My wife's been grumbling that she'd rather just sit on the porch and watch with the flu and all, but she might be feeling better in a few hours."

"Okay, no problem. I'll be here till ten o'clock, so just give me a call once you've decided. I like to take off by nine or nine thirty, but by ten thirty at the latest. We'll be up for at least an hour, maybe two, so usually around nine o'clock is the best time to be in the air."

"All right, well, thanks for the information. As soon as I know something for sure, I'll give you a call," Stan replied.

Jack filed the flight plan. No one else had called, and this late it was doubtful anyone would. He checked again on the forecast—still the same. *Shoot,* Jack thought, *I might even go up by myself if this doesn't pan out.* He did this every so often, but only when it was worth it. He had seen so many, only something that really grabbed his eye was of any interest anymore.

It was starting to get dark and he had finished everything on the plane that needed to be done, so he sat down at his desk and pulled out a book. He didn't want to leave the airport in case Stan and his wife wanted to come over, so he sat and read. The book was one of his favorites, *Zen and the Art of Motorcycle Maintenance.* A book about the relationship between a father and his son as they rode across the country on a motorcycle, but it was so much more. The book was a journey about transcendence and philosophy and about finding oneself. He had read it several times, but during these waiting periods, it was one of his favorite ways to relax.

There were a few people still around. One of the mechanics was out in the hangar working on a plane, and another guy was doing some paperwork—but it was mostly quiet. He read for several hours, and finally about a quarter past eight, Stan called. "Jack, I'm sorry, but I'm not going to make it tonight. My wife's still ill. We're from New Mexico, and my wife just wasn't quite prepared for this Alaskan cold. She got a bug almost as soon as we got off the plane. She doesn't like the idea of being alone on our vacation, so I think I'm just going to sit on the hotel porch and watch instead."

"No problem. I understand. You never know—we might have something again next week. If not, if you ever find your way back to Alaska, don't hesitate to call. We'd love to have you join us."

"I'll do that. Thanks."

"Take care, Stan, and maybe we'll talk again some other time."

"Take care, Jack."

Oh well, Jack thought, *he seemed like a decent fellow; it's too bad it didn't work out.*

It was dark by now, and Jack had been inside for several hours. He hadn't had a chance to look at the night sky, but at nine o'clock he walked out of the hangar building. As he looked up, his eyes were caught by the most brilliant aurora borealis he had ever seen. There were multiple colors dancing across the sky. Typically the auroras were in one color, usually light green or a pinkish red, but this one consisted of multicolored ribbonlike fingers that stretched from one side of the sky to another, almost like a cosmic artist had taken his paintbrush and painted long, wide, vertical streaks across the heavens.

"My god!" Jack exclaimed. "There are reds and greens, and violets and blues, and even a tinge of yellow there."

Jack had seen over a hundred auroras but nothing quite like this one. Not only was it brilliant; it covered over 70 percent of the night sky—most cover only 30 percent of the sky at best. It seemed to be so low in the sky as well, almost like you could reach out your hand and touch it.

"Fascinating!" Jack exclaimed. "Wow!"

It was only nine o'clock, and Jack didn't have much to do—other than go home and watch the local news or something. *What the heck,* he thought, *might as well go up for a joyride.* He went back inside to get the keys to his airplane, grabbed a digital camera out of his desk, and wondered if anyone wanted to go up with him. The old mechanic, Ralph, was still in the hangar working on the plane, but Jack remembered he didn't like to fly, especially at night, and no one else was around. He thought he'd give Ralph a try at least.

"Ralph, have you seen the spectacle out there?"

"Yes, I did just a few minutes ago. Never seen anything quite like it."

"Me neither," Jack replied. "I don't have anything to do tonight, so I'm heading up for a joyride. Not interested, are you?"

"Nah, you know me, those small planes scare me. But have fun, okay, Jack?"

"I sure will. Talk to you later."

Well, it looks like a solo flight this time, Jack thought to himself.

He climbed into his plane and took off. During his preflight run-up, he had made sure all the radios worked and he could track to the VOR beacon he used for navigation at night. Sometimes his customers would ask if the auroras disturbed his instruments. No, he would always assure them, the auroras were typically 250,000 feet up, or about fifty miles, too far up to cause any problems—and in any case, the preflight run-up would catch any anomalies. As any good pilot would, Jack did his preflight run-up as if passengers were on board; his routine was the same regardless.

As he climbed, he looked up into the brilliant night sky. The aurora seemed to hang unusually low—Jack suspected a height of one hundred thousand feet or so—but as he climbed and could begin to see the texture of its lower surface, he noticed a strange aberration, something even more peculiar. Off in the distance, probably twenty to thirty miles away, there was a fingerlike portion of the aurora that stretched down toward the ground. Like the rest of the aurora, it was multicolored, with thin strands of colored light that wrapped around each other like different colored yarn that had been twisted to make a strand. *No,* Jack thought, it reminded him more of a tornado funnel cloud stretching down from the rest of the aurora, but the funnel cloud was opaque. He could see through it, but at the same time, could make out distantly colored wrapped ribbons of light that formed the funnel. *Fascinating,* Jack thought. He flew toward it, captured by its presence.

As he flew, he took out his digital camera and took several photos of the aurora, first banking steeply to the right and then momentarily taking his hands off the controls as he snapped a shot from the left side window. He then pointed the nose of the aircraft in a steep climb and took several shots out the front window. As he got closer to the funnel, he took a few more photos as it came into clearer view. As he approached, it appeared that the bottom of the funnel was only a few thousand feet above him. He was at twelve thousand feet, and he put the plane in a steady climb, hoping to get level with the bottom of the funnel. It was still forming, and by the time he was a few miles away, he could see that the funnel stretched down below him, his altitude now at sixteen thousand feet. The aurora seemed to take on a power all its own, and Jack was drawn toward it, foregoing the thoughts in the back of his mind to keep his distance. Its beauty and uniqueness pulled him closer, like someone or something was taking over his mind, beckoning him to experience the phenomenon completely.

He pointed the nose of his airplane toward the funneled aberration and flew straight through it. Despite the funnel shape of the aberration, the wind was calm as he passed through the aurora. The colored light danced all over his airplane like multicolored fireflies that were swarming around his plane. It took him just over a minute to fly from one side to the other.

As he flew through it, he thought to himself, *Are you nuts, Jack? What are you doing?* But he continued on, seemingly oblivious to his inner thoughts, which emphasized caution. As he exited the funnel, he turned his plane to the left and circled the aurora funnel, staying a few hundred yards away from its edge. He checked his instruments and radios to see if anything unusual had happened to his plane. Everything appeared normal.

He turned sharply and headed back into the aurora and began a spiral climb up through the center of the aberration, climbing steadily as the colored light danced across his wings. It was much brighter in the aurora than in the night sky, but it was not as bright as daylight. It reminded him of an amusement park ride at night, with flashing lights that lit up the ride and made the rider forget that darkness was only a few feet away. He kept climbing until he was close to his maximum altitude of eighteen thousand feet, where the plane struggled to gain additional altitude. Then he turned his plane to the right and began a long spiral descent through the aurora. As he picked up speed, the display of light across his wings was spectacular. The air flowed more quickly across his wings, taking the light from the aurora with it, appearing almost like colored caramel that flowed across the wings as they sliced through the air.

He descended until he came out of the bottom of the funnel at around twelve thousand feet, and then he turned his plane around and began another ascent back to 17,500 feet. When he got to altitude this time, he pulled the nose up at a steep angle and waited for the airplane to stall; then, as the nose dropped, he applied full left rudder and sent the airplane into a controlled spin. He had done this maneuver many times, first as a student pilot twenty years prior as part of his training, and then periodically throughout his time as a pilot to keep his skills intact. In fact, during the check rides he needed every two years to keep his license current, several examiners had asked him to demonstrate entry into and recovery from a spin. It was a common maneuver, one any good pilot could perform successfully.

Beyond that, Jack mused, *it's also a lot of fun.*

Jack spun his airplane down through the auroral funnel. With the spectacular display outside his window and the sensation of g-forces as he spun, he began to laugh. He was on a natural high; in fact, he felt a little giddy.

"I haven't had this much fun flying in years," Jack laughed as his plane descended.

He exited the bottom of the funnel, applied full right rudder, and brought the nose of the airplane up gently to recover from the spin. Then he turned and began another ascent. He climbed back to seventeen thousand feet and performed the maneuver again, dropping down to just below thirteen thousand feet. As he climbed this time, though, he could see the aberration beginning to recede back into the night sky. He was able to fly his plane to the bottom edge of the funnel before it started to quickly dissipate back into the heavens. By the time he reached seventeen thousand feet again, the funnel was almost gone; he could just glimpse its dying embers as it was sucked back into the flat texture of the full aurora.

"Now that was an experience!" Jack exclaimed.

He looked up at the full aurora, and in fact, it was starting to dissipate as well. As he watched, he could see the yellows and blues and greens being replaced with a red pinkish glow, similar to so many other auroras he had seen in the past. *I think I've seen the best of it,* Jack thought to himself, and he turned his plane toward the airport.

When he was close to the airport, he called in his intention to land.

"Fairbanks traffic, this is Beaver 45656 Tango inbound for landing." Jack's radio didn't work, he could tell by the lack of feedback from the mike. He tried again after tapping the mike against his leg.

"Fairbanks traffic, de Havilland Beaver 45656 Tango inbound for landing," but again nothing. He tried to contact the intercom controller on the ground at Fairbanks but got no response. *Well, maybe this wasn't such a good idea,* he thought to himself. This wasn't the first time his radios had malfunctioned, so he tried to remain calm.

I'll just have to deal with this tomorrow, Jack thought; *it's getting late, and I'm low on fuel—time to get this plane on the ground.* All his aircraft lights were still working, so after looking all around him to make sure there was not any other traffic in the area, he entered the traffic pattern. As was standard procedure for a plane without a working radio, he rocked his wings as he turned into the pattern. He continued to look for other aircraft, but since it was so late at night, he doubted he would see any. The air was calm, and he brought the plane down gently and without incident. He taxied back to the hangar, parked the plane, and walked inside to get the keys to his truck and grab a few things. Ralph had gone home by now. He was alone. He was tired. It had been a long day, but he had enjoyed himself. As he drove home that night, all he could think about were those dancing multicolored fireflies he had played with earlier that night, fifteen thousand feet up in the sky.

Chapter 2

The next morning was crystal clear just like the night before. Jack was in no rush, so he slept in till nine o'clock and then did a few odds and ends around the house. He also checked his digital camera for the photos he had taken the night before, but unfortunately, his camera had malfunctioned and none of the photos were saved. *That's odd,* Jack thought, *just like the radio.* It was too bad—he was looking forward to seeing how they turned out. He decided to head back to the airport.

When he got there, he noticed something odd about his plane, but he couldn't quite put his finger on it. As he walked to the back of the plane, he saw the problem. On the back of his plane, mounted to the top of the vertical tail, was a static discharge antenna, commonly referred to as a "discharge rod." It was standard equipment on all planes. On Jack's plane, the main antenna was on the vertical tail, but he also had smaller rods mounted on his wing tips. Their purpose was to discharge static electricity that the plane picked up from the surrounding air. Over time, the rods would erode away, sacrificing themselves to prevent any malfunction in electrical equipment from any electrical overflow.

About every two years, Jack would replace the discharge antennas on his plane because of normal wear, and he had done this only three weeks prior. The odd thing was that the twelve-inch-tall discharge antenna he had mounted on his vertical tail just weeks ago was gone. The only thing that remained was a stub of material left where the antenna was mounted. He walked around to the discharge antennas on his wing tips, and he saw the same except they were completely gone; the only things left were the mounting brackets and screws that attached the antennas to the wing tips.

Well, that explains the problem with the radios, Jack muttered to himself. *There must have been a heck of a lot of electricity floating around my airframe to do that to those antennas, or maybe some type of magnetic field. Of course, it must have been the aurora borealis,* Jack thought. *What else would explain it? Well, the antennas are easy to replace; I just hope my radios aren't shot.* He climbed into the pilot's seat, turned the power on, and checked his radios and electrical equipment. Oddly, everything was functioning properly.

He miked a message over to the Fairbanks control tower, and they responded, "Yeah, Jack, you're coming in loud and clear, doesn't seem to be a problem, not as far as we can tell."

Well, that's lucky, Jack thought, *it must have been some type of surge, a brief anomaly that's corrected itself. It might be a good idea to change out my fuses just in case.* He went into the hangar building and bought a new set at the pilot's shop, went back to his plane, and replaced all of them. *I'll keep my eye on it, but there's no use in doing anything else right now,* he thought to himself.

Jack climbed in his truck and drove into downtown Fairbanks, where there was a fairly well-stocked airplane supply house located in the industrial area of town. Jack bought equipment from them periodically; the parts there were more expensive, but when he needed something in a hurry, it was his best shot.

"Hey, Frank, how's it going?"

"Good, Jack. What can we get for you?" Frank replied. Frank was an older gentleman whose face was weather-beaten from years of exposure to the Fairbanks wind and cold, but his blue eyes were still bright and he smiled warmly when he saw Jack. Frank had been working the store for twenty years, and he and Jack had developed a casual friendship.

"I need some discharge rods. One for the tail and for the wing tips as well."

"No problem, we've got them in stock."

Frank went into the back and came out with the rods.

"Did you get a chance to see the northern lights last night, Frank?"

"Sure did, Jack, quite a sight. Were you able to line up a tour? It would have been a good one to see from the sky."

"No," Jack replied, "but you know, in fact, I went up myself. It was one of the most incredible experiences I've had flying. I actually flew right through part of the aurora."

"Come on now, Jack, we all know those lights are fifty miles up. What'd you do, buy yourself one of those space planes or something?" Frank replied, a comically skeptical look on his face.

"No, I'm serious, it was some type of anomaly, like a funnel cloud, that stretched down below fifteen thousand feet. It only lasted for thirty minutes or so."

"I've never heard of such a thing," Frank replied.

"Yeah, it's why I'm replacing those rods. Don't you remember, I bought a set only a few weeks ago."

"Not from me, you didn't. Are you pulling my leg again, Jack? Like the time you told me you did a double loop in that hang glider of yours?"

Jack had tried to do a loop in his hang glider earlier that year, in July, but he had pulled out when his airspeed dropped off too quickly. He was just having fun with Frank about it during a round of beers, trying to make the escapade a little more interesting than it really was. Later that night, George had told Frank the real story. George had been Jack's chase driver that day and had seen the loop attempt.

"No, no," Jack chuckled, "this was for real, it was."

"Anything you say, Jack. You want me to put this on your line of credit?"

From Frank's tone, Jack could tell there was no point in trying to convince him, and there were other customers waiting in line.

"Sure, Frank, that's fine. See you again soon, okay?"

"Okay, Jack. Talk to you later."

Jack was halfway back to the airport when it dawned on him. *That's right, isn't it,* Jack thought to himself, *I bought those discharge rods mail order, not from Frank. No wonder he was so skeptical.*

★★★★★

By three o'clock that Wednesday, Jack had installed the new rods. He went inside to check and see if any auroras were forecast in the next several days. There were none expected, and no one had called that day about going up for a flight. He decided to head back to Anchorage. It was pointless to stay in Fairbanks, and he had a tour set up in Anchorage on Sunday. Sometimes potential and even scheduled customers would want to come to the airport and meet with him, so it helped if he was available the few days prior to a tour. *Besides,* he thought to himself, *a few friends are going to meet up on Friday night.* With nothing much to do, it would be a fun way to spend the evening.

★★★★★

Jack was running a little late on Friday, but he got over to the bar by eight o'clock. The bar's name was the White Elephant; it was one of George's favorite hangouts. It sat on the outskirts of Anchorage, where a lot of the men and women involved in the oil business came for an evening drink. It had a rugged but friendly atmosphere, a perfect setting for George and his friends. When Jack got there, he ordered a drink and then wandered over to the table where his friends sat.

"Hey, boys, how's it going?"

"Jack, what's going on? We didn't think you'd make it tonight."

"I wouldn't miss it for the world," Jack replied in a jokingly sarcastic tone. His eyes wandered across the table, and he noticed that George was sitting at the end of the table. His leg, propped up on top of one of the wooden chairs, was covered in a cast.

"George, what the heck happened?"

"Ah, you know, just a little scratch."

"You break that leg or something, George?"

"Aw, come on," George replied, "do I have to keep explaining this to every one of you guys? Maybe you should have all shown up at once so I wouldn't have to keep repeating the story over and over again."

The others laughed—it was so typical of George to act this way. He had a proudly masculine demeanor about him, and to have to describe this type of mishap repeatedly was not something he took delight in doing.

"All right, George, well, you can tell it one more time. There's no one else coming tonight, I promise. Just lay it on the line one more time for your friend Jack."

"Aw, you know," George replied, "just one of those little accidents at work."

"When did it happen, George?" Philip asked. Philip was a regular at these social gatherings; he had known George and Jack for ten years now.

"Oh, about four days ago. Mind you, I was at work the next day," George proudly replied.

"Just like my old George, that is," Jack said with a playful boisterousness. "So what happened, old boy—did you fall off a ladder or something?"

"Not quite."

The others sat and waited while George took a gulp of beer from his mug. Sensing the others didn't mind listening one more time, he began his tale again.

"Well, like I said last time we met, we've been pumping a lot of oil recently. And you know how those things go—when you're working that hard, sometimes those maintenance things you should do every day get missed. Well, as usual, all week I was working my butt off and the other guys were slacking, and this was part of the problem."

Right, Jack thought, *you mean you were smoking a cigarette while the other guys were working,* but it didn't matter, he wanted to hear the story.

"Well, you see," George continued, "one of largest pumps on the site blew a hose. The guy the night before forgot to shut one of the valves off, and this overloaded a worn hose and caused it to blow. So, of course, when I got on the site in the morning, I noticed it immediately and got to changing it right then and there. It wasn't an easy job, so I had Shawn, our foreman, helping me. I was leaning over the pump trying to tighten down a bolt, but I couldn't quite get to it so I asked Shawn to get me a socket extension. Well, it was a little cramped up there on the platform, and when Shawn got up to find one, he knocked my leg from the side. Well, with the snow mixed in with the spilled oil, it was slick as a willy up there, and I began to slip."

"That leg fold up underneath you, George?" Jack asked.

"No, no, I began to slide, but then I caught myself, then caught myself again, and by this time, I was inches from the railing. Well, I grabbed Shawn to stop myself from going over the edge, but when I grabbed him, he starting coming over too. Well, instinctively the bastard pushed me away, and before I could react, I careened over the rail and fell to the platform below."

"The bastard," Darrell repeated, nodding his head. Darrell was a schoolteacher from Anchorage who shared Jack's passion for flying and hang gliding.

"You can say that again," George said. "I must have fallen a good twenty feet, and when I finally hit the platform below, my ankle took a bad turn and twisted my leg around. Well, when my leg twisted, it smacked right into the side of an oil line fitting sticking out from the platform, and I heard a snap and then just felt massive pain."

"Man," Jack said, "that sounds bad; it's a good thing you didn't hit your noggin on that platform—it could have been a lot worse. So where did you break it exactly?"

"Oh, right in the middle of the femur, about ten inches down from my hip," George replied casually as he took a swig of his beer. "Broke it clean in two. Once I got to the hospital, the doctor braced it up really well. He said if it heals up well, I could be back on the job in five to six weeks."

"They must have given you some strong painkillers, George. Are you sure it's okay for you to be drinking beers with us? Those things don't mix too well with alcohol, you know," Jack said.

"Don't be my mother, okay, Jack?" George said in an irritated tone. "Yeah, I was pretty doped up for a few days there, but I stopped taking the painkillers they gave me. That stuff's just not good for you, and besides, I like the taste of beer."

Everyone chuckled.

"Yeah, I can't argue with that one, George," replied Sam as he took a gulp of beer and leaned back in his chair. Sam worked out at the oil rigs with George.

"You're going to stay at home for a while then?" Jack asked.

"Well, you know, they said I could work in the office for a while and keep my current pay. Do stuff like figure out how much we pumped that day, see who came into work and who didn't, you know the kind of crap I hate to do, the bean-counting stuff, but it will keep me busy until my leg heals up."

"Yeah, that's the way it is sometimes," Jack said. "You should be a little more careful next time, George."

"Yeah, yeah, Jack, I don't need that crap. I get it from everyone I work with; I don't need it from you too."

Jack chuckled, "Okay, George. I'm sorry, buddy; I was just trying to console you a bit."

"I don't need consoling, Jack. I'm a big man. I don't need someone crying for me, and I sure don't need someone trying to patronize me either," George replied sternly.

Oh boy, Jack thought, *I shouldn't have said anything. It doesn't take much to touch him off, especially when it has to do with his masculinity.*

"Okay, George, I'm sorry you broke your leg, but you know I still wish I could be you, even for just a few moments!"

Suddenly Jack felt a shooting pain run through the middle of his leg. *My god, what was that?* Jack thought. It lasted for just a split-second, but it was an intense, concentrated pain. At the same time, he saw images flashing before his eyes, so quick he couldn't quite make sense of them. It shocked Jack, and he came outside of himself for an instant and into a daze momentarily. When he recovered, he looked up, and everyone around the table was staring at him blankly.

"What's wrong, Jack?" George said. "You look like you've just seen a ghost or something."

"What? Oh, I mean ... god, I just fazed out there for a second; something strange came over me."

"Yeah, right, Jack," George said, "you playing with us or something?"

"No, no, I just … um …"

"Anyway," George said, "I'll get over this in a little while. Can't we pick on someone else now? I know, let's talk about how Jack crashed his plane a couple of years ago. Yeah, let's do that—what do you say, Jack?"

Jack had crashed his plane several years back during an emergency landing after an engine failure. He was attempting to land on a country road at dusk when his left wing tip clipped a tree and spun the plane around, damaging the wing and landing gear.

"Okay, okay, George, enough tit for tat. Come on now," Jack said as he raised his hand, "we're all friends, aren't we? It's Friday night—let's try to have a good time, all right?"

George eased up after that. Jack and Darrell began to talk about hang gliding and how they were looking forward to the following summer, when they could break their hang gliders out in earnest again. George talked with Sam and Philip at length about a nurse he had met while he was in the hospital. Jack felt a little light-headed the rest of the night—it might have been the beers or maybe just the atmosphere—but he was enjoying himself. By twelve thirty and after his fourth beer, he decided to head home.

"What's the matter, Jack? Leaving already? Come on, buddy, we're just getting started. Tomorrow's Saturday—you don't have to get up early," Sam said as Jack got up to leave.

"Yeah, that's true," Jack said. "Aw, what the heck, maybe one more round."

Jack sat down for another beer. When he was through, he finally got up to leave. "All right, guys, see you next time around, okay? And, George, take care of that leg."

It was the first time anyone had even mentioned George's leg since Jack and George's friendly little confrontation earlier that night—and George didn't appreciate getting reminded of his accident.

"Yeah, yeah, why don't you just take care of your brain, Jack, okay? That's what you need to take care of."

"Very funny, George. All right, guys, see you later."

Jack hadn't driven that night. He had just walked over, since his apartment was only fifteen minutes away by foot. He wasn't very sleepy when he got home, so he sat on his porch for a little while thinking. He thought back to earlier that night when he seemed to come out of himself for a split-second; even now, he continued to see brief flashes shooting across his mind. The most vivid image was of a woman singing a Gaelic folk song, and he remembered the stinging pain that shot through his leg earlier. It was strange, and it bothered him that he couldn't understand it.

Before Jack went to bed, he filled up the bird feeder he had on his porch. The feeder was almost empty, and often in the morning, birds would come for a meal. Sometimes, especially this time of year, Jack would see eagles flying near his apartment, so he decided to fill the feeder with a meat-based feed similar to dog food but with fish chunks added as well. On a good morning, Jack would sit on one side of the porch, and the birds would feed on the other side, unfettered by his presence.

He was tired, but he didn't sleep well that night. He tossed and turned, and woke up several times in the night with images floating in his head. The image of a woman singing Gaelic kept reappearing, but he also saw others, more distant and faint but there nonetheless. Another image that reappeared was one of a beautiful coral reef with dolphins swimming nearby, in an ocean with a dark, almost ghostlike appearance.

When he awoke late the next morning, he fixed himself a cup of coffee. It was another clear morning, with temperatures in the low fifties, unusual for October. Jack took his cup of coffee and sat down on the porch, hoping to see some birds feeding. He had a nice view of the landscape from his porch. Out to his right was a flat plateau, with a tall ridge of mountains beyond it.

As he sipped his coffee, off to his right toward the ridge of mountains, he saw a beautiful black eagle flying. Its wings were spread out, catching the morning breeze as it glided effortlessly through the air. The eagle flew closer and closer. Jack sat very still, hoping not to scare the eagle off. As the eagle flew closer, Jack sensed it was growing suspicious of his presence, but it continued to fly toward the porch, a few times turning its head quickly to see if the shape sitting in one corner of the porch had moved. Finally after several minutes, the eagle set its feet down onto the porch railing.

Jack had set up the feeder so that a big bird such as an eagle could sit on the rails and lean over to feed. The eagle started to feed but periodically would look up and stare at Jack. It was a beautiful bird. From its size and wingspan, Jack could tell it was a male. On its back, Jack spotted two unusual markings. There were two red splotches of color on his tail section just behind his wings, each about the size of a quarter. *That's unusual,* Jack thought, *they're so symmetric as if they had been placed there on purpose.* Jack suspected the eagle was getting ready to migrate and was having trouble finding food. In a couple of weeks, he would be gone.

The eagle stared at Jack quizzically, and Jack stared back at the bird's dark penetrating eyes. They stared at each other for what must have been five minutes, it seemed, as if the bird were waiting in anticipation of something. It was strange to Jack, and it made him think back to the night before. Jack started to put the pieces together. Of course, the pain in his leg matched George's pain, the pain so intense because George hadn't been using painkillers. Then he thought about that image of the Gaelic singer, and he remembered George talking to Sam and Philip about one of the nurses he had met in the hospital. George had struck up a conversation with her, commenting on her thick Irish accent, and after she felt relaxed talking with him, she told him she had been rehearsing every night as a Gaelic singer and her first live performance was going to be at a local club that showcased new talent. After George was released from the hospital, he headed to the club to listen to her perform. *How could I forget?* Jack mused; *he talked about her all night.* And it had only been a few weeks since George returned from a vacation in Australia along the Great Barrier Reef. Jack recalled a story George had told about how he had been scuba diving when a brief but strong storm had blown in. George decided to stay in the water and watch as a few dolphins played nearby. It all seemed to make sense.

Am I losing my mind? Jack thought to himself. *How could this be?* Jack hadn't been paying attention to the eagle, but when he heard a ruffling of feathers, he looked up to see the bird jumping off the railing as he flapped his wings and began to fly back toward the ridge.

Jack looked at him as he flew away and thought to himself, *I wonder, I wonder if I could live as this bird lives, if I could fly as this bird flies.*

"You're thinking crazy, man," Jack said out loud. "Whatever nerve fiber you have that keeps you from losing it, well, you just lost it, man." But there was another voice in his head that told him to move forward and experiment—something incredible was happening to him. The eagle was only forty feet away, well within hearing distance, and Jack stood up quickly as if on a whim and yelled at the bird, "Come back, you beautiful bird, come back! Can we play for a little while? Let me play with you; let me fly with you!"

And suddenly Jack was flying over the city, atop the eagle with its wings spread wide. He looked behind him and saw a man standing on the porch with a cup of coffee in his hand, and then he looked ahead as they flew closer and closer toward the ridge. It was a beautiful, gorgeous sight. He had done this type of thing in his hang glider, but it wasn't the same. There was nothing around him, just the sleek beauty of the eagle's body. It was the reason Jack wanted to fly in the first place—to feel the freedom of the sky, the sense of tranquility, and the rush of the air. He pointed the eagle's beak down and descended quickly, then pulled up as he turned swiftly to the left. It was spectacular to fly freely through the air, not encased by a big metallic chunk of structure or covered overhead by a bulky canopy.

Jack started to manipulate the eagle's wings to see how it flew. He brought the eagle's right wing tight to his side, and then tipped his left wing up to send the bird into a series of tight rolls.

"Wow!" Jack exclaimed. "That's amazing!"

Then he flew up into a long arch, but when he reached the apex, just as he started to become weightless, he tipped the bird's tail down and sent the bird over his head, falling flat onto his back. He then slowly pulled the eagle's left wing in, rolling his torso into a long, graceful, arching descent before arresting the descent with a slow, gentle pullout.

Jack wanted to reach the ridge and look over it across the great Alaskan wilderness, and he flapped the bird's wings faster and faster to gain speed. Suddenly he was sitting back in his chair on the porch sipping his morning coffee.

"Whoa, what was that?" Jack said out loud. "Was that a dream?" It seemed too real to be a dream, but what was it then? Some type of strange aberration?

Jack got up and looked for the eagle. He looked toward the ridge but didn't see anything. Was this some type of fantasy he had experienced? Maybe there wasn't an eagle at all that morning—it was all dreamed up in his head. He kept looking and then suddenly, far off in the distance, he saw the eagle flying gracefully away from the city and toward the ridge. By now the eagle was just a speck in the sky; Jack guessed he was at least half a mile away.

Jack stood up quickly and yelled out at the eagle again, "Let me fly with you!" but the eagle was so far away that Jack was sure it couldn't hear his voice.

What was this strange power he seemed to have acquired? It didn't seem real, but he remembered what happened with George the night before and now the eagle. *It couldn't just be some type of coincidence—it's happened twice now,* Jack thought.

Jack finished his coffee and then got up and went inside to fix himself some breakfast, but he was out of eggs. He threw some jeans on and headed downstairs to a grocery store down the street. The store was run by Phyllis, an older woman Jack knew through her son, Scott. When Scott was a young teenager, he would spend his afternoons after school at the airport in Anchorage and had asked Jack one day if he needed some help with his plane. Jack could sense his enthusiasm, and although Jack didn't really need a helping hand, he told Scott he could use him part-time. Jack paid him a decent wage for a young teenager, and Scott had worked diligently with him over the next several years. In fact, Jack had been quite impressed with Scott's mechanical aptitude. They had been working together for six months when Jack had to leave Alaska for an emergency. His father had suffered a mild heart attack, and he went to see him in Oregon. Scott and Jack had just started an engine overhaul, and Jack told Scott he could continue pulling the engine and they could finish the overhaul and reinstallation when he got back. Jack was quite surprised when he returned to see that Scott had finished the overhaul and the plane was ready to fly again. In fact, when he cranked the engine and took the plane out for a taxi test, it ran better than it had ever run.

Scott had had a bit of a troubled childhood: his father had left Phyllis when he was five, and Phyllis struggled to support herself and raise Scott at the same time. Scott would sometimes complain about Phyllis, and Jack had tried to comfort the young teenager as best he could during those times. When Scott was seventeen, he left Alaska for California. Jack didn't speak to him often, but about twice a year, Scott would call Jack. Scott seemed to be doing well. He had taken a job as a mechanic at a prestigious car dealership in Los Angeles and was living in a condo near the beach. Scott would rarely talk about his mother but would ask about her sparingly during their phone conversations. Jack could sense a rift there but decided it really wasn't his place to probe. Phyllis herself was quite moody, and Jack had never gotten to know her well. At best, she was a casual acquaintance.

When Jack entered the store, he saw Phyllis sitting behind the counter in the front of the store, staring at nothing in particular. At first she didn't notice him. Jack could see she was deep in thought.

"Hi, Phyllis, how are you?"

"Oh, oh, Jack, just fine, thanks, and you?"

"Good."

Jack walked to the back of the store and picked up the eggs, along with some bacon, bread, and orange juice. It was early, and he was the only one in the store. As he walked back toward the front, he saw now that Phyllis was sitting with her head in her hand, staring down at the floor.

"What's troubling you, Phyllis?"

"What? Oh, nothing, nothing, just a little sleepy, that's all."

Jack could tell by her sunken shoulders and vacant eyes that it was more than that, but it had always been so hard to get Phyllis to talk to him. She would keep to herself, making it difficult to communicate with her.

"Now, Phyllis, it's okay; just tell me what's on your mind."

Phyllis glanced at Jack quickly, then looked away and began to ring up his items.

"Need anything else today, Jack?" she asked.

Jack stared back at Phyllis and smiled; then he said, "Now, Phyllis, if you're not going to tell me what's wrong, I'm just going to have to find out myself one way or another."

Suddenly Jack was sitting behind the counter staring back at a fit man in his midthirties with dark black hair, with a rugged but handsome look about him.

What an odd thing to say, Phyllis was thinking; *it's not like Jack to ask me such personal questions.*

Jack could see it all before him now, what was troubling her. She was thinking about Scott and asking herself what she had done wrong that her only son hadn't talked to her in seven years. He had left at the end of a screaming match, telling Phyllis that he hated her, that she wasn't his mother, and that she'd never see him again. She had taken it as any parent might in dealing with an angry teenager: he'll get over it, lighten up after a while, and things would return to normal. But for Phyllis, it didn't turn out that way. After Scott left, he never did talk to her again; she only knew he had left Alaska for the continental United States. After so many years, she began to fall into a state of depression, not knowing where he was and how he was doing. For all she knew, he could have been killed in a car accident long ago. The two men she loved the most, her husband and her son, had left her; and all the thoughts that antagonized her mind about what had happened dragged her deeper and deeper into depression, causing her to slowly withdraw from the people around her. *How sad,* Jack thought to himself, *no wonder I could never get to know her. If I had only known, I could have told her how Scott was doing, let her know that he was doing well.*

A few seconds passed, and then abruptly Jack was looking back at Phyllis across the counter. Phyllis had a stoic expression on her face, but beneath it, Jack could feel that shadow of sadness that she suppressed so well in her facial expression. Jack had seen that look before, a look that was difficult to traverse, one that would end the conversation quickly and send him on his way.

Jack didn't know what to say. How could he navigate across the barrier that Phyllis used to shut others out? Jack pulled out his wallet and paid for the groceries, then stared at Phyllis for a few seconds. Noticing the stare, Phyllis turned her head and looked at him, then quickly looked away. She sat still, waiting for him to leave.

"Well, Phyllis, have a nice day, okay?"

"Sure, Jack, see you again next time."

Jack grabbed his groceries and walked toward the door. As he opened it, he turned back to Phyllis and said, "Don't worry, Phyllis, Scott is alive and well. He's living in Los Angeles. I talked to him only a few months ago. He's a good kid and thinks of you often. I'm sorry—I just didn't realize you two weren't talking to one another."

Phyllis turned her head and looked at Jack, a surprised, quizzical expression on her face, but then for the first time Jack could remember, she smiled at him with a brilliant, radiant smile. Jack smiled back at her, and as he turned to leave, Jack could see that along with her smile, there was a sense of peace in her eyes.

As Jack walked home, he wondered how Scott could behave to his mother that way. *That little punk,* he thought to himself, *that boy needs a talking to.*

Chapter 3

When Jack got back to his apartment, he checked his phone messages. Sandy—the woman he had been seeing for seven months—had called.

"Jack, darling, how's it going? Are you out hunting a polar bear or something so early in the morning up there in the Alaskan wilderness? Listen, Jack, I'm coming up on Tuesday, got to make a few house calls, so I'd love to get together. I'll be out of the office most of today, but try me on my cell phone, okay? Look forward to hearing from you, sweetie."

Sandy was a pharmaceutical rep and worked the Northwest region, which included Alaska, Washington, and northern Oregon. Her office was in Seattle, but a good majority of her clients were in Alaska at the hospitals in and around Anchorage. Jack decided to fix breakfast before he called back. Sandy usually had her cell phone turned off in the mornings, but often he could catch her by midday.

Jack pulled out his address book and looked up Scott's number. He wanted to give Scott a call and talk to him about Phyllis and try to convince him to contact her, but when he looked up his phone number, he remembered Scott had recently moved to the beach and that he didn't have his current number.

Ah shoot, Jack thought to himself, *I'll just have to wait until he calls me; I don't even have his new address.* Jack felt empathy for Phyllis and wanted to somehow help. Since Jack was Scott's only contact back to Alaska, Jack felt some responsibility to help sew up their broken relationship.

Jack's mind wandered as he sat and ate breakfast. He could see images of Phyllis sitting alone in her house crying. *Such a sweet woman,* Jack thought. To see such a scene was painful, and he forced himself to think of something else.

After finishing his eggs and pancakes, he gave Sandy a call, but she didn't answer so he left her a message.

"Sandy, how are you doing? Yeah, it would be great to see you. Listen, I'll give you a ring back in a couple of hours. I'm going to head down to the gym and lift weights. I'll be back in a little bit, and I'll give you a call then. All right, sweetie, I'll talk to you later. Great to hear from you. Bye."

Jack was full but he could lift weights on a full stomach—he had done it many times before—so he headed down to the gym. While he was working out, he contemplated this strange power he seemed to have acquired. It had worked three times now—maybe it was a temporary anomaly, maybe not, he didn't know. He decided to head over to the library that afternoon and see if he could find out any information that might shed some light on this strange phenomenon.

When he got back to his apartment, he gave Sandy another call. After five rings, she answered.

"Sandy!" he began.

"Jack, you big boy, how are you doing?"

"Good, good, and yourself?"

"Oh, doing fine, just fine. I've been out hopping from hospital to hospital trying to sell these doctors some drugs, you know."

"Well, they need those drugs, Sandy," Jack replied.

"Yeah, you know, I guess so. Keeps me employed, that's the best part."

"So you're coming up for a trip?"

"Sure am, Jack. I'll be there Tuesday morning. Let's get together. What do you say?"

"Sounds great. I'll be here. Listen, after you make your rounds, I'll just swing on by your hotel and we'll head out, okay?"

"Sounds great, Jack. It will be wonderful to see you. I'll give you a call on Tuesday when I get in, if I don't talk to you before then, and we'll take it from there."

"Great. What time do you think you'll be done?"

"Oh, I don't know. I'll try to cut it short. You know those doctors—they want you to hang around all day long, but I think I can give them the quick easy-over routine and be done by three or four o'clock, so maybe we can get together by five or six."

"Great, Sandy. Look forward to seeing you, sweetie. I might talk to you before then, but if not, look forward to hearing from you."

"Sounds good, Jack, I'll talk to you later."

"All right, sweetie, I'll see you soon."

"Bye, Jack."

Jack smiled. It would be good to see Sandy. He didn't see her as often as he would like since she lived in Seattle, but between him going south and Sandy coming up for business trips, he saw her usually every two or three weeks. She was a fun person to be around. She had an upbeat, bubbly personality, with a slight bit of sarcastic wit that would catch Jack off guard and make him laugh. Jack wouldn't have described Sandy as a deeply thoughtful person; she wasn't the type to sit and ponder things at length. Instead, she would be off dreaming about her next adventure, or laughing and giggling about nothing in particular. She was a fun, high-spirited type, who could pull Jack along with her for a ride. She was slim, about five feet six inches, in her late twenties, with reddish-blond hair and beautiful green, mesmerizing eyes.

They had met at a bar near the main hospital in Anchorage. Sandy was up for a business trip and didn't have much to do, so she had decided to grab a drink. Jack was by himself and wanted to sit and relax at the bar before heading home. He noticed from the corner of his eye someone staring at him. He didn't want to be too obvious, so he had gotten up to go to the bathroom. When he headed back to his barstool, he saw Sandy sitting at the bar, looking down at her drink, casually stirring her vodka martini with a straw. Jack sat down with his eyes on her, and after several seconds, she looked up from the bar searching for the man who had left a few minutes earlier. When Sandy saw Jack, she gave a quick smile, then turned her head back to the bar. Then she looked at him again, put her head down, and continued to stir her drink, a faint smile across her lips.

During this time, Jack had kept his eyes on her, and by the time she took a second glance, he had a broad smile on his face. Jack took a gulp of his beer, walked over to her, and asked her how she was doing that evening. They hit it off really well and laughed and giggled the rest of the night. It was obvious to Jack that Sandy was attracted to him. Jack, for his part, found her sexy. They were like two schoolkids frolicking in the playground that evening, each drawing off the other, bringing them to an energy level each had experienced only rarely.

From the onset, there was a strong sexual attraction between them, and Jack had gotten the impression that if he had asked, Sandy would have been happy to go back to his apartment that night. Jack had thought about it, but he didn't want to ruin a potential relationship with a one-night fling. Instead, he walked Sandy back to her hotel and told her he would love to see her again and that he had had a great night. Sandy joked that he could see her to her room, but Jack sidestepped the invitation and instead they exchanged phone numbers and addresses. Before leaving, Jack put his arms around Sandy's slim waist, and they kissed. It was a long, sensual kiss, a kiss that much more exciting because they had only met a few hours earlier. Then Jack said good-bye and walked back to his apartment in the dry, chill Alaskan air.

After that evening with Sandy, Jack talked to her almost every day for the next few weeks over the phone, and they saw each other again on her next business trip to Anchorage three weeks later. They went out for dinner, had a great time, walked around the nice parts of the city, and then headed down to the harbor and sat on a bench overlooking the bay. It was cold, and they snuggled. The snuggling led to a kiss, and then another kiss, and then to laughter. At the end of the evening, Sandy went back to Jack's apartment, and they made love. Their lovemaking was exceptionally heightened since it was their first time together and there was such a strong physical attraction between them.

They had been seeing each other for seven months now. Their relationship was fulfilling to Jack, their lovemaking was always good, and their friendship had begun to blossom. But she was gone a lot, and when they were together, they didn't really talk about any meaningful, deep subjects. With Sandy, it was more about fun and laughter; everything was kept on the light side. Jack didn't mind that—it was just her personality. *No one person can satisfy all your needs—just be happy you have her,* Jack would say to himself. In any case, he was looking forward to seeing her on Tuesday.

After talking with Sandy, Jack showered and then decided to head over to the library. He wanted to read up on telepathy and extrasensory perception to see if he could make any sense of this strange power. When he got to the library, he looked at every book he could find on telepathy and ESP, trying to find some description that would correlate to the type of experiences he had been having.

A lot of the stuff he found was just junk, like reading the horoscopes in the Sunday morning paper. Much was fabricated garbage based on sketchy science written by someone trying to make a buck off people's curiosity. He searched for several hours, and then he came across an obscure book written by a scientist in the early 1980s concerning telepathy. It discussed a phenomenon that had been supposedly documented—though based on very limited data—about telepathy and how it was correlated to a process not unlike a television remote signal. When a person presses on a television remote, it sends out an ultrasonic or infrared signal that is picked up by the TV. The book indicated that this same type of phenomenon could also occur between human beings if particular tones or syllables were presented in a certain way.

Interesting, Jack thought, *like a signal that opens up a door between two minds.* He continued to read through the worn pages about the few experiments described. They weren't well documented, and it was obvious there wasn't nearly as much time or money spent on the study as the author would have liked. In the description of the study, the author made a comparison to talking. When someone talks, it creates vibrations in the air, and these vibrations travel across the room, impacting the ear of another person. This, in turn, causes vibration of the eardrum of the person listening, which the brain picks up and interprets as communication. The experiments were similar to that, except instead of traveling through the vibration of air, the median of travel was faint electrical impulses given off by the brain as patterns of thought traveled through the cerebral cortex. In essence, the electrical impulses generated during human thought could be detected and interpreted through a communication channel to another individual. It was common knowledge in the medical community that thought traveled through brain synapses as electrical nerve impulses; the purpose of the experiments was in part to detect and then interpret these electrical patterns.

The idea is plausible, Jack thought, but it almost seemed that a "sixth sense" was needed to be able to "listen" to the other person's thoughts. The author's premise was that this "sense" already existed. The author stated that deep in the cerebral cortex near the top of the spinal cord, there existed a gland called the corpus callosum, which was used as a "switching station" for thought traveling between the left and right sides of the brain. The gland's purpose was to connect the right and left sides so that brain impulses could be turned into cohesive thought by sending the impulses in the brain and spinal cord to the correct area of the brain for interpretation. The author speculated that under the right circumstances, this gland could be used to "connect into" someone else's thoughts instead of just the thoughts of the brain where the gland resided.

The function of the gland was well documented; for example, individuals who suffered from schizophrenia had glands with certain chemical imbalances. In essence, the gland malfunctioned, sending impulses to the wrong parts of the brain and causing symptoms well documented for schizophrenics. Examples were the hearing of voices or seeing of images that didn't really exist, psychosomatic pain, or the comprehension of fictitious individuals created inside the schizophrenic's brain. Chemical imbalances could exist in other parts of the brain as well, but the malfunctioning of the corpus callosum was well documented in schizophrenic behavior.

The book was simply titled *Experiments in Telepathy.* Jack turned to the last page of the book for information about the author. His name was Robert Weldon, an accomplished doctor who had spent his career studying the brain. His biggest accomplishment had been the development of drugs to treat schizophrenia, and he had been involved in the development of the first brain scan machines used for tracking electrical impulses throughout the cerebral cortex. In part due to his success in the treatment of schizophrenia, he had obtained funding to study the phenomenon of brain communication between people.

The experiments Weldon conducted involved having two individuals sit in a room together, with their heads in close proximity to one another. All moisture in the room was removed to improve the ability to detect the other person's thought patterns, and the individual trying to receive the patterns was blindfolded and his ears were muffled. In one set of experiments, the other person was given information to induce a strong emotional reaction. Several different methods were used to induce the reaction, such as reading text in a book, viewing photographs, and watching television. Sometimes the emotion induced was joyful, such as watching the image of children playing; other times, anger or fear were induced through images of suffering or death. In a similar experiment, the person was asked to solve a complex mathematical problem or write text in a given period of time in an attempt to induce rapid and complex thought patterns.

The experiments were run over a one-year period in the early 1980s. Weldon created a drug not unlike the one he had developed to treat schizophrenia; this drug actually enhanced the sensitivity and increased the capacity of the "switching station" gland.

There were approximately one hundred individuals involved in the initial experiments, and these initial hundred were given a small dosage of Weldon's drug. After running some preliminary tests, it appeared that certain individuals had a greater innate ability to detect others' thought patterns. Under extreme emotional or analytical activity of the brain, these individuals could not "read" another person's thoughts; however, they could comprehend general thought patterns emanating from the other mind. At the end of the experiment, the subjects were asked to write down any thought patterns or general impressions they perceived. These certain individuals could give a general description of the strong thought patterns experienced by the other subject, whether it be a strong emotion such as great joy or anger or the other person was working a math problem or writing text.

Out of the one hundred individuals, a handful who showed the most promise were selected for continued tests. These individuals were administered a more potent version of the drug developed by Weldon to see if their ability could be further enhanced. The selected individuals were paired together and both were administrated the drug, the thought being that increased activity in both brains would lead to more successful results.

The experiments presented in the book looked promising. There were some indications that with the use of the drug, patterns of thought could be transmitted between the two subjects. As in the previous tests, a strong emotion or intense activity in the brain produced the best results. In some cases, the subject "listening" could perceive an emotion and could describe what created the emotion. For example, when questioned, the listener would say that he or she perceived joy; when asked why, he or she could describe a scene where the individual was sitting in a field in the springtime, surrounded by flowers, with the sky beautifully clear and a pleasant breeze blowing in the air. This description would match the stimulus the other subject was given to create that emotion. In another successful test, the subject "listening" perceived fear because he or she experienced the sensation of falling from a cliff—and this was the exact image the other subject was shown on a television screen during the experiment.

In a surprising finding that Weldon hadn't expected, when one individual was given a complicated math problem to solve, the other subject in the test, given the same problem later after the two subjects were separated, could work the problem five times faster than expected. In other words, the subject appeared to have maintained the "memory" of the other individual working the problem. In further tests, it appeared that the memory of the emotion or analytical thought pattern could be invoked by repeating words that had been recited to the other person during the experiment. It was shown that these words improved the ability of the "listener" to describe the detailed thought patterns of the other individual.

Fascinating, Jack thought to himself, *there definitely seems to be something here.* At the end of the book, Weldon summarized his findings and recommended that further research be done. Jack searched for additional books under Weldon's name and he found several, some written in the 1970s and a few written in the late 1980s and early 1990s, but none dealt with ESP. The other books concerned either the treatment of schizophrenia or Alzheimer's disease. It appeared that in the 1980s, Weldon spent considerable effort developing drugs for the treatment of Alzheimer's. *Interesting*, Jack thought. *The ESP experiments had looked so promising, I wonder why no other research was published.*

It was getting late, and Jack had a few things to do to prepare for his flight the next day. He checked out the book from the library since he wanted to read it in further detail. It was still light when Jack went outside. It was early October, but even at 6:00 p.m., it would be another hour before night began to descend in the Alaskan sky.

When Jack got back to his apartment, he checked on the weather. It was going to be a cold, crisp morning, with winds out of the northwest at a leisurely five knots. *Excellent*, Jack thought, *perfect conditions for a soft landing on the glacier.* When the weather was clear and cold, Jack sometimes mounted small skis beside his plane wheels and would land on a glacier located on the south face of Mount McKinley. The glacier sat at 8500 feet on a long and wide plateau that looked over Denali National Park.

Jack loved to land there, but it depended on the clients he was taking up that day as well as the weather. Some passengers preferred to fly into the valley below, to a small town that had a pleasant atmosphere, with several small but friendly restaurants and shops near the airport. A more adventurous group would choose the glacier, even though they would have to bring their lunches with them. Many times, the glacier was not accessible due to cloud cover, wind, or soft snow; but when Jack checked the forecast, it said the glacier would be available for landing the next day.

★★★★★

Jack collected the group the next morning at 7:30 a.m. There were five people going up with him that day: two young men in their early twenties, a married couple in their late thirties or early forties, and an older man, probably retired, in his early seventies. It was still dark outside as Jack gave the preflight briefing inside the small airport office.

"Good morning, everyone, it's great to have you this morning. My name is Jack. Looks like we have an absolutely beautiful day ahead of us. It's going to be cold, but the winds are very calm and it's going to be crystal clear so it should be a perfect day for flying—and a perfect day for sightseeing. I just want to make sure everyone keeps themselves nice and warm."

When Jack said this, the older man patted his heavy down jacket and fumbled with the zipper, and the married woman playfully showed Jack her heavy gloves. Jack looked at them and the rest of the group, and everyone seemed to be reasonably well dressed for the coldness of the glacier.

"Now we have two choices this morning for our route, and I'll describe each to you and we'll try to come to a group consensus as to what we want to do," Jack continued. "The plan today is to leave here and head north toward McKinley, as mentioned in the brochure. We'll circle the mountain from the west and see some spectacular views of the mountain and Denali National Park. We'll do a full loop around the mountain. After that, we have two choices. There's a small town in Denali National Park down near the base of the mountain, and ... uh ... we can land there at a small airport just off a beautiful lake next to the town. It's a beautiful little town with several shops and restaurants, where you can buy some things if you'd like, souvenirs and the sort. We can stop there for lunch before we fly back here.

"The other option is to land on a spectacular glacier at 8500 feet. The glacier is halfway up the mountain on a plateau that stares right into the face of McKinley. There's a snow runway there, and the forecaster said it's open for landing. When the weather is warm or there's a strong wind, they will not allow landings, but the weather today gives us a wonderful opportunity to visit there. You'll see some spectacular panoramas, but if we go, everyone will have to bring their own lunches on the plane, and you will probably want to bring a few more warm clothes with you since it will be cold on the glacier once we leave the plane. If you have any extra clothing in your cars, I would suggest you bring it with you if we decide on the glacier. I have some spare gloves and hats I can loan out as well. There are a few shops down the street where you can buy a packed lunch, and once we get to the glacier, we'll get out and have lunch in the snow."

The married man smiled briefly when he heard this and then moved his hands over his back and legs, pretending to knock snow off his backside.

Jack saw this and smiled, and then said, "Joking aside, I have a few mats we can lay down, and we can have a kind of picnic out on the glacier. There are some opportunities to do a little hiking also for those interested, or we can just relax near the plane. So those are the two choices for the trip today. The glacier in my mind is an absolutely spectacular spot, but if you want to get a feel for the culture and people of this area, the town is very nice as well."

Jack stood silent, waiting for some response.

The married woman spoke up first. "Hi, Jack, my name is Christine. Let me ask you, do we need to bring any special hiking boots if we go on the glacier?"

"Not really, Christine. If you do want to do a little hiking, it might be better with some sturdy boots, but even running shoes would work if you're not going to be hiking very far. We'll only stop there for about an hour and a half, so what you're wearing should be fine," Jack replied as he looked down at her below-the-ankle hiking shoes.

Christine nodded her head, understanding. Jack paused and looked at the others and then asked, "Are there any other questions I can help with?"

Jack stood still. It was early in the morning, and Jack could see that the group was still trying to wake up and were not quite with it yet. The two young men looked like they had stayed out way too late the night before and were suffering from a hangover or the like. The older man was expressionless; it was hard to get a reading on him. Christine looked the most alert, but her husband had his arms crossed and was staring at the floor, a vaguely concerned look on his face. Jack looked around, turned his head and looked out the window, and then looked back and waited.

"All right, folks," Jack finally said, putting his hands in the air. "Well, listen, if you're not going to tell me what you want to do, I'll just have to read your minds to find out!"

They looked at him with puzzled, slightly amused looks on their faces when Jack said this. Jack could tell what they wanted to do; he guessed they were just a little timid about what they preferred. The only hesitation he read was from the husband—he was a little wary about going to the glacier, but if everyone else agreed, he was willing to do it.

"All right, the glacier it is," Jack said. "It's obvious everyone wants to go there."

When Jack said this, Christine smiled and nodded her head, and then turned to her husband and nudged him. Her husband looked at Jack and narrowed his eyes slightly, then looked at his wife and said, "Sure, sure."

The two young men came out of their daze when they heard the word "glacier," and they smiled broadly at Jack and then looked at each other, nodding their heads in agreement.

The older gentleman looked at the others to see their reaction, then looked at Jack and replied smiling, "Yes, the glacier it is!"

The sun was just rising twenty minutes later when the group reconvened outside the hangar by Jack's plane. Jack had been busy mounting the skis alongside the plane's wheels, but during that time, he began to understand why the woman's husband, Phil, was wary about going to the glacier. He had had a heart attack two years earlier, when he was only thirty-nine, quite unusual for a man that young, especially given his level of fitness. He hadn't told Christine about it; it was unclear why, but Jack sensed it had to do with their relationship. Christine was quite athletic, and she pushed him sometimes. Since the attack, he had scaled back the intensity of his workouts, preferring to take a brisk walk instead of trying to keep up with her on runs they used to do together. Christine never really understood it, and in her ignorance, she would prod him even more, making him that much more uncomfortable. Jack decided that once they got to the glacier, he would watch over Phil and make sure he didn't overexert himself. The air was thin, but as long as he was relatively sedentary, Jack didn't perceive that there would be a problem.

★★★★★

Jack landed the plane on the glacier two hours later, after they had done a routine but spectacular transit around Mount McKinley. The glacier sat on a plateau that had been carved out over thousands of years by melting ice and snow. On one side of the glacier, Jack and the others could look down into the valley below. Half the mountain below was snow covered, but then it transitioned into rugged green terrain as the mountain melded into the rest of the landscape. Far off in the distance was the small town Jack had described earlier. Next to the town sat the pristine lake, a popular spot for amateur fishermen in the spring and summer. When Jack looked up from the plateau, the beauty of McKinley was staring in his face. It was a spectacular scene—first the wide expanse of the glacier, and then beyond and above it sat a wide, jagged rock face that seemed to stretch out over the glacier. On that clear day, above the rock face, the rest of the mountain could be seen stretching up to the summit of McKinley at 20,320 feet.

As they climbed out of the plane, one of the young men exclaimed, "This is awesome!"

"Amazing!" replied the other, "high five, buddy, high five!"

The two joyfully smacked their hands together in their giddy excitement.

Jack pulled out the mats from the back of the plane and laid them down in the snow.

"Not the most comfortable lunch tables in the world," Jack said, "but you can't complain about the scenery."

"You can say that again," Christine replied.

The group sat quietly as they ate their lunch, soaking in the mesmerizing scenery before their eyes.

Toward the end of their lunch, Phil asked, "So how long have you been doing this, Jack, giving plane tours of Alaska?"

"Oh, about twelve years now. It's been a lot of fun."

"You've been doing this all your life?"

"Well, no, actually. I graduated from the University of Washington with a degree in aerospace engineering what seems like ages ago. I took a job as an engineer with Boeing for a while, you know, but I left a few years later."

"What happened?" Phil asked. "They didn't turn out the lights on you, did they? You know the old saying during those huge layoffs they had in the seventies—the last one to leave Seattle, please turn out the lights."

Jack chuckled, "No, no, I just couldn't see myself stuck behind a computer screen all day long for the next thirty years. You know, designing a new airplane sounds so exciting, but when it comes to the actual work, a lot of the time is spent on the computer inside a small cubicle working on some nitty-gritty little detail. Just not my bag, if you know what I mean. So how about yourself, what line of work are you in?"

"Oh, I work for Nextel at the main West Coast development center in San Francisco," Phil replied.

"So are you an engineer then?"

"Well, I used to be. My degree is in electrical engineering, but after ten years at the company, I went down the management track so I don't really do a lot of engineering anymore. Most of my work involves working with suppliers and the development team, writing contracts, and developing and managing budgets and schedules for new product introductions."

"That must be interesting— seeing the whole process, looking down from a bird's-eye view and pulling the whole project together."

"Yeah, I guess you could say that, but it's a lot of pressure trying to get everyone on board and working to a specific schedule and budget. Three years ago, I was promoted to a director's position for one of our product lines. 'What an opportunity,' I said to myself back then, but it's been hell. I'm always having to deal with crisis situations. The people who work for you don't come to you unless they have a problem, and my management is constantly giving me heat, making sure we're on track. I'm kind of like the guy in the middle taking the crap from both sides. I'm getting old beyond my years in this job—it's just wearing me out."

Jack could see the stress all over Phil's face; he was tense, and Jack suspected his blood pressure had increased twenty points just talking about it. *No wonder he had a heart attack,* Jack thought.

"Well, you're here on this beautiful mountain in Alaska a thousand miles away from all that. Don't think about it—just relax and enjoy yourself."

"Good advice, good advice, but easier said than done, if you know what I mean."

Christine had been sitting ten feet away with the two young men during their conversation, but she had gotten up and was standing before them now.

"Hey, Jack, you said there were some hiking opportunities up here?" she asked.

"Yes, of course. You see that bluff due right of the rock face?" Jack gestured to his right toward the other side of the glacier. "It's about a thirty-minute hike at a brisk pace from here. Once you get to the bluff, you can stand on the top of it and see the full mountain without the rock face in front of you; you can also see a good twenty miles more of the valley than from here. If you're going to go, take your camera because you'll want some memories of it, and of course, be careful."

"Sounds great."

Christine turned toward her husband. "Phil, darling, do you want to go? These two kids over here are up for it. Don't you think it would be fun?"

"Oh, Christine, sweetie, I'm not sure I …"

"Come on, sweetheart, when's the next time you'll be on this mountain? I know if these two young guys can keep up with me, you can too," she said jokingly.

Phil looked down at the snow.

Poor guy, Jack thought. *He's not just getting pressure from both sides, is he? It's coming from all three.* As they stood there, the elderly man approached, apparently overhearing the conversation.

"You wouldn't mind if an old man like me tagged along, now would you?"

"Of course not," Christine replied, "the more the merrier! Come on, Phil, it looks like everyone wants to go. You wouldn't want to spoil the party, would you?"

Phil looked up and over to the bluff, two miles off in the distance, with a concerned and slightly miserable look on his face, and then returned his eyes to the snow in front of his feet. "I don't know, I …"

"Phil and I were having a fascinating discussion about his line of work, Christine," Jack interjected. "I was thinking about setting up a more sophisticated marketing network for my business, maybe a website hooked up to a cell network or something. I was hoping Phil might be able to fill me in on something like that."

Phil looked over at Jack, a slightly relieved look on his face.

"Besides," Jack continued, "it's always good to have someone else here with me in case the wind picks up and I need to tie the plane down in a hurry."

Phil eked out a brief smile, happy that Jack had given him an easy out.

"You all go ahead," Phil said. "I'll stay here and keep Jack company and give him some info on the network. Have fun, Christine, and don't wear these guys out too much, okay?"

Christine looked at Phil with a disappointed look on her face, and Jack could see a trace of pain as well, as if Phil had hurt her in some way.

"Okay, have it your way. We'll see you two in an hour or so."

Phil watched as the group walked away and then turned to Jack. "Yes, Jack, I can help you with that network. We do this stuff all the time; it shouldn't be too difficult."

The two sat back down on the mats that were laid in the snow. After getting a good feel for what Jack was looking for, Phil gave him a few recommendations to enhance the system, handed him his card, and told Jack to call him in San Francisco in the next few days. "I'll put you in touch with one of our best service agents, and he'll take it from there."

"Thank you, Phil, I appreciate it."

The two sat quietly for the next thirty minutes, relaxing and taking in the beauty of the mountain.

After a while, a bird flying overhead caught Phil's attention, and he said casually, "Well, the wind never did pick up. We really did get a nice day, didn't we?"

"Oh, yes," Jack replied, "I didn't think it would get windy; you can usually tell these things."

"Well, I'm glad you asked me about the network. It gave me a good reason not to plod along with Christine. You know it's just push, push, push with her. She can never just take it easy and relax. After eleven years of marriage, I'm starting to get sick of it—you know what I mean, I'm just getting tired of her."

Jack tilted his head up and stared into the clear blue sky not saying anything, then closed his eyes, contemplating a response.

Phil continued as if he were trying to squeeze a reply from Jack. "I don't know, she just never gives me a break. If it's not this, then it's that, and it just goes on and on. It's like walking on eggs all the time. I try to keep her happy, but it just seems to be going downhill with her."

Jack looked over at Phil. His arms were crossed over his knees, and his head was tilted down. It was obvious he was very unhappy.

"Look, Phil, I don't mean to interfere, but I think it would help if you told your wife about your heart attack. She just doesn't understand why your behavior has changed so drastically since then. She thinks you just don't want to spend time with her anymore, as if you don't love her as much as you used to."

Phil looked over at Jack, surprised at his insight. "How did you know I had a heart attack? And how do you know I never told her about it?"

Jack shrugged his shoulders. "Oh, just a hunch," Jack replied. "With the pressures from your job and everything, it seemed likely; and if she knew, she wouldn't be pushing you so much."

Phil frowned and sat silent for the next fifteen minutes until the two young men, the elderly man, and his wife returned from their hike.

As they approached, Phil stood up and tried gallantly to put a smile on his face. "Did you enjoy your hike, Christine? It must have been beautiful!"

"Oh yes, Phil, it was beautiful. I just wish you had come with us," she said glumly.

"Yeah, well, I'm glad you all had a good time."

★★★★★

On the flight back to Anchorage, the two young men were playful and happy. They had gotten over their hangovers and were now on a natural high from being on the mountain. They sat in the back of the plane, talking about their plans for the upcoming ski season, discussing what mountains they wanted to ski, and reminiscing about great ski trips they had done in the past.

The elderly man stared out the window, seemingly content, having enjoyed his time on the mountain. Phil and Christine sat silent, as if not to bother one another, hoping the silence would help repair their strained relationship.

After they landed at Birchwood airport, Jack gave his best regards to everyone and thanked them for choosing his flying service. As he shook Phil's hand to say good-bye, he said, "Thank you, Phil, for the card and the info on the network. I'll be giving you a call next week once you get back to San Francisco."

"Okay, Jack," Phil replied solemnly. There was something on his mind, and his wife, although pleasant, seemed distant.

*****

It was a thirty-minute drive to Phil and Christine's hotel from the airport, and as Phil drove back, the two sat silent for a while. Phil finally said how beautiful the flight was, and Christine replied that the mountain was majestic and that she liked their tour guide. They drove down the winding, scenic road in silence for the next twenty minutes, and then Phil turned his head to his wife and said, "Christine, I have something to tell you."

"What, Phil?"

"I know I've been a little distant from you over the last year or so, and I think it's time I should help you understand."

Christine sat still, not saying anything.

"Two years ago, I had a heart attack."

"What?"

"Yes, it was during the time I was working eighty hours a week for months on end. One evening, I just keeled over and dropped to my knees. I struggled to my chair and sat with my head on my desk until I had the strength to get myself to the hospital. I didn't exactly know what happened, but at the hospital, the doctor told me I had had a heart attack."

"Oh god, why didn't you tell me?"

"I'm sorry, Christine, I'm so sorry, I just couldn't get myself to tell you. I don't know why. I know I should have."

"Oh, Phil, I can't believe it. Are you okay now, I mean, have you been treating it?"

"Yeah, I've been taking medication, and the doctor told me to back off rigorous workouts. He put me on an exercise schedule and diet, and we've been working closely together to make sure it doesn't happen again."

"All this time, oh god, I wish you had told me. I could have helped you, and it would have helped me understand. Oh god, Phil."

"I know, Christine. I'm sorry."

★★★★★

After he said good-bye to everyone, Jack parked his plane back in the hangar and did some routine inspection and maintenance on the plane. Once done, he got in his truck, went out to get a bite to eat, and then drove back to his apartment. It was a little after seven o'clock by then, and he decided to give Sandy a call. After four rings, her answering machine came on. Jack shrugged; it was so hard to get hold of her. He wanted to talk to her, tell her about the trip that day, how beautiful the mountain was, and tell her about Phil and how he had tried to help him out. *Oh well,* Jack thought, *not a big deal; hopefully she'll call me back later this evening.* Jack liked listening to her voice—it was so upbeat and bubbly, like a babbling creek on a warm spring day.

"Hi, Sandy, Jack. Lovely to hear your voice. Thought I'd call to see what's going on. We had a beautiful flight up to that glacier on McKinley today, pretty spectacular. The conditions were perfect for a glacier landing. We had lunch there, and then most of the group went for a hike over to that bluff I told you about. It was a lot of fun. I just wish you had been there—you would have loved it. Anyway, look forward to seeing you on Tuesday. Just give me a call when you have the chance. Miss you, sweetie. I'll talk to you soon, okay? Take care. Bye."

Jack was a little disappointed. *Well, maybe she's in the shower or running an errand or something; hopefully she'll call back soon,* he thought. In the meantime, he lay down on his bed, pulled out the book he had checked out from the library, and read some more about the ESP experiments.

It had been a long day—he had gotten up at five thirty that morning—and by eight thirty, he couldn't keep his eyes open. Sandy never did call that night. He would have liked to hear from her, but it wasn't that big of a deal to him. He lay the book down next to him, and within five minutes he was fast asleep.

It was still dark when he woke up the next morning. He walked out on the porch and stared up into the night sky. The air was dry and crisp, and even with the city lights, the stars were brilliant. Jack went back inside and pulled out his astronomical calendar. He was an amateur astronomy buff, and every once in a while, he'd check the positions of the constellations and see if he could make out the fainter stars in the sky. He sat on his porch for the next thirty minutes staring up into the heavens, until the sun began to fade the stars from view. It was a lovely way to spend the morning.

★★★★★

Sandy called that afternoon from her cell phone.

"Jack, how are you doing?"

"Sandy! I'm doing well, and yourself?"

"Good, I guess. I'm a little beat. Been running from one hospital to the next, and of course, one of those stupid doctors got all upset about one of our products. Said his patients were experiencing some bad side effects, so I had to try to pacify the guy. Pulled out the literature on all the testing we did to certify the product, and he demanded to talk to one of our scientists, not just the 'saleswoman.' Oh, what a bother. That guy is such a pain in the ass. In any case, enough about me—what about yourself, what have you been up to?"

"Oh, not too much. I took a group up to Mount McKinley yesterday—it was a beautiful day. Had a couple of young kids, a married couple, and an older man."

"Where did you fly them to?"

"Well, we did a loop around McKinley, and then we landed at that huge glacier up at 8500 feet."

"The glacier, wow! I didn't think you went up there anymore."

"Well, you know, it's not available to land on very often, but luckily with the sky so clear and the air so cold, it was open yesterday. I told you about it in my message yesterday, remember?"

"Oh yeah," Sandy replied, "I, well, I must have erased it by mistake or something. I was wondering when you were going to call."

There was a short silence. Jack hesitated, a little confused how she would have erased his message or at least not known that he had called. Sandy loved to talk on the phone; it wasn't like her to miss a message.

"So are you coming up tomorrow?" Jack asked calmly, trying to mask his confusion.

"Yeah, I'll be on a flight at six in the morning—god knows how I'm going to get up that early. Should get there by nine thirty at the latest. I'll make my rounds in the afternoon and should be back at the hotel by five o'clock."

"When are you heading back to Seattle?"

"Not till the following afternoon. Won't it be fun—we can sleep in together. Have some morning coffee, then have a little early morning lovemaking—make up for lost time. It's been almost three weeks now, Jack. You can't keep a young gal like me waiting too long, you know."

Jack smiled. "Well, I'm sure I can accommodate your needs, Sandy, or should I say satisfy all your desires?"

Sandy laughed. "I can't wait to see you, Jack!"

"Can't wait to see you, Sandy. Are you staying at the Marriott?"

"Yeah, just ask for my room at the front desk."

"What time—five o'clock or so?"

"Make it six. That will give me a chance to freshen up before you come over. I want to look good for my boy."

"You always look good, sweetheart. I'll see you at six."

"See you then, Jack. Talk to you later, okay?"

"See you later."

★★★★★

Jack thought he'd surprise Sandy on Tuesday evening, so he went out and bought her a bouquet of white daffodils—they were her favorite flower.

He then headed into downtown Anchorage to the Marriott hotel where she was staying.

"Good evening, can you tell me what room Sandy Walker is staying in?" Jack asked the receptionist at the front desk.

"Sandy Walker, let me see," the man replied. He looked up her room number, gave Jack a quick glance, and then said, "Oh yeah, that one. Yeah, I remember her from this morning."

He said this quietly but with a noticeable undercurrent of irritation in his voice. *That's odd*, Jack thought, *maybe she did something to upset the guy.*

"Yeah, she checked in this morning in a big hurry and rush, yeah, quite a gal," he said sarcastically.

"Is there something wrong?" Jack asked politely.

The man hesitated a second as if to check himself, and then replied, "No, no, all in a day's work, I suppose."

Jack could tell he wanted to say more, but he was minding his manners and stayed quiet. Sandy could be rude and unpleasant at times. Jack had experienced it on a few occasions, but he had dismissed it as part of the process of getting to know her.

"She's in room 801. She's expecting you."

"Thanks very much. Have a good evening, okay?"

"Sure thing, sir."

Jack took the elevator up to Sandy's room and knocked on her door. He could hear her reply from behind the door, "Okay, hold on, give me a second."

Jack was standing with one hand behind his back holding the bouquet of flowers when Sandy opened the door.

"Jack, my darling!"

"Hi, Sandy."

Jack walked into the room and then pulled out the bouquet of flowers and handed them to Sandy. "Thought I'd pick up something nice for you."

"Oh, Jack, you're so wonderful!" Sandy threw her arms around him. "Oh, Jack, I love you so much!"

"I love you too, Sandy."

Jack mused with himself for a brief second, and then said jokingly, "Sandy, I love you so much, I wish I could be you just for a second."

Sandy giggled, "Oh, Jack, you can be so silly sometimes."

Jack had his arms wrapped gently around Sandy's slim waist, but then as the images and sensations rushed through his brain, his hands froze, as if his blood had turned to ice.

"You, you …" Jack wanted to scream at her, but he didn't. Instead, he slowly removed his arms from around her waist, stepped back, and looked in her eyes. She was smiling with that cute little smirk on her face. Jack had seen that expression many times before, and he never quite understood what it meant. He didn't think much about it; he just thought that it was kind of cute, but now it wasn't cute at all. He wanted to yell at her, tell her she was a two-timing whore, but instead, he just turned his eyes away from her and stared into the corner of the room.

"Jack, what's wrong, Jack?"

Jack didn't look at Sandy again; he just turned and began to walk out of the room. With his back turned toward her, he said, "I've got to go."

"Jack!"

He walked out of the room, closed the door behind him, went down the hall, and stepped into the elevator.

Sandy just stood there, stunned, wondering what the hell had just happened, wondering how Jack could have possibly found out. After several seconds, she opened the door and ran down the hall after him.

"Jack, Jack! Where the hell are you going?"she yelled out.

Jack could feel her running up behind him as he entered the elevator. He didn't give her a second glance. He had his eyes fixed to the floor as the door slid closed.

"Jack!"

Very convenient, Sandy, Jack thought to himself as the elevator descended. One guy in Portland; the other guy in Alaska. When one wasn't visiting, the other was, and as she made her rounds between Anchorage and Portland, she would see both of them on a regular basis. All this time, ever since they started dating, she was having sex with both of them. *My god,* Jack thought, *no wonder I couldn't get hold of her on Sunday; she was with him, laughing and giggling all night long before they made love.* Sandy knew she had to decide eventually, but she was in no hurry. She was just having a good time, playing one off the other, telling them both she was in love with them.

Jack was filled with emotion as these thoughts and images cascaded through his brain. He was upset, he was angry, he was hurt; but as he walked the cold, rainy streets of Anchorage that night, his mind began to wander, and he knew those feelings wouldn't last very long.

★★★★★

Jack didn't get back to his apartment until one o'clock that night, and he went straight to sleep. The next morning when he woke, he noticed Sandy had called several times. He replayed the first message.

"Jack, where the hell are you? You give me a call, Jack!" she had screamed through the receiver. "How dare you walk out on me like that! Who the hell do you think you are? You can't just treat me like that! I'm not just someone you can trample on like that, Jack! You better call me, Jack, or you'll never see me again, you bastard. You better call me, Jack, you call me!" At the end of the message, her anger turned to sobbing. "You bastard, you bastard, how dare you treat me like that! You bastard."

She was crying and sobbing before she slammed the receiver down hard on the phone. Jack laughed lightly.

"God, what a joke," he said out loud. He erased that message and the other five messages she had left. He didn't listen to the other messages; he just erased them all.

Chapter 4

A few weeks later, Jack met up with his friend Darrell to go hang gliding. Darrell was an excellent hang-glider pilot, one of the best in Alaska. He competed regularly in national competitions and consistently would finish in the top three in his division. His specialty was time aloft, and he held the record in Alaska for that time—fourteen hours, fifty-five minutes. Jack and Darrell had been friends since high school.

As they were unloading their gear, getting ready for their first flight, Darrell asked Jack, "So, Jack, you still seeing that woman down there in Seattle?"

"Oh no, I'm not, I'm not seeing her anymore," he replied.

"Really? I thought you two were hitting it off pretty well. That's too bad. What happened?"

Jack took a long sigh, "Well, you know it's a strange thing, but when you date someone and get to know them better, learn about them, and learn about who they are, in a certain way you become them. You take on their views, their personality, their beliefs, and I realized that I just didn't want to be her and that I didn't want to be like her. That was enough for me to know that I couldn't see her anymore."

"That's a strange way of putting it, Jack," Darrell replied, "but I think I know what you mean, yeah, I understand what you're saying. You must be kind of sad about it, aye?"

"Oh, not really. Actually I don't feel much of anything, but if I had to put a word on it, I'd say I feel a sense of relief. I knew things weren't quite right between us; I just couldn't get myself to admit it. I just got caught up in the excitement of the whole thing, the sexuality of it all, though I knew deep down it wasn't working. In any case, I'm relieved that it's over, that I'm free."

Jack paused briefly and then said, "Listen, Darrell, it's a beautiful day. Let's get our hang gliders out and have a good time, all right? I don't want to talk about it anymore."

"Sounds like a great idea to me, Jack. Let's get in the air and fly!"

"Yeah, let's do it!"

★★★★★

Jack and Darrell were hang gliding off a high ridge that looked over a large plateau almost three thousand feet below. The idea was to take off from the ridge and then descend toward the plateau, maneuvering their hang gliders on the way to catch thermals and hone their flying skills. It was about a thirty-minute drive back to the ridge from where Jack parked his truck on the single lane road that wound its way through the plateau. They would fly for as long as possible, and then land their gliders near the truck before driving back to the ridge to pick up Darrell's Jeep. On a good day, they could stay aloft for over an hour. If they started early enough, they could make the trip back to the ridge for another flight three and possibly four times in one day.

Darrell took off first. The ridge was a great place to practice and learn because if the pilot did not take off well and could not get the hang glider aloft, he could lay the glider down into a long, gradual hill. It wasn't too treacherous. Sure, the pilot could bang up the hang glider if he wasn't careful, but it wasn't like some places where the drop-off was almost cliff-like, requiring expert skills. It was late fall and good hang-gliding conditions were rare that time of year, but it was such a nice day they decided to give the ridge a shot.

Once Darrell was safely aloft, Jack took off behind him. Within seconds, Jack caught a good thermal and was a few hundred feet above the ground only a minute later. Jack followed Darrell along the ridge and into the valley below. They descended gradually, trying to catch thermals along the way. Jack had only taken up the sport four years earlier, so he tried to mimic Darrell's flying as best he could in an attempt to capitalize on Darrell's ability to find thermals. Darrell had been flying hang gliders since high school, and Jack always seemed to pick up a thing or two when he flew behind him.

As Jack watched, Darrell turned his hang glider ever so slightly back and forth in a hunting type of motion, something Jack had never done before. *Maybe that's part of his secret,* Jack thought, and he mimicked the motion to see if it made a difference. If anything, it seemed to bleed speed away from the glider; as he began to lose airspeed, Jack straightened the glider and descended slightly to gain back some speed. *He must know something that I don't because that sure doesn't work for me,* Jack thought to himself.

Suddenly Darrell turned his glider sharply to the left, and Jack followed. Before he even realized it, his glider was ascending, caught in a strong, warm wind that lifted his canopy into the sky above him. "Wow, now that was a good one," Jack wanted to scream to Darrell, but Darrell was too far ahead to have heard it. *The boy knows his stuff,* Jack thought, and for the next thirty minutes, Jack did his best to follow Darrell's moves, even without understanding why they worked. It was a blast; Jack was really enjoying himself hanging onto Darrell's coattails.

Darrell picked up speed and gradually moved away from Jack. Even with his best efforts to keep up, Jack began to fall farther and farther behind. Over time, Jack's glider began to descend more rapidly, and he prepared himself for a landing in the valley within walking distance of his truck. Jack briefly looked above and ahead of him, and he could see Darrell gracefully and effortlessly flying his glider. Jack wondered what he was doing wrong—why he couldn't stay aloft like Darrell—but it was only a passing concern; he was enjoying himself, and he knew he would learn over time as he got more experience. Jack caught a few more small thermals, and he stayed aloft for ten more minutes before finally steering his hang glider toward a large green pasture, where he landed gently in the grass.

Jack unstrapped himself and spent the next few minutes dismantling the canopy and metal tubes of his glider, laying each piece carefully on the canopy in the prescribed order. Once he had all the pieces disassembled and packed up, he picked the whole unit up and put it on his back for the short walk back to his truck. He figured it would take him a good ten minutes to make it back to the vehicle. After five minutes of walking, he stopped, laid the glider down in the grass, and stared up into the sky, searching for Darrell. He could just make out the outline of Darrell's hang glider far off in the distance, close to where the ridge and plateau intersected. *Oh well,* Jack thought to himself, *I might as well take my time; I think I'll be twiddling my thumbs for a while.* He made his way to the road and picked up his pace since it was easier to hike on the road than in the grass. A few cars drove by before he made it to his truck, and as the occupants looked curiously at him as they passed by, Jack waved and smiled to let them know that he was fine.

Once he got to his truck, he laid his hang glider down in the back, pulled out a blanket, and laid down in the grass, enjoying the afternoon breeze and the unseasonably warm weather that day.

Jack could just glimpse Darrell from his vantage point in the grass. Darrell was still far off in the distance, but was no longer near the ridge. Instead, he appeared to be working thermals in the valley created by the intermittent cloud clusters scattered in the sky. *Amazing, just amazing,* Jack thought to himself. Once Jack was a few miles from the ridge, he lost altitude quickly, but Darrell seemed to have an innate ability to stay aloft, taking advantage of even the smallest difference in air temperature in different parts of the valley.

Over the next fifteen minutes, Darrell got closer and closer to the truck. Once Jack could clearly make out Darrell's body slung under the glider's canopy, he stood up and waved. Darrell turned his head and gave Jack a quick thumbs-up before turning his glider slightly to the left and climbing rapidly. He did a long, gradual, climbing turn, then leveled out, then turned left again, and headed back to Jack as if he were following a flight pattern around a small airport. When he came by again, Darrell was almost directly overhead about four hundred feet up. Jack yelled, "You're amazing, Darrell, absolutely amazing!"

Jack could hear Darrell laughing as he flew by. He flew about a quarter of a mile away from the truck, descending slightly before climbing and turning again. He performed the same maneuver several times, dropping fifty feet at each pass. By the third pass, Darrell was only a few hundred feet above the ground as he came by.

"You gonna stay up there all day?" Jack yelled as he passed overhead.

"As long as I can," Darrell yelled back, laughing again.

The next time by, Jack yelled out, "Hey, Darrell, mind if I hitch a ride, get inside that head of yours, and figure out how you do it?"

"Sure, buddy," Darrell yelled back, "that is if you can handle it!"

Jack smiled, but then before he could blink an eye, he was two hundred feet above the ground, his eyes fixed well in front of Darrell's glider, scanning for even the slightest change in cloud patterns not just in front of him but throughout his peripheral vision. If Darrell sensed even the slightest change, he'd turn his head to determine how he could take advantage of the shift.

When Jack had entangled with the eagle several weeks earlier, he had enjoyed taking control of the eagle's body immensely. Today, though, Jack wanted to learn Darrell's craft. Jack's mind was with Darrell, but he was there only as an idle observer, listening and observing Darrell's thought patterns and physical actions without interfering.

Darrell was completely focused on the task at hand; his mind, his senses, and his movements worked in concert to keep the glider aloft. Darrell had an uncanny ability to absorb massive amounts of information and then filter this information down to only what was needed to optimize the performance of his glider. In addition, his body was finely tuned and adaptive to wind and thermal inputs he was receiving through the glider. His eyesight was exceptional, and where Jack would see a cloud pattern, Darrell would see movements within the cloud that gave him insight into the flow of air in and around the cloud. Once he sensed air patterns that he could use to keep himself aloft, he would turn his glider ever so slightly back and forth to sense the direction and magnitude of the wind. Then he would turn gently in the direction he needed to take full advantage of the ascending warm air. That day, oblivious to Jack when he was aloft earlier, there were three faint, high-altitude, razor-thin clouds that blocked sunrays to different parts of the valley. It was the thermal currents created by these clouds that allowed Darrell to fly back and forth in front of Jack's truck that day.

Jack looked down toward his truck and saw a man standing next to the vehicle, his hands over his eyes blocking the sun. Darrell made several more passes back and forth in full control of his elevation. When he wanted to climb or descend, he could do so easily by taking full advantage of the unusual air currents that day. Before turning, he would dip the nose of the glider slightly down to pick up speed, and then he would pull his glider up, pivot the glider around, and then tip the nose of the glider down again as he completed the turn to regain airspeed. Jack was impressed with his ability to make his turns so precisely and smoothly. It was like watching a ballet dancer dancing his glider along the unseen air currents in the sky.

As Darrell passed by Jack's truck for the last time, he looked down and yelled out, "Hey, Jack, watch this!"

Jack heard himself yell back, "Okay, Darrell, I'm watching!"

Jack was there with Darrell, but there was some part of his consciousness that was still present with him as he stood by his truck. *Well, that's nice,* Jack thought, *I can be two places at once. I'm loving it.*

Up in the sky, Darrell picked up a thermal; he rose quickly over the next quarter of a mile until he was almost seven hundred feet above the ground. Suddenly Darrell pitched his glider straight down—it seemed dangerously down, but Jack could sense that Darrell had complete confidence in his ability to control the craft. The glider picked up speed rapidly until it was only three hundred feet above the ground. The glider was traveling faster than Jack had ever traveled in a glider by himself. Jack was quite frightened as the ground approached, but then abruptly, Darrell pitched the nose up, almost jerking the glider skyward. It was if he were driving in a car and then just jerked the wheel abruptly to the right or left, though in this case, he pulled straight up, keeping the glider perfectly level, with no yawing or rolling at all. Jack always felt he had to baby the glider along, but it was obvious that Darrell knew when and where he could maneuver the glider aggressively.

The nose of the glider was pointed straight up, and as the glider climbed up rapidly, Jack thought to himself, *Wow, what a ride!*

As the glider ascended, it began to lose airspeed, and Darrell forcefully but ever so smoothly continued to pull the nose back by raising his neck, arching his back, and moving his body backward. All Jack could see was blue sky in front of him and the canopy of the glider ruffling as it began to lose lift and approach a stall condition. Darrell guided the glider up and over as it continued its long arch. Within seconds, the glider was upside down and moving very slowly, but Darrell skillfully stayed in control as he waited for the glider to reach the top of the arch. Darrell knew that any slight motion could send the glider out of control, but he was not one to make a mistake. He waited patiently until the craft crested the top of the arch and began to ever so slowly pick up speed again. Jack could see the ground come back into view as the glider quickly, almost explosively, regained momentum.

They were pointed straight down now. Darrell gleefully let the glider accelerate and spontaneously yelled out, "Yeah how! What a ride!"

Darrell keep the glider pointed straight down for over five seconds as the ground approached rapidly, but then he forcefully pulled the glider out of its dive and into a long, smooth arch. At this point in the loop, they pulled several g's as Darrell pulled the glider out of the descent and leveled out only fifty feet above the ground. Jack could feel the exhilaration and satisfaction Darrell obtained from performing that crazy loop, but he also sensed his incredible ability and confidence that allowed him to perform the stunt flawlessly.

Now only fifty feet off the ground, Darrell made one final turn, headed back toward Jack's truck, and landed in the field several hundred feet away from the road. When the glider landed, Jack was suddenly back in his own skin, watching Darrell begin to unstrap himself from his glider about an eighth of a mile away. As Jack walked over to help his friend, he was thankful for the opportunity to see Darrell perform his magic firsthand and hoped that one day he could come close to that level of performance.

As he approached, Jack said, "Pretty impressive, Darrell, pretty impressive!"

"Yeah, Jack, it was a lot of fun," Darrell replied. "Maybe someday I'll teach you how to do one of those loops."

"Well, in a sense, you already have, Darrell. It's neat to watch a master at work."

Darrell smiled as he began to disassemble his glider, and with Jack's help, they were walking back to Jack's vehicle in just a few minutes. It was starting to get overcast and chilly, and it was almost three o'clock, so they decided to pack it up for the day and head over to a bar for a drink.

Chapter 5

The next morning Jack checked his phone messages, and he was pleasantly surprised to learn that Scott, Phyllis's son, had called. Scott seemed very upbeat as Jack replayed the message.

"Jack, how are you doing? Long time, no talk. Just thought I'd call to touch base. Things are going well down here. You should come down for a visit when you have the chance. Listen, Jack, I have some good news—I'm kind of excited about it. Give me a call back, and I'll tell you all about it. Hope all is well up there in Alaska. Look forward to hearing from you."

It was good to hear Scott so upbeat; he'd been through some tough times, and Jack worried about him. Many times Scott would call when he was down and needed someone to talk to for support, so Jack was thankful that he had called to share good news. Scott was an only child, and Jack in a way had been like a big brother, almost like a father figure, to Scott when he was growing up. Scott never really knew his biological father since he had left when Scott was only five, and he didn't have a good relationship with his mother either. Both Scott and Jack were fans of the original Star Trek science fiction series, and sometimes on weekday evenings after school, Scott would swing by Jack's apartment, and they would watch the old shows together before Scott headed home. Between the work on Jack's plane and the Star Trek episodes, they became good friends.

Jack fixed himself a cup of coffee and read the newspaper for a while before he called Scott back.

"Hey, Scott, how's it going?" Jack asked when Scott picked up the phone.

"Jack! What's going on?"

"Oh, not too much, just having a cup of morning coffee, and yourself?"

"Oh, just hanging. I'm going to head out to the beach in a little while, relax, and enjoy the sunshine."

"Well, it must be nice down there. You guys get a lot more sunshine than we do up here."

"Yeah, I know, Jack. Why don't you think about moving down here? You'd love it."

Jack laughed lightly. "That's funny, Scott, I love it up here—you know how it is. This is the last real piece of wilderness we have in this world. It's not warm now, but the sun is out and the air is crisp so I'm trying to soak it all in. Went and did some hang gliding with Darrell yesterday—it was a blast."

"That's good, Jack," Scott replied. Scott hesitated, and there was a brief silence. Jack sensed Scott wanted to tell him the good news but was uncomfortable sharing it with him; he wasn't used to reporting something positive.

"So what's up, Scott? You said you had some good news that you were excited about."

Scott started out slowly. "Oh, yeah, well, I just wanted to tell you, well, you know I've been working at that auto dealership for almost five years now."

He stopped and hesitated again.

"Go on, go on, it's all right," Jack said encouragingly. "Tell me, Scott, I want to hear it."

"Well, the owner seemed to be pretty impressed with my skills as a mechanic, and some of the other things I've learned, welding and fabrication. He told me about an auto racing team that was looking for a few skilled mechanics, and he encouraged me to apply for the job. He told me he thought my skills would never be used to the fullest at the dealership. He said that even though he would be sorry to lose me, that I had the ability to work as a mechanic at that level and that I could do well in that environment."

"Really, wow, so what happened?"

"Well, I went down to the race team headquarters and applied. Their team shop is not far from the auto dealership, in fact. There was an interview, and then there was a kind of tryout. I had to work on some cars and then fabricate a few parts, show them the skills I had. It was pretty competitive—I think over thirty mechanics applied for only two spots. After waiting a few weeks, they called me and told me I had the job."

"Really, hey, man, that's great, dude."

"Yeah, the owner at the dealership said that he was sorry to lose me, but he said I had such aptitude that I would get bored and frustrated working on street cars all day long. He said I had more ability than that, that it was only fair for me to at least give the auto racing job a shot."

"Really, he said that?" Jack replied. "You should believe it, Scott. You know when you were up here working on my plane, you were amazing. I'm happy for you. So what's the deal; what kind of team is it? What will the job be like?"

"It's an Indy car team. It's not a top-level team, at least not now. It's a small start-up team, but in their first year last year, they did well, had a couple of top ten finishes, and they're trying to build on their success. They've got some good sponsorship this year and have a top-notch driver, so it should be pretty exciting. It will be tough—I'll be traveling around the country from track to track. A lot of the races are on the West Coast, but there are races in Texas and Ohio and New York as well, so it will be pretty hectic, but this is something I really want to do. I think it will be fantastic."

"That's wonderful, Scott. That's really great. I'm very happy for you."

"Thanks, Jack. I wanted to tell someone about it. I just couldn't keep it all to myself."

Jack thought for a second and then said, "Listen, Scott, do me a favor, all right?"

"What's that?"

"This is a real favor—you'll promise me you'll do it, okay?"

"Sure, Jack, what?"

"Call your mother and tell her about it. I'm sure she'd love to know, and I know she'd love to hear from you."

"No, no, Jack. I don't want to talk to that woman," Scott replied in a flat, hollow tone.

"Why not? What's wrong with talking to your own mother?"

"My own mother? What do you mean? She's a bitch. I hate that woman," Scott replied, a tinge of irritation now evident in his voice.

"What?" Jack replied. He was starting to get angry, and he raised his voice. "What do you mean, you hate that bitch? What a horrible thing to say. She brought you into this world. She raised you as best she could. She's your own flesh and blood. Just give her a call."

"What do you mean, Jack? I haven't talked to her in years. I don't even know her anymore."

"What do you mean you don't know her? You don't know your own mother! Who the hell do you think you are?"

"Jack! I never heard you talk to me like that before. You just mad or something?"

"Damn straight I'm mad. What do you mean, you hate that woman? What kind of man are you to say that about your mother? I know you two didn't get along, but she misses you. It has been very painful for her ever since you left seven years ago. That was a horrible thing to do to her. You give her a call, and I mean it."

"How do you know that, Jack? How do you know anything about my mother?"

"I know," Jack replied, "I know it was she who encouraged you to involve yourself in mechanical things, and it was she who encouraged you to get a job working on my plane as a start. She saw your ability, Scott, and she was trying to guide you."

"Guide me? Come on, she was trying to get me out of the house. She didn't care about me. She wanted to get rid of me," Scott replied as he began to raise his voice.

"That's a lie, Scott, a flat lie, and you know it. Sure, she didn't show her love in a way you expected to see it. But she loved you then, and she loves you now. She only wants the best for you."

"The best for me—you've got to be joking, she doesn't give a damn about me, she never did. She's a drunk, just a damn drunk," Scott replied in a dismissive, angry tone.

"You little punk, Scott. If I could be you right now, I'd smack myself upside the head for talking that way about my mother."

Jack was surprised that even so far away and across a phone line, he was still able to be there with Scott on that Saturday morning. He was sitting outside with Scott in a bean bag chair on Scott's second-story porch looking toward the beach and the Pacific Ocean beyond. The air was warm and salty from the light ocean breeze blowing up the coast. He sat there for a brief second trying to orient himself with his new surroundings before acting. He knew he didn't have much time; across such distances, he suspected he wouldn't be there very long.

Jack had Scott stand up, and with the phone still in his hand, walked him inside the small condo into the living room. *This might cause a little damage,* Jack thought to himself, but he didn't care—Scott needed a little disciplining. He thrust Scott's head hard against the drywall, hard enough to put a three-inch dent in the wall. Jack could feel the sharp pain of the hit as small pieces of paint and drywall scattered their way into Scott's hair and onto his forehead. The hit was hard enough that Jack saw stars and began to gray out for a few seconds. Scott stumbled slightly and had to put his hand on the wall to stabilize himself, accidentally dropping the phone on the carpet as he waited for his head to clear.

"Ouch!" he heard Scott say just before he was back in Alaska, his morning coffee sitting on the kitchen table in front of him, the pain in his head gone.

"Scott, are you there, Scott?" Jack said into the phone. There was a long silence, and Jack waited for a response. "Scott, pick up the phone—it's just a little bump on the head, just pick up the phone."

Jack could hear some muffled moans in the background, and he suspected the pain was now spreading into the nerve centers in Scott's brain. It took Scott a good twenty seconds before he picked the phone up from the carpet.

"What the hell?" Jack heard Scott say. "Man, that hurt! Something just came over me; it feels like I just got smacked in the side of the head."

"Look at your wall," Jack replied.

"What?"

"Look at your wall," Jack repeated.

Scott turned and saw the dent in the drywall, then moved his hands up to his forehead, feeling the small pieces of debris on his skin.

"What the hell just happened? Man, that hurt. Jack, what the hell is going on?"

"You needed to have someone smack some sense into you, Scott. I just had to take it upon myself to do it," Jack replied.

"What's this all about, Jack? Are you crazy? All I know is my head hurts like hell."

"Well, take the pain in your head, Scott, and multiply it by a thousand. That's the amount of pain you've inflicted on your mother by never calling her, never telling her what you were doing. For all she knew, you could have been dead," Jack replied. "Just sit down for a little while. Your head will be fine. I just smacked it into the wall, that's all."

"I know, Jack. I don't know how in the hell you just did that, but I saw what you did. I feel what you did. Are you some kind of telepath, man? What have you been doing, Jack—learning the skills of Trekian mind control? This is strange, very strange," Scott said, bewildered, as he gently rubbed his hand over his forehead.

"Don't concern yourself with me, Scott," Jack replied. "Focus on your new job—it sounds like a perfect fit for you. And call your sweet mother—she misses you so much. She's terribly hurt and would love to hear your voice. Tell her all about your life in California and the excitement you feel now. Share what you've shared with me with her."

Scott stood dazed for a few seconds, but with the pain in his head and the distant images he now saw of his mother alone in her house crying, he replied, "All right, Jack, I'll give her a call."

"Good, Scott. Do you still have her number?"

"Yeah, I got it. I have it written down in my old address book. I didn't throw it away."

Scott paused for a few moments and then said, "You're right: it was a terrible thing for me to do to Mom. I'll call her today."

"Great, and, Scott, again, congratulations on your job. Well done."

"Thanks, Jack, thanks a bunch. We'll talk again soon?"

"Sure, Scott. Talk to you soon."

Jack got up, walked into the bathroom, and looked at himself in the mirror. He felt no pain, so he was surprised to see a swollen, red welt on the topside of his head. He smiled. *Don't worry, Jack,* he said to himself, *you'll be fine—you just hit your head into a wall, that's all.*

Chapter 6

After Jack hung up with Scott, he pulled out the book he had checked out from the library and read more about the experiments that had been performed by Robert Weldon. It was fascinating, and he was so intrigued by this power he had acquired that he wanted to find out more and possibly discuss it with a doctor. He thought about going to a local doctor, but he thought, *you know, they won't be able to tell me anything. They'll probably just look at me sideways and think I'm going insane.* He looked at the back cover of Weldon's book. Weldon at the time had been a professor at the University of Montana in Bozeman. He had his own practice, but he served as a professor as well.

Jack thought he might try to look him up—possibly he was still there. He logged onto his computer and did a search for faculty at the University of Montana. He went through the list of names, but it appeared Weldon wasn't on staff anymore. He wrote an e-mail to the university requesting information on Weldon, saying that he had reviewed several of his books and would like to discuss some of the information contained in them. He asked the university if there were a way he could contact Weldon.

★★★★★

Over that weekend, Jack was busy. He delivered supplies to two remote Eskimo villages that were only accessible by plane, so he didn't take the time to log onto his computer. Finally, on Monday evening, Jack checked his e-mail and found that the university had responded, saying that Dr. Weldon had retired several years earlier but he could be contacted through his university e-mail. Weldon checked it periodically to see if people had questions, and Jack could try to contact him that way. Jack was a little surprised that they were so forthcoming with the information, but he thought it probably had something to do with the fact that Weldon liked to communicate with people around the country regarding his work.

Jack sent him an e-mail telling him he had reviewed several of his books and was most curious about his experiments regarding extrasensory perception. Jack didn't directly discuss his newfound abilities, but he hinted at it slightly by saying that he thought he might have experienced on rare occasions some of the behavioral patterns that the people in the experiments had perceived. He wasn't sure, though, and he wanted to get a better understanding of the experiments and determine if there were a relationship to what he had been experiencing recently.

★★★★★

Robert Weldon must have been reading his e-mail regularly, because he responded back to Jack the next morning.

The e-mail read, "Thank you for sending me an e-mail and for reading some of the literature I have published. Yes, we can discuss this further, but first I would like to get a better understanding of your background, where you live, and what you do for a living. Please just send me a brief biography of yourself to help me understand your situation so that we can get to know one another better before we discuss the behavioral patterns you mentioned. Thank you again for contacting me, and I look forward to hearing from you."

Jack was a little surprised and very pleased that Weldon had responded. He seemed like a pleasant guy, open to listening to Jack's tale, which was refreshing. Jack responded back, telling him about his life. How he had grown up in Alaska and the continental West Coast. He had become a pilot at a fairly young age, getting his license at the age of seventeen with encouragement from his father. He had majored in engineering, and then decided to open up a charter service in Alaska, which he had been doing since then. He gave Weldon the name of his charter, "Alaskan Sky Beauty," in case Weldon wanted to look him up. He mentioned some of his hobbies, such as hang gliding and astronomy. He told him he was single, that he had been living in Alaska for quite a few years now, and that he, in general, had a good life and was happy.

Jack wasn't sure why Weldon had asked about his background and life. Maybe he was just being a good doctor, trying to get an understanding of his patient before his evaluation, or maybe he was trying to make sure Jack wasn't a mental patient suffering from schizophrenia or the like. In any case, Jack responded as he had asked. As Weldon had requested, he didn't discuss the behavioral patterns he had been experiencing; he just described his life and who he was.

At the end of his message, he did refer to Weldon's books, especially the one describing his ESP experiments and how the drugs he had developed affected people's ability to pick up on others' thoughts. He quoted a specific line out of the book to let Weldon know that he had done some research and was familiar with his work. *Maybe this will give me some credibility,* Jack thought, *and will give Weldon an indication that I am serious about the questions I am asking.*

★★★★★

When Jack got home that afternoon after a short flight with a few people, Weldon had already responded.

The e-mail read, "Thank you, Jack, for letting me know a little bit about yourself. I appreciate it. It must be getting cold up there in Alaska this time of year. I used to vacation quite often there with my family—it is a beautiful area. We did enjoy Anchorage, but my fondest memories were when we took a small fishing boat down the Shelikof Strait and along the Aleutian Range. The long Alaskan summer days gave us hours and hours to see the landscape and visit with the natural wildlife. It was a wonderful trip."

Jack knew the Aleutian Range well; it was one of the more favorite spots for his Anchorage passengers, second only to Mount McKinley. Jack was a little surprised about how direct Weldon was in his next series of questions.

The e-mail read, "Now let me get to the business at hand and ask you a few questions concerning your previous correspondence. You hinted at some of the symptoms you've experienced. If you feel comfortable, please describe to me in detail the experiences you've been having; when they started, how often they occur and under what situations, and any other information you feel would help me better understand your condition. It is difficult for me to do an assessment of your condition unless I have an understanding of these things. The brief description of your experiences was quite fascinating and sparks my memories of the research I did thirty years ago, and I'm curious to know more. Look forward to learning more about your condition and trying to relate your experiences back to the work I did. Take care, Jack, and look forward to hearing from you."

Jack spent that evening and the following morning writing a lengthy e-mail back to Weldon describing his trip through the aurora borealis and his recent experiences. He described his ability to feel the pain in George's broken leg and recall some of George's recent memories, as well as the ability to take control of the eagle's body and fly through the sky as if he were the bird, directing the eagle's body and psyche to his every whim. He described how he had hitched a ride with Darrell as he performed a loop in his hang glider, not disturbing Darrell's control of his glider but instead just being there with Darrell, observing his thoughts and movements. He recalled his flight up to the glacier and how he had perceived Phil's heart attack, which Phil had later confirmed. He touched on his episode with Sandy, finding it difficult to recount since this had been quite a painful experience for Jack, but he gave Weldon enough information to get a good idea of what had happened. He described at length his experiences with Phyllis and Scott and how he had felt the pain rush through his own head when he had thrust Scott's head against the drywall. He noted that the pain was short-lived and actually vanished once he came back into his own body, but the welt on his head remained. He also described the lingering depression he felt as he experienced Phyllis's sadness over losing touch with Scott.

He tried to recall the periods of time these phenomena had lasted. Sometimes it would last for a few minutes, as with the eagle; other times it was brief, lasting only a few seconds, but long enough for Jack to perceive the person's thoughts and feel the sensations he or she felt. Jack tried to recall if there was any particular time of day the experiences were more vivid than others, but he couldn't put a logical connection to it—but then again, he wrote, he hadn't been paying that much attention either. After four pages, Jack felt he had summarized his experiences as best as he could.

He felt a little anxious about disclosing all this detail, but Weldon was a doctor, a good one at that, and even though they had only communicated back and forth a few times, he felt comfortable with Weldon, as if they had already begun to form a bond of trust. He thanked Weldon for spending the time to communicate with him, and then he ended the message as Weldon had started the previous one, describing Alaska and mentioning that he had flown the Shelikof Strait many times and that it was one of his favorite destinations. He mentioned a trip he had taken to Montana to see Glacier National Park a few years earlier and how, even though he lived in Alaska, he had never seen anything quite so beautiful. They seemed to share a common interest for the outdoors and earth's natural wonders, so Jack felt it was a nice way to end his correspondence. Jack sent the e-mail off, hoping that Weldon would reply in turn shortly.

★★★★★

Jack checked his e-mail every morning for the next six days but did not receive anything from Robert Weldon. He felt somewhat disappointed, but then on a Wednesday morning, Jack was pleasantly surprised to see Weldon had responded. Weldon first apologized in a very pleasant manner that he hadn't gotten back to Jack earlier, but said that it had been quite a few years since he had performed his experiments and he wanted to refresh his memory and try to assimilate what Jack had described and compare it to the observations and results he had collected thirty years earlier. He had spent some time reviewing his work in detail to draw a connection to Jack's experiences.

Jack read on. Weldon told Jack that some of the symptoms he was experiencing were similar to the results of his experiments, but it appeared that Jack's were more intense and pronounced than anything Weldon had observed. However, the underlying behavioral patterns were similar to what Jack had described. As published in his book, Weldon had documented the ability of one participant to perceive another's thoughts and this ability was greatly enhanced by Weldon's drugs, but those thoughts had to be in the forefront of the other participant's brain. For example, a television scene that induced strong emotions of either joy or pain could then be perceived by the other person. In addition, there had been several experiments where one person would feel specific bodily pains of the other participant for brief periods of time, especially if that pain were intense. Weldon had not published those results because he had seen it only a few times and had not spent the time to investigate it further, but in questioning some of the participants, it had been mentioned on a few occasions. Weldon said, however, that he had not observed the ability of one person to perceive scenes buried deeper in the other person's brain, such as images from several months or years earlier. Nor had he observed the ability of one person to actually take control of the other's body, though he had never specifically performed such tests. In fact, he said that he had intended to conduct such experiments before he decided to discontinue his work on ESP and focus, instead, on developing drugs for brain disorders such as Alzheimer's and schizophrenia.

Jack paused for a moment after reading this, wondering why Weldon had discontinued his work on ESP—obviously the drugs he had developed were promising; Weldon did not elaborate on this point in his e-mail.

Weldon went on to say that thoughts were transmitted through the brain by small electronic currents or waves and that there were small gaps between brain cells called synapses that the electrical current had to traverse or jump across. It was these jumps that helped to direct the electrical pulses to the correct portion of the brain for interpretation and appropriate action. The idea was that under certain conditions, these synapses could be modified or altered, giving the brain the ability to pick up on electrical signals other than just those traveling through an individual's brain. When altered, the synapses could pick up on specific patterns outside of the individual's body, and this was essentially what his drugs had tried to achieve. It had to do with slightly modifying the chemical nature of certain synapses so that they could "tune in" to a different frequency of brain waves.

Jack was hoping Weldon would elaborate on this, but he did not. Jack got the sense that Weldon was hedging a little, unwilling to divulge too much information regarding his drugs, as if there were a lingering concern in the back of his mind that inhibited additional openness. Weldon went on to ask Jack more about his encounter with the aurora borealis.

"Jack, I find this encounter particularly interesting, and understanding it better will help me to better assess what has happened to you. This event was quite peculiar, so try to think back to that night and give me any additional detail that comes to mind. Anything unusual or out of the ordinary that you didn't describe before would be helpful. I find this entire phenomenon you've described to be quite fascinating, and I hope we can continue to discuss it. In fact, Jack, if you have the urge, it would be useful if we could meet at some point. I understand that you've described to me some very personal events, and I appreciate your willingness to share these events with me. Rest assured that I consider this to be strictly confidential between you and me. I have no intention of sharing this with anyone else. I hope I can trust that you will do the same for now. Thank you again, Jack, and I look forward to hearing from you again soon."

★★★★★

Jack replied the next day. He responded first to Weldon's hope that their correspondence remain confidential.

"Yes, I understand your desire for confidentiality at this point. You're the first person I've shared this with, and until some later time, once I better understand what has happened to me, I do not intend to discuss this with anyone else. Yes, I do hope that we can meet at some point; I think that would be helpful for both of us."

Jack went on to describe some further details about his encounter with the aurora borealis. Previously he had failed to tell Weldon that his radios stopped working after he had flown through the auroral funnel, and that the next morning he had noticed that his newly installed static discharge rods were completely gone. He described how his radios had worked the next day, and that besides having to replace all his discharge rods, the plane did not appear to suffer any permanent damage. Jack mentioned that he was encouraged to hear that some of Weldon's experiments did produce similar, although not as dramatic, behavioral pattern changes not unlike Jack's own experiences. He mentioned that he would like to make a flight out to Montana sometime in the near future to meet with Weldon, and that hopefully something could be arranged.

★★★★★

Weldon responded the next morning.

"Jack, your encounter with the aurora borealis and the effect on your radios and discharge rods do, in some ways, agree with my experiments, because the drugs I developed stimulated the ability of the synapses to pick up electrical thought patterns traveling through another's brain. It's kind of like taking a radio receiver, extending the range, and then adjusting the frequency of the receiver to tap into another's thoughts. If your body and mind were somehow overloaded with electrical stimuli during your flight through the auroral funnel, it's possible that your synapses, especially those buried deep in your corpus callosum, have been altered. You see, the synapses in the corpus callosum act as the central switching station for the entire mind, telling which electrical brain waves to go where. If this 'station' now is receiving signals from someone else, your brain could perceive their thoughts. I'm speculating, but it's possible that the synapses in parts of your nervous system have been altered so that when you receive thought patterns that perceive pain, injury, or in general feedback from the other person's body, these sensations are reproduced in your own body. Once this pain is experienced, it appears your nerve centers retain the memory of this pain, thus possibly explaining why the welt remained on your head, as you described to me concerning the incident with your friend Scott. Again, this is speculation that can only be validated with experimentation."

He went on to tell Jack that they could continue to correspond via e-mail, but it was difficult for him to do a further assessment of Jack's condition unless he were actually able to do some tests on him. These tests could include taking blood and tissue samples, doing some tests on Jack's brain functioning, and possibly taking a brain scan to track electrical thought patterns as they traveled through his brain and nervous system. Some of the more simple tests could be done in Weldon's office, but the more sophisticated tests would have to be done in Bozeman at one of the hospitals Weldon worked with while a professor. He suggested that if Jack wanted to pursue this more, he could make a trip out to Montana.

Weldon mentioned that he'd had some bad experiences thirty years earlier with people leaking information regarding the development of his drugs and talking with individuals behind his back, so he hoped Jack understood his desire for confidentiality. He gave Jack his phone number and told Jack to call him if he so desired.

Experiments and tests, Jack thought to himself. *Man, this sounds like something out of a mad scientist story.* He felt shivers run down his spine, but he understood that from a medical perspective, this was what Weldon needed to do to collect more data. Jack had a flight that morning. During the day, he thought more about where he wanted to go with Weldon. Weldon sounded like a decent, competent doctor, but maybe a little voice-to-voice over the phone would help Jack feel more comfortable before he pursued a face-to-face meeting.

When he got home that evening, he replied to Weldon.

"Thank you, Dr. Weldon, for taking the time to do your assessment of my condition, and thank you for keeping this confidential between you and me. Yes, sometime in the future, I would like to travel to Montana, so I'll see if I can plan something in the next several months. I would like to talk over the phone before then as well; I would enjoy that very much. If you don't mind, if I could contact you if I have any unusual or alarming symptoms, I would really appreciate it. I'm still trying to understand what has happened to me, but thus far, it's actually been quite enlightening and enchanting, and I hope it stays that way. Some additional feedback from you as things progress would be much appreciated. Thank you again, Dr. Weldon, for your time and insight. Take care, and I'll be in touch soon."

Jack included his phone number at the bottom of the message and told Weldon he'd be happy to hear from him if he so desired.

★★★★★

Jack had e-mailed Weldon back and forth quite a few times now. All the e-mail traffic sparked his memory of the couple he had met during the flight to the glacier near the base of Mount McKinley. *Ah, yes,* Jack thought, *I said I would contact Phil about a website and business network for booking flights.* The next morning, Jack went through a pile of notes on his desk and found Phil's card. It was nine o'clock in the morning, *probably a good time to catch him,* Jack speculated, and he picked up the phone and made the call.

Phil picked up the phone after one ring. "Hello."

"Hi, Phil. This is Jack, from Alaskan Sky Beauty."

"Ah yes, Jack, Jack from the tour service, how are you doing?"

"Very fine, thank you, and yourself?"

"Great, great! Thanks for asking."

Jack could sense a little bounce in Phil's voice, and he seemed more upbeat and alive than when they had met during Phil's vacation in Alaska.

"So how are things back in the Bay area? Are you settled back into work now?"

"Oh, of course, Jack. I love going on vacation, but it's nice to get back to your real life if you know what I mean. Whenever I'm gone for a while, I have a hundred e-mails when I return, and it takes me a full day sometimes to go through all that junk. Are you sure you want to sign up for a more sophisticated network, Jack?" Phil asked jokingly. "What will happen is you'll get hundreds of e-mails each day, and it will drive you crazy sifting through all that crap. We have ways of blocking some of that junk e-mail with software routines, but they always figure out ways to get around it. You know, don't let me scare you off, because I know we can set up something to help you streamline your business and get you more clients. We'll work up something really nice."

"Yeah, I know what you mean about the junk stuff," Jack replied. "I don't use e-mail all that much, but every once in a while, I'll get some stuff, especially those pop-up ads. It'll drive you crazy if you're not careful. But you know, if there's something we can do, that would be great."

"Sure, sure, my pleasure. So how's it going up there in Alaska, Jack?"

"Oh, it's going well. Thanks for asking. Things are starting to slow down a little bit here in Anchorage. I'm going to start flying out of Fairbanks more often now. I have a night flight, a tour if you want to call it, up to see the aurora borealis. It's quite popular, especially in the winter during peak season for the auroras. Other than that, not too much else is going on."

"Well, good, Jack. If I ever make it back to Alaska, I'll look you up for one of those night flights. All right, well, let me look up this guy's number to call about that network. It's probably best to just give this guy a ring directly. We'll set up something good for you, Jack—it shouldn't be too difficult. You could probably set it up yourself, but we know some shortcuts and tricks to it. It would probably take you much longer to get it up and running. We do this stuff all the time; you just tell him what you want, and he'll get you going. It will be well worth your nickel, and don't worry, it won't cost you much. Let me see—ah, there's his card. His name is Gordon Phillips, and he works out of Anchorage. His number is (907) 475-8910. I've worked with him on quite a few occasions; he's very good and a very nice guy to work with."

"Great, Phil, thanks for the referral. Do appreciate it."

"Sure, Jack, look, it was a pleasure to meet you. Christine and I really enjoyed our flight; it was a lot of fun."

"Well, that's good to hear. I enjoyed having you two as well."

"By the way, Jack, I took your advice."

"What's that, Phil?"

"Oh, I told Christine about the heart attack I had two years back."

"Really! Well, that's great."

"Yeah, well, ever since I told her, we've been getting along a lot better.

She understands now why I was behaving the way I did. I wasn't trying to distance myself from her or anything like that. It was just that I was afraid of exerting myself because of my health. It really sank in with her once I told her about my attack. She was taking it very personally, if you know what I mean, but she finally realized it wasn't about her—it was about my health. She's helping me a lot now with maintaining a healthier lifestyle. After I told her, we went to the doctor together. The doctor gave me some additional exercises I can do and suggested I make improvements in lifestyle, eating habits, stuff like that. It really shocked her when she found out I had been seeing him for a while now, but with us together talking with him, it was great. It's a help to both of us, and Christine has been following his advice as well. She's been wonderful, and since she's been making some of the same changes, it gives us something to talk about and share together. We've been eating more fresh fruit, staying away from fatty foods, and such, eating in more often, and it's been fun when we go shopping together. She's kind of a health fanatic as it is, but now she's even more into it and she's really taking it to heart to make sure I'm following doctor's orders. We've been getting along so much better, and it's really been a joy spending time with her again. I was really in the dumps there for a while, and our relationship was quite strained. I think you could see it between us when we were up in Alaska."

"Yes, Phil, I could sense something was troubling you, and I'm very happy for you that things are working out."

"Yeah, it's like a big weight has been lifted off my shoulders. We can share our thoughts so easily now, I don't have to conceal anything from her anymore. It's been quite a change, but a wonderful one. I do appreciate it, Jack. It was a good piece of advice. Listen, we'll keep in touch, okay?"

"Sure, Phil, that would be great. We'll talk again soon."

"Okay, Jack, sounds good. I'll talk to you later."

"Talk to you later, Phil. Good-bye."

Chapter 7

Jack had three flights that week, but nothing scheduled for the following week in Anchorage. He decided to head up to Fairbanks after his last flight to try to set up some tours and work on his house. On Wednesday afternoon, after an early morning tour, he flew to Fairbanks.

He felt like doing something social that weekend, but he checked the local paper when he arrived and there was nothing much going on. It was early dusk, but even then, the stars were brilliant, so he decided to check and see what the local astronomy club was doing that weekend.

He was a casual member of the club in Fairbanks, fittingly called the Astronomical Unit. Every month in the fall, winter, and spring, the club would get together for stargazing activities. They would set up several small to medium-size telescopes in a large field a short distance from the Museum of the North, the Fairbanks museum of science and art, and gaze at the moon, the planets, and star formations. The museum itself was a swooping combination of grand, graceful shapes that reminded Jack of moving icebergs, or perhaps even the northern lights, and was a beautiful backdrop for the event. On occasion, the club would schedule time at the Fairbanks Observatory, about a thirty-minute drive outside of the city, but that weekend the club was meeting on Friday night at the museum. The weather forecast predicted a cool, crisp night, perfect for gazing, so the club had scheduled an activity. The club mentioned that it was one of the rare occurrences where Mars, Jupiter, and Saturn were lined up in their orbits

84

around the sun, and Friday would be one of the rare opportunities to gaze at all three planets at the same time through one telescope.

Jack got there early Friday night, and people were still setting up their telescopes, although a few were already set up. Jack wandered over to the small gathering, occasionally looking up at the stars trying to find the three bright dots of light that were Saturn, Jupiter, and Mars. There was one telescope pointed in the direction of the three planets, and Jack waited patiently in line behind four other observers. Each took his or her time as more people gathered for the occasion and the other telescopes were set up to observe other points in the night sky. After about twenty minutes, Jack got his turn. This particular telescope was focused on Jupiter, but as Jack gazed through the eyepiece, he could make out the blurred images of Saturn and Mars behind and in front of the giant planet. As Jack stared more closely at Jupiter, he could just make out two small moons of Jupiter orbiting near the planet's equator. *Amazing,* Jack thought to himself, *here we are millions of miles away, and we can peer into the workings of another world.*

There were two other telescopes sitting close to this telescope; one was set up on Saturn, and the other on Mars. There were also several other telescopes in the field that night; one was focused on the crescent moon, and others were focused on various constellations and star clusters.

Jack casually walked from one telescope to another, saying hi to a few people and talking politely about that night and how the stars and planets were so brilliant. While chatting with a fellow astronomy buff, something caught his eye, and he looked to his left. He saw a woman by herself staring up into the night sky, a serious but somewhat curious look on her face. It was cold that night and she was wearing a down coat, but even with it on, Jack could tell she was a slim woman. Her light brown hair was in a bow on her head and she had some earmuffs on, but it didn't hide her striking and somewhat mysterious attractiveness. Jack hesitated—he didn't know exactly why, but possibly because he immediately felt an attraction to her. She appeared to be in her midthirties, give or take a few years, he guessed.

Jack stared at her, her features lit up by the light of the crescent moon, his interest in her growing as the seconds passed. His gaze must have caught the woman's attention, because she looked down toward the ground and then turned her head and caught Jack's gaze just for an instant. It caught Jack off guard, and as she looked at him, he continued to stare back at her, his face expressionless. Before he even had time for a gesture or smile, she turned her head again and looked back up at the sky. Her expression was one of interest, Jack could tell, but there was also an expression of solitude, as if she didn't want to be interrupted with what she was doing. That expression made Jack hesitate. Jack put his hands in his pockets, turned, and walked to some of the other telescopes set up in the field, but she had captured his attention and his mind was no longer focused on the stars that night. *You should strike up a conversation with her,* Jack thought to himself. *You never know, this might be your only chance; you might never see her again.*

After several minutes of lingering, pretending he was still interested in just looking at the stars, Jack looked for her, hoping she hadn't already left. He saw her just a few yards from where she had been before, but now she was standing in line for one of the telescopes. Jack walked up behind her.

"Beautiful night for stargazing, isn't it?"

"Why yes, yes, it is," she replied quietly.

"So how are you doing tonight?"

"I'm doing fine, fine, thank you, just enjoying the stars and planets."

"Yes, I noticed earlier you were just gazing up at the heavens without the aid of the telescopes, just looking up."

"Yeah, I do that often to get a better perspective. Lets my mind capture the whole image before I get behind the telescope, so that I can better understand the beauty of what I'm looking at."

"Yes, that's a good idea, lets one better appreciate the image captured by the lens."

"Yes," she continued, "if you look up there in the northwest corner of the sky, you'll see how the Seven Sisters are canted toward the Big Dipper. You'll get that perspective only in late fall, something to do with how the earth's magnetic field distorts the view."

"Really? I never noticed that before, but now that you point it out to me, I can see what you're talking about."

"Yeah, it is a subtlety, but it's something you'll pick out if you look at the stars over an extended period of time."

"Fascinating," Jack replied, "I remember a few years ago, I was on vacation in Australia. I did some stargazing down there, and I looked up at the heavens and noticed that Orion the Hunter was upside down. It caught me off guard at first, but then I realized that Orion the Hunter wasn't upside down—it was I that was upside down! I was figuratively standing on my head down there!"

She laughed, "Yes, of course."

There was a brief silence, but Jack didn't want the conversation to end.

"Well, let me introduce myself. My name is Jack."

"Nice to meet you, Jack. My name is Helen."

"Nice to meet you, Helen."

She's very pleasant and quite conversational, Jack thought to himself, the type of person he would like to get to know better.

There was a brief silence again, then something crept into Jack's brain and he said, "You know, sometimes I do this stargazing and it's just spectacular and beautiful, but then I start to think about the expanse of outer space, how huge it is out there and how small this tiny planet is that we live on. It just seems we're so insignificant relative to the vastness of the universe, the vastness of the Milky Way galaxy, even the vastness of our own solar system—we're such a small piece of the puzzle that I can't even attempt to really comprehend."

Jack was looking at her as he spoke. He didn't quite understand why he had spurted that out, but there was something that came over him as he gazed at her.

She looked down with a slight frown, but a thoughtful expression on her face as well.

"Yes, I've felt that way at times myself," she replied, "but then I think about this planet that we live on, this jewel we call Earth. There's probably millions and millions of planets out there, but think of a planet like ours that can support life, that can harbor the diversity of life that we see here, trees and plants, dolphins and fish, giraffes, elephants, kangaroos, monkeys, you name it, and of course, human beings. This planet and the world it has created are amazing. It's a one in a hundred million shot, maybe one in a billion shot. It's like we don't realize how lucky we are to be part of it all. I consider myself to be very fortunate to be part of this wonderful oddity—some would call it a miracle. I just call it an absolutely amazing phenomenon that I am so grateful to be a part of."

Jack was taken aback by her insight, but then he collected himself and said, "That is a beautiful way of looking at things. I have never thought of it in that way, but you know, you're right, you're absolutely right. I wish I could have that perspective, so beautiful and pure. Maybe if we could swap minds, then I could ..." Jack stopped in mid sentence.

She was looking down at the ground, an almost frightened and distinctly disappointed look on her face. He couldn't quite comprehend it, but it was almost as if she were thinking to herself, *oh god, not another one of those types, some Alaskan screwball.* Maybe she was starting to like him, thinking they might spend some time together, but not now, she couldn't waste her time with some whacked-out character, someone she wouldn't have any interest in. She wasn't a young woman, in her midthirties, and she turned slightly away from him as if to say, "Look, my time is limited, and I can't waste it with someone who would say such an odd thing as that."

Don't screw this up, Jack said to himself. *You better think fast before she puts you down as some flaked-out, screwball idiot.* He got nothing from her either, nothing from her mind that he could read, but that was okay, he thought, he didn't need it to find out more about her.

"I'm sorry, Helen, I'm sorry. I'm just being silly. Don't take it the wrong way. It's just sometimes when I'm enjoying the evening—I mean, here I am enjoying such a beautiful night as tonight, talking to such an elegant woman as yourself, I start to lose myself, my mind drifts thinking of possibilities. When I think this way, I can spit out silly things like that. Don't take it in a bad way. I would like to talk more with you, about astronomy and some of the things you like to do, and learn how you developed such a wonderful perspective on life."

She smiled faintly, and then batted her eyes a few times as if to say, "nice recovery, you haven't lost me yet."

"Yes, I'd enjoy that," she replied.

During the rest of the evening, they did talk. They talked about a lot of things, about astronomy at first, but then about Alaska, and their jobs, their hobbies, and many other things, so many that Jack couldn't remember them all—but they each learned a lot about the other, and Jack couldn't remember a more wonderful evening than that evening. They enjoyed each other's company for hours, but it was starting to get late and Jack could tell that Helen was getting tired, that she was thinking about going.

"Listen," Jack said, "I've had a wonderful evening, and I'd like to see you again. Maybe we could go out for coffee, spend some time together, do something nice."

She looked back at him and then said, "Yes, let's do that, I'd like that. I've had a wonderful time as well."

They exchanged phone numbers. She worked in Anchorage at the main hospital there, but was visiting her parents, who lived just outside of Fairbanks, for a few days. She told Jack to call her at the hospital; it was the easiest way to reach her.

"I'll do that," he replied. "Listen I've really enjoyed spending some time with you tonight."

"I've enjoyed it as well, Jack. Look forward to seeing you again."

He put her number in his pocket, and as she walked away, for one last time that night, Jack looked up at the stars, his mind wandering, and he started dreaming.

Chapter 8

"Josh, it's time to come in now. Come on, Josh, you need to get inside and get some sleep!"

"Okay, Mom, okay. I'll be in when I get done," Josh replied as he rummaged through the gear and clothing he had scattered out on the back porch of their house.

"Josh, I'll give you five minutes. You'll need to be up at four tomorrow morning, three hours before the crack of dawn, and you need a good night's rest. You can't afford to be dragging all day tomorrow."

"All right, Mom, all right. I'll be in when I'm done."

"Five minutes, and I mean it!" his mother, Linda, replied.

"Yeah, yeah," Josh mumbled. It was almost ten o'clock and he did need to get some sleep, but his mom was driving him crazy. He resented his mother treating him like a little baby; he was going to be seventeen in another few months. Josh and his parents lived in a small fishing village on the north side of Anchorage. Josh's father was a fisherman and kept his boat docked there most of the year.

That evening Josh was preparing for a four-day, three-night camping trip he planned with two of his teenage friends. No parents, no counselors, no chaperones—only him and his buddies. Josh was looking forward to it, to be out on his own in Denali Park with only his friends. No one to tell him to be careful and watch for this and watch for that, or to tell him not to do that and don't go there and don't do anything foolish. He wanted some freedom to hike where he wanted, ski where he wanted, and camp where he wanted.

Their plan was to hike in the morning up the backside of one of the big mountains and then use their telemark skis to ski down the other side. They'd do that three or four times the first day, camp out, and then hike to another mountain and do the same thing the next day. His mother was going to drive them to the park the next morning and then they were on their own. It was a solid two-hour drive from their home to the park trailhead and they had to pick up his friends as well, so Josh knew he needed to get up early—but he didn't care, he hadn't finished packing.

Josh had done similar day trips before, and once they had done a trip with their older friend Jack for a couple of nights. On that trip, they had not skied but did a lot of hiking, kind of like a boy scout outing but without parents. He liked Jack—he was a cool guy—but even then Jack had started telling them what to do and to be careful, especially toward the end of the trip as they all got tired.

He just had a few more things to pack and then he'd be ready. He was trying to keep it light with his camping supplies—he didn't want to hike with a big load on his back—and he was having a hard time figuring out what he wasn't going to take.

It was almost eleven o'clock when he finally got in bed, but luckily his mother had given up bugging him in frustration, so he was able to organize everything to his liking. He was so excited he didn't fall asleep until a little after midnight. It seemed like he was asleep for less than an hour when the alarm went off the next morning. Josh hit the snooze button and went back to sleep.

His mother came in ten minutes later.

"Come on, Josh, time to get up. This is your big adventure. You can't start off like this, you little slummer," she said jokingly. "Get up and face the world."

"Okay, Mom, okay, just give me another twenty minutes."

"Twenty minutes!"

"Yeah, twenty minutes," he said coldly.

"Okay, I guess, but this is no way to start your big adventure with your buddies."

★★★★★

It was two hours past sunrise before his mother finally got them to the trailhead.

"Good work, Josh," his friend Scott griped. "We were supposed to be here three hours ago. We're starting so late we'll be lucky to get two ski trips down the mountain today. I was hoping for at least three."

"Oh god," Josh snapped back, "you're just as bad as a grown-up. Let's just not worry about it, okay, bud? Let's just try to have a good time."

Josh's mother kissed him on the cheek and gave him a big, warm hug to say good-bye.

"Oh, Mom, come on now," he sighed.

"You three take care, you take care of each other, okay?" Linda said in a sweet, motherly tone. "I checked the weather forecast and it looks good, but there's a chance of snow tomorrow so be careful."

"All right, Mom, it's not like we haven't hiked in snow before."

"All right, sweeties, take care and have fun, bye, bye."

Josh's mother drove off, leaving them at the trailhead. Josh and his friends Scott and Bruce headed out on the trail with a young, almost foolish exuberance, knowing they were finally hiking alone. The trail started in a valley with mountains in the distance, but after several hours of hiking, the trail narrowed and started to climb as they made their way into the mountain range proper. They wanted to get far into the park to get to the higher peaks, so they hiked along the dirt trail for a good four hours that morning, though their progress slowed as the trail became snow covered. There was a group of medium-sized peaks they planned to ski that day, and they didn't get to the base of the first one until one o'clock. They then spent the next two hours slowing drudging up the mountain, ascending the slope until they reached a gentle ledge where they could rest. They turned around and enjoyed the view, then put on their telemark skis and made their first trip down the slopes.

As he made his way down, Scott yelled out, "Yahoo, all right, now this is the way to live!" Josh and Bruce followed, skiing with that young exuberance that made the long hike and climb all the more worth it.

Josh was loving it. It was slightly hazy, but it was a beautiful day and the powder on the mountain was deep and soft. As he picked up speed, he made several long, sweeping turns, gently churning his skis back and forth in the deep powder. As he made his way down the mountain, he came upon something, a small lump in the snow, but by the time he could see it clearly, he was already on top of it. Something caught his ski—it felt like a tree branch but he wasn't sure—and he turned suddenly and then tumbled hard down into the snow. It yanked his leg out from underneath him, and he winced in pain as his knee twisted awkwardly to the left.

"Ah, that hurts!" he screamed.

His friend Bruce was behind him.

"Josh, you fool, are you okay?"

"Oh man, yeah, yeah, I think I'm okay. Just got caught up on something."

"You need some help?" Bruce yelled as he skied on by.

"No, no, I'm okay, I'll manage. Keep going, I'll catch up with you in a little bit."

He worked his leg out of the tree branch and stood up. His knee ached, and he lay back down in the snow, working his leg back and forth to see how his knee felt. It hurt, no doubt, but after a few minutes, he gathered up his skis and poles, and slowly and gingerly made his way down to the base of the mountain, where his friends were waiting for him.

"How you are feeling, Josh?" Bruce asked as Josh snapped off his skis. "We've been waiting here for a while."

"Oh, not too bad. Just had to catch my breath a little. I twisted my knee a bit, but I'm okay. It feels better now. I'll be all right."

"You sure?"

"Yeah, don't worry about it. I'm good. Don't want to ruin our trip. Come on, let's find another hill to master."

It was almost four o'clock, but they decided to make another run partway up the mountain on the other side of the narrow valley. They would need to hike for at least an hour to get a reasonable run in. They were tired, having hiked six hours, but they went ahead and drudged up the slope. Josh's knee hurt, but he didn't want to ruin his friends' trip, and although he struggled to keep up with them, he managed.

It was starting to turn dark by the time they skied back down to the base of the mountain, but not just because of the sun setting. Cloud cover had started to roll in. They hurried to set up camp before complete darkness set in, and then prepared a hearty meal of chili, onions, and cheese. After a busy day, the food tasted wonderful. After cleaning up, they all climbed into their sleeping bags and fell into a deep sleep.

★★★★★

At four o'clock the next morning, Josh woke up to the gentle patter of snowflakes against his tiny pup tent. He had to go to the bathroom, and as he made his way out of the tent, he felt the tiny snowflakes gently falling on his face. *Hmm,* he thought to himself, *the chances of snow were low, but here it is. No matter,* he thought, *we'll just have more powder to ski on later today.* His knee ached and he was still tired, so he climbed back into his tent and fell back into a deep sleep. He didn't wake up again until eight o'clock.

By the time the three woke up in earnest, the snow was falling at a steady pace, and the wind was starting to pick up. The snowflakes were small, indicating it would snow for a while. When they got up and looked at each other, they were all a little shell-shocked. They were tired from the day before, and now they had to deal with the snow and wind—but being young kids, they brushed it off, packed up their stuff, and proceeded to hike along the trail in search of another mountain to ski.

It was Scott who had the idea of picking a huge mountain that day to ski. There was a beautiful one several miles away that had really sparked Scott's interest the day before, and they made their way to its base. They couldn't see the top of it very well because of the snow and wind, but it was steeper than the others and was pointed at its top.

"It's the Matterhorn's cousin," Scott joked. "Looks like it needs some ski tracks to pretty it up a little."

They hiked for three hours up the mountain, pressing on to ensure they would have a long ski down. The snow and wind made it that much more difficult, but finally after almost three and a half hours, Josh piped up, "Come on, Scott, this is far enough; we don't need to go any higher. It's starting to get hazy up here—I can't even see very well."

"How about up to that next plateau? It's only another twenty minutes at most. You up for it, Bruce?"

"Yeah, why not?" Bruce said, shrugging his shoulders. "Come on, Josh, it's just a little longer."

Josh didn't say anything but just fell in behind his friends. When they reached the plateau, Josh wanted to rest his aching knee for a while, but Bruce and Scott were ready to get going.

"Let's go, Josh, we don't have all day," Scott said as he strapped on his skis.

"You guys go ahead; I'll meet you at the bottom. I just need to rest for a second."

"You sure?" Bruce asked. "I don't mind waiting."

"It's okay, go ahead. I'll get going in a little bit."

Bruce hesitated, but Scott had already started on his way down the steep terrain.

"Okay, Josh. We'll see you in a bit," Bruce said as he followed Scott down the steep incline.

Josh's knee ached, and he was anxious about following the two. The terrain was steep, so after sitting for five minutes, he strapped on his skis and headed to the left to an area that looked a little easier to ski. Visibility was poor, but Josh skied down at a gentle pace. After several minutes, however, the section he was on began to narrow, and he had to tighten up his turns to stay on the slope. As he looked to his left and right, he could see considerable drop-offs on either side, and he slowed his pace further.

Suddenly he heard a crack and a pop below his feet, and before he knew it, he was tumbling down the mountain, down toward a cliff-like crevasse. When he landed at the bottom of it, he hit his head hard against the snow, and he lost consciousness quickly.

★★★★★

Josh's friends skied down the mountain unaware of Josh's accident. It was challenging traversing the mountain with the snow coming down and the low visibility, but the powder was fantastic and they were both having a blast. Josh was an experienced skier, so they both were confident he'd catch up with them at the bottom, if not before. They skied down the slopes without stopping, and twenty minutes later, they were at the bottom of the mountain. They gave each other a high five.

"Wow, that was wild!" Scott exclaimed.

"Fantastic!" Bruce replied.

After a few minutes, Bruce turned back toward the mountain and looked for Josh.

Scott looked over at him.

"Don't worry, Bruce, he'll be here in a jiffy. He's the best skier of the three of us. He'll pop out of the snow in a second."

"Yeah, I know. We can just sit and wait."

They sat down on the snow and waited. After twenty minutes of waiting, however, they were starting to get worried.

"Where the heck is that boy?" Scott asked.

"Maybe he went down another slope, came out at the bottom somewhere else," Bruce replied.

"Yeah, that must be it. He's probably walking around now trying to find us. Why don't you go left and I'll go right, and we'll meet back in a little bit; I'm sure one of us will hook up with him."

Half an hour later, they got back together. As they approached, each thought he'd see the other with Josh tagging behind, but this was not the case.

"Shoot! Where is this guy? Think he's still on the mountain?" Scott said.

"Oh, I don't know. Let's hope not. He was complaining about that knee. Maybe something happened up there. Maybe he couldn't make it all the way down, at least not right away."

"Yeah, we should probably wait for a little while. Why don't we try again, see if we can find him if he doesn't show up in the next twenty minutes or so. If that doesn't work, we might have to hike back up the mountain."

Twenty minutes later, they split up again, picked out a good landmark, and decided they would meet back in thirty minutes. Visibility wasn't good, but they went their separate ways. Thirty minutes later, Scott was back at the landmark, but Bruce didn't show for another ten minutes. Each could tell by the look on the other's face that Josh was still out there.

"Shoot, we should have never gone down the slope without him; we should have waited," Bruce said in frustration.

"He's the best skier of all of us. He didn't need us to wait."

"Oh yes, he did!" Bruce replied.

"Come on, Bruce, don't get down. He's got to be around somewhere. Look, why don't we retrace our steps up the slope now?"

"But it's getting late. We're not going to make it all the way up."

"Well, hopefully we won't have to. Let's just get up as high as we can, and we'll probably see him. He's probably somewhere up there. We can't just wait around here, and we should stick together, especially since it's going to be dark soon."

"Okay, Scott, let's give it a shot."

They started back up the mountain, but it was slow going. Within thirty minutes, it was getting dark, and the snowstorm didn't help. As they hiked, they called out his name over and over again.

"Josh, where are you, Josh? Josh!" but to no avail.

After an hour, it was late dusk, and they decided to strap on their skis and go back down.

"What are we going to do, Scott?"

"Man, I don't know," Scott said defensively as he shook his head and stared down at the snow. "Think about what they're going to say to us. My mother, oh, she'll just freak out. Say how we were just a bunch of irresponsible kids—you know, the same old story."

"Come on, Scott, what about poor Josh out there? He might be injured. We know he's lost. He's properly going out of his mind right now," Bruce replied, raising his arms in exasperation.

"Yeah, I know, I know. We'll just have to set up camp, and let's keep calling out his name. Maybe he'll show up. If he doesn't, we'll get up at the crack of dawn and continue the search."

★★★★★

Josh lay unconscious throughout the night at the bottom of the shallow crevasse along the steep mountain slope. At five in the morning, his eyes popped open. He was facing down in the gulley, blood oozing from his forehead, but he could move his arms and legs, and even though his twisted knee ached like hell, it didn't appear he had broken anything.

Thank god, he thought to himself.

He slowly sat up and dusted the snow off his head and back that had fallen on him that night. He couldn't see where his skis were—it was too dark—but his head ached, and he wiped the blood off his forehead with his ski glove. He felt dizzy, so he sat there for quite some time, breathing heavily. Finally he stood up. He was disoriented and couldn't maintain his balance; he stumbled back down and rolled onto his back. Luckily, because it was so cold, the snow was dry and he was comfortable, if you could call it that, lying there on his back waiting for his head to clear.

After an hour, the night sky started to turn into morning dusk, and he finally got up. He saw one of his skis had broken in half, and his other ski was ten feet away. He walked over slowly and picked up his good ski. His head was still bleeding, and he pulled an old shirt from his knapsack and wiped the blood off again. He had a deep gash above his left eyebrow, but the bleeding had almost stopped.

He didn't want to stay there in that gully, so he slowly climbed his way out. The walls of the gully sloped back up to his left toward the hillside proper, and using his single ski as a prop, he scrabbled his way up the gulley to the mountain slope. He looked around to see if he could find the others, but they were nowhere to be seen. He was on quite a precarious slope, but it was still skiable. He slid his lone ski into the backside of his knapsack and walked a little to see how he felt. Once the terrain leveled a bit, he stopped and put the one ski on his good leg and tried to hobble down the mountain, this being faster than hiking. He didn't know where he was exactly, but he thought if he could just make it down the side of the mountain into the flatlands, he could wander around and hopefully find Scott and Bruce. It took him a good hour and a half to make his way down, but when he reached the bottom, the terrain didn't look familiar. Before him was a long sloping valley on one side and the steep ridge he had just descended on the other. He scanned forward and noticed the ridgeline sloped down and then leveled briefly before climbing again to an adjacent mountain peak a half mile away. Although he didn't know exactly where he was, the sloping plateau to his right looked far more appealing than the ridge to his left. He was in no state to try to hike his way over that ridge, so he turned to his right and started to make his way along the plateau.

He called out for his friends. "Bruce, Scott, are you there? Bruce, Scott! Where are you?"

The wind was howling that morning, and his voice didn't carry very far. He wasn't optimistic he'd find them anytime soon, but he kept trying as he hiked his way along the plateau.

★★★★★

On the other side of the mountain, Bruce and Scott were just getting up. They looked at each other, both worried. There was no sign of Josh.

"Maybe we should just hike back out of the park now, Scott, and call for help," Bruce said.

"No, no, let's not," Scott replied back quickly. "We got all day today. Let's see if we can find him."

"Are you sure?"

"Yeah, I'm sure. Think about it. We hike out of this park, the first thing they'll say is—"You stupid morons, you dumb kids, you just can't take care of yourselves, can you?" God, like I need that crap. We'd never get to go out by ourselves again; they'd ground us. It will be the biggest pain. You know how these grown-ups are."

"I know, but Josh could be hurt; he could be dying for all we know."

"Yeah, probably not. He's probably just out trying to find us."

They spent the whole next day looking for Josh. They hiked all the way back up the mountain from the day before, yelling out his name as they hiked. It was windy and the snow had blown over all their ski tracks, so there was no way of knowing what direction Josh had taken. They skied back down and then hiked all around the base of the mountain, but to no avail.

That evening they decided to get up early the next morning and continue to look for him, but if they hadn't found him by midday, they would hike back down the trail, since that next day they were scheduled to meet up with Josh's mother. They were both tired and short on food, and they knew it would be even more difficult and alarming if they missed the rendezvous with Josh's mother the following afternoon even if Josh wasn't with them.

As they started to fall asleep, Bruce said, "Look, maybe we should just hike back tomorrow morning. We can find someone near the park and alert them. The park ranger could get a rescue team going that much earlier."

"Yeah, but you know whether we get there at ten o'clock or four o'clock ain't going to amount to a pile of beans. They won't get anything going till the next day regardless, and we still have the chance we'll find Josh tomorrow and not have to tell anyone this whole mess happened," Scott replied.

Bruce groaned slightly, and they both fell to sleep exhausted, hoping that Josh would appear the next day.

★★★★★

It was six o'clock in the evening the following day when Jack got the frantic call from Josh's mother on his answering machine.

"Jack, damn it, Jack. I went to pick up the kids a little while ago, and Bruce and Scott were there but Josh was gone, My god, they lost him—he's lost out there somewhere in that wilderness. I don't know where he is; they don't know where he is. They lost him two days ago. Those dumb kids, they tried to look for him for two days instead of trying to get someone to help. Crazy kids, crazy. He's out there, Jack, he's out there. Please call me. I'm going to call the police, the rangers, whomever. You know these kids better than I do when it comes to this kind of stuff. He's been out there by himself for three days. God knows what he's doing or if he's all right.

Oh god, Jack, I'm going to lose my mind—we've got to find him. Please call me, Jack, please, I need your help!"

Jack called her as soon as he listened to the message. She was still frantic.

"All right, Linda, all right. Calm down, please calm down. I'll be up there early in the morning. I'll get my plane out. I'll be out there at the crack of dawn looking for him. Did he have any sort of tracking device we can use to find him?"

"No, Jack, no. You know those kids. They don't care about that sort of thing; they're too carefree, thinking that nothing can happen. Oh god, Jack, I should have never let them go by themselves. Young kids—they don't know how to handle themselves. It's all my fault, it's all my fault—oh god."

"It's okay, Linda, it's okay. We'll find him. It's okay. I'll call the park ranger and the police sergeant right now, make sure we're all on the same page. We'll have a rescue team out there immediately. We'll find him. Don't worry; we'll find him. How about Bruce and Scott, are they all right?"

"They're okay. A little hungry and tired, but otherwise all right."

"Good, Linda, that's good. I'm making some calls as soon as I get off the line. Don't worry."

"Thank you, Jack, thank you."

Jack called the police sergeant, and they agreed to meet the next morning at the airport where Jack stored his plane and arrange a search party. The police station was only a few miles from the airport.

"How long have they been out there, Jack, do you know? I haven't had the chance to talk to Linda directly yet."

"From what I gather, he's been out there four days now. About three days by himself."

"Four days. That's pushing it. How many days was the trip planned for?"

"I think about three and a half days."

"Well, he's probably getting low on the food supply. That's a problem. But you know, it ain't like we haven't done this before."

"How's the weather looking, do you know, Sarge?"

"It's clear tomorrow morning, but after that, it's not looking too good. This storm has been off and on, but by noon tomorrow, it will be here for a while, maybe three or four days. It's going to be steady as far as I can tell, but we'll see what we can do."

"Well, I'll be up in the air before it gets here. If we're lucky, by noon, he'll be at home with Linda, safe and sound."

"Let's hope so, Jack. We'll see you in the morning, okay?"

"Sure thing."

★★★★★

The next morning, the conditions were horrendous. The wind was howling, and the snow was coming down hard. It was stormy, almost blizzard-like conditions, and it was very cold. The team met briefly at the airport, but since it was impossible to fly that day, they drove their vehicles to the trailhead parking lot.

"Looks like an early winter storm, hey, Jack?" the sergeant said as he stepped out of his cruiser. "The visibility out here is terrible—I'd say fifty feet at best."

"Yeah, it's pretty bad," Jack replied.

Ten people were gathered that morning at the base of the trailhead.

"Have you talked to the boys yet?" Jack asked the sergeant.

"Yeah, they're awful cagey about the whole thing, you know how that goes. They don't want to admit they screwed up, but Bruce was a little more responsive. He told us they were skiing down the mountain, he wasn't sure which one, but Josh was lagging behind and told them he wanted to rest for a little while. Bruce mentioned Josh had twisted his knee and couldn't ski quite as quickly as he and Scott. They went ahead of him down the mountain, and that was the last time they saw him. They looked for him all the rest of that day, and the next day and then the following morning."

"How far into the park were they, did he say?"

"Well, they had hiked quite a ways in. It was on their second day, so they were quite a good way into the park. All Bruce could remember was a real sharp peak of a mountain, he couldn't recall which one, but it was a mountain just off the trail."

"All right, well, that's better than nothing," Jack replied.

They proceeded to hike down the trail. It was slow going, but it looked like there would be a break in the weather in a few days. Jack was planning to take his plane out if the foot search wasn't successful.

Jack knew the terrain well. He had done quite a few hikes up this trail, and flew the area regularly as well. Most of the people in the search party were volunteers and didn't know the area as well as Jack and the sergeant, so they lead the party.

*****

After a full day of searching, there was nothing, not even snow tracks of any of the boys. The weather was bad and the visibility was poor, but even so they hiked well into the park. By the time they hiked out of the park that evening, it was pitch-black.

"We'll just have to try again tomorrow," Jack said to the sergeant.

The sergeant just shrugged. They both had read the forecast. Nothing could fly for at least a few days. The forecast called for continued heavy snow, with temperatures between zero and ten degrees Fahrenheit.

*****

Fifteen miles from the search party, Josh was starting to get frightened. He woke up that next morning not knowing where he was. His hands were numb, and he felt groggy. He hadn't slept much at all the night before because of the cold; he couldn't keep himself warm in his tiny pup tent. He was haggard and tired, but stayed well hydrated by eating the snow. He would put a small clump in his mouth and wait for it to melt before he swallowed to avoid chilling his throat. He had run out of food the day before and was starving. His knee ached and it hurt to walk, but he kept going, hoping he would see something he recognized to help him find his way back to the trail. That afternoon, he started to shake from the cold, and he tried to walk more briskly to keep his body temperature up.

★★★★★

Jack, the sergeant, and the rest of the search team gathered again the next morning, though the party was smaller now since some of the volunteers had returned to work that Monday. The weather was still unsuitable for flying, and Jack and the sergeant started to feel a sense of desperation as they hiked again down the snow-covered trail. Josh had been out in the park for six days now, and they both knew he was out of food.

It was that morning that Jack tried it. He was ahead of the others and a good quarter mile off the trail, panning the landscape for a lonely figure in the snow.

Josh, if I knew where you were, if I could sense your presence, please let me see where you are, he thought to himself, and then he started to repeat it out loud. He waited, but there was nothing, absolutely nothing. There was no response, no feedback at all.

Eh, Jack said to himself, *no help there.* He tried several more times during the day, but he wasn't getting anything.

The search party gathered in the late afternoon when dusk was settling in, and discussed what they would do the next day. The forecast showed another terrible day, but Jack was hoping by the day after, he could get his plane out. The police department had a helicopter and a search plane as well, but they had to wait for the weather to break.

★★★★★

That night in the blistering cold and howling winds, Josh was starting to shake uncontrollably. He had no idea where he was at; nothing looked familiar. He was starving. He had finished all his food two days earlier, and his fingers were frostbitten. He could hardly sleep given the cold and his state of mind. His knee was aching, but he could still walk and travel.

When he got up the next morning, it was overcast and snow was still falling. He looked around, but no landmark stood out; the landscape was nothing he recognized, and he didn't know which way to travel. He was confused, but he kept moving, not sure which direction he was heading but hoping he'd eventually get his bearings and make his way out of the park.

★★★★★

That day, the search party was frustrated again. The snow subsided in the early morning, but by midday, it was coming down hard again. The party consisted of only five people now, and Jack had several charter flights planned later that week. The forecast showed the snow would subside soon, either the next day or the day after, and Jack didn't want to cancel his flights. This late in the year, he was lucky to get people to book with him at all, and to cancel would hurt his reputation.

I've got one good day tomorrow, it looks like, he thought to himself, *we've got to find that boy soon.* He knew that Josh was surely struggling to hold up given the cold and lack of food.

Jack kept trying to find Josh in his mind throughout the day. He was getting desperate; he knew neither he nor Josh had much time left.

"Josh, Josh, if I could see where you are, if I could be with you for one brief moment, I know I can find you, let me find you," he kept whispering to himself. There was nothing; his mind was just blank. Jack speculated that he was losing his powers—maybe they were fading, or maybe it was just a temporary thing. He was sad, he felt so terrible for Josh, and he could sense the desperation and horrible acceptance that Josh might not make it in the minds and hearts of the other search party members.

★★★★★

Finally the next day the weather broke. Jack had his plane out at sunrise and searched for Josh from the sky all day. The police helicopter was out as well, along with another rescue plane, and they all communicated with each other to cover as much area as possible, but by dusk they had to call off the search.

It's not surprising, Jack thought to himself. *It's a huge park, and it might take several days to find him—that is, if he's not buried under the snow somewhere,* he thought sadly. He heard so many stories of people getting lost in the wilderness, and if they didn't have a tracking device, there'd be a search for weeks with no success, and eventually the search would be ended. Jack speculated that Josh had two or three more days at best before he would be incapacitated. He was a young man, yes, but there was no food available and the weather had been harsh. He had been out there eight full days now.

Jack had a charter flight scheduled for 9:00 a.m. the next morning, and he told the sergeant he could make a quick loop at sunrise but wouldn't be available again until late in the day.

"We appreciate it, Jack, we really do. It looks like we're going to get another plane out from the coast guard base in Kodiak to help. We'll have three of us out searching tomorrow. There's still hope, Jack, there's still a chance. You've done more than we could ask, Jack—we really appreciate it."

"Okay, Sarge, the charter will be over by three o'clock. I'll make some search passes after that. Just don't hesitate to call me if you need my help before then, okay?"

"Okay, Jack, sure thing."

★★★★★

During that day, Josh was more hopeful since the skies had cleared, but he was terribly weak, and even with the clear skies, he wasn't exactly sure which way to move. He headed in a generally southern direction in the hope he could find the park boundary and a road. He was so weak, though, he only made it a few miles—he was delirious now, and by midday he had to stop. He wanted to keep moving to keep his body temperature up, but instead, he packed himself under a pile of snow to stay warm and he tried to get some rest. He dozed in and out of consciousness under the snow, but he never could quite fall asleep since the cold kept him awake.

That night he slept for one hour at most, but the next morning at sunrise, he struggled and got himself up. Both his hands and all his toes were frozen, and he tried to get some feeling back into them, but it was difficult. He didn't dare take his hiking boots off, but after ten minutes of shoving his hands deep into his gut, his fingers started to tingle and move. In the hope of getting some feeling back in his toes, he started to move slowly. After a few steps, he stumbled and fell down. He waited a few minutes and then tried again. He stumbled several more times but kept moving. Because of his state, he didn't see the deep rut in the snow, and he stepped awkwardly into a shallow ravine that twisted his leg violently. In a normal state of mind, he would have caught himself earlier, but he was so tired he didn't balance himself before his leg popped out from underneath him.

"Ah, ah crap!" he yelled out. His bad knee was twisted painfully to the right, and he fell down exhausted in the snow. He shifted his weight as best he could to get the pressure off his knee. He was so tired he just lay there in the snow, his knee throbbing painfully. After several minutes, he tried to get up but he couldn't. His body was aching, he was starving, he was freezing. He put his face in the snow and started to cry. He sobbed and moaned, and then something came over him and he started to think about what was going to happen to him.

Those thoughts had never really crossed his mind before. He always believed he could find his way back, but now he couldn't help it anymore. He started to imagine himself dead in the snow, his stiff body lying there for days on end until the snow covered him. He'd be buried under the snow, entombed forever in this wilderness, forgotten.

"My god, I'm going to die out here. I'm going to die," he sobbed. Fear flowed through him. It was a deep fear, a bone-chilling, hair-raising fear that encompassed his whole body. He started shivering and shaking violently, the thought of his frozen, dead body exploding in his mind.

"Oh god, I'm going to die, I'm going to die ..."

★★★★★

At that instant, Jack was getting in his plane for one final flight in the hope of finding Josh. He had been trying for days now to see Josh. It hadn't worked for the last five days, but he tried it again.

"Josh, if I could just see you, find you, be with you, everything will be okay, let me be with you."

Then, clear as day in Jack's mind, there was Josh, lying facedown in the snow, his body shivering and shaking, his mind full of fear and pain. That deadly fear in Josh's body caught Jack off guard as he shook and shivered frantically himself. The stinging pain in Josh's knee grabbed him as well, and he tumbled back away from his plane and onto the snow, grabbing his knee in pain as he fell.

"Oh god, you poor boy, you poor lad," Jack said out loud as he lay on the ground, shivering and shaking violently, his mind full of Josh's fear and pain. Josh was extremely weak and destitute.

He doesn't have much time, Jack thought to himself. After a few moments, Jack gathered himself, fighting off the intense fear that filled his mind. He forced Josh to roll over on his side and brought Josh's head up so he could scan the landscape. He was in the middle of a big snowfield, mountains off in the distance to his left, and mountains farther off in the distance ahead of him.

He struggled to get Josh to stand up. His knee was in bloody pain, but it didn't matter. Jack's mind was focused on the landscape, pushing Josh's fear and pain into the back of his mind. He did a three-hundred-and-sixty degree turn around trying to get his bearings. He squinted his eyes and looked to the nearby mountains. There, off in the distance to his left, was Glaciers Peak, the pointed mountaintop clear as day—yes, yes, he knew that mountain. He scanned forward, and next to it was Emeralds Peak, exactly where it should have been if he were east of the park trail. He looked north now, and far off in the distance was Guldens Peak, its rounded mountaintop clear in the morning light. To his right was an open glacier field, but there was a snow-covered forest only a few miles distant. *Of course, he's wandered to the north and east of the park trail,* he thought to himself. Jack knew the area well: he had landed onto that field for a summer hiking trip through the nearby forest.

Jack had Josh sit back down in the snow, letting him get some rest. Jack got in his plane, and within thirty minutes at full throttle, he was flying over the top of Emeralds Peak. He descended and made a turn to the southeast across the open snowfield, then turned south as he neared the tree line of the forest. He flew low, only one hundred feet above the snow, scanning the landscape for Josh. Within five minutes, he saw him. There he was lying in the snow, his red parka standing out against the white background. Josh was so weak, he didn't even notice Jack's plane when he first flew by.

"My god, he's delirious," Jack said out loud. "He didn't even notice me."

Jack made a quick one-hundred-and-eighty-degree turn and landed within thirty yards of Josh, but now as he touched down in the snow, he could see Josh waving his hand frantically. Jack trotted briskly over to Josh, picked him up from the snow, and loaded him into the back of his plane. As they took off, Josh muttered, "Jack, Jack, you found me, how did you find me, how did you see me?"

Jack radioed to the sergeant that he had Josh, and when he landed forty minutes later, the emergency team was there at Birchwood airport waiting for them. Josh was loaded into the back of the ambulance and taken to the hospital.

★★★★★

Later that day, Jack checked in with the sergeant.

"He's going to be all right, Jack," the sergeant said with a sense of relief as well as gratitude in his voice. "He's scared and frightened and is suffering from a bad case of hypothermia. He tore some ligaments in his knee as well, but a few weeks on crutches and some tender loving care, and he'll be okay. He'll be in the hospital for a few days to get his strength back, but he's going to be all right. Fantastic job, Jack, just fantastic—one more day and he wouldn't be with us now. Just incredible."

Chapter 9

J ack had been seeing Helen regularly over the last four months. She was a beautiful woman in a lot of different ways. She wasn't quite as vivacious as his previous girlfriend, but she was very thoughtful, insightful, and intelligent. She could be moody at times, but as they got to know one another, she blossomed more as she began to know and trust him. Jack was happy about it; they were developing a really good relationship. She lived in Anchorage but made frequent trips to Fairbanks since her parents lived there, and was a member of the Fairbanks astronomy club.

At the hospital in Anchorage, Helen worked in the child development ward, working mainly as a physical therapist. She helped children recover from accidents and broken limbs, and some who had been very sick and needed to regain their strength. She worked with adults as well, but her emphasis was on children, ages four to fifteen. She was also certified as a nurse, which she helped with at times, depending on the workload at the hospital. She had been working second shift for quite some time now. She would go into work at 5:00 p.m. and work until one o'clock in the morning.

On occasion, Jack would meet up with her for a late-night dinner. Jack would work on his plane or do some paperwork after taking a group up for a flight, but then late in the evening, he would make his way over to the hospital after picking up dinner for the two of them. He'd call her beforehand and ask her what she'd like, and then go over to the local sub shop or sometimes an Italian or seafood restaurant and grab some food. She couldn't leave the hospital on her break, so they would sit together in the ward on the eighth floor. It was very pleasant and relaxing for them both. Working second shift was quiet—there weren't many people around—so it was fun for her, and it was a nice way for Jack to get away from his business and spend time with her.

It was a Thursday evening, and Jack and Helen had planned to meet for dinner. Jack had a flight that day, and it had taken him awhile to clean up the plane. It was a full flight, with six people in the plane, and during the flight, one of his landing lights had gone out, so he spent an hour afterward replacing it. One of the young boys on the flight had spilled his drink on the floor as well, so Jack had to soak and scrub the floor to get rid of the stain and smell and clean up any fluid that had leaked down below the floor. By the time he finished, it was almost eight o'clock, and the hospital was a good half hour from the airport. Jack considered canceling his dinner with Helen, but then decided he didn't want to hurt her feelings by canceling at the last moment.

On his way, he called Helen on his cell phone. "Helen, how are you doing?"

"Jack, I'm doing fine, thank you. Just tending to the kids. One boy had a pretty bad leg break, fell off a bobsled, needs a lot of support since he's in quite a lot of pain, but he'll be okay."

"Well, that's good. So what would you like to eat tonight?"

"Well, let me think. Let's see, how about some good old-fashioned salmon, with lots of butter, mm, that sounds tasty."

"Salmon? Yeah, salmon, it's that time of season, isn't it? That sounds fantastic. Jerry's Seafood?"

"You read my mind, Jack," Helen replied. "They've got the best takeout seafood in town."

"Sounds great, Helen. See you at nine o'clock."

Jack made his way over to Jerry's Seafood. It was a little out of his way, but it was the best seafood place in town. It was one of those tiny places no one would know about unless they had lived in Anchorage for some time. When he got there, there was a line, *must be because of the beginning of salmon season,* Jack thought as he waited. He waited impatiently; he didn't want to get to the hospital late. Jack had been late a few times, and he could tell Helen didn't appreciate it. She wouldn't really get upset; she'd just quiet down and become withdrawn. It wasn't much fun when she became moody like that, so Jack always tried to get there early—there was really no excuse for him to show up late. After waiting in line for fifteen minutes, he finally got their food, hurried back to his truck, and made his way to the hospital.

By now it was ten minutes before nine, but the roads were beginning to collect patches of snow so he drove cautiously. He was a little distracted, thinking that possibly the boy's spill in the plane had something to do with his landing light going out, but he had done his best to clean off everything under the floor and doubted the drink would have caused a short circuit. He hated the thought of that sticky soda drying up under the floor, but it was difficult to clean it off completely due to access and his lack of time. When he got to the hospital, he was contemplating removing the entire floor panel and almost missed the turn into the visitors' lot. The abrupt left he made to make the turn caused his drink to spill over and the food to tumble to the floor.

Oh, you dummy, he thought to himself as he stopped in the parking lot and picked up the half-spilled drink and the food. He rushed to get it cleaned up, and then grabbed the food before he jogged over to the hospital entrance. He made his way to the elevator, but in his haste, he pressed the ninth-floor button instead of the eighth. As the door opened, he quickly stepped out and made his way down the hall in the direction of Helen's break room, not realizing he was one floor up. He noticed there was no one at the reception desk, which was odd. *Maybe they're just taking a break or something,* he thought. The hallway was dimmed to save electricity, and it gave the hallway a spooky feel.

Jack was about halfway down the hall on the way to the break room when it happened. He was thinking about his plane, when suddenly his mind was filled with vivid thoughts and emotions he had never seen before.

"Whew," he said out loud, and he stopped in the hallway. He was seeing someone's life flash before his eyes, and at the same time, he felt a sharp pain in the left side of his brain that traveled down the side of his arm to his abdomen. It was so painful, he leaned over and slumped his body against the wall to catch his breath.

Oh man, that hurts, he thought, but through the pain, he was being taken on a journey through the life of a woman born in the early 1930s. He saw her growing up in Wisconsin, the daughter of a corn farmer. She spent a good portion of her early life being a farmhand, but at eighteen, just when her father expected her to take over the farm, she left for California to pursue her dream of becoming a surgeon, a rare profession in those days for a woman. She worked her way through school, earning a degree in molecular biology before enrolling in medical school in Oregon. At the age of thirty-two, she finally realized her dream by taking residency at the Portland medical school, where she pursued a career in heart surgery, becoming one of the pioneers of open-heart surgery, heart replacement, and bypass surgery.

Fascinating, Jack thought to himself as he gazed on her amazing journey, *such a brave and talented woman.*

It was in Portland that she met her husband, a doctor as well, but also an avid outdoorsman, and it was through him she became an avid hiker and mountaineer. They had two children together, and for the next twenty years, she spent long hours balancing motherhood with the demands of her career as a surgeon. As her children became older, she and her husband would take them on trips to the national parks throughout the United States, and it was through this process that she came to love Alaska and its rugged wilderness. Her fondest memories were the times they had vacationed in Alaska, and after her two girls left home, she and her husband moved to Alaska, taking up practice in Anchorage, where they worked for the remainder of their careers. They became the first husband and wife to scale McKinley together and developed some notoriety as the mountaineering doctors. Sadly her husband passed away not long after they both retired, and her daughters had stayed in the continental United States, one in New Mexico and one in Florida, where they both married and started families. Her stroke was sudden, and it had taken her daughters several days to schedule their trips to Anchorage, not realizing that their mother was deathly ill.

Her journey was nearing its end now with her lying in her hospital bed on the ninth floor of the Anchorage hospital alone, recounting her life as she laid in agonizing pain, hoping and praying that she would see her daughters one last time before she died. She had been crying, but now she just lay numb, saddened by the thought that she would probably die alone.

Jack was slumped up against the wall seeing her life unfold before him, but he finally saw her lying in her hospital bed in the next room down the hall. Jack cracked the door open to the room and walked inside. She turned to him at first surprised, and then a relaxed, almost tranquil look came over her face. Jack walked up to her and took her hand gently, staring into her tired but brilliant eyes, and smiled.

She smiled back and waited a few moments. Her voice was barely audible, and Jack leaned over, hoping that his actions would keep her going for a while even though he already knew what she wanted.

"My name is Ingrid. My daughters, they've just arrived this evening, but I don't think I can wait until tomorrow, I don't want to …"

"No, Ingrid, you won't be alone; they'll be here tonight, don't worry, they'll be here shortly."

She squeezed his hand and closed her eyes. "Thank you, Jack, thank you."

Jack was surprised she called him by name, but he suspected her mind had gotten a glimpse of his thoughts as he watched her life unfold before him. Jack left the room, walked back to the empty reception desk, and made his way down to the eighth floor. Helen was waiting for him, wondering if he was going to make it.

"Helen, sweetheart, I'm so sorry." Jack hugged her and kissed her cheek. "I'm so sorry. Can you forgive me? I brought you your favorite dish."

"Oh, Jack, you don't have to be so dramatic, you silly."

Once Helen was settled in, eating her reheated salmon and looking comfortable, Jack asked her, "Helen, can I use the phone up here? It will just take a second. I need to touch base with someone. I left my cell phone in the truck."

"Sure, Jack, it's just down the hall at the reception desk; dial one to get out."

During Jack's entanglement with Ingrid, he saw that her daughters had called earlier, letting her know they had just checked into the Ramada Inn ten miles away and that they would come by in the morning to see her. Their names were Kathy and Stephanie. Jack picked up the yellow pages sitting on the desk, looked up the hotel's number, and made the call.

"Hello, this is the Ramada Inn. May I help you?" the receptionist answered.

"Yes, I need to talk to Stephanie McMahon or Kathy Logan. I believe they've just arrived."

"Surely; I'll get them on the phone," the receptionist replied.

"Yes?" Jack heard over the phone a moment later. "This is Kathy Logan."

"Yes, Mrs. Logan, I'm a nurse here at the hospital. I work second shift here in the trauma ward. It's your mother, Ingrid, she is very ill. She wants to see you tonight. Please, can you make it over now? I don't think you should wait until tomorrow."

"Tonight? Oh god, tonight. Yes, yes, of course, we'll be there tonight. We'll be leaving now."

Jack could hear over the phone Kathy talking to Stephanie. "We better get over there now; I don't think we should wait until tomorrow."

"What room is she in?" Kathy asked.

"She's on the ninth floor, Room 916. Someone should be at the reception area, but if not, just make your way to the room. She's waiting for your arrival now."

★★★★★

Kathy and Stephanie were both exhausted from their long flights, but they made it to the hospital that evening and were able to spend the night with their mother. They had both brought pictures of Ingrid's grandchildren, and Ingrid nodded and smiled as they told her the stories behind each picture. Ingrid was pale and very weak, but there was nothing in the world better than spending her last few hours with her lovely daughters. Early the next morning as her daughters dozed off in their chairs sitting next to their mother's bedside, Ingrid passed away.

★★★★★

The next day, Helen called Jack.

"Jack, did you hear the news? It's so sad. Ingrid Samualson passed away last night. She had a stroke not long ago and was up in the trauma ward. I paid her a visit on several occasions; she was so nice. She was an incredible doctor and amateur climber, such a wonderful woman."

"I'm so sorry to hear that; that is sad. Was someone with her when she died?"

"Yes, Jack, in fact, her two daughters were at her bedside. The nurse receptionist talked to them several hours after they arrived. The receptionist told me she had to leave abruptly for a family emergency earlier that night, but they told her a male nurse called and told them to come that evening. It's odd, I didn't know a man was working there on second shift, but in any case, it was a good thing her daughters came that night—it would have been too late the next day. At least she got to see her daughters before she left us."

"Yes, that's a good thing. Dying alone would have been dreadful for her. She was quite a woman, wasn't she?"

"Yes," Helen paused. "Did you know her, Jack?"

"Well, I have heard of her. She was one of the first women to scale McKinley, I believe, and was quite well known as a heart surgeon. She'll be missed."

"Yes, she will," Helen replied.

"Are you going to make it to the funeral?" Jack asked.

"You know, I was thinking about it. I got to know Ingrid quite well when she was in the hospital, and I think she enjoyed my company. I know I enjoyed hers. Her daughters are making the arrangements now. I'll find out when the service will be. I would like to go."

"I'm sure they would appreciate it, Helen," Jack replied.

Chapter 10

Jack had been spending more time at his house in Fairbanks. He was to the point that he was ready to sell the small trailer home he had set up next to the house and move into the almost-completed home. Jack had been working on the house in his spare time for over four years now, so he was happy he would be able to finally move in and enjoy the place. That evening, when he was able to finally sleep in his home for the first time, he thought more about his experience with Ingrid Samualson. For the first time, he had made contact with someone, but had not initiated the encounter in any way. In fact, it appeared Ingrid had reached out to him in her desperate attempt to see her daughters one last time before she died.

Jack decided to contact Robert Weldon and see if he could offer some insight. It had been quite some time since they had corresponded. Jack had kind of dropped the ball with Weldon several months back. They had agreed to stay in touch, but Jack was so wrapped up with his business, the house, and seeing Helen, that he hadn't taken the time to stay in touch with him. Jack didn't have his computer with him, but he found Weldon's number in his wallet and decided to give him a call the next morning. Jack remembered Weldon's offer to go visit him and was still somewhat reluctant, but if he talked to him directly, he thought he might warm up to the idea. The next morning, Jack called Weldon, but no one picked up, so he left him a message on his voice mail.

That day Jack had planned to buy some lawn furniture for the back porch of his house. The view from the back was beautiful. There was a large meadow behind the house, and off in the distance was the Chena River, with a forest behind it. The mountains from the Alaska Range lay miles off and were obscured by cloud cover most of the year, but on a clear day, they completed a most spectacular view. Jack's plan was set up a bird feeder so that he could sit on the back porch in the morning and enjoy his coffee while watching the birds play.

Helen was up visiting her parents and was planning to pay Jack a visit that evening, so he wanted to have something set up that they could enjoy together. He decided on a dark birchwood table and chairs that were in contrast to the lighter-colored maple oak that made up the porch. The bird feeder was tall dark birchwood, as well, and Jack planted it twenty yards back from the porch in the hope of attracting the wilder birds, who wouldn't want to get too close to the house. The feeder had two locations for feed, and in one Jack put bird seeds to attract the smaller vegetarian birds. In the other, Jack filled it with the meat- and fish-based food he also used at his apartment in Anchorage in the hope of attracting an eagle or an owl. By the time Jack had everything set up, it was turning dusk. When Helen arrived, they both were tired, so they just had a small meal inside and went to bed.

★★★★★

Jack slept in the next morning, but Helen woke up early and made herself some coffee. An hour later, Jack felt Helen tapping on his shoulder. "Jack, wake up, wake up. You've got to see this," Helen said.

"What?" Jack grumbled as he grabbed his pillow and rolled onto his side. "Helen, I'm tired; let me sleep awhile longer."

"No, Jack, come on. Just get up. It's really neat. I don't know how much longer he'll stay. Come on."

"What is it?"

"Come on, Jack. I'll show you. I've fixed you a cup of coffee; come on out to the porch, and I'll show you."

"Okay, okay, let me brush my teeth."

Jack brushed his teeth and then made his way to the back porch. Helen was sitting there in one of the chairs, and when Jack opened the sliding door, she whispered, "Shee, be quite, Jack, you might scare him off."

Jack walked gingerly over to the next chair and sat down.

Helen handed him his coffee and then pointed her finger toward the bird feeder in the back and said, "Look, Jack."

Sitting perched atop the feeder was a beautiful black eagle casually eating the feed. It was a large bird, and from its size, Jack could tell it was a male. The bird sat atop the feeder with his head down, but a few moments after Jack sat down, the bird lifted and turned its head toward Jack and Helen. For an instant, he froze, almost surprised it seemed, and then cocked his head and stared directly at Jack. Their eyes met, and they stared at each other as if they somehow knew one another. Helen was looking at the eagle, but then turned her head to Jack, surprised to find he was staring at the bird as if in a trance.

"Jack, what's going on? Are you okay?"

"What? Yeah, oh, I'm just a little groggy, still trying to wake up, Helen, sorry."

Helen distracted Jack, and when she turned to look at the eagle again, the bird had pivoted on one foot around the feeder and was now facing away from them.

"Wow, look, Jack, do you see those red markings? I've never seen such a thing," Helen said to Jack once the bird's backside was visible. There were two red splotches of color on the eagle's tail section just behind his wings, each about the size of a quarter. They were symmetric, as if they had been placed there on purpose.

"Isn't that unusual, Jack? Have you ever seen anything like that?" Helen asked.

Jack sat silent for a few moments and then said, "He must have found his way back. I've seen this eagle before."

"What, what do you mean?"

"The bird, I've seen this bird before, last fall. Those distinct red splotches—I'm sure he's the same one."

"Really? Here at this house? But you just put the feeder in yesterday."

"Yes, he's the one. It wasn't here; it was in Anchorage at my apartment."

Jack hesitated. "But how? How did he find me here? How could he have known to come here?"

"What, Jack, in Anchorage? How could it have been in Anchorage? What's the chance the same bird would be here in Fairbanks at your house— it couldn't be. You must be mistaken, Jack. Are you dreaming, Jack?"

Helen giggled and patted Jack on the shoulder.

"No, he's the same one. I know it. I can feel it."

Helen didn't say anything. It was curious: she heard in Jack's voice a pureness she had not heard before, almost like she was experiencing an event she was not supposed to be a part of, but here she was.

She smiled and said, "Okay, Jack, I'll just go with the flow on this one."

Jack smiled and took her hand, and they stared at that lovely black eagle in silence the rest of that morning.

★★★★★

Helen had an appointment later that day, and after the eagle flew off after getting his fill for the morning, Helen told Jack she had to leave; she had an appointment with the family doctor.

"Anything wrong, Helen?" Jack asked.

"No, no, just a routine checkup. He's been our family doctor for as long as I can remember. When I'm up seeing my parents, I like to pop in for a visit. He's an old friend; we like to catch up on things."

"All right, I'll see you tonight then?"

"Sure, Jack, around sevenish. See you then."

Chapter 11

That day Jack worked some more around the house; he had plenty of cleanup work still left to do. In the afternoon, Jack checked his voice mail, and to his pleasant surprise, Robert Weldon had returned his call. Jack went inside and cleaned up a bit, and then gave Weldon a call.

"Dr. Weldon," Jack said warmly when the doctor answered the phone, "so glad you returned my call. It's been awhile since we've corresponded, and I thought it would be nice to finally have a one-to-one chat."

"Well, Jack, it's good to hear from you. I was so fascinated by the e-mails you sent, but I didn't want to bother you too much. I thought when you're ready, you'd contact me. So how's Alaska treating you? Have you made any trips down to the Aleutian Range recently? That's such a beautiful stretch of landscape and sea."

"No, not recently. I've been doing a lot of flights around Fairbanks and Mount McKinley, and through the Denali Park in general, but come spring, we usually do a few tours through the Aleutian Range. If you can make it up this way, Doctor, I'll give you a free tour courtesy of Alaskan Sky Beauty."

Dr. Weldon chuckled. "Thanks for offering, Jack, but at my age, just getting out of the house is an adventure for me. By the way, just call me Robert—Dr. Weldon's just a little too formal for me. I'm just an old country doctor, you know."

"Far from it from what I've read, but okay, Robert."

"So what can I do for you, Jack? Any more news you want to share with me?"

"Well, yes, Robert, in fact, I do have some more stories to tell."

Jack went on to describe his experience with Ingrid Samualson, how she had reached out to him in her attempt to see her daughters before she died, and how even though they had never met before, she knew his name once they had made contact. He also described at length the search and rescue of his young friend Josh, and how he was only able to make contact with Josh once the poor boy was completely destitute and scared into a frenzy, fearing his own death. Dr. Weldon listened quietly, only interrupting Jack for clarification on specific details leading up to the mind and body entanglements.

Jack went on to tell Weldon about the events that morning, certain that the same eagle he had seen the year before at his apartment in Anchorage had visited him now at his house in Fairbanks, and how they had made a connection that morning.

"Fascinating, Jack, quite fascinating. Sounds like it's been quite eventful since we last corresponded. I've thought about this, Jack, and at this point, I can only speculate without doing some tests, but it sounds like you have, at the least, a super-developed corpus callosum. If you recall, the corpus callosum is a part of the brain structure that runs forward and aft and connects the left and right cerebral hemispheres, the two main lobes of the brain. It is the largest single piece of white matter in the brain, consisting for a normal person of 200 to 250 million nerve fibers. It is a wide, flat bundle of nerves beneath the brain cortex. Much of the interhemispheric communication between the left and right sides of the brain is conducted across the corpus callosum.

"My drugs stimulated the corpus callosum, but it's entirely feasible that it could have been altered or enlarged in your brain. Your power is so strong it appears you can reach outside of your own skull to tap into others' brain waves, especially when you're communicating with them directly. When you do this, you leave remnants of your own thoughts in the other's mind. I speculate that when someone is in distress or is very emotional, those strong emotions can open up a pathway to your own brain, tapping into its superpower. Now when it comes to you experiencing their aches and pains and in some cases their bruises, I've not seen or heard of such a thing. It's as if because your brains are connected in a certain way, this leads to a type of mind and body sharing that allows you to feel what they feel. I would like to find out if, in fact, their bodily pain diminishes during those times; some tests would help to define what is happening at those moments. This may sound a little funny, Jack, but I'd love to study your brain's functioning. I spent my entire life trying to understand the brain, and a case like yours would be quite a fascinating study."

Jack laughed. "Yes, I'm sure it would be; it's not like you run into a case like mine every day, is it?"

"Seriously, Jack, as we've discussed before, I can give you some educated guidance on your condition, but without actually seeing you, there is not much additional insight I can provide. I think I have somewhat an idea of what has happened to you, but as a good old country doctor might say, I need to see you before I can heal you, though in your case, I don't think you need healing, maybe just some understanding."

Jack chuckled again. "Yes, I understand. I do appreciate your insight already; some would have taken me for a loon by now, so I can't thank you enough for letting me bounce these events off of you."

Jack paused. "I would like to pay you a visit in the near future, Doctor, I mean Robert. Look, we have a trade show every year, and I've been several times, though I missed it the last few years. I know this year it's being held in Montana, so can we try to meet then? It's in the early spring before the summer season starts, usually early April, several months from now, so that might work out. How does that sound?"

"Fine, Jack, just fine. After seeing all the family over the holidays, I usually lay low for a while and then do some spring planting in the backyard come March, so April would work for me. Just keep in touch, and when you firm things up, let me know. To make further progress in understanding your condition, I'll need to run some tests, so I'll need to make some arrangements with the university to use their facilities. Just let me know specific dates a month or so before you plan to be here. How does that sound?"

"That sounds good, Robert. Let's plan on it; I'll look up those dates right away."

"And Jack, you don't have to be a stranger before then. If you want to talk or send me an e-mail, don't hesitate. It's always a pleasure."

"Thanks, Robert, I appreciate that very much. I'll be in touch soon. Thanks again."

"Sure thing, Jack, good talking with you."

"Good talking with you."

Jack hung up the phone. *What a pleasant man, and very knowledgeable too,* he thought to himself. Jack wandered over to his computer and started to look up the dates for the recreational airplanes and bush pilots trade show.

★★★★★

Around six o'clock, Helen called.

"Helen, darling, how are you?"

"Oh, okay, I guess. Listen, Jack, I'm not feeling that well. I might just spend the night with my folks. I'm heading back to Anchorage tomorrow, so I'll see you back there—would that be okay?"

Jack was disappointed. "Oh, Helen, come on. I was really looking forward to seeing you. Listen, we don't have to do anything special—just relax, maybe watch TV for a while."

"Oh, I don't know, I ..."

"Listen, I have an idea. I'll fix us a nice meal, and by the time you arrive, it will be all ready—you won't have to do anything. We'll have a nice dinner together, and then you can just relax. I'll even do the dishes."

Helen sighed, "Oh, Jack, I don't know, I ..."

"Oh, come on, darling, I'll even give you a nice back rub. Please?"

"Oh, gosh, Jack, well, okay."

"I can pick you up—would that be better?"

"No, that's okay, Jack. I'll see you in a bit."

"Wonderful, darling. I'll get on that meal right away."

She seems a bit down, doesn't she? Jack thought to himself. Jack had experienced that before with Helen. She would seem tired and slightly depressed, and he struggled with how to deal with her during those times.

★★★★★

Helen arrived an hour later. Jack decided to be upbeat to try to get her in a better mood.

"Helen, sweetheart! My darling! The chef is at your service. Please come in; I have a fabulous meal waiting!" Jack wrapped his arms around her and gave her a big hug.

"Hi, Jack," Helen replied glumly, returning his hug but only halfheartedly.

"My darling, don't be down. It's a beautiful, clear, crisp evening, and I have your favorite meal waiting. The chef is ready to serve you hand and foot!"

"I'm not down," Helen replied defensively.

Oh man, I shouldn't have said that, Jack thought to himself as Helen walked past and into the house. *When she's down, the last thing she needs is for me to tell her she's down.*

★★★★★

Helen remained that way throughout their meal. Jack tried to make some small talk, but Helen's answers were brief, and in the middle of one of his questions about how her work was going, Helen said, "Listen, Jack, I'm tired. Can we just be quiet for a while?"

"Sure, Helen," Jack replied, a slight twinge of pain noticeable in the back of his voice.

Jack finished up his meal and then picked up the dishes as Helen wandered into the living room. She sat down on the couch and picked up a magazine as Jack cleaned the dishes and put them away.

Once he was done, he came into the living room and sat next to her. Then he grabbed the remote and turned on the TV. He was flipping through the channels when Helen said, "Can we just turn that thing off for a little while, Jack? It's all a bunch of garbage anyway."

"Sure, Helen, no problem."

Jack turned the TV off and picked up a magazine himself and started thumbing through the pages. They sat that way for some time, each reading through their magazines, not saying a word to one another.

After twenty minutes, Jack remembered he had promised Helen a back rub, so he put his magazine down and scooted his way over to her. He gently started rubbing her shoulders, saying, "I promised you a back rub, didn't I? You know the chef always keeps his promises."

Helen stayed still, and Jack could sense by her posture that she wasn't enjoying it. After a few minutes, Jack stopped rubbing her back.

"Helen, what's wrong? Bad news from the doctor today or something?"

"No, Jack, everything's fine. I'm sorry; I'm just beat. I better get some rest."

Helen stood up and made her way to the bedroom, leaving Jack alone on the couch. *I better just leave her alone for a while,* Jack thought to himself as he picked up the remote and turned the TV on, turning the volume all the way down so it wouldn't bother Helen.

★★★★★

Jack flipped through the channels trying to find something interesting to watch and luckily caught the last hour of a good sci-fi movie, but he was bothered by Helen's behavior that evening. She seemed so sad, and Jack didn't quite know what to do to help her. He didn't want to probe, but she definitely was not her usual, sunny self. He pondered this as he watched the end of the movie, but by ten, he was feeling tired himself and got up to go to bed. Helen was asleep as he walked into the bedroom, her body curled up away from him facing the edge of the bed. Jack gingerly climbed into bed, trying not to wake her up. He then scooted his body over to hers, put one arm around her waist, and slowly stroked her hair with his other hand.

"Sweet Helen, my darling," he whispered, "you're such a wonderful woman."

Helen stirred briefly and mumbled something that he couldn't quite make out, as if she were dreaming, but was half awake as well.

"My sweetheart," Jack continued, "please don't be sad. If only I could help you and see what's ailing you—please let me understand."

Then as Jack continued to stroke her hair, the images from her mind filled his mind, and he felt her pain and sadness as well.

"Oh, Helen," he said softly, "I'm so sorry. That is so sad. I'm so sorry."

He continued to stroke her hair, then rolled over to the other side of the bed and put his hands behind his head, looking up at the ceiling. He stayed that way for some time, but he couldn't sleep, so he got up and went into the living room. He sat down on the couch, his head in his hands, and cried softly, feeling Helen's sadness as he tried to understand the feelings that she felt.

Chapter 12

Once he was back in Anchorage, Jack made arrangements to be at the recreational airplanes and bush pilots trade show in April. He then called Robert Weldon and let him know his plans and followed up with an e-mail. It had been several years since Jack had taken a real vacation, so he thought it would be fun to make a holiday out of the trip. After some arm-twisting, he convinced Helen to go with him. Jack knew Helen wouldn't much enjoy a long airplane flight in his small plane and that wouldn't be much of a holiday, so after some bantering back and forth, they decided on a cruise from Anchorage down to Vancouver, Canada, and then a historic train ride from Vancouver to Calgary. The cruise ship would take them down the Alaskan and Canadian coastline over five days, and then they would board a train in Vancouver. The small historic train would take them through the most beautiful areas and towns in the Canadian Rockies, including Jasper, Lake Louis, Banff, and Calgary. From Calgary, they would board another train en route to Bozeman.

Neither he nor Helen had vacationed along the Canadian coastline and through the Canadian Rockies, and they thought the trip would be an excellent way to experience both and hopefully meet some interesting people along the way. In addition, they both thought it would be a wonderful way to spend some time together. Helen didn't have much desire to stay for the trade show, so she arranged to fly back to Anchorage the evening before the show, leaving Jack to work the show, learn from the others there, and hopefully generate some additional business. It worked out nicely, because it gave Jack a few days to visit with Robert Weldon as well.

*****

The cruise that April along the Alaskan and Canadian coastline was disappointing, to say the least. They were able to get a reasonable fare since it was so early in the year, but for most of the cruise, the weather was overcast and colder than expected. April could be hit or miss, but the temperature stayed below forty degrees most of the way, and unfortunately they got caught in that overcast and rainy Northwest weather. It was with a sense of relief that after four days of that, they finally got a break on the morning of the fifth day as they made their way into the port of Vancouver. Jack and Helen took as much advantage of that day as they could. They made their way into Vancouver proper and did some shopping, then headed over to a nice Italian restaurant overlooking Stanly Park, with a beautiful view of the Lion's Gate Bridge and North Vancouver farther off in the distance. They were relaxing and enjoying themselves, but when Jack finally looked at his watch, he realized they only had twenty minutes to get to the train station to catch the train to Calgary.

"Come on, Helen, we better get going!" Jack said as he hastily paid the waiter and grabbed his luggage. "That train's going to leave without us."

*****

Jack and Helen caught the subway just in time to make the train, and as the subway doors opened at the central terminal, they rushed to the train dragging their luggage behind them.

"All aboard! This is your last call. All aboard!" they heard the train conductor bellow out.

"Come on, Helen, we're going to miss the train!"

"Oh, hush up now, Jack. If you wanted to help me, you'd take my bag here, you silly goose."

Jack grabbed Helen's bag and ran ahead of her, flagging down the train conductor as he made his way toward the back of the train.

"We're here. Don't leave without us," Jack yelled. "My girlfriend is just behind me!"

"Hurry up, you two! We can't wait all day, you know!" the train conductor chuckled. "Can't you move a little faster?" he said, chuckling again.

The train conductor was an older gentleman, with a Scottish accent and a curled, gray mustache. He had a small potbelly and wore a light gray conductor's suit and hat, with a brass belt and cuff links on his jacket. On another day, with a red hat and suit, he would have made a good Santa Claus, handing out candy to the young children who passed his way.

"Hurry along, young lady, my dear," he said as he reached out and took hold of Helen's luggage.

"We're so sorry, sir, it's just we were enjoying the day so much, we must have lost track of time," Helen said apologetically.

"No troubles, my young lady, just jump on board. I was about to leave without you two. Everyone else is on board."

"Well, thanks for waiting. Gosh, we're almost twenty minutes late."

"No worries. I handed out some drinks to the others on board, settled them down for a little while. I couldn't think to leave such a lovely couple as you two behind. Why don't you two get settled in and we'll get on our way? You wouldn't mind terribly if my assistant brings you something to drink. I'm heading to the locomotive, and we'll be moving in just a few minutes."

"Well, thanks so much," Helen said as she made her way inside. "Of course, drinks from your assistant would be wonderful. Thanks again."

Jack had already stowed his luggage by the time Helen was in the cabin.

"Helen darling, let me get that for you. My gosh, I'm glad they didn't leave without us. We're quite late, aren't we?"

"Yes, twenty minutes to be exact. The train conductor was so nice. I'm his "young lady," you know. He was so sweet."

"Yeah, he seemed like quite a character, didn't he? I think we must have looked quite comical rushing to the train like that. He got quite a chuckle out of it, didn't he?"

"Oh, he was just playing with us. He even apologized for not being able to get me a drink—such a nice fellow."

The train they were taking to Calgary was an old historic train, one of the few left that operated the route from Vancouver to Calgary. It was a small train, with only four boxcars and the locomotive, seating sixty people comfortably. Their brochure emphasized the personal touch, and with a small number of passengers, the crew could take the time to get to know the folks as they stopped in small towns along the route.

Five minutes after the train was on its way, a young man dressed in a black conductor's suit and hat greeted them.

"Well, hello there, so glad you could join us today. How are things?"

"Great, great," Helen replied. "We're so glad you didn't leave without us—it's such a gorgeous day for a train ride."

"Well, don't think anything of it, we're so happy to have you. Can I get you something to drink, ma'am?"

"Why yes, let me see. Do you have any wine, say a zinfandel?"

"Of course. And you, sir?"

"Well, let me think, a beer would be nice, but it's a bit early for that. How about some ginger ale."

"I can get you a beer, sir, if you'd like—we have quite a selection."

"That's tempting, but maybe a little later. Ginger ale is fine for now."

"Ginger ale it is, sir. I'll be right back."

"They're so nice on this train, aren't they, Jack?" Helen said after the young man walked away.

"Yes, they're quite personable. He's a young fellow, isn't he? He doesn't look a day over twenty."

"Yes, he's quite young, but he does look quite smart in that conductor's suit, doesn't he?"

Jack smiled, then turned his head to the window and watched the countryside fly by.

★★★★★

Late that evening, the train stopped in Kamloops, a small town halfway between Vancouver and Jasper, for the trip's first overnight stay. As Helen and Jack exited the train, they ran into the old train conductor.

"Well, hello, you two! So how are you getting along? I hope you've been enjoying yourselves."

"Oh, very well, thanks so much," Helen replied.

"Yes, the countryside and mountains are spectacular," Jack added.

"Well, I'm glad you're enjoying the trip, but just wait for tomorrow. The mountain pass along the way to Jasper is quite amazing. We'll pass by Mt. Sir Wilfred Laurier—we call it Wilfry for short—making a steep climb before descending down to Kinbasket Lake. The train tracks wrap right around the lake, so you'll love it. It is such a romantic ride—it will be a wonderful ride for such a lovely couple as yourselves."

"Well, that sounds beautiful," Helen said.

"So you two look so good together. You must be engaged—such a beautiful pair."

Helen blushed a bit and smiled sheepishly as she turned her head to Jack. Jack turned to Helen and smiled as well.

"Well, I'm sorry, I didn't mean to probe," the conductor said heartily. "I'm just glad you're enjoying yourselves. Is there anything I can do for you on the train? Anything that would make the trip more pleasant?"

"I can't think of anything, but so kind of you to ask, Mr.—?" Helen cocked her head slightly and smiled, then said, "Well, I don't think we've introduced ourselves. I'm Helen."

"Helen, so nice to meet you, and such a lovely name. My name is Sean McCree."

Jack extended his hand as he said, "Hi, Sean, my name is Jack."

Jack and Sean shook hands, then Sean turned and shook Helen's hand as well.

"So are you Scottish? You have such a nice accent," Helen asked.

"Well, yes, I am. I was born in Perth, Scotland. It's just an hour north of Edinburgh, but I've lived in these parts for quite some years now;

it's been over twenty-five years since I moved from the homeland. And yourselves?"

"We're from Alaska," Helen replied.

"Alaska, my word. This must seem like timid terrain compared to what you have up there."

"Well, yes, less rugged, I would say," Jack replied.

"But I think more beautiful and green," Helen added. "We're having such a nice trip."

"Well, I'm so happy to hear that. Do you need any help finding a bite to eat? There are several nice places in town."

"Well, in fact, yes," Jack replied. "I was hoping to find a nice pub in town where I could get a good home-brewed beer."

"A beer drinker, are you? Just like me. Yes, there's a nice pub just around the next corner, called the Green Lion. Just up the way—when you turn the corner, you'll see it on the left."

"What do you say, Helen? Do you want to give it a try?"

"Sure, Jack, that would be great. I hope they serve wine as well. Care to join us, Mr. McCree?"

"Just call me Sean, and thanks, my dear, but I best get some rest; we've got a long train ride tomorrow. But listen, you two, have a nice time. You might try their Scottish Pale Ale, Jack—they brew it on site—and Helen, their wine selection is quite good as well."

"Well, thank you, Sean, we'll see you tomorrow," Helen said.

"I'll see you then. So nice to meet the both of you, and good night."

"Nice to meet you," Helen and Jack replied together.

As Helen and Jack walked down the street together hand in hand, Helen said, "Isn't he nice, Jack? I'm so glad we decided on this train ride together."

"Yes, he's very nice. Such a pleasant fellow."

★★★★★

That evening, as Sean McCree went through his luggage and personal items, he realized he had just run out of his medication. He had a mild stroke several years back, but ever since he had been taking the medication his doctor prescribed, he had remained healthy and was cleared by the medical authorities to continue to operate his train.

Well, I'll have to refill my prescription when I get into Jasper, he thought to himself. *No worries; I'll get some more tomorrow evening.*

He took the medication now as more of a precautionary measure, not as a prescribed requirement, but in any case, he had been taking it regularly to be safe. Once he had recovered from his stroke, his doctor recommended he exercise regularly, and Sean had been going to the gym ever since. After a year of a good exercise routine, his doctor told him to take the medication if he wished, but it was not required. In his younger days, Sean had become quite well-known as a boxer, so he had returned to the boxing gym, doing some light sparring with some of the younger men in the gym who shared his passion for boxing. He had also been walking regularly and had even taken up jump roping, one of his favorite exercises during the peak of his boxing career.

★★★★★

The next morning, the weather was much like the day before, clear and crisp, and Sean McCree felt chipper.

Maybe that medication is holding me back, making me less energetic than I would be otherwise, he mused. *Maybe I should just get off the stuff for a while and see how it goes. I'll run it by my doctor and see what he thinks.*

Sean met up with his younger counterpart, Jason, for breakfast. As they ate, they discussed the schedule for the day, first discussing the maintenance procedures that needed to be performed on the train before getting on their way. Then Sean made sure Jason was prepared to keep the passengers comfortable and satisfied. Sometimes Jason joked with Sean that he felt like an airline steward, serving drinks and food to everyone, instead of being more of a conductor trainee. Sean would reply jokingly that before making the train happy, he had to learn how to make the customers riding the train happy. They joked back and forth this way through their breakfast before collecting their things, and then made their way to the train. They wouldn't be leaving the station until 9:00 a.m., but they had a couple hours of work to do and it was almost seven, so they got started with their preparation.

Sean and Jason first worked in the engine compartment, going through their detailed checklist and making sure everything was operational. Then they both walked the train cars, cleaning as they went. After this, Sean helped Jason stock the food they would be serving later in the day, and helped him prepare the coffee and breakfast snacks Jason would serve after they got underway. They had been operating this way now for several years, just the two of them running the train. Jason was not yet certified to operate the locomotive, but was accumulating training hours so that in a few years, he could operate the train himself. After attending to the passengers, he would make his way to the locomotive and help Sean with the duties there, working the radios among other things. One of his favorite jobs was to blow the horn as they approached road intersections; he loved the sound of the bellowing horn, and often as the historic train made its way past the intersections, he would wave to the people in their cars as they waited for the train to pass. Sean would joke that he needed to keep his eyes on the train track, not on the road.

★★★★★

That day the air was cool and clear, and as Jack and Helen boarded the train, they ran into Sean as he made his last round cleaning the passenger cars.

"Well, hello, and good morning, you two! We've got quite a lovely day ahead of us. With the weather this clear, you'll have some beautiful views of the mountains, and you'll especially love Lake Kinbasket. So how did you get on last night? Did you make your way to the Green Lion?"

"Yes, we did," Helen replied. "Such a lovely place, a perfect little pub, and the decor was quite amazing. I loved that painting of the green lion sitting on the mountaintop. That place had character."

"And don't forget the beer," Jack added. "That Scottish Ale was spot-on. It went down smooth."

"Well, I'm glad you enjoyed yourselves. With this weather, today will be even better!"

★★★★★

"He's right, isn't he, Jack?" Helen said to Jack later that day. "The mountains are spectacular. Is that the mountain he mentioned—what did he call it, Wilfry or something?"

"Well, let me see, here's the map. Yes, I think that is it. It sits 11,500 feet high. It's pretty, isn't it—prettier than most mountains in our neck of the woods."

Helen cuddled up next to Jack as they both peered out the window enjoying the view. The train was making a long, steep climb now up the mountain track that passed by Mount Wilfred.

Ahead in the locomotive, Sean and Jason were busy. The long steep climb taxed the locomotive engine, and they remained diligent, ensuring they kept their speed at a slow twenty miles an hour to prevent the train engine from overheating. They didn't want to slow too much, however, because if the train came to a halt, they would have to tax the diesel engine to its limit to get the train moving again. It was the trickiest part of the journey from Vancouver to Calgary, and during this time, they always worked together in the locomotive. Jason stood by Sean's side, but as they made the long ascent, he remembered he had forgotten to bring one of the passengers the dessert she was waiting for.

"Sean, I need to head back to the passenger cars and attend to one of the passengers—gosh, that was almost thirty minutes ago. I hope she's not getting upset."

"Go on, laddy," Sean replied. "We're almost to the top. I'll be okay from here."

Jason turned and rushed back to the kitchen area at the front of the third boxcar, closing the door to the locomotive behind him. He hated it when he forgot about the passengers—it was the one thing that Sean would give him a hard time about, and it took away from his true love of operating the train. He went about fixing an oversized helping of the raspberry cobbler pie, putting a huge spoonful of whipped cream on top, and he rushed back to the last boxcar.

★★★★★

As the train reached the apex of the long climb, Sean gradually moved the engines back to half throttle in preparation for the long descent toward Kinbasket Lake. This was Sean's favorite part of the trip. After the long descent, the train took a long, spiraling turn on a train track that wrapped its way around the base of Mount Wilfred. The train track was built into the side of the mountain and was elevated above the lake, giving a spectacular view of the water. Then it turned and headed over a bridge that crossed the northern part of the lake.

Sean felt exuberant, in fact, he felt almost a bit light-headed. *I haven't had this much energy in years, ever since the stroke,* he thought to himself as he turned on his heel and moved to the left to get his hand on the brake lever. It was at that moment that he suddenly felt dizzy; he tried to catch himself with his left hand, but his heel hit a slick portion of the floor. Sean and Jason cleaned the floor regularly, *but apparently not regularly enough,* Sean thought to himself, because there in the locomotive, it wasn't unusual for a slippery mixture of oil and soot to coalesce in spots, with the engine directly in front.

"Oh my," Sean spit out as his leg slid underneath him. He tried again to catch himself with his left hand, but he was already falling backward. Before he could grab anything, he fell cleanly on his back, his head striking the hard steel floor with a solid thump.

"Urh," he heard himself say as stars filled his eyes and he saw blackness creeping up the sides of his eyeballs. He lay there for a few moments in a semiconscious state, his mind wandering back to a similar event twenty-five years prior.

It was the world middleweight title fight taking place in London, England, and Sean lay on the mat, having taken a wicked blow from his opponent moments earlier. It had been a grueling boxing match, with both competitors exchanging heavy blows throughout the fight, and it was now the tenth and deciding round. Sean had cut his left eye earlier in the sixth round, and the crowd as well as his coach were shocked and awed that he continued. In the next three rounds, blood seeped from his cut, but he continued even with the blood seeping down his face. He was thirty-two years old at the time, and this was his last chance to win the title.

At my age, no one is going to give me a second chance, he thought to himself as he peered across at his opponent between the ninth and tenth rounds. The bell rang, and he wiped the blood off his eye one last time, knowing he was behind and that he had to go for the knockout. He went for his opponent's body and then moved up to his head, hammering away until he had his competitor on the ropes. Blood was dripping down into his left eye, and it obscured his vision enough that he didn't see the right hook coming. The blow landed solidly on his left cheekbone with a resounding thud.

Sean fell flat on his back and onto the mat next to his corner. As he lay there in agony on the mat listening to the count, he could hear his coach yelling at him, "Stay down, Sean, stay down! It's over, it's over! Just stay down!"

But Sean didn't stay down, and after nine counts he struggled to his feet, telling the referee he was good. The referee hesitated, but the roar of the crowd was so loud he let the fighters continue. The next blow to Sean's face thirty seconds later knocked him out cold and ended his boxing career forever.

As Sean lay on the floor of the locomotive, he remembered those words from his coach, "Stay down, Sean, stay down! It's over!" but he knew as well that the train was picking up speed as they headed down the long, steep incline toward Kinbasket Lake. *I can't wait here too long. I'm still at half throttle, and I've got to get on those brakes before it's too late,* he thought to himself. He struggled to his feet, but he was disoriented and before he could catch himself, his body fell forward and he knocked his head solidly against the edge of the engine controls cabinet, opening up a deep gash on the side of his forehead that knocked him out cold.

*****

"Well, madam," Jason said as he put the dessert in front of her, "I'm so sorry this took me so long. Please forgive me. I got caught up with Sean in the locomotive."

"Well, it has been almost three quarters of an hour now, and I don't like that much whipped cream on my cobbler, either," the woman replied as she stared at the dessert in front of her.

"Well, I'm so sorry, madam. I can get you another serving if you'd like without the whipped cream."

"Oh, don't bother, I'll just take it off myself."

The woman scraped some of the whipped cream off the top and then took a large chunk of the cobbler with her fork.

"Oh my," she said, "that's quite good, even though it did take so long. That's quite tasty."

"Well, madam, I'm very glad you like it, and I'm so sorry again about the long wait. It won't happen again."

The woman didn't say anything. It seemed to Jason she was too busy eating the dessert to notice a word he said.

Jason started to walk back to the locomotive, but an elderly gentleman returning from the bathroom stopped him and asked, "Excuse me, would it be possible I could get another cup of that lovely coffee?"

Jason hesitated. "Well, sir, I'd have to brew another pot, but, uh, well, yes, of course, sir, yes, another cup coming right up. Would you like some cream and sugar with your coffee?"

"Yes, please, that would be lovely. Thank you," the elderly man replied.

Jason made his way to the kitchen in the third boxcar and made another pot of coffee. He waited there as the pot brewed for several minutes. He noticed the train seemed to be moving faster than normal during this stretch, but the pot of coffee was almost finished. When it was through brewing, Jason put the pot, sugar, and some cream on a tray and made his way back to the elderly man.

As he walked, he looked out the windows of the boxcar, alarmed that the train was moving faster than he ever remembered for the descent toward Kinbasket Lake.

"Well, here you are, sir," Jason said to the man. "Coffee right up."

"Well, thank you," the man replied.

Jason poured the coffee into the man's cup and then waited impatiently as the man poured his cream and took some sugar. When the man was finished, Jason hurriedly made his way back to the kitchen, getting more nervous with every step as the train moved faster and faster. When he got back to the kitchen, he put the tray down, stuck his head out of one of the windows, and peered up and down the track to see if he could tell what was going on. By now, the train was halfway down the descent to the lake, and Jason whispered to himself, *Sean better get on those brakes quickly, because there is no way we're going to make that bend at this speed. I better get up there and see what is going on.*

Jason was nervous. He opened the door to the next boxcar but didn't close it as he started running up to the front of the train.

"Oh my," one woman said as he rushed by. In his haste, Jason ran into the back of another woman who was making her way to the bathroom.

"Well, excuse me," the woman said as Jason pushed his way around her, not saying a word. Jack and Helen were sitting at the back of the first boxcar, and were caught by surprise when they heard the back door of the boxcar slam as Jason pushed it open wildly. Jack turned his head and saw the young man running away from him toward the front of the train.

"Wow, he looked awfully nervous," Jack said to himself as much as he did to Helen.

"Yeah, that seemed pretty odd," Helen replied.

"This train does seem to be moving pretty damn fast; there must be something wrong. I'm going to check this out."

"Jack, wait, Jack," Helen instinctively said, but by then Jack was out of his seat and briskly making his way to the front of the train. Jack could see the young man ahead of him grab the door leading to the locomotive and yank on it, then frantically yank it again. "Oh god," he could hear the young man say, and then again he tried to yank the door open.

Jack trotted up to the young man trying to remember his name. *It started with a J,* Jack thought to himself, *Ja, Jason, that's it.*

"Jason, what is going on here?"

Jack could tell by the young man's expression that he was frantic.

"The door, it's, it's locked; I must have locked it behind me."

"Well, don't you have the keys?" Jack asked.

Jason looked at Jack with a bewildered look on his face. "Yes, I think so." Jason searched his pants pockets and then all the pockets in his jacket as well.

"Oh god, I must have left them in the locomotive. The train, the train, it's moving too fast. Why isn't Sean hitting the brakes? I don't understand. He needs to hit the brakes. We're going too fast, there's a curve ahead, and we're going too fast. We're going to come off the tracks. Oh god, the train's going to derail. Oh god, no, no, this can't be happening!"

"Jason, get ahold of yourself. There must be a way to get to the locomotive. Think, man, can we get on top of the train?"

Jason stuck his head out of one of the side windows.

"There's no time; we're moving too fast. The curve is just ahead. There's no time!"

By this time, several others had gathered behind Jack and Jason, wondering what on earth was going on.

"Try to kick the door in!" one man yelled from behind. Since it was an older train, the door was solid wood with no window and looked pretty sturdy to Jack. Jason looked back briefly, and then with a heaving kick, smashed his foot into the door as hard as he could, but it didn't budge.

"It's solid," Jason screamed. "What is Sean doing? Why doesn't he hit the brakes?"

Another large man made his way to the front.

"Let me try—I'll bust this door down." Jason moved out of his way as the man got a running start and smashed himself into the door with his right shoulder. He hit the door hard, but bounced back, falling to his knees—and the door held.

"Where's a crowbar? We'll smash it in," a third man said.

"Crowbar, crowbar," Jason said. "We keep the heavy tools in the locomotive. There's nothing in the boxcars. Oh man, we're running out of time!"

"Get out of my way," the large man said, "I'm trying again." He took a larger running start this time, but the aisle was narrow, making it difficult to gather speed. He hit the door again, but it still didn't move.

As this was going on, Jack backed up several feet behind the men gathered around the door and tried to concentrate. He closed his eyes and tried to get an image of Sean in his mind.

"Sean, where are you?" he whispered. "Sean, we're in trouble, where are you?"

Slowly over a period of a few seconds, a hazy image of Sean lying facedown in the locomotive appeared. Jack could see that Sean was bleeding profusely from the deep cut on his head and was struggling with all his might to regain consciousness and stop the train. Jack could make out some images of the train's controls, the throttle, the brake, but he had never been inside of a locomotive and now was no time for him to learn how to operate a train.

By this time, Helen had made her way out of her seat and was standing behind Jack.

"Jack, what's happening?"

Ahead, Jason was screaming, "We've got to stop this train! We're out of time!"

"Sean, we're out of time; come on, get up," Jack said under his breath, but Sean didn't move. Jack waited a few more seconds and then closed his eyes.

"Oh god, this is going to hurt," he said, and then he rolled his eyes backward and concentrated.

"Jack!" Helen screamed as Jack collapsed in front of her and onto the floor of the train. He fell face-first, and his head struck the floor with a thud.

"Jack!" Helen screamed again. She knelt down on the floor and rolled Jack over onto her legs and torso, cradling him with her arms. "Oh, Jack!"

Above his left temple, there was a deep cut, and blood was streaming down his face and onto his clothing.

Ahead in the locomotive, Sean's eyes suddenly popped open. He was at first surprised, but his head was clear and he quickly stood up. He looked briefly ahead of him, seeing that the train was screaming down toward the sharp curve above Kinbasket Lake. With the skill of a man who had been operating a train for twenty years, he moved the engines to idle and simultaneously grabbed the brake handle. The train braked suddenly and violently, throwing the passengers in the boxcars hard forward. Smoke billowed from the brakes from the blistering heat, and the brakes made a screeching hiss as Sean worked them to their absolute maximum. Once the train had slowed to seventy miles an hour, Sean rammed the engines into reverse and applied the emergency brakes. The locomotive shuttered violently, but the massive jolt helped to slow the train down considerably. As the train entered the sharp curve, the passengers were thrown hard against the walls of the boxcars. For a moment, Sean was afraid the train would come off the tracks and plummet down the steep embankment below, but he modulated the brakes perfectly and the train exited the sharpest part of the curve without incident. The train was well in Sean's control now, and he took the engines out of reverse and then slowly and patiently brought the train to a halt, making sure the emergency brakes were applied fully.

He then turned around, moved to the back of the locomotive, and unlocked the door. Jason was there white as a ghost, but he was still present enough to catch Sean as he collapsed in front of him.

"Sean, my god, Sean, you did it. You came through when we needed you most."

Sean didn't say a word. By then, the deep gash on his head had again spun him back into unconsciousness.

★★★★★

Jack's head ached, but he opened his eyes slowly and peered up toward Helen.

"Did we make it? Are we safe?" he asked her.

"You missed quite a ride, Jack, but we're still here. The train stopped safely," she replied.

Jack slowly stood up and then took a napkin and wrapped it around his head, covering up the gash on his head.

★★★★★

Jason and the other men at the front of the boxcar laid Sean down into one of the seats, and then Jason went to the kitchen area and brought back an emergency medical kit and attended to Sean. He cleaned off the blood as well as he could, and then applied some antibiotics to the wound before wrapping Sean's head with bandages. Jason then went to the locomotive to see if the train was still in working order. Other than the smell of the brakes, nothing appeared amiss. The other men waited with Sean, and after fifteen minutes, he started to come to. One of the men went and got Jason from the locomotive.

"Jason, he's coming to. Do you want to speak with him?"

"Of course, yes," Jason replied as he made his way back to the boxcar.

"Sean, how are you doing, are you all right?"

"Oh, Jason laddy, I'm okay. Don't worry about me. How's the train?"

"As far as I can tell, everything looks operational. What should we do, Sean? Do we need to wait here to get a tow to Jasper? What do you think?"

"No, Jason, we could be here for hours, if not longer. Go and make sure all the passengers are okay, and then let's get on our way slowly, very slowly. We'll be in Jasper in less than an hour."

"Okay, Sean."

★★★★★

Farther back in the boxcar, Helen was perplexed and worried.

"What happened to you, Jack? You just collapsed all of a sudden, and then that bad gash on your head—are you going to be all right? Let me take that napkin off your head and clean up your wound properly, Jack."

"Oh gosh, Helen, I just don't know what happened. I felt a little flustered with the train moving so fast and all, and then all of a sudden, I just lost my head. I'm feeling okay now, darling, you're so sweet. It's okay, I'll just get something from Jason and clean myself up. I'm just so glad Sean was able to stop this train. Can you imagine if we had derailed? That would have been horrendous. Why don't you see if Sean or Jason need some help, sweetheart? I'll be okay."

"Are you sure, Jack? You took a big blow when you hit the floor."

"Go on, darling, I'm okay."

★★★★★

Over the next hour, Jason limped the train to Jasper and then radioed in for some medical help for Sean when they arrived. Sean was taken to the hospital while the passengers alighted from the train, and then Jason had the train taken over to the maintenance depot for inspection. The train trip had a planned overnight stay in Jasper, so Helen and Jack checked into their hotel along with the other passengers. A few hours later, Jason made his way to the hotel and told all the passengers that the train would be in the maintenance depot for several days and that he would arrange to have another train take them to their final destination in Calgary. Jason told everyone that the train, however, wouldn't be available until midafternoon and that he had arranged a late checkout with the hotel for all the passengers.

Jack and Helen caught up with Jason as he was about to leave.

"Jason, hope you are doing all right. That was quite a scare we had on the train."

"I'm fine, Jack, I appreciate you asking."

"So how's Sean doing?"

"Oh, he's okay, I just paid him a visit at the hospital. He's still a bit disoriented and he was so concerned about the train and the passengers, but I assured him everyone was okay and the train would be ready for service in a few days."

"Where's he staying?"

"At the Jasper hospital—it's just a short walk from here."

"Do you think he's up for a few visitors?" Helen asked. "I think it would be nice to pay him a visit."

"Yes, I'd like to see how the old Scotsman is doing," Jack continued.

"Well, I don't see why not. I think he'd appreciate that," Jason replied.

"We have some time tomorrow morning. We could come by, say, around eleven?"

"Yes, I think that would work out well," Jason replied.

"All right, Jason, well, get a good night's rest—it's been quite a day.

Maybe we'll see you tomorrow at the hospital," Jack said, patting Jason on the shoulder.

"Yes, hopefully I'll see you then, but in any case, have a good night, Jack, and you too, Helen—and thank you."

★★★★★

When Jack and Helen walked into the hospital room the next morning, Sean had his spectacles on and was buried in a book, but when they caught his attention, a big smile came over his face and he put the book down on his lap.

"Well, hello, you two! So wonderful to see you!"

"So it looks like you're getting on quite well," Jack said. "Catching up on some reading, are you?"

"Well, yes, it's just a book on some of the great boxers of our time—one of my passions, you know. So how are you two getting on? I hope that train ride wasn't too much for you, and I'm so sorry about what happened. I heard you took quite a bump to your head as well, Jack," Sean said as he pointed to the patch above Jack's left temple.

"Well, yes, I did, but I'm feeling fine today. It wasn't nearly as bad as the one you took—that must have hurt."

"Yes, it sure did. I slipped, and next thing I know, I'm flat on my back. I tried to get up, not wanting the train to get away from me, but I slipped again, and then I'm flat out cold. I feel much better today. Hopefully they'll release me tomorrow or the next day. I just don't know what happened to me. I suppose I shouldn't have tried to get back up so quickly after the first slip, but I just felt I had to with the train descending and all."

"We're just so glad you were able to stop the train, Sean. Your dear friend Jason was in quite a tizzy, as was I," Helen said.

"Yes, I was out cold. Then the next thing I know, my eyes pop open, and I feel as fresh as a daisy and was able to bring the beast to a halt. I suppose it was only temporary, because Jason tells me I collapsed right in front of him once the train was stopped."

"So did you use to box, Sean?" Jack asked, pointing to the book.

Sean laughed, but then put his hand up to the big bandage wrapped around his head.

"Oh my, I better not laugh too much—that hurts my head. Well, yes, I used to throw a few punches back in my day, but that was ages ago."

"Throw a few punches? That's quite bashful of you, Sean. I was told you were at the top of your sport, and were only one fight away from the world championship title."

Sean was caught by surprise. He no longer discussed his boxing career with anyone, not even Jason. He was still disappointed with the way his career had ended, so he usually kept his boxing stories to himself.

Sean looked down. "Well, yes, Jack, that's true, but that was twenty-five years ago. I threw my boxing career away like I almost threw the train away yesterday. The match was his after he floored me in the tenth round. I should have let him have it to box another day, but instead, I struggled to my feet to try and hold on. After he floored me a second time, I could never box again, at least not at the level to be a champion. Yesterday reminded me of that—how I almost lost it all in my haste to save the train."

"Come on, you old brave Scotsman," Jack replied. "You were just trying to do your best. No one can blame you for that, so please don't beat yourself up over it. It was worth it then, twenty-five years ago, and it was worth it yesterday."

Sean had his head down, frowning, but after a few moments, he looked up at Jack and a faint smile came across his face. "Well, that's nice of you to say, Jack. Yes, I suppose you're right, yes indeed, I believe you're right."

Chapter 13

D espite the drama on the train, Helen and Jack had a wonderful trip together, so Jack was sad to see Helen board the plane back to Anchorage the evening before the trade show. Jack had things to do to prepare for the show that evening, so he kept himself busy, but the next day he checked in with Robert Weldon. They agreed to meet at the university hospital in Bozeman the day after the show ended. Dr. Weldon had reserved some time after normal operating hours at the hospital were over, at 5:00 p.m.

Jack kept busy over the next few days meeting and connecting with a wide variety of people at the trade show. On Tuesday evening, it was with some anxiety that Jack made his way over to the university. He didn't know what to expect, having never met Dr. Weldon, and he was afraid the doctor might tell him something he didn't want to hear. He had heard of stories, maybe old wives' tales, but stories nonetheless of people who acquired some type of magical power only to lose it after some time or become stricken by it eventually. These powers altered the person's mind, enhancing its ability, but that same alteration would be too much for the mind and body to handle, leading to a turn of events Jack disliked contemplating. Jack didn't particularly like the idea of having tests performed on him either, but he knew Dr. Weldon needed those tests to determine how his mind and body had been altered. Dr. Weldon agreed that there would be no assistants during the tests; he would be the only one meeting with Jack that evening.

Jack walked up to the third floor of the hospital to the central brain and nervous system department. Dr. Weldon was sitting in the reception area of the office reading a medical journal when Jack arrived. He was wearing a white doctor's coat with blue jeans. He was quite old—Jack put him in his late seventies or early eighties. His hair was white, and he wore big, round glasses; in fact, the image of an old country doctor seemed to fit him quite well.

"Jack, it's a pleasure to finally meet you," he said as he stood and shook Jack's hand.

"It's a pleasure to meet you as well, Robert."

Dr. Weldon's demeanor put Jack at ease. He seemed friendly and quite personable. His voice was soft and low, and he smiled easily when they met.

"Well, Jack, why don't we sit down in my office; let's get caught up on things."

"Sure thing, Robert."

His office was a small room, but was overfilled with medical textbooks, journals, and notebooks.

"Well, Jack, how was your trip down? You told me you were taking the train, isn't that right?"

"Very nice. We actually took a cruise ship from Anchorage to Vancouver, but the weather was overcast most of the way. The train from Vancouver was quite fun. It was an historic train run by an old Scotsman and his young apprentice. The weather was perfect, and the landscape was spectacular."

"Yes, that's a beautiful area, especially from Jasper to Banff. It's such a beautiful stretch of glaciers, lakes, and mountain peaks. My wife loved that area; we'd vacation there almost every year."

"Yes, I never realized how beautiful the Canadian Rockies are. We had quite a scare on the train just outside of Jasper, but luckily everything turned out okay."

"Is that right? What happened?"

Jack went on to tell Dr. Weldon about what occurred on the train, how Sean had been knocked out as the train accelerated down the steep mountain track. Jason, his apprentice, had tried to get into the locked locomotive, but as time was running out, Jack made a desperate attempt to contact Sean to understand the situation at hand. Seeing that Sean was knocked out cold in the locomotive and with no time to learn how to operate a train, Jack had taken Sean's injuries onto himself, giving Sean the needed seconds to stop the train before it would have plummeted off the mountain track and down the mountainside below.

"Fascinating, Jack, absolutely fascinating," Dr. Weldon said inquisitively as he raised his eyebrows and wrinkled his forehead in thought. "And this injury, this deep cut to his head, can you describe what happened exactly and how long it was transferred to you? Seconds, minutes, hours?"

"Well, the gash was transferred to me almost immediately, as if, in fact, I had been hit in the head the same way Sean was hit when he fell. When I saw the image of Sean on the floor and realized there was no time to spare, I closed my eyes and concentrated, and then the next thing I know, I'm on the floor and out cold. It was quite painful, and I was told I was bleeding quite badly. After Sean stopped the train, he made his way into the front boxcar and collapsed, and over the next few minutes, I slowly regained consciousness. The gash to my head began to dissipate, but it wasn't immediate; it took several hours to disappear, and during this time, I had a splitting headache, but by the next day, it was completely gone, as was my headache."

"And what about Sean—did he remember all this?"

"I saw him in the hospital the next day, and he remembered waking up and stopping the train, but as far as I could tell, he wasn't aware of the entanglement between him and me. Parts of his memory did stay with me, though. I recalled a boxing match he had twenty-five years prior, and in the hospital we talked about it. It was something he was mulling over in his mind when he collapsed, and those thoughts stayed with me."

Robert Weldon sat still, trying to make sense of Jack's story. After a few moments, he said, "All right, Jack, well, thanks for sharing that with me. Why don't we get started? I have the machines set up to run various tests in the laboratory."

They walked into the medical laboratory. In the room sat a large rectangular machine, with a circular hole at one end with a table attached. On top of the table was a sliding pallet that allowed the subject to be moved partially into the rectangular machine. At the front of the pallet, there was a location to position the subject's head for the purpose of scanning the brain.

"This is called a functional magnetic resonance imaging machine, or fMRI for short," Dr. Weldon said. "It works like any other MRI, using a magnetic field to first align and then alter the alignment of hydrogen atoms in the water of your body. This change in alignment creates a faint rotating magnetic field detectable by the scanner. The fMRI is tuned to monitor blood flow to different parts of the brain, and therefore tells us which areas of the brain are active during a certain thought, action, or experience."

"Okay," Jack replied.

"Don't worry, Jack, it is noninvasive and harmless. I've probably told you more than you wanted to know, but it's great technology. This technology has only been available in the last twenty years. Before that, we needed to inject a chemical into the subject's bloodstream and then monitor the chemical, but with the fMRI, this is no longer needed. All you need to do is lie on the table, and we can get started. It does use magnetic fields, so you'll need to remove any ferromagnetic objects such as your watch. You haven't had surgeries where they inserted permanent bone plates or screws, have you?"

"No, luckily not," Jack replied. "I broke my arm once when I was learning to hang glide, but that was quite a few years ago and nothing like that was needed."

"Good, Jack. Why don't you lie on the table, and I'll move you into the scanner. I'll first ask you several questions, and we'll see how that goes. Try to remain as still as possible; we'll get better results that way."

Jack lay down on the table, and then Dr. Weldon moved to the operating console located several feet from the machine and turned a knob. The sliding pallet moved until the upper half of Jack's body was in the scanner.

"Can you hear me all right, Jack?"

"Sure, no problem, Robert," Jack replied.

Dr. Weldon proceeded to ask Jack a series of questions regarding basic math and reading skills. He was asked to solve various addition, subtraction, multiplication, and division problems. Then Dr. Weldon asked him to spell various words, and then performed a reading comprehension test on Jack by reading several passages from a book and asking Jack to answer questions on the passages that were read.

"I feel like I'm back in high school, taking an SAT test," Jack said after a while.

"Yes, it's very similar to that, isn't it? I'm trying to establish a baseline for your brain patterns, and to see if I detect anything out of the ordinary. At this point, everything looks normal, which is good. Okay, now let's try something new. Go ahead and describe some of the events and memories you encountered during these entanglements. Let's just start with one for now. Try to pick an especially vivid one, one of the more extreme events you've encountered."

"Well, okay, let's see," Jack replied.

Jack went on to tell the doctor about his encounter with young Josh, how he had been trying to make a connection with him over several days, and how he was finally able to break through. He recounted how Josh's crippling fear and dread of dying flooded Jack's brain and body when they finally made a connection, and how he was immobilized momentarily when he experienced Josh's shivering body and frenzied emotional state. He then described how he was able to get control of the situation and direct Josh to stand up and pan the landscape so that Jack could locate his whereabouts.

"Okay, Jack," Dr. Weldon said patiently and calmly as he quickly scanned the images from Jack's brain. "Try another one, say in a situation where you were making face-to-face contact at the time."

Jack described his very first encounter, several evenings after he had flown through the aurora borealis, when he was at a bar with his gregarious friend George. He recounted how he had joked with George about being him, and then suddenly he had experienced a shooting pain through his leg, feeling the pain of George's broken leg, and he told how George's recent memories had stayed with him.

After this, Dr. Weldon spent a few minutes examining the brain scans in more detail, seeing if he could detect the patterns in Jack's brain that gave him his ability.

"Jack, I appreciate you recalling these events to me, but it appears these thoughts and feelings are now just a part of your normal memory, as if you had experienced them yourself. There's nothing particularly unusual there—they're just a part of your own memories now."

Dr. Weldon turned a knob, the pallet Jack was lying on moved out from the machine, and he told Jack he could sit up.

"Listen, Jack, can we try something else? Can we try to exercise your ability now? As I did when I was performing tests on my own drug years ago, we can run some tests to see if you can pick up my thought patterns. Would you be okay with that? If everything goes well, we can try the same thing with you in the fMRI."

"Well, I suppose so. I don't see why not; let's give it a shot," Jack replied.

First Dr. Weldon got out a deck of cards, pulled a card from the deck and looked at it, and then asked Jack to tell him the card he had in his hand. Jack closed his eyes and concentrated as Dr. Weldon performed the test, but after Jack rattled off the correct card thirty times in a row, Dr. Weldon stopped.

"Quite amazing, Jack, that's quite good. Let's try something else."

They sat next to each other, and Dr. Weldon told him he would think of something and ask Jack to tell him what he was thinking about.

"So what am I thinking about now, Jack?"

"You're thinking about your garden, how you planted the tulips and roses together this year and how their contrast was quite beautiful."

"And now?"

"You're thinking about your son, Ted. How you're looking forward to seeing him and his family in a few weeks, and how you adore your grandchildren."

"And his children's names and ages?"

"Stacy, age six, Phillip, age eight, and little Samantha, age three."

"Well, you're spot-on, Jack. Let's try it with you in the machine and see if we can determine what's going on. I don't think the machine will have any effect on your ability, but if something unusual happens, we'll stop."

Jack lay back down on the pallet, and Dr. Weldon moved him back into position inside the fMRI scanner.

"All right, Jack, let's start with the card recognition again. Let's do it slowly so I can watch the images in your brain as you call out the cards."

Dr. Weldon shuffled the deck and then pulled out the first card and looked at it.

"What do I have, Jack?"

"Ten of clubs," Jack replied.

"Wow!" Dr. Weldon exclaimed as he moved his head closer to the image, studying it in detail. "The center of your brain lit up like a candle in an area toward the backside of the corpus callosum. Quite amazing. Let's try again."

Dr. Weldon proceeded with the experiment, and Jack named the next twenty cards spot-on.

"What I'm seeing, Jack, is first the area in the backside of the corpus callosum is being exercised, and then it appears that image is sent to the area of the brain normally responsible for interpretation of visual images, in the backside of your cortex, called the occipital lobe. How do you feel, Jack—is everything all right?"

"I feel fine, Robert, let's keep going."

"Okay, let's try the thought recognition exercise again. I'll put a thought in my mind, and you tell me what I am thinking. And now?"

"You're thinking about your last patient, the one with Alzheimer's. You're glad that the drug you prescribed slowed the advancement of the disease in her brain in the last few months."

"What about now?"

"You're thinking about what you had for breakfast. Three scrambled eggs with ham, along with toast and butter and your favorite homemade rhubarb jam."

"Excellent, Jack."

"What are you seeing from the scanner now?" Jack asked.

"Well, as before, the area in the backside of your corpus callosum is being exercised, but now that information is being sent to the temporal lobes of your brain where memories are stored. From there, the memories are simply accessed and recounted by you in the same way all our memories are recalled. In other words, Jack, it appears you are accessing my memories and storing them in your brain as your own."

"Have you seen anything alarming, Robert, anything I should be concerned about?"

"Not really, but I'd like to have the fMRI do a complete scan of your brain to give a better and more educated answer to that question. I'll need some time to look at and evaluate the images. If it's okay with you, I'd like to perform those more detailed scans in a little while."

"I think that would be fine, Robert. I very much appreciate you performing these tests on me."

"The pleasure is mine, Jack. I'd like to continue with our experiments for now."

"Sure thing. What would you like to do next?"

"I know you've had experiences where you have sensed and shared pain from another person, and in fact, it appears that during those times, you have the ability to take that pain temporarily and keep it within your own body, as was the case with the train conductor, Sean. I'd like to try a test relating to that ability. Let's try something simple. I'm going to pinch myself to the point where it hurts a bit, and then I'll ask you to tell me what I'm doing exactly and see if you can experience the pain yourself. What do you think, Jack, do you want to give it a shot?"

"Yes, let's give it a try. Okay, Robert, go ahead."

The doctor put his right thumb and index finger around a piece of loose skin on his left arm just below his elbow and squeezed hard.

"Okay, Jack, can you sense it?"

"Yes, you're pinching your skin below your left elbow ... ah yes, I can feel the pain now. Don't pinch too hard, Robert, I might start bleeding."

"Amazing, Jack. It's as if I've gone numb suddenly. I don't feel a thing, but I'm pinching hard so I know it must sting. I'll keep a constant pressure on my skin, but let me know if it hurts too much."

Jack lay still, feeling the sting in his arm, waiting for further instructions from the doctor.

After a minute, Robert said, "Can you take control of my arm, Jack? Do you have the ability to control my motor skills?"

The doctor was quite surprised when he saw his arms being lifted above his head, even though he still had the ability to pinch his skin.

"Is that easy for you to do, Jack, or did that take a lot of effort?"

"It's quite easy, maybe just a little more effort than commanding my own body," Jack replied. "Do you want me to try something else?"

"Yes, go ahead."

Jack had the doctor stand up, make a full rotation of his body, and then sat the doctor back in his chair.

"Fabulous, Jack. All right, let's see how long you can hold the pain and control it within you."

They both sat still, Jack feeling the sharp, pinching pain in his arm; but after a few minutes, the pain subsided.

"Ah yes, I feel the pain returning now," Robert said. "It came back slowly at first, but it's all there now. Did you do that purposefully, Jack, or did it just happen?"

"I was trying to hold it, Robert, but then it just dissipated. It wasn't a conscious decision; it just left me."

"Okay, well, let me review the fMRI images, see if I can determine what's going on. This will take a few minutes. Do you want to get out of the machine, Jack?"

"Sure. I'd like to see what those scans look like as well."

The doctor moved the pallet out from the machine, and as Jack got up, Robert accessed the scanning data and began examining the images.

"There, Jack, do you see it?" the doctor said after several minutes of running the brain scans back and forth on the computer screen. "You can see how the image lights up brightly toward the back of your brain, in the area of the corpus callosum, when you first told me where I was pinching myself. After this, though, the image changes. Actually I don't think I've ever seen anything quite like this. There's an area of the brain called the anterior cingulate gyrus that appears to, well, what would the word for it be? It's almost as if it's glowing, or stimulated, as you experienced the pain from me pinching my arm. The anterior cingulate gyrus is a collar-shaped brain tissue that is wrapped around the base of the corpus callosum, where the spinal cord attaches to the base of the brain, and in fact, pain is registered there."

"I see," Jack replied. "It's as if my brain is registering the pain and is somehow taking it away from the other person."

"Yes," the doctor replied, "you can see the images; the gyrus is dancing with activity during those minutes that you took and felt the pain in my arm. Let's take a closer look, see what is happening when you directed my body to move."

The doctor rewound the images and then played them back slowly, trying to find the period of time when Jack raised the doctor's arm and had him stand.

"Yes, there's the activity—the gyrus maintains its glow, but then I see as well activity in the parietal lobe of your brain. The parietal lobe is associated with movement, orientation, recognition, and perception of stimuli. It plays an important role in integrating sensory information from various parts of the body, as well as commanding movement."

Something caught the doctor's eye, and he rewound the images again, playing them back even more slowly.

"Look at that. Do you see it, Jack, the activity in the corpus callosum? First there's the activity in the parietal lobe formulating the movement and then almost instantaneously, the back of the corpus callosum lights up. Your corpus callosum, it appears, is acting as a pathway, connecting our minds and bodies together, sending the neural command signals from your parietal lobe across the room and into my mind, which then performs the motion you commanded."

Jack sat still, fascinated but also a bit frightened about the doctor's prognosis of his mind's ability.

The doctor continued. "At the end, when the pain returned to me, the gyrus slowly dissipates its activity, like a dying ember of light. Quite fascinating, and I suppose it does make sense, though I've never seen this level of ability before, nothing even close. My experiments from years ago,

I was able to boost the functioning of the corpus callosum in a handful of people, those who were most receptive to my medication, but their ability was nothing compared to yours, Jack. They could pick up brain signals from someone else on occasion, but it was spotty and unreliable, and I did not pursue developing the drug further. I've never seen anything close to this level. You've been given a great gift, Jack, a great gift."

Jack didn't say anything for some time as he gathered his thoughts, but then he asked the doctor, "Do you want to perform some further experiments, Robert?"

"No, I don't think any more are necessary, we can stop here. I do want to answer your previous question and see if there is anything you should be alarmed about. To answer that, I'll need to perform a detailed brain scan with the fMRI, as I mentioned before. It's painless and noninvasive, but you'll have to be under the machine for a good half hour. How does that sound?"

"It sounds like a wise thing to do," Jack replied.

"All right, let's take a break for a little while. I brew a great cup of coffee, Jack. We can sit in the break room and relax for a bit. What do you say?"

"Sure thing, Robert; coffee sounds good."

★★★★★

After a relaxing conversation over coffee, the two headed back to the lab, and Jack lay back down inside the fMRI machine.

"All right, Jack, just remain still as I take the scans. I'll be taking scans from the front at first, then will move to the right and left sides of your head, and then for the last set of scans, I'll have you lie facedown in the scanner to get a good picture of the back side of your brain and upper spinal cord. You'll hear a small motor running as I take the scans, and you'll see a purple colored light as the scanner makes its way across your face. It's not too bright but is noticeable."

"Okay, Robert, ready when you are," Jack replied.

The doctor proceeded to take the scans, and Jack lay still, only moving when Robert told him to do so. Thirty minutes later, Robert told Jack they were done and moved the pallet back so Jack could get out from the machine.

"Well, that wasn't too bad," Jack said. "What's next, Robert?"

"We're done for the day, Jack. I'll need some time to look at the scans, which I will do tomorrow morning. What I'd like to do is meet again tomorrow afternoon, say, after lunch. We can go over the scans together and see what else we need to do, if anything. Do you have a place to stay for the night, Jack?"

"Yes, I have a hotel room in the same hotel where we had our conference. My flight back to Anchorage is in the morning the day after tomorrow. Tomorrow sounds good. I can come by, say, at one o'clock?"

"Perfect, Jack," Dr. Weldon replied as he looked at his watch. "Look at that—it's already nine o'clock. Time flies when you're having fun, as the saying goes. I'll lock up and then we can walk out together."

"It was fun," Jack replied, "and I do very much appreciate it, Robert."

"The pleasure is mine, Jack. It's not like I get to study a subject like you every day. Just give me a minute, and then we can head out."

★★★★★

That night as Jack lay in his bed trying to get to sleep, a series of images unfolded in his brain. He saw why Robert Weldon had stopped his extrasensory perception experiments thirty years earlier. It wasn't that he lacked the curiosity or technical ability to continue; in fact, his mind had been full of ideas to make his stimulant more effective. It was something else, something the doctor had no control over.

They had come into his office early one morning unannounced, telling him his work was too valuable to be shared with his colleagues and the general public and that he would no longer be allowed to publish articles on his findings. The three military officials standing in his office that day were polite but uncompromising, telling him his work was important, in fact, crucial to national security. His work would be well funded, they assured him, but it would now be under the control of the military, and all tests and future developments would be held under the cloak of secrecy. He would not be allowed to share his results with anyone, and all his work would be closely scrutinized by military personnel, who would work closely with him on all further development. Robert Weldon had protested, saying he wanted to understand what this was all about, and the top marine in his office that day had simply said he was a valuable scientist who would now be helping to modernize national security.

After further assurances and with the promise that his research would be funded for years to come, the doctor had reluctantly agreed. He had been working on his studies off and on when time permitted, but they told him he would now be working on them full-time. He was given a large budget, in excess of fifty million dollars per year, funded by military research and development dollars. The assistants assigned to him would be required to track the funding closely, but he was given freedom as to what tests he wanted to perform and what changes to his stimulant would be made, as long as his research was directed to further enhance ESP abilities in his subjects.

The first thing that happened was all his research was moved off campus into a military facility near the university. He was no longer allowed to do any work at his office at the university, but he was allowed to keep his office there. He was given a security badge to access the facility and was required to go through a background check. He could no longer pick his subjects at random either; the military now picked who he would administer his stimulant to.

He never liked the setup; he felt stifled and anxious, not knowing what his research would be used for. He had to sign a series of documents stating that he gave full use of his research to the military and that he was not allowed to share the information with anyone else. Anything he wrote down or developed had to be reviewed by the top assistant, and then appropriate markings were put on all documents, making it clear those documents were explicitly for military personnel, on a need-to-know basis only.

He grudgingly continued his studies, but over the next several months, he proceeded cautiously, making enough changes to his stimulant and experiments so that his assistants wouldn't become suspicious, but not proceeding with the more ambitious ideas that could potentially make his drug more reliable and powerful. He wanted to feel his way around and try to get a handle on what the military had in mind before he really strove for any major breakthroughs.

As the weeks and months went by, it became quite apparent what their plan was. His drug would be used to develop an army of mind-reading soldiers. All his subjects were young, well-trained military officers, and whenever he asked them what they did in the service, each would dodge the question. Their hesitation and secrecy bothered the doctor, so one day, he broke into one of his young assistant's files, trying to learn more about his research grant. His research was code-named operation Mind Manipulation Matters, or MMM for short. Although not clearly stated, it was quite obvious the soldiers would be trained as mind readers and would be planted throughout the world as the military saw fit. The doctor suspected they would be stationed in foreign embassies and military facilities, but the paperwork hinted at something more—there would be plainclothes civilians as well, planted on US and foreign soil to monitor anyone the military considered suspicious. If successful, there were plans to train law enforcement in the same techniques, using the doctor's drug as a surveillance tool to sidestep the cumbersome laws that protected citizens from government scrutiny.

Dr. Weldon's research was in its infancy—they realized that—but if his experiments proved successful, there were explicit plans to move the entire operation to a military base in Nevada. Weldon's eyes opened wide as he read that plans were already afoot to center the studies at the facility called Area 51 at Groom Lake, a secret military facility ninety miles north of Las Vegas that the military denied even existed.

Dr. Weldon had heard about Area 51 through several of his colleagues. Though never confirmed, it was common knowledge in the medical community that mind and telepathy experiments had been going on there for years. *A better description was mind control experiments,* Weldon thought to himself. He had heard several stories of captured foreign military personnel who had been planted with monitoring devices in their brains to extract technical and scientific data. Weldon remembered one of his colleagues describing how scientists there had modified the DNA of a rat so that a single wing, similar to a bat's wing, had grown up out of the rat's spine. Brainwashing, psychological torture, genetic engineering experiments, and the development of secret weapons were par for the course at the facility.

★★★★★

A few weeks later, when the doctor didn't show up one morning at his makeshift office in the military compound, his assistants informed their superiors, and a search party was formed to find the doctor's whereabouts. They found him a few hours later in the school library, reading up on some of the most recent developments in the treatment of schizophrenia.

When they demanded he return to his military office, he quietly refused, saying he had decided to stop development of his ESP drugs. The lead assistant was furious and stormed off to notify his superiors, leaving the other officers to watch over the doctor. That evening, he was put under lock and key at the military compound until the head of the MMM project could be notified and brought into town.

"So you've decided to stop development of your drug, have you?" the tall, brawny man dressed in civilian clothes asked that next morning.

"Yes," the doctor replied, "I will not pursue any further development."

"And what brought this about, Doctor? You know your research is very valuable."

"It's just not what I want to do. It's not the direction I want to take with my work. I am quitting, as they say."

"You know others will eventually develop this drug fully, Doctor. They will get great praise for their accomplishments and will have research funds available to them whenever they want them. You're missing out on a tremendous opportunity to further yourself and your research, Doctor."

"Perhaps," the doctor replied. "I understand the ramifications."

"You know you will never receive one dollar of government funding from this day forward, do you understand that, Doctor?"

Robert Weldon had simply looked away, staring out the window, wondering when he could leave the facility.

"Are you sure you want to do this, Doctor?" the man said loudly.

Weldon simply nodded his head, staring down at his hands, wanting the meeting to be over.

"You understand, as well, that if we ever find you developing your drug in the future, we'll have you arrested in direct violation of US law and military protocol. We'll put you in jail for years to come. Do you understand that, Doctor?"

"Yes, I understand."

"Is that it, Doctor? Is that all you have to say? I expected more from someone like you."

"That's all I have. I would like to leave the facility now."

They had let Dr. Weldon leave the facility that morning, and he returned to his teachings and research at the university, keeping his promise to them and to himself to never study or develop his ESP mind stimulants again.

★★★★★

When Jack arrived at Dr. Weldon's office the next day, the doctor was quite upbeat.

"Jack, good to see you again. Did you have a good evening last night, well, what was left of it?"

"It was okay, Robert. I had a hard time getting to sleep last night, had a few things on my mind, but I slept in so I feel quite fresh today. And yourself?"

"Fine, Jack, fine. I was up early this morning trying to get through all the data we took last night, and I think you'll find it quite fascinating. Did you get a chance to eat yet, Jack?"

"Yes, I had a late breakfast at the university café—a nice place. The omelet there was excellent."

"Yes, the café, I used to go there every so often when my wife didn't get a chance to fix my lunch in the morning. Yes, a very nice place."

Jack paused. "So what did you find out, Robert? How are things looking?"

"Sit down, Jack. Why don't you scoot your chair around next to me. We can go over the images together."

Jack scooted his chair around and then looked at the images. They were colored, but looked like normal X-ray scans he had seen before, when he had broken his arm years earlier.

"I started to look at these closely, Jack, and everything appeared relatively normal until I got to the backside of your brain. You can see it most clearly with the images we took of the side of your brain and of the backside of your head when you were lying facedown on the table. As expected, your corpus callosum is larger than in most humans, but that's not what surprised me. You can see it clearly in this image. At the backside of your oversized corpus callosum, there are two growths, almost tentacle-like fibers, that are integral to the backside of the callosum but extend backward to the backside of your lower skull. You see, the corpus callosum ends about two-thirds of the way toward the backside of your skull, but in your brain, I see these two tentacle-looking fiber bundles extending backward to the rear of your brain."

The doctor looked at Jack, and he could see that Jack didn't understand his description clearly. Robert pulled a textbook down off a shelf and opened it, showing a sideways cross section of the brain.

"Behind the callosum lays the cerebellum just below and aft of where the callosum ends, and above and aft is the cuneus. These tentacle-like fibrous growths from the backside of your callosum have worked their way between these two segments of the brain to the back of your skull."

"How large are they?" Jack asked.

"Well, at the beginning, where they extend from the callosum, I would say each is about three quarters of an inch in diameter, but they taper down to about an eighth of an inch at the back of your brain. They are approximately four inches in length."

"So something really has happened to me, I mean, physically. What do you think they are made of?"

"Well, it appears they are nerve fibers like the rest of your callosum; it looks like they are just extensions to the existing fibers." Dr. Weldon paused and then said reflectively, "You know, it's interesting, I've seen these fibrous strands before—oh, nothing as well developed as yours, but I've seen small, pin-sized wound nerve fibers extending to the back of the skull in the brains of patients we've diagnosed as schizophrenics. This morning I looked through some of my patients' files and found a few cases where I've seen this."

"Are you saying I'm suffering from some form of schizophrenia, Doctor?"

Robert Weldon smiled. "No, Jack, what I'm saying is these patients we diagnosed as schizophrenics may not have been schizophrenics at all. You see, common symptoms of schizophrenia are the hearing of voices that others don't hear, or tastes, or images, and in some extreme cases, unexplained pain. In these rare cases, some of my patients or my colleagues' patients have been, in fact, diagnosed with schizophrenia, but they did not exhibit some of the other common symptoms associated with the disease."

"Such as what, Doctor?" Jack asked.

"Most schizophrenics lack the ability to live normal lives. They have trouble concentrating and cannot put information together into coherent thought. You see, schizophrenia is a disease associated with the synapses in your brain. You receive information through your senses, and then this information travels through your brain and your nervous system to the appropriate area for interpretation. Brain waves can be thought of as electrical signals, and these electrical signals travel through the brain by jumping minute gaps in your nerve fibers called synapses. In the mind of a schizophrenic, these synapses do not operate properly, and these electrical signals get rerouted, or you could say, they take detours. Instead of a nice, orderly pattern, thought patterns become disorganized and jumbled because the electrical signals are getting rerouted into areas of the brain not typically associated with that pattern of thought. These jumbled brain patterns result in the symptoms typical of a schizophrenic, as I have described.

"In the rare instances I encountered, however, the patients appear to be quite normal, except for these errant thoughts that appear in their mind on occasion. They have described instances where they hear voices or see images and they can't explain their origin, but despite this, they seem to lead healthy and happy lives, unburdened by the other, more debilitating symptoms of schizophrenia."

"So you suspect these thoughts are being transmitted in their mind through these nerve fibers in the back of their brains?" Jack asked.

"Yes, that's what I'm speculating. It's possible they are picking up signals outside of their body from other humans, but unlike yours, their ability is sporadic and unreliable, so we as doctors interpret these events as symptoms of schizophrenia."

"That's fascinating, Robert, but it seems to be such a drastic deviation from what we consider to be normal. I just have a hard time comprehending that these bundles of nerve fibers could be so powerful, so mind altering. That these fibers could give me the ability that I've developed, and these other people the ability to pick up others' thoughts."

"It's really not that unusual; it's just something that we're not used to. Take, for example, our ability to see, which we all take for granted, and then explain that ability to someone who is blind. The blind man can barely begin to comprehend what eyesight enables us to do and experience."

From Jack's expression, Robert could see that he wasn't convinced.

"Look at it a different way, Jack. We perceive the world through the five senses we have, and this is how we interact with the world and the people around us. Take, for example, therapy, or more generally support groups, whether it is a psychiatrist or a group of friends you know well. If someone is having a hard time, is upset about something that has happened in their life, often they'll share their feelings with a close friend. They'll share their experience, their sadness, their pain. The friend who receives this information hears their voice, sees their demeanor; they might take their hand and feel the coldness of their touch. Through this process, the feelings that the person is experiencing are passed to the other. The other person's shoulders shrug, they visualize the experiences in their own mind, and they take on the sadness the other is feeling. The sadness is shared, and this sharing relieves the pain that the person suffering is experiencing. This relief may be temporary, but for that period of time, it helps the individual get through a difficult situation. We typically call this interaction 'empathy.'

"The ability you've developed is an extension of the ability we all have as humans or creatures in general—just more developed, more focused, more powerful. I recall that you told me the black eagle you had interacted with was able to locate your home in Fairbanks even though he had never been there before. As you share another's thoughts and take temporary control of their body, your minds share information, and this is how I suspect the bird could locate your whereabouts months later. It's a two-way street: you see their thoughts, experience their pain, help them in a difficult situation, but the remnants of your own thoughts remain with them.

"In the case of Dr. Samualson, alone on her deathbed, her emotions were so strong, so intense, that she was able to tap into your mind, utilizing your incredible telepathic ability to help her see her daughters one last time before she died. I suspect your immense telepathic brain somehow stimulates another's mind to the point where a pathway can be opened even if that pathway is not initiated by you."

Jack sat still listening to the doctor, trying to comprehend what he was saying, but after a few minutes he said, "What do I do now, Robert? What should I do from here?"

"Let me ask you, Jack," Robert replied, "have you been having any worrisome symptoms since your developed this ability—headaches, thoughts you can't control, any inability to behave appropriately in situations you find yourself in, for example, flying your charter service or with a loved one?"

"Sometimes I see things, Robert, events come into my mind. I can't control when they appear; they just appear."

"Like what, Jack? Give me an example."

"Last night as I tried to get to sleep, I saw why you stopped your experiments years ago. I had read your journals, and I could never understand why you had stopped your research—the work looked so promising— but last night, the whole story unfolded in my mind."

Dr. Weldon looked down, a thoughtful look on his face. "I thought I had buried those memories long ago, but I suppose these tests and the discussions we've had have rekindled the memories of those events."

Robert paused, searching for something more to say. "That was a very difficult time for me, Jack. I wanted to continue my work, but I always suspected it might end up down the path the military forced me to take. I just didn't want my work to be devoted to that; I didn't want to go down that route, you know. I wanted to be a doctor, someone devoted to curing disease, not a military scientist."

"I understand, Robert, you don't have to explain yourself to me. We all have to make choices in our lives. You made the right decision in your own mind—that's the most important thing."

"I appreciate that, Jack," Weldon replied as he smiled slightly and nodded his head up and down slowly. Then he said, "Let me ask you, when these images come into your mind, can you control them? I mean, can you function normally, or do they overwhelm you to the point that you have to stop doing whatever you were doing before they appeared?"

"It's almost like they are my own memories, like I'm recounting something that actually happened to me. Like my own thoughts or memories, I can stop thinking about them, shut them off as I need. Last night I had nothing to do and I wanted to see the story, so I lay in bed, seeing the story unfold."

"That's encouraging, Jack. So would you say you've had any symptoms that you find alarming, that concern you then?"

"Not really. It's been quite an experience, as you can imagine, but I haven't had anything that I have found to be particularly alarming or disturbing. In fact, it's been quite a colorful and enlightening set of experiences in many ways."

"I can imagine it has been. Do you have any questions for me, Jack, that I might be able to help you with?"

"Well, Robert, I guess I'd like to get your thoughts on how this whole thing started—I mean the experience of flying through that low-hanging aurora borealis, and how I've developed this ability since then. What happened up there? How could flying through an aurora borealis have sparked this growth that you've detected in my brain and that's given me this ability?"

"Well, it's hard to say, Jack, and I can only speculate, but it's very possible you had some tendency there before the event happened. Possibly in your brain you had these small strands of nerve fibers I described earlier, which I've discovered in some of my patients, and somehow that event of flying through the aurora borealis sparked their growth. It's like a seed: the potential is there, but it needs water and nourishment to grow. Another example is disease. Many diseases can sit dormant in a host's body for years, and then a set of chemical reactions initiated by some set of random events allows the disease to grow and develop in the host's body.

"I'd like to think of your ability more as a seed that's sprouted than a disease that's developed, but you get the picture—the process is similar. The brain and central nervous system are driven and operate through electrical impulses, so the nourishment that allowed those strands to grow could have come from the electrical currents contained in that low-hanging aurora borealis. Quite possibly that ion funnel started a chemical reaction in your brain that allowed those strands to mature into what we see now."

"You know, Robert, that's interesting you say that. For quite a few years now, long before the flight through the aurora, sometimes I'd pick up tastes in my mouth, though I never put much thought into what was happening. At first I speculated I had an oversensitive nose and the smell of food seemed like a taste, but the tastes were so strong I had a hard time believing it was all from my nose. It was especially strong if I was sitting in a restaurant—these flavors would just appear on my tongue, like I was tasting someone else's food. So I wasn't imagining it; it must have been real."

Dr. Weldon chuckled, "That's funny, Jack, tasting someone else's food. My, the things we run into. Sounds or visions are more common; it's quite rare where you hear a story like that, where someone tastes another person's food. Though if you, in fact, did have these small strands of nerve fibers extending from your corpus callosum, it would seem to make sense, wouldn't it?"

Robert Weldon paused.

"Look, Jack, I'm glad we've had the opportunity to meet, and I'm happy that we were able to run these tests to see what has happened to you. Being a research doctor of sorts, I of course would love to study this more, but speaking as your physician, I think we can stop for now. From everything I've seen and heard, you appear to be quite healthy and well adjusted to your newfound ability. Do you have any other questions, Jack? I'll do my best to give you an educated answer."

"Oh gosh, I can't think of any right now, Robert. I guess the only thing is, do you have any advice for me? I mean, do you think I need to be doing anything special? Should I be taking some form of medication, or do I need to change my lifestyle in some way? Maybe change my eating habits or stay away from certain activities?"

"Well, Jack, I don't see any need to. I haven't seen anything that indicates medication is needed, and as long as you are able to maintain your normal routine, live a pretty normal life, I wouldn't worry about it too much. Just go about your life as usual. Of course, if something happens that worries you comes up, don't hesitate to call me, but right now, just be yourself. You've been given a very unique, wonderful gift—just enjoy it. I suppose my only advice would be to put it to good use. Do something worthwhile with your newfound ability, something that helps others, makes the world a little better place to live. From the stories you've told me, it appears you already have, but continue on. That's really the only advice I have for you, Jack."

"That's good advice, Robert, I appreciate it," Jack replied. "Well, I guess we're done for now. I can't thank you enough. If you do ever consider making it back to Alaska, I can be your tour guide. I know of some great places to visit—some of those remote places you wouldn't know about unless you've been piloting around there for years."

"I might just take you up on that, Jack, thanks. Listen, the only other thing, let's just keep this to ourselves, our encounter and the tests we've done—I think that might be best."

"I understand, Robert. Yes, I agree, this is just between you and me."

"All right then, let's keep in touch," Robert replied. "It's been a pleasure."

Robert extended his hand and they shook.

"The pleasure is mine," Jack replied.

Chapter 14

When Jack got back to Alaska, he and Helen talked and decided to move in together. Jack moved out of his apartment in Anchorage and moved into Helen's beautiful, well-kept house built in the 1970s on the outskirts of town. Jack liked the surroundings much more than his cramped apartment, and it was nice being closer to Helen. They agreed that in the summer, they would spend more time together in Fairbanks as Jack put the final touches on his house there.

A few weeks later, as Jack was at the airfield preparing for a Saturday flight from Anchorage for a tour down to Kodiak Island, Helen called.

"Jack, he's back!" Helen exclaimed on the phone.

"Who's back? What are you talking about, Helen?" Jack replied.

"The bird, you know, that beautiful black eagle. He's found us again, Jack."

"Are you sure?" Jack replied. "Maybe the bird just looks like the one from Fairbanks."

"He's the one, Jack. I've never seen those distinctive red spots at the base of the tail except on this eagle, and I've been studying birds for years."

"Is that so?" Jack replied. "I guess he must like us, well, maybe he just likes your house."

"He's been in the backyard all morning. He got his tummy full from the feed I put out, but now he's just perched atop the feeder, just waiting there. He'll look around, then stare back at the house like he's looking for something or someone, and then he'll turn again and just sit there. I think he's waiting for you, Jack, do you think?" Helen asked lightly.

"Maybe so," Jack chuckled. "He's a persistent little creature, isn't he?"

*****

Jack didn't get home until after dark that evening, but the next morning, he and Helen were up early fixing coffee, trying to get an early start to their day off. Helen had an elevated porch attached to the second floor, giving them a nice view of her garden and the landscape behind it. They would sit on the porch, enjoy the view, sip coffee, and just relax.

As Jack and Helen stepped out on the porch, the eagle was sitting there perched atop the feeder waiting for them. When the eagle saw Jack, he let out a loud, deafening screech, then spread his large wings and lifted off, flying into the sky above the house. He circled the house several times, climbing higher and higher, and then dove straight down, pulling out of his dive just a few feet above the treetops, and flew right by the porch at eye level to Jack and Helen, rocking his wings as he flew by. He then climbed, flapping his wings vigorously to quickly gain altitude until he was several hundred feet above them. Then he dove, but this time he tucked his wings and barrel rolled as he descended; then he pulled out gracefully to fly by Jack and Helen again.

"Look at that, isn't that spectacular? I think he likes you, Jack. It's almost as if he's trying to get you to play with him," Helen said.

Helen took her eyes off the eagle and looked over at Jack. His coffee was sitting on the table next to him, his arms were by his sides, his eyes were closed, and he had a smile on his face.

"Jack? Isn't that so neat? Jack, are you there? Do you hear me?"

Jack didn't hear Helen; he was too busy enjoying his time again with the eagle.

*****

Over the next several months, the eagle was a frequent visitor to Helen's home. For a while, he was showing up every day; then he would be gone, and then he would show up again several weeks later. Helen enjoyed seeing the bird, and she could tell that the eagle and Jack had developed a special friendship, almost like a bond between two good friends.

Chapter 15

Later that year in the early summer, Jack took his hang glider out of storage and prepped it for his first flight that year. Spring was over, the weather was more predictable, the winds were calmer, and it made for some excellent hang-gliding conditions. Since he hadn't flown for five months, he planned to take the glider out to some small hills and practice to get back into the swing of things. It usually took three or four flights before his skills were back to a level where he felt comfortable handling the longer and more complex flights. He was going to meet Darrell, his longtime hang-gliding friend, in a grassy plateau not far from Birchwood airport north of Anchorage. They would then take Darrell's Jeep and drive up a country road that took them to the top of a hill that sat five hundred feet above the plateau. Since the elevation of the hill was relatively modest, it allowed them to make short but frequent flights in one day, which was a good way to get in takeoff and climbing practice. Each would land within walking distance of Jack's truck so they could parley their gliders back to the top of the hill as often as time permitted.

"Darrell, how's it going?" Jack said as he stepped out of his truck. Darrell was leaning against his Jeep, waiting for Jack in a large gravel pull-off area that sat beside the country road.

"Great, Jack, great. Let's get these birds up in the air and get some practice in. What do you say?"

"Let's do it," Jack replied.

After Jack loaded his hang glider atop Darrell's Jeep, they both got in and made their way to the top of the practice hill. The winds were a bit gusty that day, but the temperature was perfect; a few minutes into his first flight, Jack felt quite comfortable. Jack could see Darrell ahead of him catching a thermal, so he turned his glider in the same direction, hoping he could ascend as well. He caught the thermal, and it lifted the glider up quickly. He worked it for all its worth, weaving the glider back and forth slightly to find the greatest lift. The time he had spent with the eagle made him more relaxed and more in tune with his hang glider, and he was able to catch and pass Darrell a few minutes later.

"Come on, you old boy! What's holding you back?" Jack playfully yelled out as he passed Darrell.

"I'm just getting started," Darrell yelled back. "Have fun while it lasts, Jack. I'll be back by soon!"

They got in five flights that day, each lasting thirty to forty minutes. Jack felt particularly comfortable.

"Have you been practicing on me in the winter, Jack?" Darrell jokingly asked as they made their way back up the road leading to the practice hill one last time to get Darrell's Jeep. "You looked great up there today."

"Thanks, Darrell, just trying to keep up with you, buddy. Yeah, I felt good today. Everything seemed to just click. I can't wait until we go up again. What do you say, in a couple of weeks?"

"Sounds good to me. School will be out by then, and I'll have plenty of time. Let's plan on it."

★★★★★

That evening when Jack walked through the door into Helen's home, he noticed a framed poster on the wall. It showed a female rock climber hanging precariously off a rock ledge, with a steep backdrop behind her. She was hanging there with one hand, her feet dangling off the edge of the face, and her other hand was reaching up, trying to grab a small nub of rock above her head. At the bottom of the poster, in bold letters, it read, "When you think it's all over, reach for higher ground."

Oh god, make me gag, Jack thought to himself. *Neat picture, but I could do without the words. Is that supposed to inspire me? Give me a break.*

When Jack walked into the kitchen, Helen was doing the dishes.

"Hi, darling," Jack said as he kissed Helen on the cheek.

"Hi, Jack. Did you see it?"

"See what?"

"The framed poster in the hallway—isn't it neat? Ira, my second cousin, gave it to me this morning. She's an accomplished rock climber, you know. Isn't it inspiring?"

Oh god, if only she could read my mind, Jack thought to himself.

He frowned and hesitated for a moment, but luckily Helen was busily loading the dishwasher and didn't notice.

"Oh yeah, I saw it as I walked in. Wonderful, Helen, quite amazing. What a spectacular shot. Is that her in the photo?"

"Oh no, I don't think so. In any case, it still gets me going. I'm so glad you like it as well, Jack."

Chapter 16

Three weeks later, Jack met up with Darrell to go hang gliding again. It was a perfect day to hang glide. There was a slight breeze, with small clouds scattered in the sky, and the temperature was sixty-five degrees. They decided to head over to Angel's Peak, a good launching site forty miles northeast of Anchorage near the town of Palmer. The peak stood at 7200 feet and was surrounded by smaller mountains around it, but the terrain to the east was rolling hills and flatlands, with a beautiful rustic river situated in the valley between the mountains. On a good day, after a tricky launch off the small launch site, they could hug the mountains in the beginning of the flight and gain elevation by catching the updrafts coming up the side of the mountains adjacent to Angel's Peak. Once they gained sufficient altitude, they would then turn east and have a pleasant, relaxing flight over the rolling hills and river valley, taking their time to enjoy the scenery. Jack also planned to use this time to practice the more difficult maneuvers in the glider, such as steep turns, steep ascents and descents, and stalls. Mastering those maneuvers helped him hone his skills, especially when it came to finding and capitalizing on thermals. Of course, the added bonus was that it was fun as well.

Ten miles from the launch site, in a large plateau there was a common landing area that many of the glider pilots used, located just a few miles east of the town of Palmer. Because of its central location, with tall mountains surrounding it on both sides, pilots from different launch sites would gather there at the end of their flights. Next to the large, level, well-cut grassy field where people would land, there was an old abandoned airfield strip. In June and July during peak season, drivers would be stationed there to ferry people back to their cars, making the logistics of a long flight simpler. The chase drivers would park their cars along the abandoned runway with their coffee and breakfast and wait for the gliders to show up.

★★★★★

"What do you say, Jack, are you ready to glide?" Darrell asked at six that morning.

"Sure am, Darrell. I checked the forecast, and it looks like it's going to be a great day."

"Yes," Darrell replied, "light winds blowing east. If things go well, I'm going to head up the river valley along Highway 1 as far east as possible to where the river begins near Glennalien, then turn around and head back to Palmer."

"You're a master, Darrell. That's difficult terrain, especially if you try to fly back west to Palmer, so if you don't make it back, just give me a call. I'll work with one of the chasers, and we'll come and get you. I'm going to hug the mountains, then fly back and forth over Palmer—at least that's the plan."

Darrell chuckled. They would both try to lay out their flights in their heads, but once they were in the sky, things changed sometimes because of the weather, sometimes because the beauty and freedom of the flight made them forget their plans and just fly.

They made their way up the winding mountain road leading to the launch site. Even though they had left early, by the time they pulled Darrell's Jeep into the small gravel parking area a few hundred feet from the launch area, there were already several cars parked there. They unpacked their gear and walked to the flat grassy opening that looked out onto the edge of a steep drop off of Angel's Peak. If for some reason the glider launch were not successful, it was possible to ditch the glider onto the terrain below the launch area. The drop-off was steep enough that ditching could easily result in damage to the glider and injury to the pilot, but after the steep drop, the terrain was gradual enough that a severe accident was avoidable.

"How are you feeling, Jack?" Darrell asked as they waited their turn to launch, with four gliders ahead of them.

"Good, Darrell, fresh, I feel fresh. Hopefully we don't have to wait too long," Jack replied. "How about yourself?"

"Fantastic. Don't worry, Jack, as long as no one ditches, we'll be in the air in thirty minutes, no more."

They waited patiently for their turn, enjoying the cool, sunny morning. Luckily everyone ahead of them got off cleanly, and they both got their gliders ready for launch.

"What do you say, Jack, do you want to flip a coin to see who goes first, or do you want to lead this train?"

"Man, I can't wait to get this bird in the air," Jack replied. "I'd love to go now."

"Go for it, Jack."

Jack looked out over the edge of the launch area to the steep terrain below, then looked to his left and to his right to clear the area and soak up the beautiful mountain ridge before them. As he jumped off the ridge, he let out a big scream, then dropped the hang glider down slightly to pick up speed, then gently pulled the glider up as air flowed over the canopy and gave it lift. He brought the glider several hundred yards from the ridge and then stabilized it in level flight before turning his head back to the launch site to see Darrell preparing to launch.

"Awesome, absolutely awesome!" he screamed out, and Darrell in turn gave him two thumbs-up. Seconds later, Darrell was in the air and following Jack. Jack turned his glider to the left and ran parallel to the ridge for half a mile before turning toward the ridge in search of mountain updrafts. Jack turned his head to see Darrell following. They both wanted to gain as much altitude as possible before they headed their separate ways, and catching the mountain updrafts was the easiest way to do it. It made for amazing scenery as well.

Before him, Jack could see rugged granite mountain cliffs carved from the mountain over millions of years of natural erosion. The mountains were high enough that the cliffs stood above the tree line, but only a few hundred feet below, evergreens dotted the landscape, and farther below a full forest filled the mountainside. It was a calm day, so luckily the air wasn't too turbulent as Jack got closer to the ridge. As he caught an updraft, he moved his body back, and the glider gracefully climbed. As he got closer to the ridge, the power of the updraft increased, and he moved his body forward slightly to reduce his ascent. The glider crested the top of the ridge, and he moved his body forward to maintain his airspeed as the glider lost lift and started to descend. He was well above the ridgeline now, so he had altitude to play with. He circled back around and then entered the ridgeline at a forty-five-degree angle so that the updraft wouldn't lift his glider up too rapidly. When he entered the mountain updraft, he swung his body to the right abruptly to avoid getting pushed back toward the ridgetop below him. Flying away from the ridge was more difficult since the glider was lifted abruptly upward at first and then the ascent rate decreased rapidly, but done properly, the glider could still gain good altitude.

Jack flew a thousand feet away from the ridgeline, circled again, and headed back to the ridge to gain more altitude. When he turned this time, he could see Darrell a few hundred feet above him and to his left. Darrell saw Jack as well and waved at him, and Jack gave Darrell a thumbs-up in return.

They both worked the mountain ridges this way, gaining as much altitude as possible. Thirty minutes later, Jack was at ten thousand feet; now he was far enough above the mountains north of Palmer that he wasn't gaining any more altitude by flying along the ridgeline. The air was thin as well, pushing the limitations of his hang glider to climb higher. He looked around him to see if he could spot Darrell, and after a few seconds, he caught sight of him far off in the distance to the east. Darrell was heading up the river valley, now on his way toward Glennalien.

Jack turned his glider south and headed toward Palmer. Once he moved away from the mountains, the air was calm, and he glided in complete silence as his glider descended gradually over the flat landscape surrounding Palmer. There was a beautiful river that wrapped its way around Palmer to the west, and Jack could see sailboats and powerboats scattered in the clear light blue water. To the southwest, the river flowed into a wider river bay, which eventually made its way back to Anchorage to the west. On the other side of the bay, another set of majestic snow-covered mountains beckoned Jack closer. He turned southwest and headed over the river bay toward the mountains, hoping to catch some updrafts and gain altitude again. The mountains were taller here, only allowing Jack to fly parallel to the mountains and not over the top of them. The wind updrafts were more turbulent and unpredictable, and Jack struggled to keep his glider level as gusts jostled his glider to the right and left. He climbed back to nine thousand feet, but it was difficult flying, so he made a two-hundred-seventy-degree turn and headed back to Palmer.

Fifteen minutes later, he was flying right over the town center, and he could hear bells ringing from city hall signaling nine o'clock that Sunday morning. Jack headed slightly east in an attempt to find the common landing area.

★★★★★

"What do you say, Joe, how's it going this morning?" Mike asked as he pulled his Jeep up alongside Joe's flatbed truck parked on the abandoned runway by the common landing area.

Joe was lying in his flatbed with the bed facing toward the grassy field. He had a blanket laid out under his back, with a pillow propped up behind his head and a cup of coffee in his hand.

"Ah man, I've got a bit of a hangover from last night, drank too much and stayed out a little too late, but coming out here always clears my head, you know what I mean?"

"Sure do, Joe," Mike replied. "Beats lying in bed all morning. You got some breakfast for me?"

"Come on, man, I bought both rounds of shots last night, can't you just get your own? Janet's bakery is just up the road."

"All right, Joe, sure, man. I'll be back in a few. Seen anyone out yet?"

"I've seen a few fly by. There was one guy landing when I first got here, but another guy picked him up. They'll be showing up soon enough."

★★★★★

When Mike got back, coffee and muffin in hand, Joe was still sipping his coffee.

"You haven't moved a muscle, buddy. Not much action, hey?"

"I've seen several guys, but they're working the updrafts flying back and forth between the mountains. The air must be good up there. I don't mind—it's kind of fun to watch these guys, especially if I can get my binoculars on them before they begin their stunts. I've seen a few guys doing some acrobatics, steep turns, stalls, spirals, all that kind of stuff. They'll drop pretty low, then catch some air and climb back high again."

"Cool, man, I'm just going to sit back and enjoy my breakfast. By the way, how are those huskies of yours doing? Don't you have to feed them in the morning?"

"Oh yeah, they're great. In October, we'll start training hard again, when there's more snow on the ground. I'll take them on some long trail rides and get them into shape. My dad's tending to them this morning."

"Cool, man," Mike replied, and then he pulled out a blanket, dropped it on the grass and lay down, and started chewing on his muffin.

★★★★★

High above, Jack spotted the abandoned airfield to his left. He turned his glider to fly over the large grassy field. He could see a few vehicles parked on the edge of the runway. *Probably some chase drivers waiting for someone to park it,* he thought to himself. He was at 6500 feet now, and he felt great. He thought this would be a good time to practice some of the more difficult maneuvering, so he banked his glider into a steep turn and did a seven-hundred-twenty-degree spiral to his left and then turned right and did a seven-hundred-twenty-degree spiral to his right before pulling out at four thousand feet. The glider felt nimble and responsive in his hands, and once he pulled out, he was able to easily catch a thermal and climb back to five thousand feet. He then made his way back north to the mountains, caught an updraft, and climbed back to eight thousand feet.

*****

"Did you see that, Joe?" Mike exclaimed. "That guy knows how to work a glider."

"Pretty cool," Joe replied as he laid his binoculars back down by his side. "That guy must have had that glider banked seventy degrees in that spiral. Did you see how he flipped from right to left? He was working it."

"Here comes another one," Mike said, pointing to the south. "Let me borrow those binoculars a second, Joe; I want to get my eye on the next one."

"Aw, come on, bud," Joe said he as he grudgingly handed him the binoculars, "just this once, and then I want them back."

*****

Jack was at 8500 feet now, having worked the mountains north of Palmer, so he turned around and headed back to the airfield to practice some more maneuvering. This time as he approached the practice area, he pointed the nose of the glider down and picked up airspeed until his indicator showed seventy knots. He then moved his body back as far as possible and pulled the nose of the glider up and climbed quickly. He kept the nose of the glider up until he was climbing almost vertically. He held the glider there, waiting for the airspeed to bleed off, and then at twenty knots, he felt the glider flutter as it approached stall speed. He waited a few more seconds, the glider stalled, and he brought the nose down, with wings level, gently guiding his craft into a long, sloping arch. The idea was to descend enough to recover from the stall, but to bring the aircraft back up after recovery to avoid losing too much altitude, to simulate appropriate stall recovery procedures close to the ground.

The practice maneuvering felt particularly effortless that day, and Jack brought the glider back up into another stall, then dropped the nose again, repeating this several times. For the last stall, he kicked his body to one side. As the glider stalled to the left, he lowered the nose and went into a long, sweeping spiral, not pulling out until his altitude was four thousand feet.

★★★★★

"He's at it again," Joe said, having gotten his binoculars back from Mike several minutes earlier. "See him, the guy with that red, yellow, and purple glider? He's the same guy we saw earlier."

Mike got up and started digging in the cluttered backseat of his Jeep.

"I know I've got some binoculars back here somewhere—where the heck are they?"

Buried far under the backseat, he finally got hold of them.

"Here they are! All right, Joe, let me see, yeah, there here is, I got him. That's a pretty glider, isn't it? It looks like he's heading back to the mountains again, probably trying to get some altitude back."

"Yeah, you missed it, Mike. He did one of those hammerhead stalls, pretty, real pretty, then he went right into one of those spirals again."

★★★★★

Jack was enjoying himself. The air was calm around the practice area, the temperature was pleasant, and once he got his glider back close to the mountains, he found he could gain altitude without much effort. He was actually feeling a bit giddy, having obtained a natural "glider's high" from the maneuvering he had done, and from the ease and beauty of flying that day. He flew his glider back to the mountains, descending slowly until he was at 3500 feet, but once he was within a quarter mile of the mountain ridges surrounding Angel's Peak, he picked up an updraft and climbed again. He worked the ridges back and forth for the next twenty minutes until he was at 7500 feet. He felt great, so this time when he turned his glider back to the practice area over the abandoned airfield in Palmer, he thought he'd have some real fun.

He glided effortlessly for the next ten minutes as he headed south, descending to 2500 feet, but once he had the airfield in sight, he went into a sweeping turn and caught a thermal that took him back to 3500 feet. Once he was there, he looked all around him to make sure there was no other traffic in the area, be it hang gliders or small planes. The area was clear, so he dipped the nose of the glider down into a shallow descent. As the glider picked up speed, he continued to dip the nose down until he was descending rapidly. He kept a close eye on his airspeed indicator, and it began to climb, first fifty knots, then sixty, then seventy knots.

At seventy knots, he dipped his nose down slightly more as the glider encountered more drag. He continued to pick up speed until his airspeed indicator was reading ninety-five knots, and then he took a deep breath and pulled the nose of the glider into an abrupt but deliberate pull-up. He remembered back to that spectacular day when he literally took a ride with Darrell as the master performed a full loop in his glider, and he tried to duplicate Darrell's precision and skill as he attempted a loop himself. Unlike Darrell, though, he started the loop at a higher altitude to give him some distance to recover just in case he had to abandon the loop attempt.

He continued the pull-up, but once he had the nose of the glider heading straight up toward the sky, he gently pulled back more, to guide his glider into an inverted trajectory. The glider shook slightly as the canopy began to turn topside down, but he continued the loop and over the next few seconds, his airspeed dropped rapidly. He concentrated on keeping the glider level to avoid a stall and certain spin, and as he reached the top of the arch, he felt his body go weightless momentarily as the g's he generated from the loop were balanced by the weight of his body. He wasn't thinking about keeping his legs rigid, and as he crested the top of the arch, his knees bent backward toward the canopy. He felt his feet ruffle the nylon material briefly, but once he realized what was happening, he straightened his legs, and the glider continued through the loop unfettered. He gradually and gently brought the nose of the glider down and began to pick up airspeed again. As the glider began its descent, he relaxed a little and smiled, then began to laugh.

"Fantastic! That's beautiful!" he screamed out.

★★★★★

Down below by the abandoned runway, Joe and Mike had their binoculars glued to Jack as he did his loop.

"Wow, do you see that, Joe? He's doing a full loop. What a wild man; he's a crazy man!"

"He's a brave soul," Joe replied. "Pretty crazy. He must be loving it. I've got to get one of those gliders. Man, it's got to be a thrill."

"You got it, bro. Look how fast he's coming out of that loop. He's booking."

Joe put his binoculars by his side to get a better overall image of Jack's speed and proximity to the ground; he could see he was still a safe distance above the flat grassy field.

"How high do you think he is now?" Joe asked.

"Don't know, man. You're the math dude—you tell me," Mike replied.

"He's got a few thousand feet, I'd guess."

Joe kept looking up and brought his binoculars back to his face to get a clear image of Jack.

★★★★★

High above, Jack was ecstatic. He had never done a full loop in his glider, and it felt effortless. He had tried several times before, but had to back out as he lost too much airspeed too quickly and had trouble controlling the glider at low speed, but not this time. The glider felt so nimble and responsive in his hands; it moved in concert with him now, like a world-class musician playing his finest instrument. As he completed the second half of the loop, he loosened his grip and let the glider fly free, like a horseman letting his horse gallop without rein. He was flying almost straight down now toward the grassy field below him, and he kept the nose of the glider pointed to the ground to accentuate the thrill of his ride.

Wow, incredible! was the only thought he could gather in his mind, but as he picked up airspeed and descended rapidly, he looked down at his airspeed indicator and noticed with surprise it read 110 knots. At that instant, something came over him—he wasn't sure if it was the joy of gliding that glorious morning or just the challenge of doing something that he'd never even dreamed of doing, but it dawned on him, he had plenty of airspeed to go for a second loop. He smiled a glorious smile and laughed, then moved his body backward and pulled the glider into a graceful, sweeping arch upward.

★★★★★

"What the heck!" Joe yelled out. "Look, Mike, look! It looks like he's setting up to do a second loop. Now that is crazy—two in a row back-to-back!"

Mike put his coffee down and grabbed his binoculars again.

"Wow, I see him, man!" Mike exclaimed. "He's doing it; he's going for number two!"

"Sure hope he makes it in one piece!" Joe replied with his eyes glued to his binoculars.

★★★★★

Jack climbed rapidly, and then as before, he brought the glider toward him, and the canopy started to ease upside down. He was slightly off-kilter as he got two thirds into his arched climb, but he straightened the canopy and continued to ascend, bleeding off some airspeed in the process. He felt comfortable and relaxed, though, so he wasn't concerned. There was turbulence now, unlike the first loop, and it jostled the glider side to side a bit as he got close to the top of the arch. *How strange, it's such a calm day,* he thought, but he was focused on the loop and didn't have time to ponder what was causing it. There was a second, heavier turbulence pocket a second later, and it caught him off guard as the glider yawed thirty degrees to his left, but he caught it quickly and continued on, now almost completely upside down.

Man, that was close, he thought to himself, *another one like that, and I'll be in trouble.*

A split second after that thought passed through his mind, it happened. The glider caught a third, more violent pocket of turbulence, and it rolled the glider to Jack's left. He tried to catch it, but it was too late. The glider shuddered, then yawed as it rolled, and it swung Jack's body awkwardly sideways above the canopy. Before he could react, his body slammed sideways into the upside-down, tilted glider, and as he fell into it, he heard and felt something snap. The weight of his body had crushed the middle forward and aft running crossbar that gave the glider its form, and the glider buckled around him. The flailing canopy wrapped itself around Jack's left arm and legs, and he lost his left-hand grip on the control bar as the glider collapsed and nosedived straight down.

Jack still had a grip on the control bar with his right hand, and he tried to stabilize himself as best he could as he used his left hand to reach around and grab the small emergency parachute strapped to his side. Somehow he got hold of it, but he was spinning now as the glider spiraled down, out of control. He grasped the small parachute as best he could, and then he threw it hard to his left, hoping it would clear the glider. Once it was open to the air, a small leader chute would catch the wind and deploy. Then Jack just had to pull the rip cord, and the parachute would open fully.

The leader chute never got its chance to catch the air. Jack threw the parachute hard, but the glider's canopy spiraled right into the trajectory of the parachute and caught it. The small parachute slid down into the crevice made by the buckled glider behind Jack, and the line that attached it to Jack's midsection got tangled around the broken crossbar.

"Aw, crap!" Jack muttered helplessly. He then reached behind him and tried to free the parachute, but the harder he pulled, the more the line tangled its way around the crossbar. The glider was plummeting to the ground; he was two thousand feet above the field now and falling fast. He kept pulling the line, to no avail. He tried to spread his arms to get the canopy to open and catch some air in the hope of decreasing his descent speed, but it was useless. The canopy had folded over on itself and was worthless; it was like holding a rag out in the wind of an open car window, lots of flapping, but it was doing hardly anything to decrease his descent rate. As much as he tried, he couldn't get it to open up.

Jack started to panic.

"Crap, what can I do now?" he said to himself out loud. He was spinning wildly now, and at that instant, the grassy field below him caught his eye directly and he looked straight down. He froze in sheer terror.

I'm not going to survive this, he thought to himself. He had no time and was descending rapidly. His eyes widened, his mouth went dry, his skin started to crawl, his heart started racing, and his mind filled with fear. It was a deep, frightening, bone-chilling fear, one that wrapped its way around his body and mind, so strong that his body tensed up and his thoughts jumbled.

He heard himself muttering, "What can I do, what can I ...," until the instant he blacked out and his body went limp.

★★★★★

On the edge of the abandoned runway, Mike and Joe were looking up, seeing Jack's failed attempt at a second loop unfold before their eyes.

"He's almost at the top of the arch now, steady as she goes. He looks a little shaky, but he's just over the top now. There you ... whew, did you see that, Joe, what the heck?" Mike said.

"He's in trouble," Joe replied. "He better abandon it now, but it's—it's too late; he lost it."

Joe took his eyes from behind the binoculars. "Oh man, he's really in trouble now. He's falling like a brick, he's, he's free-falling."

"The glider, the glider, it's collapsed," Mike exclaimed. "I can see it; it's folded over and wrapped around the poor guy. Oh crap."

They both stared in shock as Jack and the collapsed glider plummeted to the ground.

"He's a dead man," Joe said quietly, and Mike shook his head frantically from side to side in response and yelled, "Oh, man!"

Jack hit the ground at 120 miles an hour only a few hundred yards from where they stood. They both froze there in horror as they heard a loud thud and then saw Jack and the collapsed glider bounce back in the air a few feet before finally settling down in the grassy field.

A moment later, they both took off running through the field toward Jack.

"We're not going to like what we see," Joe yelled back to Mike, but instinctively they couldn't help but run to the crash site. When they got there, they saw a man wrapped in the canopy of his glider facedown in the grassy field. The aluminum tubes that gave the glider its form were in a mangled mess scattered here and there next to the canopy, with some still tethered to the nylon. Jack's body lay still, with his face buried in the grass.

"My god, what do we do now, Joe?" Mike asked in a sickened voice. "I've never seen someone die before."

Joe knelt down next to Jack and took his wrist, feeling for a pulse. He knelt there for quite some time, not expecting anything, and was surprised when he began to feel a pulse.

"I feel something," he said after a minute. "It's very faint, but there's something. I can't believe it—how could someone have survived that wreck, how could he possibly ..."

He hesitated, surprised again.

"What is it, Joe, what are you feeling?" Mike asked.

"His pulse—it's getting stronger, much stronger. Look, Mike, look, he's, he's breathing. My god, he's still breathing."

Joe stood up in shock, but was even more surprised when he saw Jack begin to move his arms and legs back and forth, moaning. Seconds later and with a lot of effort, Jack propped himself up on one elbow, but then collapsed back to the ground and clumsily rolled onto his back, his arms flailing through the torn canopy as he did.

Joe and Mike knelt on the ground next to him. Jack's eyes were still closed and his breathing was erratic, and the two young men hesitated, not sure what to do next.

As they waited, Joe asked, "Did you see something out here, Mike? I swear I saw something out in this field just before the guy smacked the ground."

"Really?" Mike responded, still shaken by what he had just witnessed.

"Yeah, some types of forms, almost ghostlike, appeared just before he hit the ground—at least I think they appeared. It all happened so quickly, maybe I was just imagining it."

"I was so focused on this poor sucker smacking the ground, I didn't see anything else, Joe. God, that was frightening."

"It sure was frightening," Joe replied, but as he said this, Jack's breathing stabilized, and they both watched as he slowly opened his eyes.

★★★★★

Jack saw two young men staring at him like they were looking at a ghost, an expression of shock and confusion on their faces. Jack rolled his head to the left, then to the right, trying to gather in his surroundings, and then he looked back at the two young men.

"What the heck happened—where am I?" he asked.

"You lost control of your glider, sir," the young man closest to him said. "Don't you remember? You plummeted from a few thousand feet above us. We can't believe you're still with us. You hit the ground hard, really hard."

"Here? Now? But it can't be. I was asleep, dreaming. It was so quiet and tranquil. I felt so at peace."

"We saw it with our own eyes, sir," the young man replied. "You were doing aerobatics in your glider. You were at the top of a second loop when you lost control at the top of the arch and fell into the glider. Then it collapsed, and you plummeted to the ground."

Jack looked at the man in disbelief. "How could that be; how could it be?" Jack said, almost to himself.

"Believe it, sir. We just witnessed the whole thing."

Finally, searching for something to say, Jack asked, "What are your names?"

"My name is Joe, Joe Lawson, and this is my friend Mike. We're chasers; we ferry people back to their cars after they land here in the field."

"It's a pleasure to meet you," Jack replied. "My name is Jack."

The two young men stood there, still shocked that Jack had survived and that he was talking to them at all.

Finally Joe asked, "Is there something we can do to help, Jack? Can you walk, or are your legs broken? And your glider, it's in pieces."

Jack got up on his elbows and looked around him.

"Well, it sure is, isn't it?" he said with a slight chuckle. "Well, if one of you could help me to get out of this canopy, I'd appreciate it. It's wrapped pretty tightly around my torso, but as far as I can tell, my legs feel okay. I'll need some help getting this mess cleaned up as well."

Joe pulled out his keys and handed them to Mike.

"Can you run back and get my truck, Mike? I'll help Jack get himself out from the canopy."

"Sure thing," Mike replied, and then he trotted back toward the vehicles.

Jack struggled to get himself out from the canopy. Joe helped pull the torn nylon away from his body and then helped him unbuckle from the glider's harness and unzip from the leg cocoon pouch. Seconds later, Jack was sitting on the grass, his knees bent up in front of him, his arms behind him supporting the weight of his upper body.

"Are you okay to get up?" Joe asked.

"Well, I think so, but I could probably use a hand," Jack said.

Joe put out his hand and helped Jack to his feet. Jack stood up quite easily, but as he stood up, he felt a dull pain running across his ribs.

"Ah, that hurts," Jack said, grabbing his ribs gently as he bent forward slightly to ease the pain.

"Are you okay?" Joe asked.

Jack slowly bent backward, stretching his ribs the other way, and then he raised his arms and bent his torso slightly to the right and left.

"That's a little better—just seems like I clobbered my ribs somehow, kind of a dull pain running across my ribs diagonally. I think I'm okay."

Joe looked at Jack's glider poncho and saw that it had a rip in it across the rib area. He helped Jack remove it, and then he saw a bit of a bloodstain on Jack's shirt across his right rib cage.

"It looks like you're bleeding," Joe said, gesturing toward Jack's ribs.

Jack looked down and saw the blood. "Well, so I am," he replied. "It doesn't hurt too bad—maybe it's just a scrape."

Jack pulled up his shirt and saw a brazen pizza burn running diagonally across his right rib cage about five inches in length. It was only an inch wide but oozed blood like something had rubbed up against his skin hard enough to make it bleed. He could see some black and blue marks running diagonally adjacent to the pizza burn as well.

"Well, that's strange, isn't it?" Jack said.

It was Joe who made the connection. He started to look around the mangled glider until he found the buckled forward-aft running aluminum tube that had previously given the glider its form. Joe pulled the aluminum tubing toward him, looking at it closely. Right in the middle of the area that got bent sharply, presumably from the impact with Jack's body when he fell into the glider, he saw little stains of blood.

"Look," Joe said, showing the mangled tubing to Jack, "see the bit of bloodstain? When you fell into the glider, you must have hit the tubing hard enough to braze yourself and bruise your ribs. I mean, you hit it hard enough to buckle the tubing, so I'm not surprised you got a little taste of it as well. Do you see?"

"Well, yes, I do," Jack said thoughtfully, looking closer. "It's strange—I can't recall any of this. It's like it was a dream."

"I've heard of that before," Joe replied. "Your mind develops a sort of built-in temporary amnesia for the time leading up to some traumatic, life-threatening event, like people who are in a car crash who can't recall anything prior to the crash or the crash itself."

"Yes, I've heard of that as well," Jack said, slowly stroking his bruised ribs to see if any were broken. Although they were tender, he didn't feel any sharp pain as he moved his hand across them. Jack stretched his arms out again and moved his body from side to side, seeing if that motion added to the pain.

"Well, my ribs feel okay," he said. "They're a bit tender, but I don't think anything's broken. I guess I was lucky—that tubing isn't very stout and really isn't designed for that type of impact."

"Yeah, you were lucky," Joe replied. He hesitated as it dawned on him again what he had just witnessed.

"Lucky?" he continued. "Lucky? Man, you just get a little bruise after what I saw happen, well, that's not luck, it's, it's—man, I can't even describe it. You should have seen how hard you hit the ground, and you don't have a scratch other than a little trouble with your ribs from buckling that bar. Man, it's unbelievable, just fricking unbelievable."

"I don't know what to say, Joe; I feel just fine," Jack replied.

★★★★★

A few seconds later, Mike pulled up with Joe's truck, and all three pitched in to pick up what was left of the hang glider.

"It's too bad, man," Mike said as he picked up the pieces of the broken craft. "That was a pretty glider, and we sure did get a kick out of watching you perform your stunts."

Joe offered to drive Jack back to his house east of Anchorage, and Jack gladly accepted.

"Are you sure you don't mind, Joe?" Jack asked. "It's a good forty minutes from here."

"No problem, man, we're both just relieved to see you in one piece and talking to us—not a big deal. Come on, jump in, we'll be there in no time."

"I'm just going to hang out here," Mike said to them both, "see if anyone else shows up this morning. I don't want to leave someone hanging out here by themselves waiting for a pickup."

"Sure thing, Mike," Joe replied. "I'll be back in a little while."

"Oh, and Mike," Jack said, now remembering his drive up to Angel's Peak earlier that morning, "if you run into a guy named Darrell, can you tell him I had to go home? He might be landing here in a little while."

"Sure thing, man, no problem," Mike replied.

As they were just about to leave, Mike said, "Glad to have met you, Jack, and I'm sure glad to see you survived that wreck. Man, we thought you were a goner. Maybe we'll see you out here again sometime, but I'll think you'll be needing a new ride for yourself," he said as he gestured to the glider pieces in the back of Joe's truck.

Jack chuckled. "Yeah, it might be awhile, but hopefully I'll see you again. Can't thank you enough for your help, Mike. See you later."

"Take it easy, man."

★★★★★

Jack and Joe drove in silence most of the way back to Helen's place, the quiet being interrupted when Jack needed to give directions to the house. Jack was in a daze. He tried to remember the events that Joe and Mike had described leading up to his accident, but he couldn't. The only thing that came to mind was the conversation he had with Darrell when they discussed what a glorious day it was going to be. He did at some point, though, remember being asleep in a peaceful, restful dream, but he couldn't make any connection between that and the rest of his day. He felt at ease now, and comfortable with Joe sitting beside him, like they were good friends. Joe, for his part, was cordial and pleasant, making Jack feel at home as he drove him back to Anchorage.

When they arrived, Joe backed his truck up the driveway and helped Jack unload what was left of the glider into the side of the garage. When they were finished, Jack found his wallet packed inside a zipped-up pocket in his glider poncho, grabbed fifty dollars, and handed it to Joe.

"Can't thank you enough for your help, Joe," Jack said as he handed him the fifty dollars.

Joe waved his hand. "Don't worry about the money, Jack. I'm just glad to see you in one piece and talking to me. It's the least I can do to get you back here. Just catch me on the next go-around. It's been a pleasure."

"Are you sure?" Jack replied, surprised.

"Dude, it's cool. I'll see you around."

Joe stretched out his arm, and he and Jack shook hands.

"And take care of those ribs, okay?" Joe said as he turned to walk away.

"Sure will, Joe. You've been amazing. Thank you so much."

"Sure thing," Joe replied.

★★★★★

Well, that was awfully nice, Jack thought to himself as he made his way into the house. Helen's car was parked out front, so Jack suspected she was somewhere inside.

"Helen? Are you here?" he said as he walked down the hallway. After looking for her for a few minutes inside the house, Jack found her in the back of the yard doing some gardening.

"Helen, darling, how are you?" he said as he walked up to her.

"Jack dear, you made it back, alive and well and in one piece," she replied without taking her eyes off the potted flower she was now planting in the ground.

Jack chuckled nervously. "Well, I made it back in one piece, but I can't say the same for my hang glider. I can't remember any of it, but the chasers say that I was doing aerobatics in my glider and I was on a second loop and upside down when I ..."

Helen interrupted him, "When you lost control and fell into the glider, snapping it in half, and then you plummeted two thousand feet until you smacked into the ground at terminal velocity."

"Well, yes, but how would you have known such a thing?" Jack asked, confused.

"I was there, Jack," Helen replied as she stood up slowly and faced him. In her expression, there was a calmness and peacefulness that Jack had never seen before.

"You were there? What do mean you were there? It was just me and the chasers," Jack replied. "You weren't there."

"I was there, Jack, I saw it all happen before my eyes. I experienced the whole thing."

"What are you talking about? You're talking crazy, Helen. You were here doing some gardening, not in Palmer."

"I was there, Jack," she repeated. "Don't you understand, Jack? We took your body."

"What?"

"We took your body, Jack. No one could have survived that fall, so we took your body."

"I don't understand," Jack said, bewildered.

"I was here gardening, just minding my own business and enjoying my day, when it hit me like a freight train. This mind-boggling, terrible fear entered my psyche, and it was horribly frightening. It filled my entire mind it was so powerful, and it froze me in my tracks, like I was in some type of suspended animation. Then over the next few seconds, things started to clear as if I was stepping out of a fog. I stepped out of the fog into this beautiful grassy field, and I looked up, sensing the fear coming from above. That's when I saw you, Jack, plummeting from the sky. I gasped, 'Oh my god!' I shuddered, realizing what was happening, and I was spellbound for a moment.

"Then I heard someone else gasp, and I looked to my right and I saw this old man. I knew who he was as soon as I saw him—it was the doctor you talked about so much, Dr. Weldon, and beside him stood George, your oil-rigger friend, and beside him young Josh, the boy you rescued in Denali Park. I turned to my left, and there was Phyllis, who owns the grocery store, and beside her, her son Scott, who was holding her hand. Next to them was a tall man—I had never met him, but being there, we all became immediately connected, and I knew him as Phil, the man who helped you with your website, the man who had a heart attack. Then I turned and looked behind me, and there was Darrell, your hang-gliding friend, and beside him stood that friendly old conductor, Sean McCree, and that beautiful black eagle was sitting gently on his shoulder. And next to him stood the two sisters, the daughters of Ingrid Samualson, Kathy and Stephanie—I had met them at her funeral.

"It was so wonderful to see all these people gathered together, and for a moment I felt so happy—but then that fear, that horrible fear, just grabbed me again, and I looked back up. We were all there, Jack, looking up at you, seeing you free-fall from the sky above us, knowing you'd die when you hit the ground. I was mesmerized in fright for a few moments, but then I screamed, 'We've got to do something! We can't let him die! We've got to do something!'

"It was Robert Weldon's idea, Jack—he's such a brilliant man—and of course, we all agreed immediately; we only had a few seconds to spare."

Jack was looking at Helen with a look of shock and disbelief on his face.

"Don't you understand, Jack?" Helen continued. "No one could have survived that fall, no one, so we took your body. Oh, it hurt, Jack—don't get me wrong—but when the impact of one is shared among twelve, it's a survivable event. It was a massive jolt to all of us, like being in a violent car crash with your seat belt on, but we shared the impact of your body among all of us, so we made it through okay. Do you see now, Jack? Do you understand?"

Jack stood stunned for a few seconds, but then he said, "My god, this power I've acquired, somehow it reached out, or should I say allowed me to reach out to all of you in desperation. The chasers told me they were sure I was a dead man when I hit the ground. Unbelievable, I mean incredible, absolutely incredible."

Jack paused for a moment, and then he asked, "Is everyone okay? I mean, did anyone get hurt?"

"We all checked in with each other right after the impact, and everyone responded that they were okay. Oh, we definitely had some bumps and bruises, but luckily nothing serious."

"And the eagle?" Jack asked.

"He didn't make out quite as well, Jack. He broke one of his wings. He was in the back eating from your feeder before this whole thing happened, and I found him in the grass a little while ago flailing his wings to no avail. I fixed him up as best I could and put him in my birdcage. He'll be staying with us for a while, but I think he'll heal up eventually."

"After the impact, what happened after that, Helen?" Jack asked.

"Well, we all waited to see if you were okay, but we were all a part of you and could sense you had survived. I could feel your heartbeat, could sense that you still had feelings in your limbs, that your mind was still present, and that you were breathing, and then the next thing I knew, I was back here in my own body, my flowers waiting for me to plant them. I didn't even get a chance to say good-bye to everyone."

"Oh, Helen, I don't, I don't know what to say."

"It's okay; I can understand. My god, Jack, to die in a silly hang-gliding accident! Just be a little more careful next time, okay? I'm not going to let you get away from me that easily, you know."

"Oh, Helen," Jack responded. Then he wrapped his arms around her and gave her a loving hug.

"I love you, Helen, darling, I love you so much. Thank you so much for what you've done."

"I love you too, Jack."

When Jack went back into the house, he walked into the room where Helen kept her birdcage and saw the eagle sitting quietly on the hay floor. When the eagle saw Jack, he fluttered his wings and starting squawking over and over again.

"Easy, boy, easy," Jack said to the bird. "You don't want to make that wing worse. It's okay, I'm here; it's wonderful to see you, too."

Jack opened the door, gently picked up the eagle, and held him in his arms.

"Let me see that wing. Well, Helen did a nice job of wrapping it up for you. You take it easy, old boy. It'll heal up all right as long as you let it."

The eagle turned his head toward Jack, squawking again to let him know he was happy to see him.

After setting the eagle back down into the cage, Jack walked down the hallway to the kitchen to grab a bite to eat. It had been quite a day, and he'd only had a light snack that morning. As he walked down the hall, he noticed the picture of the female climber with the corny saying was gone. *Well, that's nice*, he thought to himself as he opened up the refrigerator to make himself a sandwich.

★★★★★

Later that evening, as he and Helen got ready for bed, Jack mentioned it to Helen.

"Helen, that picture of the climber with the saying below it, I noticed it was …"

"I took it down, Jack," Helen interrupted. "You know, if you didn't like it, you could have just said so; it wouldn't have hurt my feelings."

"Oh, Helen, I didn't want to say anything," Jack replied.

"You know, the more I thought about it, the more I agreed with you, it was kind of corny," Helen said, trying to not make a big deal about it. "Look, it's been a long day, and I'm tired. Come on, that bed's waiting for us."

As Helen was putting on her nightgown, Jack noticed the long black and blue bruise running down a portion of her back.

"Oh my god, Helen, are you okay? I didn't realize, I mean, oh gosh, I'm so sorry—and I'm, I'm so grateful."

"It's okay, Jack. I just got the wind knocked out of me. It's a little sensitive, but it will heal up. It just hurts a bit when I stretch out my back too much."

Jack went into the bathroom and pulled out some ointment from the bathroom cabinet.

"Lie down on the bed, sweetheart; let me rub some of this ointment around that bruise. I'll be really gentle. It will make it feel better."

"Promise?" Helen replied as she lay down on the bed and pulled up her nightgown.

"Promise," Jack replied as he proceeded to gently rub the ointment onto Helen's exposed back.

Chapter 17

Over the next few weeks, Jack contacted all his friends who were there that morning in the grassy field outside of Palmer. He wanted to say hi and to thank them, and more importantly he wanted to make sure they were doing okay.

On a Monday morning, Jack drove out to the oil rig George was working. George was his usual stoic self, shrugging it off like it was just a walk in the park.

"Don't worry about it, Jack. You're my friend, aren't you? What else could I do but help out my friend, and you needed some help. I know you would have done it for me."

"Are you feeling okay now, George?" Jack asked.

"Me? Come on, Jack, I'm fine. Man, I'm out here every day, aren't I?" George replied as he flung his hand in the air gesturing to the rig. "Not a big deal."

"But is there something I can do to show my gratitude, George?" Jack asked.

"Gratitude? Come on, man, what are you talking about? Listen, why don't you just buy us old boys a few rounds at the bar next time around, all right? And make it a good brew, Jack, that's what I need, yeah, a nice strong brew."

"You got it, buddy, you got it," Jack replied, grinning as he grabbed George's shoulder in friendship.

★★★★★

The next day, Jack called Phil at his office in San Francisco.

"Jack! Great to hear from you, you old hang-gliding fool. I know you made it through that crash okay, but it's sure good to hear your voice nonetheless. How are you feeling, Jack?"

"Well, I feel great, but I can't say the same for my glider. It's going to be awhile before I fly again. But me, I feel good, never felt better actually. I wouldn't be here if not for all of you. I can't thank you enough."

"That was quite a journey, Jack, quite an experience. I was sitting at my desk in the office when it hit me—god, that was intense. I stood up and looked out the window, and then the next thing I know, I'm standing in that field with Helen and your other friends around me. It was like we were all one, sharing our minds together, and somehow we all knew we could save you, Jack, we all knew."

"How did you know, Phil?"

"I really don't know how to describe it, but when Helen screamed and Dr. Weldon said we had to take your body, it just crystallized in our collective minds. It was almost as if we were just reaching out our hands to catch you, but instead, we reached out and took your body, sharing it among all of us. I know I can't capture the feeling completely in words, but that's the best way I can describe it."

"Incredible, isn't it, Phil? Just incredible," Jack replied.

"Yes, it is incredible. That's quite an extraordinary gift you have, Jack, quite extraordinary."

"I can't thank you enough," Jack said. "So how have you been, Phil, and are you doing okay after taking that fall?"

"The fall, Jack? Oh, I'm fine. I was a little stiff for a few days, the way I used to feel after doing those marathons years ago, but Christine practices massage and one night I conned her into giving me a wonderful two-hour massage and since then I've felt great."

"How's she doing by the way? You two must be getting along well, I would guess."

"She's great, Jack, thanks for asking. She's expecting in just a few months, and we're both looking forward to having our second child."

"She's pregnant, wow! Well congratulations," Jack replied.

"Yeah, we both had been talking about a second child for a while, but she's thirty-nine and we weren't sure about it. We gave it a try, and a few months later, voila, she was pregnant."

"It will be nice having another little one around to keep you company," Jack said. "How old is your other one?"

"She's ten now. It will be a big change for her; she's gotten so used to being an only child."

"Is it a boy or girl, Phil, or do you know?"

"It's a girl. I'll be the only man in the house, well, me and the dog. I hope I can handle it."

Jack chuckled, "You'll be able to handle it; just be sure to pitch in on those diaper changes."

"That's the one thing I'm not looking forward to," Phil replied, "but the rest of it, it will be great."

"Well, I'm sure you'll have fun with it, Phil, and thanks again. Be sure to send us some baby pictures when the little girl arrives. Helen especially would love that."

"Will do, Jack, it's been a pleasure."

★★★★★

The next day, Jack went over to Phyllis's grocery store to say hi and was pleasantly surprised to find out that Scott was in town visiting.

"I'll buy both of you dinner tonight, what do you say, Phyllis? How about over at Rocky's Burgers—I used to go over there with Scott when he lived up here."

Just then Scott opened the door to the grocery store and walked inside.

"Jack, great to see you!"

"Scott, how's it going?"

They hugged, and then Jack said, "I was just inviting Phyllis over to

Rocky's for a burger, so you showed up just at the right time. What do you say, Scott? I'm buying."

"Do you want to go for a burger, Mom? They make great burgers and have some good catfish as well, and it's not every day that Jack offers to buy, you know," Scott said jokingly. "What do you say?"

"Sure, why not?" Phyllis replied. "Let me finish up a few things, and then let's head over."

"What do you need, Phyllis?" Jack asked. "We're here to help."

"Well, sure. I just need these boxes moved to the back, and I'll close out the register in the meantime."

"No problem, Mom," Scott said. "You should have told me about the boxes earlier; I would have gotten them."

"Thanks so much, boys," Phyllis replied as Scott and Jack grabbed the eight boxes of canned goods and moved them to the back of the store.

★★★★★

After buying the burgers for everyone at the counter at Rocky's, Jack sat down with Phyllis and Scott at a corner booth in the pleasant, well-lit burger joint.

"Does Rocky still own this place, Jack? He's got to be getting on in years now," Scott asked.

"Yeah, he does, I talked to him a few weeks ago. He's still at it—you can tell by the taste of the burgers—but that's all he does nowadays, the cooking; he leaves the rest up to his daughters. They really take care of the place now."

"Well, these burgers sure are good," Phyllis said, having just taken her first bite from her mushroom burger.

"Sure are, aren't they?" Jack replied. Jack took a bite from his chili burger and then said, "Well, it sure is good to see both of you together after all these years. Any special occasion?"

"Oh, nothing special," Scott replied. "I just wanted to come up and see Mom and say hi to some of my old buddies. I was going to give you a call tomorrow, Jack, but you beat me to it. You know I lost touch there for a few years, so I wanted to reconnect."

"It's been wonderful having Scott here," Phyllis said. "He's still my boy, Jack, still got that sparkle in his eye and kick in his step."

"He sure does, doesn't he?" Jack replied. "So how's the auto racing team gig going, Scott? That sounded so exciting when you told me about it, and perfect for you."

"Ah, it's great, Jack, pretty hectic but great. There's a lot of travel involved, you know, going from one racetrack to the next all over the country. But the great thing is the race cars—what incredible machines. I love working on them, and I'm working on them constantly. An Indy race car is like working on a street car in some ways: you've got to do the regular stuff, change the brake pads, bleed the brakes, change tires, put gas in the car, change oil, tune up the engine, you know, the routine stuff—but there's the added dimension that makes it so challenging."

"What's that, Scott?" Jack asked.

"The racing, the search for speed. We're always tweaking something trying to get the car to go faster. One time it might be the shocks, the next time the suspension setup, and there are the wings we're adjusting depending on what the car's doing, often right in the middle of the race. We've gotten to the point now where we collect data all over the car, forward-aft and lateral g's, tire pressures, throttle position, you name it, and we work with the driver and others on the team to see what we need to do to the car to go quicker."

"Sounds exciting. How's the team doing, Scott?" Jack asked.

"We're improving. It's a new team that only was started three years ago, but we got our first top five finish earlier this year, so we're making headway."

"Wow! So you got any races coming up on the West Coast?" Jack asked.

"Yeah, there's a race at Laguna Seca near Monterey, California, in August."

"That's right, Jack," Phyllis interjected, "and Scott has invited me down to be a special guest of the team. I'll get to hang out with Scott that weekend and a few days after."

"You're not going to be out there changing tires in the middle of the race, are you, Phyllis?" Jack quipped.

"That's funny, Jack," Phyllis replied. "No, I'm just going to enjoy myself, have some of that California wine in the guest area, and enjoy the racing. If they really need me, maybe I'll give one of those race cars a nice wax job just before the race."

"That's right, Mom," Scott replied. "It will make the car slip through the air that much faster."

"Well, it sure sounds like a lot of fun," Jack said. "You'll have a great time down there together."

"Yes, it will be the first time I've left Alaska in ages," Phyllis said.

"You'll love it, Mom," Scott said. "It's more crowded than up here, but there's so much to do, so much to see, and the people are a bit crazy. California is beautiful country as well."

There was a pause in the conversation as they ate their food, and then Jack said, "Well, it's so nice to see you two together and enjoying yourselves. Listen, I really wanted to thank you for what you did in that field in Palmer a few weeks back. I wouldn't be here talking to you if you hadn't helped me that day."

Scott and Phyllis smiled and nodded their heads, and then Scott said, "Look, Jack, it's the least I could do. If it wasn't for you, I would have never gotten into working on these mechanical things, airplanes and cars. It was with your encouragement that I pursued it, and now I'm working on Indy race cars, my dream job. I never really got to thank you in any right way, so I guess it was my way of saying thanks. I'm just so glad it worked and you're still here with us."

Phyllis smiled as well and nodded her head in agreement, then said, "You brought my boy back to me, Jack, my wonderful Scott, and now I'm going to get a chance to see him at work and visit the wine country in California. Come on, Jack, what else could I do but help you when you needed it most?"

Jack looked at them and smiled, nodding his head, and then he took another bite of his burger before asking, "So are you two doing okay? I mean, it must have been quite a jolt."

"I'm fine, Jack," Scott replied. "I was a bit sore for sure, but I'm a young man, I can handle it. No worries, Jack."

Jack and Scott both turned their heads to Phyllis, waiting for a response.

"Come on, boys," Phyllis said. "I'm an Alaskan woman, born and bred. We're built tough, you know. What else can I say? I'm good."

★★★★★

Jack was able to get the phone numbers of Ingrid Samualson's daughters, Stephanie and Kathy, from Helen. Luckily Helen had exchanged numbers with them during their mother's funeral, and in fact, Helen had kept in touch with them periodically via e-mail over the last eight months. Jack tried several times unsuccessfully to reach them, but then one day he was able to get Kathy on the phone in New Mexico. He was pleasantly surprised to find out her sister, Stephanie, was visiting that week from Florida.

"Jack, so wonderful to hear from you," Kathy said enthusiastically on the phone. "Your girlfriend, Helen, is so wonderful, such a doll. We've both been keeping in touch with her ever since our mother's funeral. She's so nice."

"She's quite a woman, isn't she?" Jack replied. "It's nice to hear you've stayed in touch."

"Jack, would it be okay if I put you on speakerphone?" Kathy interjected. "I've just walked into the study, and Stephanie is here as well. That way we can talk to you together."

"Sure, of course," Jack replied.

"Hi, Jack," Stephanie said once they were on speakerphone, "I've heard so much about you from Helen. It's nice to finally talk to you."

"It's nice to talk to both of you together. So how are things in New Mexico? I've never been down there, but I hear it's beautiful country."

"Great, Jack, great," Kathy replied. "It's so wonderful when Stephanie comes and visits. We try to get together at least twice a year—I'll go to Florida and then she comes here—but this is the first time since our mother's funeral. We always get so busy, but we finally made a point of getting together. I love New Mexico, much better than Florida, I might say. When are you going to convince that husband of yours to move out here, Stephanie?"

"I've been twisting his arm for years," Stephanie replied. "One of these days, he'll say let's do it, and then I'll be here in a heartbeat. It's quite spectacular, New Mexico is, Jack. It's got that rugged desert beauty, with beautiful mountain terrain in the northern part of the state, and the people are just genuinely nice, maybe because it's not so crowded like Florida. It's quite different from Alaska—not so green, and snow mainly north of Santa Fe around Taos, but I'm sure you'd love it, definitely for the outdoorsy type."

"Well, that's me for sure," Jack replied. "I should talk to Helen; maybe we can arrange a trip down there soon."

"That would be wonderful, Jack," Kathy replied. "You're always welcome here."

"Well, I called to say hi to you both," Jack said, "and to also say thank you for what you did in Palmer several weeks back. If you hadn't shown up in that grassy field moments before I hit the ground, I would have never gotten the chance to talk with you—never gotten a chance to do much of anything, for that matter."

"Ah, yes, Jack," Kathy replied, "that was quite an extraordinary experience."

"Yes," Stephanie added, "I call it an out-of-body, out-of-mind encounter. Quite spectacular—what a trip. I'm just sitting on the back porch on a Sunday morning drinking my coffee and watching the kids, and then it's like this giant hand comes along and whisks me across to the other side of North America. There I was, standing in that field, transfixed by that bone-chilling fear. That was powerful, Jack, really powerful."

"You know we dreamed about you, Jack, long before that morning in Palmer," Kathy added.

"What's that?" Jack replied. "What do you mean?"

"Both of us," she continued. "We had a recurring dream about that evening before our mother died, when she made contact with you. The dream was always the same. We could see our mother reaching out to you, and then we saw you stumbling with her pain, then the joyful encounter she had with you, then the phone call a few minutes later to us. And the emotion from our mother was always the same—a brief relief of that agonizing pain, and then the elated anticipation of seeing us before she died. The dream ended with us sitting at her bedside showing her pictures of her grandchildren."

"Yes, Jack," Stephanie said, "but it's not the first time Kathy and I have shared dreams. For years now, we've called each other in the middle of the night, sharing our thoughts as if we had both been there in the same dream together, at that same moment in time."

"Ah yes, I've heard of stories like that before," Jack replied. "Special telepathic powers between siblings, as if you share the same mind together. Are you two twins?"

"Identical twins, in fact," Stephanie replied. "Kathy was born three minutes before me. I call her my Old Sis; she can't stand that name, but three minutes is three minutes."

"We've been telling our husbands and friends for years about those dreams," Kathy said. "Everyone just seemed to laugh it off or shrug their shoulders and walk away, but there was something to it all along."

"Indeed," Jack replied. "In fact, I'm surprised my mind was able to reach out to the two of you that morning in Palmer. I had never made contact with you prior to that morning, unlike the others who responded to my plea for help."

"True, Jack, but our mother made contact with you the evening before she died," Kathy replied. "We've both been talking about that. We think somehow that encounter was passed on to us during those precious hours we had with her before she passed away. It would explain the dream we've both been having ever since."

"Yes," Jack replied, "your mother reached out to me, not I to her, and during that time I saw her life flash before my eyes and shared the intense physical pain she was experiencing. Obviously her power of telepathy was impressive; somehow she knew how to open up a pathway to my mind, asking me to call for you. That power of telepathy has been handed down to the both of you, it appears, and it was that power I was luckily able to tap into that morning in Palmer. I can't thank you enough for helping that morning. I wouldn't have survived that fall without you."

"Jack, you answered our mother's dying wish that evening, and we're just grateful we were able to see her that night before she died," Kathy replied.

"Yes, Jack, I wanted to thank you for giving us that call," Stephanie continued. "I know seeing us that night brought our mother much joy, and I'm glad to know I haven't been crazy all these years. Kathy and I have, in fact, really been sharing our thoughts and dreams; it's not just a figment of our imaginations or some kind of strange coincidence."

"Far from a coincidence, that's for sure," Jack replied. "It appears you have telepathic powers you weren't even aware of, at least not until that morning in Palmer. You can now see how powerful they really are. It's quite an amazing talent you have—enjoy it."

Jack paused briefly and then asked, "So how are you two doing? I know you didn't have a lot of time to decide what to do that morning, and from what Helen and the others have told me, it was quite a jolt."

"Oh, I'm fine now, Jack, but I was bedridden for a few days there," Kathy replied. "My husband took a week off from work to take care of the kids while I recovered, but nothing serious or permanent, just a lot of aches and pains. Look, Jack, don't worry about it. You took us on a journey we would have never experienced otherwise and opened a door to something we've only begun to understand. We're just glad we could help."

"How about yourself, Stephanie?" Jack asked.

"Much the same as Kathy. I was in bed for four days getting over the aches and pains, but it gave me and Kathy time to reconnect on the phone and talk about my trip to New Mexico now. It's so nice to get away and see my Old Sis. I'm doing fine. In fact, we went together on a hike in the mountains yesterday, and it was gorgeous. I think you'd like it down here, Jack."

"Well, it sure does sound beautiful. I'm just so glad you two are doing well," Jack replied, breathing a sigh of relief. "I was concerned about you there for a while, especially after seeing the big bruise on Helen's back. Don't worry, she's doing much better now. I'll tell her I spoke to both of you. Don't be surprised if she gives you a ring; I'm sure she'd love to chat."

"That would be wonderful, Jack," Kathy said. "Stephanie's here until Sunday. Tell Helen we said hi."

"Great talking to you, Jack, and we look forward to chatting with Helen," Stephanie added. "Take care of yourself."

"You two as well, take care," Jack replied.

★★★★★

Jack caught up with Darrell a few days later at his home. Jack rang the doorbell, and Darrell's wife answered the door.

"Jack, so good to see you, how have you been?" Wendy said as she smiled and gave Jack a hug.

"Good, Wendy, thanks. How are you doing?"

"Great, great. Enjoying the summer. You know it's so nice we're both teachers and have the summer off together. Well, I heard you took a nasty spill in your hang glider. You don't look any worse for the wear. You're very lucky, Jack, very lucky."

"You can say that again," Jack replied. "Wendy, is Darrell around? I just wanted to come by and say hi."

"Oh, of course. He's in the back working on, what else, his hang glider. Do you want something to drink, Jack?"

"Sure, how about a beer?"

"Beer right up. Darrell always keeps the refrigerator well stocked with some type of microbrew in the summer. I'm sure he wouldn't want you to drink alone, so I'll get him one as well."

★★★★★

Darrell was busily sanding a small detail on his hang-glider frame when Jack walked into the backyard.

"Darrell, buddy, that glider looks beautiful, beautiful. Come on, take a break. Wendy's coming with a beer."

"Jack! How you been? I just can't keep away from this thing; you know how it is."

"I'm good," Jack replied. "I know what you mean about wanting to tinker with the glider, but given the shape mine is in, well, I'll have to find something else to keep me busy for a while."

Darrell laughed. "Aw, come on, Jack, you'll get back in the air sooner or later, but I think you'll need a new bird—that one is toast."

Wendy opened the back porch door and walked up with two beers in her hands.

"Here you go, boys," she said, "two cold Red Hook Pale Ales."

"Thanks so much," Jack said, and then asked, "Aren't you going to join us, Wendy?"

"Oh no, little Josephine needs someone to play with, and I don't like beer too much, at least not in the afternoon," she replied. "You two have a good time."

"Thanks, honey," Darrell said as she walked back inside.

"Well, Darrell, how are things? What's the deal with the glider, trying something new?"

"Yeah, you know, I thought I'd try a few things, reconfigure the canopy attach points a bit. I just want to see if I can squeak a tad more lift out of this bird. It's great at high altitude, but when I'm close to the ground and I get some ground effects, well, it could be better."

"You're a real tactician, or should I say perfectionist," Jack replied, "always trying to eke out that slight improvement."

"So how are you feeling, Jack? That fall several weeks back was absolutely horrendous."

"I'm feeling great—well, other than the fact that I hurt my pride that day. But you know I wouldn't be here at all if not for all of you showing up in that field that morning to save me from the impact. I can't thank you enough, Darrell."

"My pleasure, Jack, what else could I do but help out a good friend? That was quite an experience."

"I'm curious, Darrell, what was your story? Were you still flying your glider those moments before I hit the ground?"

"Oh no, Jack, I was sitting in a field by the river; I had landed there twenty minutes earlier. I made it all the way to Glennalien, but when I turned around, the wind was strong and gusting, and I couldn't keep my bird in the air. As I got closer to the ground, it dropped like a brick, and I landed right by the river. It was pleasant, so I was taking my time enjoying the scenery."

"Well, thank goodness for that. God knows what would have happened if you had been in the air and left your glider unattended even for a brief period of time."

"Yeah, it's a good thing I was on the ground and available to help you. You know, Jack, that first loop you did was excellent, but you made a near fatal mistake on the second one."

"Well, it would have been fatal if not for all of you. I don't remember any of it, but what did I do wrong?" Jack asked.

"You started the second loop in almost the identical location where you had started the first one, and in the process flew right through the wake from the first loop. You see, from the bottom all the way up to the apex of the second loop, you flew through that disturbed air. That's very difficult to do, Jack, especially as your airspeed bleeds off as you approach the top. It's hard enough doing a loop, but flying through a shifting wake is unpredictable. I wish you had told me you were going to try a loop, well, multiple loops that morning, Jack; I could have given you some instruction."

"Forever the teacher you are, Darrell. Well, give it to me now," Jack replied.

"You see, what you need to do when you come out of the first loop is level off slightly while maintaining your airspeed, then count four seconds before starting the next loop. That way you stay far enough in front of your wake that it won't be a problem. You're not doing multiple loops on top of one another; you're doing a series of loops offset from one another, all close together but shifted enough that the glider is still stable, kind of like those amusement park rides that do one loop after the next in series."

"Yes, I understand," Jack replied, "but even then, wouldn't you still run into your wake sometime during the subsequent loops?"

"Well, you do, Jack, but you're away from the wake during the most crucial part of the maneuver up until you crest the top. Once you're over the top and start to descend, you might intersect the wake, but by then, you're picking up speed and can fly through it quite easily."

"I see, well, that does make sense. It's extraordinary you know all about my flying that day. I don't remember any of it," Jack commented.

"Oh, the memories are there," Darrell replied. "You've buried them deep in your psyche, I suppose. That built-in defense mechanism in your brain has them hidden for now, but I think they'll come back to you eventually. As I stood in that field watching you plummet to the ground, I could see them all—in fact, it almost felt like I had been taking a ride with you as you flew the glider that morning."

Jack smiled, "Well, maybe in a way you were. I don't know if you were aware, but I hitched a ride with you during that loop you did over my head last year. The memories of that loop helped guide my way that morning."

"Yes, I suppose so. You know, it was only then when I was staring up at you in that field that I realized you had ridden with me previously."

Darrell paused and then said, "When I was with you and the others, I also saw the amazing experience you had flying through that auroral funnel, and now you have this gift—quite incredible. What an awesome power to be able to call us that morning. I'm just glad we were able to save you."

"It is incredible, isn't it? All because of that spectacular aurora borealis. I'm so grateful, Darrell, I just wish there was something I could do to show my appreciation."

"Nothing is needed. I guess the only thing I would say is, be happy you've done it, Jack. But for Helen's sake and the sake of your friends, I'd think twice before trying it again. I've decided never to loop again. God, it's fun, don't get me wrong, but then I start to think about Wendy and my darling little Josephine. How horrible it would be for them if something happened to me. I've had a few close calls myself doing those crazy maneuvers, and seeing what happened to your glider that morning and being there to share that tremendous impact made me realize I shouldn't be taking this stuff for granted. It could be me up there next time, and I know I don't have your amazing telepathic ability to save me."

Jack looked at Darrell with a thoughtful expression on his face and then nodded his head in agreement.

"So how have you been getting on after that hit, Darrell? I wanted to check in and see how you're faring," Jack asked.

"Oh, I'm fine, but that morning when I came back into my own body, I was knocked off my feet, even came close to falling in the river. That was a quite a wallop, and it stayed with me. I lay on the ground for quite some time since I really got the wind knocked out of me. When I finally called one of the chasers to come and fetch me, I let them do all the work. I was in no shape to be handling my glider at that point, but I made it back to my Jeep okay and just took it real easy on the drive back. Wendy was such a doll when I got home, and unloaded my glider and gear for me. I'm okay now, no worries."

"Well, that's good to hear," Jack replied. "You're right, Darrell, about the flying—that's a good piece of advice. No, I won't be doing any more loops or the like either, but once I find myself another glider, we can still fly together, can't we? It's one of the funnest things I do, and I don't want to lose my flying buddy."

"Of course, Jack, I love it too, but let's just keep it sane. We don't need to be doing crazy stuff to enjoy ourselves."

"You got that right," Jack replied. "It's such a great endeavor, we don't need to be scaring ourselves in the process. It really ruins the joy of it, doesn't it?"

"Yeah, it does," Darrell replied.

Jack could sense that Darrell wanted to get back to work on his glider, and he wanted to see if he could catch young Josh at his home before it got too late.

"Well, Darrell, I'll let you get back to work. I better get going and see if I can catch up with our young friend Josh."

"All right, well, thanks for coming by. We'll talk again soon. If you need some help finding another glider, just let me know."

"Sure thing, Darrell."

As Jack walked away, Darrell said, "Hey, Jack, I almost forgot, but congratulations."

"Congratulations for what?" Jack replied.

"For doing that beautiful loop in your glider. There aren't many people who can say they've done that, you know."

Jack smiled. "Thanks, man, I appreciate it."

★★★★★

Jack drove to the other side of town to Josh's house. Linda, his mother, answered the door.

"Jack, so great to see you! Well, this is quite unexpected. How have you been?"

"Just great, Linda. I was in the neighborhood, so I thought I'd swing by and say hi."

"Well, I wish you had called in advance—you could have joined us for dinner. We just finished eating, and these kids eat like crazy, I don't have any leftovers. Can I fix you a sandwich or something?"

"Oh, that's okay, Linda, I'm not too hungry right now, but thanks. How's Charlie doing? He must be out on the fishing boat this time of year."

Charlie, Linda's husband, was fishing out of Juneau, where the yield was typically greater in the summer.

"Oh, he's doing fine. Yeah, he's out on the hauler somewhere near Juneau. He'll be back early next week. He called a little while ago and said the catch so far has been great. He loves being out on the water, especially this time of year."

"Well, the weather has been great for fishing, hasn't it?" Jack said.

"It sure has. It's been so nice I might have to join Charlie on one of his trips, but then again, maybe not—that's too many smelly fish in one place for me."

Jack laughed. "Oh, come on, Linda, you'd love it. So how are the kids doing?"

"Oh, they're doing well. You know, what do you do with two teenagers? I just have to let them go and hope they come back in one piece, but ever since that trip to Denali, Josh has definitely been more of a homebody. I can't thank you and the others enough for what you did back then. You guys were incredible."

"Well, thanks, Linda, we were all so glad to help. Is Josh around? I wanted to see how he's doing."

"Oh sure, he's out back, probably working on his mountain bike or something. I'm going to take him and Linzey out Saturday for some mountain biking near Denali. I might even hop on a bike myself."

"Sounds like fun," Jack replied.

★★★★★

When Jack walked around to the back of the house, Josh was sitting in a porch chair, with his arms in his lap looking west toward the sunset. He didn't notice Jack until he was just a few feet away and greeted him.

"Josh, my man, how are you doing?"

It took a few moments for Josh to come out of his gaze and respond. "Oh, wow, Jack, wow, what a surprise. Great to see you, man. How you been?"

Josh got up out of the chair and shook Jack's hand.

"Oh, been doing well. I wanted to come by and say hi and see how you've been."

"Oh, I'm fine, you know, trying to enjoy the rest of the summer. I'll be back at school in just a few more weeks."

"Yeah, that's tough, isn't it, but once you're back, you'll get into the swing of things again."

"Yeah, I hope so. I've had a great summer, been doing lots of mountain biking, and I've helped Dad out on the fishing boat a few times. Take a seat, Jack; here you go."

Josh pulled up another chair from the table, and they both sat down.

"Pretty spectacular sunset, isn't it?" Josh asked as they both looked west toward the sun. The sky was a blazing blend of blue and light and dark orange, with a reddish haze that surrounded the sun. There were some scattered clouds in the sky near the horizon, and the orange light refracted off the edges of the clouds, making it appear as if their edges were on fire.

"Pretty amazing," Jack replied.

"So what brings you out this way, Jack?" Josh asked.

"Well, Josh, I wanted to thank you for helping me out that morning in Palmer after my glider collapsed. I wouldn't be here if not for all of you, and I wanted to make sure you're doing okay."

Josh's face lit up with a glow before he said anything.

"Wow, Jack, that was damn intense. I felt like I was back in Denali Park, terrified off my ass, sure that I was going to die in that frozen wilderness. Man, all those memories just bombarded my psyche. At first, I didn't know what was happening; I thought I was having a flashback or something."

"Pretty frightening, was it?" Jack replied.

"Yeah, it felt like a nightmare, like I was going through it all again, but after a few moments I realized it wasn't coming from me. Oh man, you were one frightened dude. When I stepped out into that field, I was already shivering with fear."

"Well, I don't remember any of it, but I must have been really scared. I was struggling with all my might to save myself, and this is why somehow I was able to reach out to all of you," Jack replied.

"Yeah, Jack, after you fell into the glider, you were spinning wildly, but it wasn't until your eye caught the ground and that fear filled your mind that you reached out to me and the others. It was powerful, really powerful, and it stopped me in my tracks. I was just getting up, but Mom told me to take the trash out and I was carting it out front—then bam, the next thing I know, I'm whisked off to Palmer, wondering what the heck was happening."

"Well, I don't know what to say, Josh, other than thank you."

Josh didn't say anything for a moment, but instead lowered his head and looked down at his hands before raising his eyes to Jack. "You saved my life, Jack," he said quietly. "I could never repay you for that; at least I thought I never could. It was a wonderful experience for me to save the life of the man who saved mine. I should be the one thanking you. I was just returning the favor."

"Well, I appreciate that, Josh, well said. So how are you feeling? I mean, from what I've been told, it was quite a jolt."

"It stung, man, it really stung. We all knew it was going to be bad and it was, but what else could we do? Watch you die as we stood there and watched? How horrible would that have been after what you did for me? It hurt, like one of those bad tumbles I've taken on my mountain bike, and I'm still a little achy here and there, but nothing serious. I'll get over it," Josh said, putting his hand in the air. Then he said thoughtfully, "You know that experience in Denali and in that field in Palmer taught me something."

"What's that, Josh?" Jack asked.

"Just to enjoy life. I've always been rushing around, carrying this pent-up anxiety that I'm not doing enough, that I'm not studying enough, that I need to push harder, work harder, ski faster, beat my friends at whatever we're doing. There's so much peer pressure out there, and if you aren't anxious about the fact you're not doing enough, then there's something wrong with you. It'll drive any teenager crazy, you know."

"Tell me about it, Josh, and it doesn't end when you get older either. There's always that pressure." Jack paused but then smiled and said, "You're right, you're absolutely right. We need to stop and smell the roses, take it all in, and enjoy it."

"You got it, Jack, like sitting back on Wednesday evening and watching the sunset," Josh said as he turned his head back toward the setting sun.

"Of course," Jack replied, remembering Josh's gaze when he first walked into the backyard. "Like watching a beautiful sunset on a warm Wednesday evening."

★★★★★

Jack tried to contact Sean McCree several times but kept getting the voice mail for his locomotive business. After four tries, he finally just left a message. He didn't have a personal phone number for Sean, so it was with a pleasant surprise that several days later, he found that Sean had tried to call him back, leaving a message on Jack's voice mail. After playing phone tag several more times, Jack was finally able to get Sean on the phone.

"Sean! I finally got hold of you! How are you doing, you old Scotsman?"

"Jack! Laddie, so nice to hear from you. I'm doing very well, very well indeed," Sean replied. "So how have you been? And how's that fine lady, my dear Helen, been doing?"

"I'm doing great, Sean, thanks. Helen is doing really well. She's been asking about you, and prodding me that we need to take another one of those train rides."

"Well, you're always welcome. The train departs every Tuesday at four o'clock sharp," Sean replied, laughing. "It would be wonderful to have you two back."

"We had a great time," Jack replied. "How have you been getting on with the business, by the way? I'm sure the train needed a few repairs after what happened on our way to Jasper this spring."

"Oh yes, the train did need some repairs, that it did. We did a major overhaul of the locomotive engine, but it was in quite good shape all things considered. It was only a few hundred hours away from the scheduled overhaul anyway. The brake rotors and pads all needed to be replaced, along with a few other related parts, and of course, we had some fixing up to do in the boxcar interiors, but all things considered, it wasn't too bad—all in a day's work, as the saying goes."

"Well, that's good to hear. How about yourself, Sean, have you still been able to operate the business?"

"Oh yes, we're doing fine, but we changed the duties around a bit, you know. I've known for quite some time that Jason, my apprentice, wanted to spend more time in the locomotive, but I was just being a selfish old fool thinking he needed more training. Deep down, it was just me who wanted to hold on to that job. He's quite remarkable, that young lad is; sometimes, I think he knows more about that train than I do. Nowadays he operates the train most of the time, and I help him when he needs me. It's quite nice actually; it allows me to spend more time attending to the guests. He didn't care much for that part of the job, but me, I fancy it—so much fun to meet all these fine folks on the train, each with their own unique stories to share."

"Well, Helen and I can attest to the fact that you're a wonderful host. I'm sure everyone who takes the train feels the same way. Have you been keeping on with your medication as well?"

"Oh yes, the medication, well, I've cut my dosage in half. After what happened that day when we almost lost the train, well, I've been back at the gym and have even picked up my old boxing gloves. There's a very nice boxing gym in Calgary, and I've been spending quite some time there now. Oh, I'm not as fast as I used to be, but I can still give these young lads a run for their money once I get them in the ring. They think I'm just an old man until I pop them in the head a few times and knock some sense into them."

Jack laughed. "I'm sure you carry quite a wallop."

"Well, yes, I suppose I do. I've taken up coaching in the gym as well, and after some prodding, I've become a trainer for a couple of talented boxers there. It's quite exciting, you know, going out to the arena, getting my boxers ready for their match, and then watching the action in the ring. Reminds me of my days back in Scotland when I was a young man doing it myself. These young kids, Jack, they've got the talent, but they need direction and guidance, and an old retired boxer like me fits that bill. Training these two lads has been quite a challenge, quite a challenge, but I love it."

Sean let out a heavy sigh, glad that he had reconnected with the sport he loved so much. After a brief pause, he said, "But look, Jack, enough of me talking about myself. I'm so glad you called because it's been on my mind to check in with you and see how you've been getting on since that fall in your glider. We did our best to save you from that mighty impact, and before I left that field, I gathered you were okay, but you never know what could happen down the road so it's good now to hear your voice."

"Well, Sean, I appreciate that. I really wanted to call and thank you for what you did. I would have been down for the count, down for the count permanently that is, if not for all of you, so thank you."

"You're welcome, you're most welcome, I'm so glad I was able to help. Listen, Jack, I never really knew what happened in that train as we barreled our way down toward Kinbasket Lake until you called me to that field in Palmer a few weeks ago. All along I thought I had just gotten lucky, that somehow I had gathered my wits and snapped myself out of unconsciousness long enough to save the train, but when I was standing in that field watching you fall from the sky, what really happened materialized in my mind.

"It was you, my dear chap, who saved us all. If not for you, I would have been lying on the floor of the locomotive as we careened off the tracks and down the cliff below. I should be thanking you for giving me the time to save the train and those onboard from certain destruction. I'm so sorry you had to suffer through that horrible jolt to your head. I know it gave Helen such a scare, and I regret that deeply—she's such a lovely lady. I know it caused her such distress. I'm so grateful for what you did, Jack, thank you so much."

"Well, Sean, that's very kind of you. No worries, my friend, I did what I had to do, and I'd do it again in a second. There wasn't any time for me to save the train myself. I didn't know if the entanglement would work, but I knew if there was anyone who could stop that train, it was you. I'm just so glad it worked out for both of us, that spring day outside of Jasper and that morning in the field in Palmer."

Jack paused and then asked, "So how are you getting on, Sean? I know it was quite a blow for all of you to take the impact of my body hitting the ground."

"Ah, I do appreciate you asking about my condition, yes, I do, but remember, laddy, I'm an old boxer. I've taken quite a few blows to my head and body over the years, more than I can even remember. What's one more blow when I've taken so many already? I'm fine, just fine, but that's very kind of you to ask. Listen, Jack, I don't mean to pry, but you know that dear lady Helen is very fond of you, very fond indeed."

"Well, yes, I suppose she is," Jack replied. "I'm very fond of her as well, Sean."

"Well, then, Jack, what's holding you back? Can't a whippersnapper like yourself take that final step?"

"Well, Sean, you know we're living together now, don't you?"

"Well, yes, I gathered that when we all were standing in that field together, but listen, Jack, my son lives with me, and when I was a young man, I used to live with my boxing buddies in a big old Scottish farmhouse we rented along with a few girls. Living with someone isn't quite the same as taking their hand in matrimony now, is it?"

"Well, I've thought about it, yes, I have, but the whole marriage thing has always been a bit of a roadblock for me. I just can't seem to get my hands around it. What's your story, Sean? Were you once married?"

"I still am, Jack. I've been married to the same lovely lady now for thirty-five years, and she's given me two beautiful children. My daughter has moved out now and lives in Vancouver, but my son, well, we just can't seem to get rid of him," Sean replied, laughing. "Listen, Jack, you give it some thought. That Helen, she's a lovely lady, but you know she can't wait forever; she's a beautiful gal, but she's not a young lady either. You see, when I was married, I was a wee twenty-three years of age and my lovely wife was just twenty-one, but Helen and yourself are getting a bit older in years. Her clock is ticking, as they say; she's waiting for you, lad. You think about it. I know you won't ever regret it, not with such a wonderful lady as she."

"Well, I do appreciate that, those kind words for Helen and the advice. I will definitely give it some thought. Thanks again, Sean, for all you've done. We'll talk again soon, what do you say, Sean?"

"My pleasure, Jack. Yes, let's talk again soon, yes, I'd enjoy that very much, my friend."

★★★★★

Jack tried to get hold of Dr. Weldon at home, but he did not pick up and finally Jack left a message. A few days went by but the doctor did not return his call, so Jack tried the university.

"Ah yes," the receptionist said over the phone, "Dr. Weldon said you might be calling and told me to give you this number in case you did. It is (406) 782-8745. I've heard Dr. Weldon talk fondly of you, Jack, so it's a pleasure to speak with you."

"Well, thanks very much, that's most kind," Jack replied. "Thanks for the number."

Jack tried the number, and a woman answered the phone.

"Well, hello," Jack said over the phone, "I'm trying to get hold of Dr. Weldon. Can he be reached at this number?"

"Oh yes, you mean Robert? Oh well, yes, he and Ted took the kids out sailing, but they should be back this evening. Can I ask who is calling?"

"It's Jack, I am a friend of Robert's. I was out visiting him in Bozeman not too long ago."

"Oh, Jack, yes, Robert has mentioned your name on quite a few occasions and said you might be calling. I know he's looking forward to speaking with you."

"Well, that's good. If you don't mind me asking, who am I speaking to?"

"Oh gosh, I'm sorry, I thought Robert had told you. I'm Sarah, Ted's wife. We live in Helena. Robert comes down each year and stays with us during the month of August."

"Oh yes, Robert has mentioned to me how he loves those little grandkids—what were their names again? Stacy, Phillip, and Sa—, Sa—, Samantha, isn't it?"

"Yes, that's it, that's quite good," Sarah replied. "I guess we're not the only ones Robert talks to about his grandchildren. He adores them. It's so nice to see them together this time of year, and it gives me a little break as well."

"Well, I can imagine," Jack replied. "Three young kids have got to keep you and Ted quite busy."

"Oh, it sure does, but we love it," Sarah replied. "Robert's so great with the children, but I think he spoils them a bit too much."

"Oh, what do you expect, Sarah? That's what granddads are for," Jack replied.

"Well, yes, I suppose so," she replied, giggling. "Listen, Jack, I'll tell Robert you called when he gets in. They should be back in a few hours. Nice to talk with you."

"Nice to talk with you too, Sarah. Take care."

*****

Dr. Weldon called Jack later that evening. "Jack, old boy, how are you? So nice to hear from you."

"Nice to hear from you as well, Robert," Jack replied.

"Listen, Jack, it's been a long day. We had a wonderful time with the children, but I'm quite worn-out. Can we talk tomorrow in the evening, say around eight o'clock my time?"

"Sure, Robert," Jack replied, "I'll give you a call then."

★★★★★

Jack called Dr. Weldon the following evening.

"Well, Jack, how are you?"

"Great, Robert, just great, and yourself?"

"Fine, Jack, I'm fine."

"How was the sailing, Robert? Sarah told me you and Ted took the grandchildren out sailing."

"It was wonderful, just wonderful. Ted has an eighteen-foot sailboat, and we went out to Lake Helena. Beautiful, beautiful lake. Sarah and I packed up a nice lunch for the kids, so after an hour of sailing, we put down the sail and floated out in the middle of the lake and had a nice late lunch. The kids loved it, even little Samantha—she's four now and we were a bit worried she might get sick, but I think that Stacy and Phillip's joy must have spilled over on her because she was all smiles the whole time. Phillip is old enough now where he can help out with the sailing duties, but Stacy and Samantha just enjoyed the ride. I watched over them closely, and we had them strapped in when Ted got the sailboat up to speed, but when we stopped, that brave old Phillip jumped in the water and Stacy wasn't far behind. Of course, I made sure they were wearing their life vests, and luckily Samantha was just content to sit on the boat and relax as Ted watched over the other two. These kids, they're so exuberant and adventurous. What a joy to be with them."

"Sounds like a great time," Jack replied, "Sarah tells me you spoil those kids a bit too much."

"Well, I guess I do," Robert replied, laughing. "But that's what granddads are for, isn't it, Jack?"

"That's funny, Robert, that's exactly what I said to Sarah when she told me the same thing. We must be on the same wavelength."

"Yes, indeed we are," Robert replied, chuckling, and then he asked, "So how are you getting on, Jack? That was quite a traumatic event we all experienced a few weeks ago in Palmer. How have you been since then—has everything been pretty normal?"

"Yes, in fact, I feel fine and quite normal, Robert, thanks to all of you. I don't know how to thank you. Your quick thinking and willingness to take my fall saved my life, and I appreciate that beyond words. Really the only injury I sustained was a few bruised ribs. I don't remember any of it, but from what I've been told, I bruised them when I fell into the glider in the air and buckled the frame. But how about yourself, Robert? I've been quite worried you might have hurt yourself during that moment of impact; I've been told it was quite a jolt."

"Yes, it sure was, Jack, quite a jolt, especially for an old man like me. It's a good thing I took up that brisk walking a few years ago. After my wife passed away, I was feeling depressed and a bit isolated, and a friend suggested I take up exercise to give me a fresh outlook and improve my health, and I've been at it ever since. Nothing like a brisk walk in the morning to start the day, and I've been pretty good at getting a walk in at least four times a week. Well, it's a good thing I've been at it, because my body was in fair enough shape to take that fall. It stung, Jack—don't get me wrong—but it didn't cause any permanent damage to this old frame of mine, not as far as I can tell. I did take a week off from walking just to let myself heal up, but I'm doing fine now. In fact, I took Sarah out for a nice walk this morning, and she was more exhausted than me by the time we finished."

"Well, that's great to hear, Robert, I'm so glad you're doing all right," Jack replied.

"I just hope you don't plan on doing anything like that again, Jack. I'm not sure this old body of mine can take another impact like that, and I'd sure prefer not to find out," Robert replied back, laughing.

"Don't worry, Robert. I've made a pact with myself and my friend Darrell that we won't be doing any more crazy maneuvers like that. So what happened up there, Robert? Can you explain it? What's your take on what happened, from a medical perspective?"

"Well, Jack, as I've said before, it's hard to put my finger on exactly the process that occurs inside your mind, and I can only begin to understand your telepathic powers—obviously they're quite incredible. I don't know if you remember, but moments before you called us to that field, you in fact had blacked out, but your telepathic power was still operating in full force, and I would speculate that it was so strong that it overwhelmed your thought processes and actually caused you to black out.

"You see, Jack, we have what are called somatic nerves, which control the voluntary cells that are under conscious control. These nerves are triggered, for instance, when you want to raise your hand. In contrast, the autonomic nerves control the involuntary motions of your body. These nerves keep check of your body continuously by maintaining temperature, composition of blood, heart rate, breathing, digestion, you get the picture. Even your body's reactions to stress, when your blood pressure, pulse rate, skin condition, and blood sugar become elevated, are controlled by the autonomic nerves. The somatic and autonomic systems work together—for example, skin exposed to cold air turns blue, this is autonomic. At the same time, impulses are sent to the brain for sensations of cold, and this is somatic.

"Autonomic functioning of the brain is controlled at the base of the brain primarily in the brain stem. The brain stem sits below the corpus callosum, the area of your brain that I saw distinctly light up when you exercised your telepathic powers, so it appears your powers extend into the brain stem, which is where our survival instinct is centralized. Next to the brain stem sits the cerebellum, which is connected to the brain stem through nerve fibers called pons. The cerebellum plays an important role in motor control, but in addition, though not as well understood, it is involved in emotional functions, such as regulating fear. Just before you passed out, you became quite frightened as your eyes caught the ground and you realized you were going to impact it at a great velocity. Do you remember that, Jack?"

"No, I don't, Robert. In fact, I don't remember any of the events that occurred that morning, other than chatting with Darrell on our way to the launch site," Jack replied.

"Well, that's understandable. Our brains have a way of blocking out traumatic events; it's a protection mechanism that prevents us from shocking our minds with those memories. You see, I would liken your reaction at that moment to the fight-or-flight response. Your mind becomes overwhelmed with fear, and the autonomic nervous system takes over. The heart pounds, the eyes dilate, your skin crawls, you develop tunnel vision, muscles tense, your blood is filled with adrenalin, all in preparation for a survival response.

"A classic example is a grazing zebra, calmly maintaining homeostasis. If the zebra sees a lion closing in for the kill, the stress response is activated. For the zebra to survive, his escape requires intense muscular effort supported by all of his body's systems. Another example is the documented case of a woman who miraculously lifted her car off the ground to prevent the car from crushing her child. It's a reaction in everyday life we think is impossible, but under the right circumstances can occur.

"Well, in your case, your mind responded in this way, switching into survival mode, and your telepathic powers overwhelmed your entire psyche, allowing your mind to open up a pathway to ours, screaming for help. Fear is an intense emotion. You experienced it yourself from young Josh when he was certain he was going to die, and that fear allowed you to open up a window to his mind. Well, your fear opened a pathway to all our minds, and in fact, called our bodies as well. What's interesting to me, though, is that even in your desperate time of need, you mind was still capable of being selective, only calling those you wanted to have help you, not necessarily calling everyone you had entangled with previously. This indicates to me your somatic and autonomic nervous systems were working in concert, and that even in your unconscious state, you were still able to direct your response in a controlled manner that allowed those you called to be there together to provide assistance. In fact, I find it quite amazing that you were able to reach the Samualson sisters, although it does appear they possess some of the same qualities and powers you have in your own mind."

"Yes, it appears they do, Robert. I talked to them just a few days ago, and they were relieved to know that they haven't been going crazy all these years, their telepathic powers were real and they weren't imagining those communications they've had with each other. With regards to being selective, well, I can see why my mind didn't want to pull my former girlfriend Sandy into that situation—she was the only one I left out. My life has moved on since her, and I suppose I didn't think it was appropriate to involve her, especially with Helen being there and all that. I'm just so amazed it all came together so quickly and that all of you were able to act on it."

"Yes, Jack, it was quite extraordinary," Robert replied. "I would have loved to have seen the images of your brain at work at that moment; it must have been incredibly dynamic. It's amazing, despite all the knowledge we've gathered over the centuries about the processes of the mind, there is still so little we know about it, and your mind and its ability is proof of that."

"But how did you know what to do, Robert? Helen and the others said you were the one who understood clearly what needed to be done, that you had to take my body," Jack asked.

"Well, Jack, I really didn't know, but I had a good hunch. I felt you drawing me in when I was standing in that field. Your mind was desperately trying to understand the situation, but our response needed to be coordinated. To put it another way, you needed collective cooperation from all of us to save you. We all saw you falling and we all wanted to help, but the others hadn't witnessed the processes inside your mind quite the way I had. None of us alone could have saved you, but collectively I knew there was a chance, knowing what I had seen when you visited me at the university. It required us to come together at the same moment, and once I realized it was our one chance to save you and called out to the others in the field that morning, it crystallized in all of us. The fragments of thoughts were there, but we bundled them together into a unified response. It was as if at that moment of impact, we were all standing there holding a fireman's catch net, you know, the ones they use to save people jumping from a burning building, but that catch net consisted of the fabric of our thoughts, and ultimately the fabric of our bodies."

"During those times of transformation, Doctor, what happens to you, I mean the real you, the one who was sitting at home in Montana before I called you to that field? I've always wondered about that," Jack asked.

"Well, that's a good question, and I really don't know, but our minds and bodies have a way of going into automatic pilot even when we think our conscious mind should be in control. Have you ever been driving, and then suddenly asked yourself what you have been doing for the last half hour? You can't recall any of it, but you know you must have been in control because you and your car are still in one piece and you're still driving down the road. Well, I believe this is akin to what happens during that time: our mind and body go into a type of automatic pilot, allowing us to be transformed to another place without due harm."

"Yes," Jack replied, "I can see that, no wonder, it's happened to me on quite a few occasions. I'll be flying along daydreaming in my plane, and next thing I know, I'm about to arrive at my destination."

"What's amazing to me, Jack, is the depth and breadth of your ability," Dr. Weldon continued. "You have the ability to simply read someone's mind, but you can also extend that to what another person is experiencing and thinking without interfering with them, as you did when you rode with Darrell during the loop he performed in his glider. These powers I can comprehend; in fact, during my experiments years ago, some of my finer subjects got quite good at those things. But there's an extra dimension to your ability that goes well beyond anything I've seen or can even begin to understand. You have the unique ability to extend your power to encompass the entire person, so that you are not just sharing thoughts, you're sharing and exchanging their brain patterns and then manifesting those impulses into your own body.

"You see, humans have a thing called mirror neurons. They are cells in the brain that fire not only when we perform a particular action, but also when we watch someone else perform the same action. Neuroscientists believe this 'mirroring' is the mechanism that allows us to 'read' the minds of others and empathize with them. It's how we 'feel' someone else's pain—or joy for that matter—how we discern a frown from a smile, a grimace from a grin. Well, those mirror neurons in your brain, I suspect, are 'supercharged' and possibly have spread to encompass your entire brain.

"In fact, since that episode in Palmer, I've been reading up on the latest research into the biological sciences and their application to extrasensory perception. There are theories now that quantum physics may play a part in the processes in our brain. Quantum mechanics holds that any given particle has a chance of being in a whole range of locations and, in a sense, occupies all those places at once. This leads to the possibility of influence at a distance, something called entanglement by physicists, although Einstein himself called it 'spooky action at a distance.' This, in turn, leads to a phenomenon of hopping across seemingly forbidden gaps called quantum tunneling. Well, you get the picture, that extrasensory perception is simply the process of entangled minds exercising quantum tunneling. Do I believe it? Well, I'm not so sure, but it does provide some interesting food for thought.

"How you saved that train from certain disaster by taking Sean McCree's pain could, for example, be a case of quantum tunneling, but what happened in that field a few weeks back, well, it showed that you can as well reverse that manifestation into someone else's body—with some cooperation, of course. Quite incredible, Jack, I'm quite amazed, and I would suspect there's more potential there, something you haven't even tapped into yet."

"You really think so, Robert?" Jack replied.

"Well, it's only speculation on my part, but after being there in that field and being a part of the effort to save your life, seeing it all work before us, well, I wouldn't be surprised. Just leave yourself open to the possibility."

"Well, Robert, I don't know what to say other than thank you. All of you, but you in particular, saved my life. I don't know how I can ever repay you for that," Jack replied.

Robert Weldon laughed a kind, pleasant laugh. "No worries, Jack, really I should be the one thanking you."

"Thanking me? For what, Robert?"

"Oh, I don't know, maybe for giving me some peace, some peace in my mind. You see, years ago when I made that decision to abandon my work in the study of ESP and the like, I was never quite certain I had made the right decision. Many of my colleagues told me I was giving up an opportunity of a lifetime, that it was foolish to abandon such promising work, even if it would have been used by the military initially for who knows what. We as scientists have a certain curiosity into the way nature works, and that curiosity, in many cases, leads eventually to the manipulation of nature, and that manipulation can lead to great advances in the fields of medicine and engineering. Look at the development of penicillin back in the 1920s; that discovery alone saved countless lives by minimizing infection, and really was the beginning of what we now call modern medicine. The development of the airplane is another classic example, allowing humans to traverse the globe, a feat thought impossible only a hundred and fifty years ago.

"But the manipulation of nature and the world around us can lead to horrible possibilities as well. The development of the hydrogen bomb is a classic example, giving man the ability to annihilate the human race and the earth as we know it, but there are many others. The development of genetic engineering opens up the world to incredible possibilities, such as the ability to produce food in unlimited quantities, but opens up a Pandora's box of sticky questions as well, especially when we apply its potential to genetically altering living creatures, including human beings. Many scientific discoveries, especially those in the twentieth century, cause us to question our conscience and ask ourselves if this is a route we really want to pursue.

"I was stuck in that dilemma back then, not knowing where my work would lead, but the military convinced me that I had to stop. I didn't want to be part of the world the military had envisioned for those ESP stimulants. Sometimes it is best to let it be and let nature work at its own pace. That pace may take a few years, or ten thousand years or perhaps even a billion years. You see, I had a pretty good idea of what the military was going to do with my work, especially if it could have been fully developed, and I didn't want anything to do with that. In the back of my mind, though, there was always the thought that I was giving up research that potentially could be used for something else, something more beneficial."

"Such as what, Robert?" Jack asked.

"Oh, I don't know. I suppose for something that every doctor, well, every human wishes for: to saves lives, to make the world a little bit better place to live. Maybe it could have been used by search and rescue teams to help find lost hikers, or surgeons who wanted to better understand the illness and pain their patients were feeling, or psychiatrists who were struggling with diagnosing and helping their clients. After seeing what you are capable of, Jack, I could even envision a whole new branch of medicine, one that could have allowed us to treat disease or ailments in an entirely new manner.

"You see, your entanglements have made me realize that these things are already starting to happen; nature isn't going to take millions of years to develop these kinds of capabilities in the human mind—we are already starting to see it happen today. We don't need to push that envelope through scientific manipulation. The mind and body have evolved to the point that these phenomena are within our grasp, and you are a stellar example of that. We as humans believe that we only have five fully developed senses, but there's nothing to say that we're not capable of more—and after being in that field with all those wonderful people, I know we are capable of more. It's just a matter of time now, Jack."

"I don't know what to say, Robert, but I can see your vision. I have these abilities that have developed inside of my mind, but I would not be able to exercise those powers without the cooperation of those around me. It's as if I've been given the ability to tap into a resource that is already buried in others' subconscious. It's there in its infancy, but it's dormant, or has only been accessed sporadically. Somehow I can tap into it, channel it, focus it, and then use it."

"Yes, Jack, that's it. Quite amazing, quite an amazing talent you've developed."

Dr. Weldon paused, searching for something else to say, and then said finally, "Well, Jack, I've said my peace, and I've gone on for quite some time now. Listen, it's been a real pleasure talking with you again. I'm so glad you called. Let's keep in touch regularly, what do you say?"

"Absolutely," Jack replied, "Thank you again, Robert, and thank you for your insight into my condition—it's been very enlightening. I really do appreciate the time you've taken to study it."

"You're welcome, Jack. Thank you as well, it's been quite a journey for me, both to study your new talent and to have been a part of it. Look forward to talking to you again soon."

"Look forward to talking to you as well. Take care, Robert."

Chapter 18

Later that year, in the fall, Helen and Jack were enjoying a quiet evening at Helen's home in Anchorage. It was a cold night, with clear skies with some scattered clouds. Jack had some catching up to do on his charter service and was inside at his computer, rummaging through his receipts and painstakingly plugging the numbers into an Excel spreadsheet in an attempt to balance the books to see how he had done that month. Helen was in the living room reading, but was beginning to get restless. She got up and walked into the study where Jack was working.

"Jack, darling, do you want to take a break? Maybe we could go out for a nice walk. It's chilly but it's clear; I think it would be fun."

"Oh, Helen, I really want to get this wrapped up," Jack replied. "You go ahead, darling, if you want. I'll feel better if I just get this stuff done and out of the way."

"All right, Jack, I know how that is. Well, see you in a bit," Helen replied.

"Have fun," Jack replied as he saved his spreadsheet again. The last thing he wanted to do was lose his changes and be forced to input the data again. Helen walked down the hall and put on her coat, then wrapped a scarf around her head and neck before heading outside.

★★★★★

Helen was gone for only ten minutes, but luckily Jack was able to finish up his work more quickly than expected. As Helen walked back inside, he was inputting the last few entries.

"Well, that was a short walk, Helen."

"Jack, you've got to see this," Helen replied. "How incredible and how beautiful. Come on, Jack, hurry, you don't want to miss it."

"What is it, Helen?" Jack asked.

"A picture tells a thousand words. Come on, see it for yourself," Helen replied. "No point in me describing it; just come outside with me."

Jack hastily input the last entry, saved the file, and shut down the computer.

"Well, it's got to be better than this damn bookkeeping, that's for sure," Jack said as he grabbed his parka and tossed a wool hat on his head.

"As soon as I stepped outside, it caught my eye," Helen said as they walked out the door. "I was out front looking up, trying to take it all in, but then someone called my name and I saw Sue from down the street waving at me. She was standing in her front yard with her kids and a few friends enjoying the view as well. I walked over and we visited, all the while taking in the panorama. She's so sweet and her kids are so much fun; they're just such a happy bunch. See it for yourself, Jack, isn't it beautiful? It's almost like you can reach out and touch it."

Helen walked out to the street ahead of Jack, but then turned around and looked up, waiting for him. Jack stepped out the door and was immediately treated to the most spectacular aurora borealis he had ever seen.

Before them, in the northwestern part of the sky, the night was ablaze with light, but it wasn't just a single color. Instead, there was a tapestry of different pigments of color, including violet, red, green, purple, blue, orange, and a tinge of yellow.

"Oh my!" Jack exclaimed. "Now that's quite a sight!"

The aurora had taken the shape of folded curtains across the sky. It extended from east to west, and the folds were so deep that the light from one tangled with light from the one next to it, creating a sparkling array of light that danced vertically at each fold line.

"Wow, that is incredible," Jack said, taking Helen's hand in his. "How beautiful."

Helen gently squeezed Jack's hand and smiled, then reached over and kissed his cheek. She snuggled up next to him, putting her arm around his waist. Jack, in return, put his arm around her shoulders and smiled. They stood there together, gathering in the sparkling display of light before them. After a few moments, Jack looked to his left, and the group gathered in Sue's front yard was still there. Jack waved at them playfully, and they returned his wave in kind.

"Come on, Helen, let's go for that walk," Jack said after a little while. "Maybe we'll get a different perspective on the aurora."

"A little walking will warm me up," Helen replied. "I'm getting a bit chilly."

They walked to the west along the neighborhood street until they reached an intersection and turned right onto a rural gravel road that took them out of the neighborhood.

"I've never seen anything quite like it, Jack, have you?" Helen asked as they walked at a leisurely pace enjoying themselves, all the while staring up at the sky.

"Not quite like this one," Jack responded. "There are just so many colors."

They walked for a few more minutes and then reached a clearing, giving them a full view of the aurora to the northwest. The field in front of them was covered with a light dusting of snow, and they stopped to take in the scenery.

"The Eskimos have a name for the aurora," Helen said, "They call it the Dance of the Spirits."

"Yes," Jack replied, "that captures the feeling quite well, doesn't it?"

There were a few scattered clouds in the sky, and as the clouds passed overhead, they interacted with the aurora, causing the light to shimmer and dance as the clouds moved in front of the aurora.

"Look, Jack, look at how it plays with those clouds," Helen said, pointing to her left. Colors of light were sparkling through the clouds, and they moved together in almost a wavelike form, shimmering in red, purple, and blue.

Jack's eyes were focused on the sky above, but then he slowly moved his gaze down to the field in front of them.

"Wow, look, Helen, see the snow," Jack replied, pointing his finger out to the field in front of them. The light shimmering through the clouds danced its way across the snow, causing the snow to sparkle and light up the field in a display of glittering colors.

"Come on, Jack, let's get closer," Helen said as she took Jack's hand. They made their way across the field, leaving their footprints in the snow. After they crossed fifty feet of the field, Helen stopped and said, "This is good, Jack, isn't it pretty?"

The auroral colors danced around them, and they both looked back up at the aurora now in full display. The colored, shimmering curtains of light flowed across the sky as they stood and watched. The curtains moved back and forth gently, slowly traversing their way across the sky from east to west. The snow below their feet danced with the red, green, purple, and blue of the aurora as the light played with the clouds above them.

"Look, Jack, there's even some yellow in the colors—it's almost like the colors of a rainbow."

Jack could spot glimpses of yellow popping out of the auroral display periodically when the aurora and the cloud interacted at just the right moment.

Jack put his arm around Helen's waist, and Helen wrapped her arm around his.

"It's so wonderful," Jack said, "and it's so wonderful to share this moment with you, Helen, darling."

"Oh, Jack, you're so sweet. It's so wonderful to be here with you, too," she replied as she laid her head against Jack's shoulder.

★★★★★

That night as Jack lay sleeping in bed with Helen at his side, he had a wonderfully, spectacular dream. The memories of the loop he had done that morning in Palmer came back to him, but in his dream, it wasn't a bright Alaskan summer morning. Instead, he was doing the loop on a cool summer night through the glimmering colors of the aurora borealis he had witnessed earlier that evening. He swooped down through the aurora and then effortlessly pulled his glider up and up, then slowly over until he was inverted. Then he arched the glider down through that amazing display of colors and completed his first loop—but the dream didn't end there. Instead, he guided the glider through another loop, and then a third, and then a fourth. As he descended down through the aurora at the end of the fourth loop, only a hundred feet above the ground, he heard someone call out his name. He looked down at the field below him.

The glimmering lights from the aurora lit up the field brilliantly, and he could see Helen waving at him with a bright, playful smile on her face, a glass of wine in her hand. Around her stood the entire gang from that morning in Palmer. There was Robert Weldon, and Scott and his mother Phyllis, and Sean McCree with Jack's beautiful black eagle perched upon his shoulder. Beside him stood the twin sisters, Kathy and Stephanie, and young Josh and George, and Darrell and Phil. All of them were gazing up at him, waving and carrying on almost as if they were having a party and Jack was the last guest to arrive. Jack waved back vivaciously and then banked the glider to the right and turned around, landing just a few yards from where they stood. He unhooked his harness, and as they gathered around him, he laughed and smiled as he high fived and hugged all of them, telling them they were the most fabulous people he'd ever met.

George handed him a glass of beer, and they toasted.

"Here's to Jack!" George shouted out, and they all raised their glasses in a toast.

"Here's to all of you, my dear friends!" Jack replied as the glasses clanged together in unison.

★★★★★

When Jack awoke, at first he wasn't sure where he was. First he thought he was flying his glider, enjoying his time in the air; then he was sure he was still in that clearing with Helen, staring up at that beautiful aurora borealis he'd witnessed earlier that night; and then a few moments later, he was certain he was at a fun, lively party enjoying himself with his friends. As his head cleared, he propped himself up on his elbows and looked around. Helen was there sleeping quietly by his side. He grabbed his pillow and rolled over on his side, smiling.

"Man, what an incredible dream," he said out loud. "What an incredible dream."

Chapter 19

The following year in April on a balmy fifty-degree Alaskan afternoon, Helen and Jack were married. They chose an outdoor setting in a beautiful clearing in Denali National Park at the foothills of Mount McKinley. It was a small wedding, attended by close friends and family. Jack's father came up from Oregon, and Helen's parents came down from Fairbanks.

George attended, as did Darrell, with his wife Wendy and daughter Josephine. Jack was happy to see Phyllis as well, in the bright, pleasant mood she was getting quite accustomed to being in nowadays. In fact, she brought her new boyfriend to the wedding, a man who had been coming into her store for years; they had finally made the connection.

For the wedding, Helen wore a tight-fitting single-piece white dress that hugged her trim body and exposed shoulders, showing her olive-colored, smooth skin. Her light brown hair was down and flowed gently over her neck and back. When Jack saw her, he was struck by her beauty and grace. They had been living together, yes, but on that day, it felt like Jack was meeting her again for the first time, when her elegance and poise had captured his attention and drawn him near.

"Doesn't she look splendid?" Jack heard a familiar voice say. "Just splendid."

Jack turned, and there was Sean McCree standing behind him as they waited for Helen to approach the altar.

"Sean, so great to see you, I'm so glad you made it."

"I'm so sorry we're a bit late, Jack; we made it just in time. Jack, have you noticed? I know you've been busy with the wedding, but look," Sean said as he pointed to a large oak tree that sat only twenty feet from them. "See him on the middle branch."

Jack looked up, and there sitting quietly on the branch, only fifteen feet above their heads, was the beautiful black eagle, sporting the familiar quarter-sized red spots on his tail.

"My old boy, there you are," Jack said in joy. After the eagle's wing had healed up and he was able to fly again, he had left Jack and Helen the previous December; Jack hadn't been sure he'd see the eagle again.

"Oh, it's okay," Helen had said to Jack after the bird had been gone for several months. "He's probably just migrated south for a while, looking for longer days and warmer weather. Don't fret, Jack, he'll be back."

Jack wasn't so sure, thinking the trauma of his broken wing had scared the eagle away. Jack waited months for him to return and was saddened each day when he looked for the bird but he wasn't there. When Jack finally saw him perched on the branch, he smiled and nodded his head, but the eagle didn't respond; he just kept his eyes focused ahead, seemingly oblivious to the people below.

Helen was approaching the altar, and Jack's mind shifted to her and the wedding party around him. Darrell stood next to him, happy and honored that Jack had asked him to be his best man. Helen's sister Margery was the bridesmaid and was all smiles in her pink and light blue dress.

As Helen approached, Jack was captured by her radiance and stunning beauty, but as they said their wedding vows, the one thing that stood out above all else was her happiness. Jack had never seen her quite so relaxed and happy as she was that day, and her happiness flowed through him, putting him at ease and into a joyful state of mind as they wed.

When Jack heard the priest say, "You may kiss the bride," he wrapped his arms around Helen and they embraced in a long kiss as those gathered for the wedding clapped and smiled. Jack and Helen walked hand in hand down the grass aisle as the wedding guests threw rice in the air and at their feet in celebration. They were halfway down the aisle when Jack and the others heard a loud screech. Jack and Helen turned and looked up to see that beautiful black eagle lift off from the oak tree branch, vigorously flapping his majestic wings as he lifted himself into the air.

"There he is," Helen said, squeezing Jack's hand, "I knew he'd come back to us. He missed you, Jack. I knew he wouldn't be away from you for too long."

The eagle climbed high into the sky until he was several hundred feet above the field, and then he turned and descended, gathering speed, with his wings tugged closely to his body. As he got close to the ground, he let out his wingtips to stabilize himself, then spread his wings fully and pulled up into a long, graceful arch, ascending just above the heads of the guests. He climbed, but as his airspeed bled off, he tucked his wings in and went into a series of barrel rolls, squawking playfully as he did. He turned himself upside down to complete the first half of his loop, and then descended again, spinning easily as he descended. He finally pulled out at the perfect moment to fly gracefully by just a few feet above Jack and Helen's heads, rocking his wings as he passed by.

"Isn't that amazing?" Darrell said, standing just a few feet from Jack and Helen. "Don't you wish you had that kind of talent, Jack? What a spectacular bird."

"Sure do, Darrell," Jack replied. "That's all him; all I can do is hope for a joyride on occasion."

The eagle climbed back high into the sky and then descended again, spiraling gracefully in circles with his wings spread wide. As he got closer to the ground, he tightened the spirals and tugged his wings closer to his body, picking up speed. He was moving so fast that Jack and Helen ducked their heads as he passed by, but the eagle was precise and flew just inches above them, squawking as he flew by.

"Wow, he was moving," Jack said.

"He must be happy to see you," Helen replied. "I think he's got a bit of your wild hair in him. What have you done to him, Jack?"

Jack laughed. "He's just having fun, darling. Come on; let's head over to the reception. The people are waiting."

The eagle climbed briskly back into the sky and then turned and made his way north toward Mount McKinley. As they walked to their cars, Darrell turned to see the eagle flying away.

"There he goes. Do you think we'll be seeing him again anytime soon, Jack?"

"You never know with those beautiful creatures, but yes, something tells me we'll be seeing him again soon."

★★★★★

"Well, congratulations, Jack," Phyllis said at the wedding reception. "I'm so happy for you. I'm sorry Scott couldn't make it, but he's off at some auto race far from California. I think it's a road racing track in Alabama or somewhere around there. He told me to give you his regards."

"Sounds like Scott," Jack replied, laughing. "Who knows where he'll be next, but it sure sounds like he's enjoying himself."

"That he is, Jack, that he is."

Phil had made the trek from California and had a broad, welcoming smile on his face when Jack greeted him.

"You picked a fine, lovely lady for this affair, Jack. So great to see you, and congratulations," he said as they shook hands. Jack put his other hand warmly on Phil's shoulder.

"Great to see you, Phil, thanks for coming. How's the family doing?"

"They're doing great, just great. Christine's so busy with the little one; I'm sorry she couldn't make it, but she's very happy for you."

"How's your other daughter dealing with being a big sister now?" Jack asked.

"Oh, she loves it. Even though she's just ten, her maternal instincts are in full bloom. She loves holding and taking care of the baby; it's quite cute to see them together. I don't think we'll need to hire a babysitter when the little baby gets older, Daina loves baby Olivia so much."

Josh was there as well and brought his parents, Linda and Charlie.

"Jack, my man!" Josh exclaimed. "Great to see you've finally gotten hitched."

"Josh, great to see you. So how are things? You're graduating next month, aren't you?" Jack asked.

"That I am, that I am. High school is history in just five more weeks."

"So what are your plans after that, Josh? Are you heading off to college?"

"Well, no, not exactly," Josh replied as he looked at his parents with a whimsical smile on his face. "I've been accepted at the University of Anchorage, but not for next year—it's actually the year after that. I'm on a leave of absence, as they say."

"Really? Well, that's a bit different," Jack replied. "That's nice they'll let you do that. So what's in store for next year?"

"This may sound funky, Jack, but I'm going to bike across the country, taking odd jobs as I need to to get by, but travel and see North America. I've never spent any time outside of Alaska, so here's my opportunity."

"On a bicycle—are you kidding?"

"No kidding, Jack, I have it all planned out. I'll have two saddlebags and a tent on my back, and I know practically every campground in North America now. I've been studying up on the whole operation. I'm leaving in June, just a few weeks after graduation."

"This son of ours," his father, Charlie, interjected, "well, he's quite a free spirit, isn't he?"

"That he is," Jack replied. "What an adventure, Josh. I hitchhiked my way around the country the summer I graduated from high school with a close friend, and it was a bit crazy, but we had a blast. You'll have the trip of a lifetime. If I wasn't just married, I'd be tempted to join you," Jack said, laughing. "You take care of yourself, Josh, and you better be checking in with your mother regularly, let her know how you're doing."

"Oh, he will be, I'll make certain of that," Linda said. "We're going to pay for his cell phone bill each month, so there are no excuses."

"Aye, Mom, the point it to get away from home and see the world," Josh replied.

"You can see the world, Josh, but you can share that world with your lovely parents," Jack said.

"That's right, Josh," Charlie said. "We want to live vicariously through you, hear about your adventures, and of course, it will calm our nerves to hear your voice and know that you're doing okay."

"Yeah, yeah, I know," Josh replied. "Of course, Mom and Dad, I'll be checking in, let you know where I'm at and what's next on the agenda."

*****

A few minutes later as Jack went to get a glass of champagne, he ran into Sean McCree.

"Jack, my boy, well, congratulations. I'm so sorry we arrived late and I didn't get a chance to introduce you to my lovely wife. Jack, this is Josephine."

"It's a pleasure to meet you, Josephine," Jack replied.

"Lovely to meet you as well, Jack. Sean speaks of you very fondly."

"Well, Jack," Sean said, "I'm so happy to see you've finally taken that giant leap into matrimony. You won't regret it, my young fellow. Helen is a lovely, lovely lady."

"Well, thanks for the kind words and encouragement, Sean," Jack replied. "Our conversation awhile back really got me thinking, and next thing you know, voila, here we are."

Sean laughed and then looked to his left as Helen approached them.

"Well, here comes the lovely lady now," Sean said. "Helen, my dear, so lovely to see you again. You look splendid, absolutely splendid."

"Sean McCree," Helen exclaimed, "it really is you. Some of the other guests told me you were here. So great to see you."

Helen put her arms around Sean, and they embraced in a warm hug.

"Helen, let me introduce you to my wife, Josephine."

"Well, hi, Josephine," Helen replied. "So nice to meet you, and thank you so much for coming."

"Our pleasure, Helen," Josephine replied in her thick Scottish accent. "This is my first time to Alaska. Such a beautiful place, and you picked such a fine day for an outdoor wedding."

"Yes, it was simply lovely," Sean continued. "Helen, what a joy to see you and Jack again. You two make such a wonderful couple, but I have a feeling Jack's going to need to stay on his toes to keep up with you."

Helen wrapped her arm around Jack's arm as both laughed. "Oh, I think he can manage, Sean, but just in case I need someone to whip him into shape, I've got your phone number."

★★★★★

Later, after Jack and Helen cut the wedding cake, Jack's father congratulated his son.

"I'm so proud of you, Jack, but I wish you had found this lovely lady earlier," Jack's father said, winking at Helen, who was standing by Jack's side. "Your wonderful mother would have loved to have been alive to see this moment."

Jack hugged his father. "Thank you for coming, Dad. I know it's hard for you to travel nowadays; we really do appreciate it. I know what you mean, it would have been lovely to see Mother here on this day. She's in our thoughts."

"I wouldn't have missed it for the world, Jack. A bad leg wasn't going to stop me from seeing my only son get married, especially to such a lovely lady as Lady Helen here."

Something caught Jack's attention over his father's shoulder, and Jack gently put his hand on his Dad's shoulder, motioning him.

"Dad, come on, I'd like to introduce you to a good friend of mine. There he is getting a piece of cake. Come on, let's go by and say hi."

Jack, his father, and Helen walked over to the wedding cake. Robert Weldon was there, leisurely eating a slice by himself, caught up in his own thoughts.

"Robert, so great to see you; I missed you at the wedding," Jack said, a broad smile on his face as he stretched out his hand.

"There you are, Jack. Well, congratulations, and congratulations to you as well, Helen. I was there, but didn't get a chance to say hi before the wedding vows. That was a lovely setting out there—what a great spot. McKinley was so majestic in the background, and those beautiful, blooming trees were simply wonderful. Well done, you two, just fabulous."

"We're so glad you enjoyed it, Dr. Weldon," Helen replied. "It's so nice for you to come all the way from Montana."

"My pleasure. I've really enjoyed my trip out here; it's been quite spectacular."

"Robert, I'd like to introduce you to my dad," Jack said. "Dad, this is Robert Weldon."

"Well, hi, Dad," Robert replied, shaking his hand.

They all giggled.

"That's my son, Jack, for you. To him, I'm either Dad or Daddy, nothing else," Jack's father said. "My real name is Quincy, and it's a pleasure to meet you, Dr. Weldon."

"Please, just call me Robert. It's a pleasure to meet you as well, Quincy. If I recall, Jack told me you were quite a piano player in your day, isn't that right?"

"Well, I could play a fair tune when I was younger, I suppose, but that was ages ago."

"A fair tune," Robert replied, "well, don't be bashful. Jack tells me you were one of the finest players on the West Coast."

"Well, I could carry a song when I wanted to," Quincy replied. "Jack tells me you still practice medicine part-time. If you're anything close to my age, well, you must really love your work."

"Well, yes, I suppose I do," Robert replied, "yes, I really do love the study of medicine. So what kind of music do you play?" Robert asked as he looked over Quincy's shoulder. "Look, there's a piano over there. You know, I can play a few notes on a good day. What do you say we give it a try?"

"Well, sure, why not?" Quincy replied. Off they went chatting to each other as if they were good friends who hadn't seen each other for years.

"Isn't that wonderful, Jack?" Helen said as they walked away. "They hit it off quite well, didn't they?"

"They sure did," Jack replied. "They sure did."

★★★★★

At the end of the reception, Helen was egged on by her sisters to do the bouquet toss.

"Oh, come on, Helen, go for it. It's a tradition; it will be fun," her sister Margery said.

"Oh, I guess so, I just feel so silly," she replied.

One of her other sisters grabbed the bouquet from the wedding table and handed it to Helen with a big smile on her face.

"Come on, girls," Margery yelled out. "Gather 'round, it's time for the lovely bride to toss the bouquet!"

The ten single ladies at the reception gathered behind Helen as she stepped up onto the raised platform where the wedding cake was located. The other quests gathered around as well, and as Helen turned her back toward the group of women on the floor, George, who was now standing next to Jack, started to clap his hands, and others joined in as well until there was a rhythmic pulse of clapping hands that filled the reception hall.

"Here you go, girls," Helen yelled out as she tossed the bouquet high in the air. The bouquet flew over the heads of the girls in the front, but the four toward the back jumped together in unison trying to grab it. A tall brunette came up with the bouquet, grabbing it as she screamed out in glee.

George and Jack were standing just a few feet behind her. As she turned around waving the bouquet to the people gathered around them with a big smile on her face, George said, "Well, that was quite a catch, my young lady, well done! You've got quite a set of hands."

"Well, thank you," she replied, smiling even more brightly as the other girls gathered around her, giggling and carrying on.

"Well, there you go, George," Jack whispered. "She's cute and single, too, looks like a prospect to me."

George just smiled and turned to Jack, then winked before heading over to the reception table to grab another drink. A half hour later, as Jack and Helen prepared to leave for their honeymoon, Jack caught sight of George by the wedding cake chatting away with that tall brunette. George was smiling as if he had just told a good joke, and the tall brunette was giggling loudly, with her head down, her hand on George's shoulder as if she were trying to catch her breath between giggles, and leaning on George for support.

"There you go, buddy," Jack whispered under his breath. "Just keep her laughing, George, she'll be the one."

"What did you say?" Helen asked as they left the reception hall.

"Oh, nothing, sweetheart, come on, let's hurry, we don't want to miss our plane flight," Jack replied, taking Helen's hand in his as they walked outside. They made their way to Helen's car and drove to the airport, with tied coffee cans dragging behind their bumper and scribbled "Just Married" logos on the rear and side windows.

"Your sisters really went to town, didn't they?" Jack said, laughing, as they drove to Anchorage airport.

"They sure did," Helen replied, giggling. "But I have a feeling they got help from some of the boys."

★★★★★

For their honeymoon, Helen and Jack vacationed in New Mexico. Their flight landed in Santa Fe, and as soon as the plane touched down, Helen was on her cell phone calling Kathy Logan.

"Kathy, so great to hear your voice, we just landed. Stephanie's there as well? Well, fantastic! We're going to rent a car and then we'll come by. Give us about an hour or two. Yes, I've got the directions. So looking forward to seeing you."

★★★★★

Jack and Helen drove to Kathy's house located in the outskirts of Santa Fe. Her house was a classic deco southwestern one-story home, with cactus growing in the front yard and artwork decorating her front porch.

"Helen, darling, so wonderful to see you," Kathy exclaimed when she opened the front door. She gave Helen a warm hug and said, "You look wonderful."

"Well, thanks so much, great to see you as well, Kathy," Helen replied, smiling.

"Come on in. Stephanie's in the back with my husband. You can put your things in the bedroom down the hall. Jack, well, how are you doing? Did you two find the place all right?"

"I'm doing great," Jack replied. "No problems finding your place, and what a pretty drive. The desert is quite beautiful."

"Yes, we really love it," Kathy said. "I suppose you don't find cactus growing in Alaska, do you? It's quite different, isn't it?"

★★★★★

Stephanie was sitting in a lawn chair by the pool when they walked out back, while Kathy's husband was wading in the pool cooling off. When Stephanie saw Helen, she jumped up and walked over to her, giving her a huge hug.

"Helen, darling, how are you? So nice of you to join us to start your honeymoon. It's wonderful to see you," she said.

"You girls are just fantastic, so nice to see you as well," Helen replied. "I'm so glad you invited us to stay."

"Well, you look great, that's for sure. Jack, how are you doing?"

"I'm great, just great. It was so nice of you and Kathy to invite us."

Kathy's husband got out of the water and wrapped a towel around his torso.

"Hi, Jack, Helen, I'm Alan, it's a pleasure to meet you. Can I get you something to drink, beer, wine?"

"Well, come to think of it, a beer would be nice," Jack replied.

"Wine sounds great to me. Thanks so much," Helen said.

"Beer and wine right up," Alan replied. "Jack, light, dark, any preference?"

"Well, if you have a dark microbrew, that would be nice."

"How about a Sierra Nevada Pale Ale?"

"Perfect."

"And you, Helen, red, white? We've got both."

"Do you have any white zinfandel?" Helen asked.

"Sure do, coming right up," Alan replied as he walked inside.

"So where are the kids, Kathy?" Helen asked as Kathy walked out back, now wearing a pink bathing suit.

"Oh, they're in Spring Camp, hiking in the Sangre de Cristo Mountains. They're staying near Taos in a little town called Mars. We dropped them off yesterday. They love it, and we get a few days to relax without them," she said, smiling.

"Well, you must miss them," Helen said.

"Well, I guess, but they're getting older now—Sue's fifteen and Jasper's thirteen—and they're getting to that age where they don't like hanging out with us as much. When they were younger, I wouldn't miss a day with them, they were so wonderful, but now, well, you know," she said as she casually threw her hand in the air and took a sip of her wine.

Alan walked back outside with two beers in his hand and a glass of wine for Helen.

"Here you go, newlyweds, enjoy. Jack, care to join me in the pool."

"Well, sure, why not?" Jack replied, taking a gulp of beer before walking inside to get his swimsuit on.

That afternoon, the girls gabbed away as Jack and Alan enjoyed the water, drank their beers, and talked. It was a pleasant eighty degrees in Santa Fe, a perfect way for Jack and Helen to spend their first full day together as a married couple.

The next morning, Helen, Jack, Kathy, and Stephanie went shopping for arts and crafts in Santa Fe. Helen picked up several items for their home in Alaska and had them sent back to Anchorage for pickup. Jack bought a framed poster of a desert scene taken in the foothills outside of Santa Fe for his house in Fairbanks.

"Do you like it, Helen? Tell me the truth," he asked Helen after he picked it out.

"Lovely, Jack, lovely. Maybe beautiful is a better word, but I like it," she replied.

"Really? You know I can read your mind and really find out what you think," Jack said, winking at her.

"Come on, Jack," she replied, smiling. "I really do love it; just get it."

★★★★★

That night they were pleasantly surprised to find that Kathy and Alan were amateur astronomers and owned a large home-built telescope.

"Oh, when the kids were younger, they loved it," Kathy said when she showed it to them. "All four of us pitched in to build it. It took almost nine months from scratch until it was operational, and setting up the optics was a bear—now that's a delicate operation. We used to take it over to the science museum downtown for their astronomy night. Jasper would set it up on Jupiter or Venus or on some distant galaxy, and before you know it, he'd have ten people waiting in line to get a view."

Kathy took out a rag and dusted off the eyepiece with some cleaner before saying, "Come on, let's take it out back. It's quite powerful for a home-built telescope. The stars that make up Ursa Minor and Ursa Major are especially brilliant this time of year. Let's see how they look under the telescope."

Jack helped Alan carry the seven-foot-long telescope into the backyard. They set it up on the edge of the patio, twenty feet from the pool, in an open area. It took Kathy fifteen minutes to get it operational.

"Here you go, Helen. How about a nice shot of one of the stars that make up Ursa Minor, what do you think?" she said, gesturing Helen to take a look.

Helen bent over and fit her eye into the eyepiece.

"Wow, that is beautiful. I didn't realize there were so many stars there; it's almost like a star cluster. Jack, take a look. She's got it focused on the northwestmost star of Ursa Minor, but there's more than one star there."

"Look at that, wow!" Jack said as he moved his eye up to the telescope. "You know, this time of year in Alaska, you can't even see Ursa Minor, but you know, I don't believe I've ever seen a close-up quite like this of any of those stars, not even at those astronomy gatherings I attended in Fairbanks."

"You know, that's how Jack and I met, Kathy," Helen quipped. "I was minding my own business trying to take in all those lovely heavenly bodies, when along comes Jack to turn my world upside down and inside out."

"He sure did, didn't he?" Kathy replied, laughing. "But you're all the better for it, aren't you?"

"Of course you are!" Jack said quickly before Helen had time to reply.

Helen clenched her fist and hit Jack lightly on the shoulder before putting her arm around his waist and leaning her head against his shoulder.

"Well, yes, I sure am, you silly fool," she replied.

★★★★★

The next morning, Jack and Helen bid farewell to Kathy, Alan, and Stephanie and headed south to Roswell, New Mexico. They had heard so many tales of the UFO crash that supposedly had occurred there in the late 1940s, so they were curious to see what they would find. The tale was like folklore—unidentified alien debris found by a farmhand one morning on a ranch some thirty miles north of Roswell, reported as a recovered "flying disc" by the Roswell Army Air Field office the next day, but later described as a radar-tracking balloon by the same field office. Eventually there were claims by those who helped recover the debris that the military had covered up the discovery of a crashed alien spacecraft, and the stories took off from there. Others came forward saying they had spotted the craft, describing the debris found as "nothing made on this earth," and later there were accounts that alien autopsies were carried out at the Roswell Army base. At one point, there were claims of a huge military operation dedicated to recovering alien crafts and aliens themselves at as many as eleven crash sites, and the story was made juicier by accounts of alleged witness intimidation by a group called the "Majestic 12." There was also the 1995 video, one that Jack and Helen used to laugh about, called the *Alien Autopsy*, which showed doctors performing an autopsy on one of the aliens that had been recovered from the crash—or so the story goes. Years later, in 2006, a comedy film *Alien Autopsy* was released, a spoof of the original video.

The UFO sighting and tales were eventually dismissed by the

government as an overblown case of UFO hysteria fueled by fanatics, but there were those who claimed the mystery surrounding the crash was never adequately explained.

To Jack and Helen, it was all folly; and as they drove past Corona, a town, in fact, closer to the original crash site than Roswell, Jack and Helen talked about the crash.

"What's more likely?" Helen asked. "A crashed weather balloon used by the military to detect sound waves generated by Soviet atomic bomb tests, or an alien ship carrying cute little aliens with oversized heads and short, stubby little bodies? Those poor little guys can't steer their craft right, and before you know it, they leave a big skid mark in the desert."

"A weather balloon with a flying saucer attached—I've never heard of such a thing. That sounds like a cover-up to me. I'm going with the cute little aliens," Jack responded, a smile across his lips.

When they got into Roswell, they visited the International UFO museum downtown. There they saw recreated fragments of the craft constructed from eyewitness accounts of the actual wreckage, and saw UFO wax figures reconstructed from those that were shown in the *Alien Autopsy*.

"There are my cute little aliens!" Helen exclaimed when she saw them. "Come on, Jack, you've got to take a picture of me with them."

Helen stooped down next to one of the figures and put her arm around the alien as Jack snapped away. There was a small movie theater in the museum as well, and Jack and Helen sat through the one-hour presentation. First the movie described the whole incident from start to finish and then went into the mystery surrounding the events the day of the crash and the weeks and months that followed. Toward the end of the movie, prominent witnesses were interviewed, including Major Jesse Marcel, who was involved in the original recovery of the debris in 1947, and Glenn Dennis, a mortician who claimed alien autopsies were carried out at the Roswell base.

Helen sat in silence, amused by the whole spectacle, but when she saw clips of the movie the *Alien Autopsy* showing an alien corpse lying on a table being sliced into by the morticians, she frowned and whispered, "Ah, my cute cuddly little alien, why can't they just leave you alone?"

When she heard Jesse Marcel claim that he had found debris as "nothing made of this earth" while at the same time describing the material as tinfoil, balsa wood, rubber, and sticks, she couldn't help herself and started to giggle. She took Jack's arm, leaning her head onto his shoulder, and covered her mouth as she giggled, trying not to disturb the others in the audience, but she was having a hard time controlling her laughter.

"Isn't that funny?" she finally whispered in Jack's ear, but when she looked at Jack, he had a stone-cold stare on his face. His expression was deathly serious as he studied the men's faces intensely as they recounted their stories.

"Jack, are you okay?" she asked, but Jack didn't respond, and they sat together in silence until the movie ended.

When they walked out of the theater, Jack took Helen's hand and said, "Come on, Helen, let's get out of here."

★★★★★

They drove northwest into Arizona and headed toward Meteor Crater in the northern part of the state. On their way, Helen pulled out some information she had gathered on the crater and read to Jack as he drove.

"Okay, Jack, Meteor Crater is a meteorite impact crater located about forty miles east of Flagstaff. It's about seven-tenths of a mile in diameter, 570 feet deep, and surrounded by a rim that rises 150 feet above the desert plains. The meteor that created the crater some fifty thousand years ago was about 150 feet across at the time of impact and weighed—wow, get this—it weighed three hundred thousand tons, made up of mainly iron ore. Well, look at that, that's interesting—you being a pilot, you'd like this tidbit. In 1964, a pair of pilots in a Cessna 150 flew low over the crater, but on crossing the rim, could not maintain level flight. The pilot attempted to build up speed by circling in the crater to climb over the rim, but during the attempt, the aircraft stalled and crashed. Luckily both pilots survived, although their injuries were serious, and a small portion of the wreckage was not removed from the crash site and remains visible today."

"Sounds like they descended into the crater flying close to the crater floor, thinking they could just climb out later," Jack replied. "It's a common mistake: a pilot gets stuck in a mountain valley, and he can't gain enough elevation to climb over the mountains and doesn't have enough room to turn around. So he stalls the plane trying, usually in a steep turn."

"Well, yes, that makes sense, doesn't it?" Helen replied.

Helen could tell Jack didn't feel like talking. He was pleasant but a bit distant, and Helen herself was feeling tired, so she napped off and on during the rest of the eight-hour drive.

They didn't arrive at the crater until 7:30 p.m. Jack paid the fee at the visitor center and didn't wake Helen up until he was parked, the parking lot being only a few hundred yards from the crater rim.

"Helen, darling, wake up, we're here, sweetheart. Come on, sunset over the crater should be pretty neat."

"What time is it?" Helen replied as she opened her eyes and yawned. "Gosh, I must have been asleep for a while."

"It's 7:30, probably a half hour before sunset. Are you feeling okay, Helen?"

"I feel a lot better after that nap," Helen replied. "I'm going to hit the ladies room, then let's go take a look."

★★★★★

The crater was more rugged and moonlike than anything they had seen in Alaska.

"Has a certain rugged beauty about it, doesn't it?" Jack said as they stood at the top of the rim and looked down into the crater. Being near sunset, sunlight still hit the eastern wall of the crater, but the crater itself was dark, although they could see the bottom quite clearly with its raised center.

"Desolate beauty, I think, is a good description," Helen replied as she sat down on the desert floor. "Look at the walls of the crater—they look like they're rusting."

"Yes, the limestone and sandstone take on that color in this desert heat, kind of an ugly off-reddish, brownish tint," Jack replied, sitting down next to her.

They sat in silence along the wide rim holding hands as the sun set over the crater and darkness began to fall. Finally Jack stood up and helped Helen to her feet.

"Tell me something, Jack," Helen said as she stood up.

"What's that, Helen?"

"Those folks back in Roswell in the movie theater. It seemed like that bothered you. I know you've had some amazing experiences reading others' minds. What was the deal back there? Were those men interviewed telling the truth about that alien ship and those autopsies, or was it just an eloquent prank, just some big fabricated hoax that we can all giggle about?"

Jack stared out at the crater in front of him and didn't say anything for a few moments. Finally he said, "They spoke the truth," as a wise smile crossed his face and his eyes brightened.

Helen looked at him with shock on her face, but after a few seconds, the shock turned into a cracking smile.

"You little twerp, Jack, I'm going to get you for this," she said as she playfully wrapped her arms around Jack and tackled him, pushing them both down on the desert floor as Jack laughed loudly.

*****

They left Meteor Crater after sunset and drove to Williams, a quiet town an hour south of the Grand Canyon. The next morning, they grabbed breakfast at a nice cafe in the center of town before driving up to the Grand Canyon. The landscape on the way was nothing special, just flat desert populated with some desert brush and cactus.

"I hope the Grand Canyon is prettier than this," Helen remarked. "It's pretty barren out here."

Even when they arrived at the park, the landscape hadn't changed much. They parked the car and walked the quarter mile to the canyon edge, but when they got there, Helen exclaimed, "Oh my god, how beautiful! Seeing it in real life is a thousand times better than pictures. Wow!"

"That's amazing!" Jack replied. "Simply amazing! Come on, Helen, let's check out the trails, see if we can hike down into the canyon. No better way to see the canyon than to be right in the middle of it."

"Sure, let's go for it," Helen responded.

★★★★★

Over the next three days, they hiked the trails in the canyon. The first day they did an easy hike along a route called the Rim Trail, which took them out over some spectacular backdrops overlooking the southern part of the canyon. That night they stayed again in Williams but got up early, arriving at the park at 8:00 a.m. with camping gear in tow. That day, they took their time hiking down to the river along the Bright Angel Trail, located in the middle of the park. At a leisurely pace, it took them the best part of the day, but they arrived at the river by 5:00 p.m., giving them ample time to enjoy the water and scenery of the gorge.

When they arrived at the river, Helen turned around and looked back toward the cliffs of the canyon. "Well, look at that, I can't believe how far they're away from us. We really hiked quite a ways."

"We sure did, didn't we?" Jack replied. "My legs are sure telling me all about it; they're sore and I'm beat. What do you say we set up the tent and crash?"

"Sure," Helen replied, "but let's find a nice spot by the river so we can relax and enjoy the scenery."

"Well, okay, but let's find something fast."

★★★★★

Fifteen minutes later, Helen picked out a spot that overlooked the river and they set up the tent for the night. Jack relaxed his legs while Helen built a small fire and did the cooking.

"Nothing like canned soup and lima beans for a honeymoon dinner, hey, Jack?" Helen said as she served the food.

Jack frowned.

"Oh, I'm just joking, Jack, I'm having a wonderful time. This is such a beautiful place, and there's no one in the world I'd rather be spending it with."

"Oh, Helen, you're so sweet," Jack replied as he took a spoonful of the soup bean mix. "Wow, that's quite good; you're quite a chef."

"Thanks, Jack," Helen replied, smiling.

They stayed up and watched the sun set over the canyon before climbing into their tent for a good night's rest.

★★★★★

The next morning, they got up early and started the long hike back up the trail. The good night's rest refreshed Jack, and he found himself having to stop often so Helen could catch up.

"Those legs of yours must have really gotten a kick from my lima bean concoction. I can't keep up with you, Jack," Helen said after several hours of hiking after she had caught her breath.

"I feel good," Jack replied. "This dry air really seems to help, and the raw beauty all around us really gets me going. How are you doing, Helen?"

"I'll survive," she replied, "but I'm not exactly chipper. You go ahead if you want. I'll be up at the top of the canyon sooner or later."

"Come on, darling, I'm in no rush. Let's just take our time; we have all day."

Jack patiently waited for Helen when he got too far ahead. He'd stop and turn around and just enjoy the scenery and let Helen catch up. Jack made a point of chitchatting with her so she'd stop and rest, and then once she was ready to hike some more, he'd let her go ahead of him so that he could hike briskly until he caught up with her. It was seven that evening when they made it back to the car. They had booked the room another night in Williams, so Jack drove the hour south back into town as Helen rested. They showered and then went to bed early that night, but Jack spent an hour channel surfing as Helen slept by his side.

★★★★★

The next morning they got up late and ate breakfast at another cafe in town, but they had had their fill of the Grand Canyon and headed north into Utah to Zion National Park. It was close to a six-hour drive from Williams, but they made their way around the eastern side of the Grand Canyon, where traffic was relatively light. They arrived at Zion at six o'clock that evening and checked into their room at a nice cozy hotel located just a few hundred yards from the park entrance.

"What do you say, Helen? Want to check out the park before the sun goes down? I've heard the sunsets are really pretty over the mountains," Jack asked once they had set their luggage down in the room.

"Well, I'm getting a bit hungry, but I guess I can wait for an hour or so. Let's check it out," Helen replied.

They drove down the winding park road, passing some of the better-known sites of Zion, including Angel's Landing, the entrance to the Virgin River Trail, and the Mountain of the Sun.

"Gosh, how pretty and how cozy," Helen remarked as they got out of the car by the Mountain of the Sun. "It's a lot different than the Grand Canyon, isn't it?"

"It's not so grandiose like the Grand Canyon, but the mountains are more picturesque and there's a lot more plant life here," Jack replied. "Look! The sun is just beginning to set over the mountains—pretty cool."

They sat on the hood of their rental car and watched the sun set. The mountains created a unique contrast of light and dark across the landscape, bathing the leafy trees on both sides of the road with a radiant glow until the mountain shadows darkened the whole area. When the sun had set fully, they got back in the car and drove to the hotel for dinner, eating in the restaurant that was run by the cheerful hotel owner.

★★★★★

The next morning, they started early and visited the park in earnest. They made the short but difficult hike up to Angel's Landing, a flat, large plateau of rock set at the top of a medium-sized mountain in the middle of the park. From there, they could see the expanse of the park, and after looking at the sights, they decided their next stop would be the Virgin River Trail.

The trail was an easy hike through a valley carved out between two mountain ridges. A small river worked its way along the valley, and Helen and Jack took a slow, leisurely walk along the trail. The ridges that rose up on either side of the river were spectacular, and the animal and plant life in the valley really caught their attention.

"Look, Jack, that's a western bluebird!" Helen exclaimed, pointing toward a small tree that sat on the side of the trail. "You won't see any of those in Alaska. They only live in the southwestern continental United States, and even then, they're rare to spot."

"Look at the little fella. He looks so happy going about his business for the day. He's got quite a collage of colors, doesn't he? Let's see, his wings and top side are blue, but his chest and stomach are orange and he's got white below his belly," Jack replied.

"Yep, but look on that other branch. See the other bluebird? Now that's a mountain bluebird. You don't see any orange on her chest; she's almost all blue, but there's a shade of white below her belly. At first glance, they look the same until you look at their undersides," Helen said. "The mountain bluebirds will fly south to the mountains of Venezuela in the winter, and I bet ya they arrived from there just a short while ago."

"You sure do know a lot about birds, Helen. Let me see if I can stump you."

Jack looked up and to his right, scanning the sharp cliff just a few yards off the trail.

"Look, how about that bird with the nest on that ledge maybe twenty feet above us? See him? The one with the black head and brown wings, with the white belly."

"I see him. Well, let me take a look," Helen replied as she rummaged through her bird book. "Here it is. I think that's a cliff swallow. Pretty fitting name, I'd say; that little nest looks pretty precarious sitting there. It says the cliff swallow is a wilderness bird, but can sometimes be found in urban settings, where they will nest under bridges and overpasses."

"That's quite good, Helen, well done," Jack replied.

They went on that way as they strolled along the scenic path, enjoying their time in Zion's wilderness paradise.

By sunset, they had seen most of Zion. Since they had already checked out of the hotel that morning, they decided to make their way to Colorado. Jack drove until eleven and then found a small motel on the Utah-Colorado border, where they stayed for the night. The next morning they drove to Telluride, Colorado, and checked into a nice hotel with an outside Jacuzzi and heated pool. It was colder now as they gained elevation, so it was quite pleasant to swim in the heated pool. They both relaxed, enjoying their time, first swimming leisurely in the pool and then getting in the Jacuzzi and chatting.

"Can I get you anything, darling?" Jack asked as they sat together in the Jacuzzi.

"Well, a glass of wine would be nice ... let's see, how about Chablis," Helen replied.

"Chablis right up."

Jack returned from the bar a few minutes later with a molded plastic beer mug in his hand.

"I didn't ask for a beer, Jack—what's the deal?" Helen said, surprised.

"But I did," and then Jack brought his other arm around and showed Helen her wine in a molded plastic wineglass. "That's quite smart. These plastic glasses are quite pretty, but you can still take them in the Jacuzzi with you, don't you think, Helen?"

"Beautiful. Now just hand that Chablis here, Jack. I love the taste of wine on my lips."

Helen took a sip and sighed, "Now, that's nice, wine in a Jacuzzi, what a combination."

★★★★★

The next morning they drove to Mount Wilson, one of the highest peaks in Colorado at 14,246 feet. The road took them to 9000 feet, and they hiked for a few hours until they reached 10,500 feet. There was a beautiful overlook that gave them a spectacular view of an adjacent mountain only a mile distant, with a dense pine forest that filled the steep terrain and valley between. They decided to stop there and eat the lunches they had packed that morning. There was a sign there as well, and Jack read it to Helen.

"Any hiking beyond this point requires ice shoes and ice picks. It is strongly recommended that tie-in ropes be used on the more difficult terrain ahead. Please climb safely."

"Well, it looks like this is the end of the road for us, Helen. Beautiful landscape, but it's sure getting cold up here and I didn't bring my ice pick."

"Fine with me," Helen replied. "The hiking kept me warm, but now that we're just standing here, it sure is cold. Let's head back down."

They both turned and looked up at the top of the mountain, admiring its rugged beauty before heading down the trail. They hiked briskly, and an hour later they were back at the car.

"What do you say we take a pleasant stroll through downtown Telluride? I've heard it's quite a nice town," Jack said as they drove down the steep road that led them down the mountain.

"Sounds wonderful, Jack, but let's go to the hotel and shower first. Don't they have a film festival each year there? I remember the woman at the hotel mentioning it to me, but I think it's not until September over Labor Day weekend. If nothing else, we can grab a bite to eat there. This landscape is beautiful, but I think I've had enough of this hiking for a while."

"Yeah, some flat terrain would be nice. I've heard about the film festival. I think they have nine or ten movie theaters open in town during the long weekend, and they even set up an open-air cinema in the downtown park. A customer of mine told me about it awhile back—people just go from venue to venue, or just sit on the grass and watch the movies in the park."

"Sounds nice, doesn't it?" Helen replied. "So relaxing."

"It sure does. Also, if you're lucky, you might even run into the Sundance Kid."

"Who?" Helen asked.

"The Sundance Kid, you know, Robert Redford. He helped to organize and popularize the film festival."

Helen smiled. "The Sundance Kid, of course, from *Butch Cassidy and the Sundance Kid*. That was always one of my favorite Westerns. We should set up a film festival in Alaska. What do you say, Jack? We could have it during peak summer, when it stays light all day long and all the tourists are around. The films could come on at midnight when it's dusk, and when the movies are over, it would be bright again."

"Wouldn't that be fun?" Jack replied.

★★★★★

After cleaning up at the hotel, they strolled the streets of Telluride arm in arm, enjoying the time together. They found a small Italian restaurant and had dinner there.

"What do you say we check out the park, Helen? It's only a ten-minute walk from here according to the waiter," Jack said as they were getting ready to leave.

"That would be nice. Let's pick up some evening coffee on the way at one of those little coffee shops we walked by—they looked so lovely."

★★★★★

After getting their coffee, they walked over to the park. It was a small park but quite beautiful, with mountains directly behind the pavilion that faced away from town. There was also a large playground next to the pavilion where a few children were playing.

"That must be where they set up the screen for the film festival," Jack said, pointing to the pavilion.

Helen didn't respond. She was looking at a woman playing with her two young children in the playground. The woman had her young daughter in her arms and was gently tossing her up and down as the small child giggled.

"Up and down you go, Tracy, my sweetheart, up and down you go," the woman repeated sweetly, a loving smile on her face.

Her young son was climbing the ladder to the top of a slide. When he got to the top of the slide, he hesitated. She said, "Come on, Daniel, slide down; it will be fun."

The boy waited a few more seconds but then slid down the slide, giggling with glee, arriving at the woman's feet. She said playfully, "Bravo, bravo."

Helen stood there watching them, a gentle smile on her face. After checking out the pavilion a bit more closely, Jack walked over to her.

"Isn't that so cute? They're having so much fun together," Jack commented.

"They sure are, aren't they? Such a lovely scene," Helen replied.

They stood there together watching the young family play for a few more moments before turning to leave. When they turned to leave, Helen was still smiling, but Jack caught a glimpse of sadness in her eyes. He'd seen that look before, but he didn't say anything. Instead, he took her hand and squeezed it.

"I'm having such a wonderful time, Helen. It's so lovely being here with you. I love you so much."

"Oh, Jack, you're so sweet. I love you, too. I'm having a wonderful time as well."

"What do you say we make it back to the hotel, darling? A good beer in that Jacuzzi would be a great way to end such a lovely day."

"Sounds good to me, but I'll stick with the wine," Helen replied.

★★★★★

The next morning they left Telluride and drove to the Great Sand Dunes National Park near Alamosa, a four-hour drive through the mountains from Telluride. At two that afternoon, they arrived at the park. There was a large parking lot and a visitor's center. When they drove up, they saw twenty or so people gathered around the center or making their way down the park trail toward the dunes. The dunes were off in the distance, situated on a plateau that was surrounded by mountains on three sides.

"How odd," Helen said as they got out of the car. "Sand dunes in Colorado, I've never heard of such a thing."

"It does seem a little strange. But look, you can see their silhouette from here, near the base of those mountains," Jack replied, pointing to the mountains to their left.

They walked a good half mile up the park trail until they were standing at the base of the dramatic dunes. There was a placard at the end of the trail that gave a description of the sand dunes, and they stopped to read it.

"Well, look at that. They say they are the tallest sand dunes in North America at 750 feet," Jack said. "I would have never guessed the tallest in North America would be located in Colorado."

"Yeah, me neither. I always think of sand dunes as being near the ocean, with the waves crashing in the background and people frolicking around in their bathing suits on the beach having fun," Helen replied.

Jack laughed. "Well, we're here—might as well check them out."

They both took off their shoes and climbed the sand dune in front of them. The sand was smooth and warm but difficult to climb, and after twenty minutes they were both exhausted.

"I bet we're not even a quarter of the way to the top," Helen remarked. "But that sand through my toes sure does feel good."

"Yeah, it's pretty tough going," Jack replied, "but at least you can do *this* when you're tired of climbing." Jack proceeded to jump backward onto the sand below him and roll down the dune for a good twenty feet.

"Now that was fun. Give it a try, Helen," Jack yelled back at her once he had stopped rolling.

"Oh, Jack, you crazy fool." Helen hesitated but then said, "Well, okay."

She flung herself onto the sand, tucked her arms in, and rolled down the sand until she was next to Jack.

"Isn't this fun?" Jack said as he wrapped his arms around Helen and gave her a kiss.

"Sure, lots of fun," Helen replied. "I always like getting sand in my ears and up my nose."

They climbed for another thirty minutes, but finally Helen said, "Jack, can we turn back now? I'm exhausted, and we won't get to the top and back until after dark. I've seen what I want to see."

"Sure, Helen," Jack replied. "These dunes are pretty huge but are nothing compared to the mountains. I know what you mean; I've seen enough as well. Let's head back down."

★★★★★

They drove to Trinidad, Colorado, that evening and spent the night at a well-kept hotel by the Interstate that led to Denver to the north and Santa Fe to the south. The next morning, they drove back to Santa Fe to catch their afternoon flight back to Alaska. They had spent over a week on the road, so they were both a bit exhausted and glad to be on a plane back home.

As the plane finished its climb, a young child in the row in front of them starting crying. They both could hear the child's mother consoling her young daughter.

"Oh, my sweet darling, it's okay. Give your momma a big hug now. That's it, give me a big warm hug. Everything's just fine. You're just tired, my sweetheart, you're just tired."

They could see the mother reach around the child and pull her close as her daughter rubbed up against her shoulder.

"That's it, darling, just snuggle up against my shoulder. You just get some rest now."

The child was still crying, but her mother starting singing, "Sleepyhead, close your eyes; Mother's right here beside you. I'll protect you from harm, you will wake in my arms, guardian angels are near, so sleep with no fear. Guardian angels are near, so sleep with no fear ..." as she gently rocked her daughter back and forth. After a few minutes, the child started to calm down, but the mother kept singing to her quietly.

Jack leaned over to Helen and said, "Isn't that cute? She has a lovely voice, doesn't she?"

Helen just smiled, squeezed Jack's hand, and then looked out the window. A few minutes later, the seat belt sign went off, and Jack got up to go to the bathroom. When he came back, the child was asleep. Her mother had raised the armrest between them and had loosened her daughter's seat belt so that the young child was cuddled up on the mother's lap, with her legs resting in her own seat.

When Jack sat back down, he tapped Helen's arm. "Look, Helen, the child is fast asleep, and cuddled up in her mother's arm—very sweet."

Helen got up and went to the bathroom. On her way back, she caught the mother's eye and gave her a big warm smile. When she sat back down, she whispered to Jack, "That's lovely, simply lovely."

★★★★★

Jack was tired from all the traveling, and after eating dinner, he napped in his seat. He napped for almost an hour, but then he opened his eyes slowly and looked out the plane window as the sun set on the left side of the plane. Helen was looking out the window as well, and the expression on Helen's face caught his attention. That same sadness he had seen in the park in Telluride was there again in her eyes, but she wasn't smiling this time as she had been in the park. Her face was solemn and sad, and Jack couldn't help but feel a twinge of pain seeing her look out the window in that way. He closed his eyes slowly, hoping that Helen hadn't noticed his stare.

Later, once the sun had set and Helen had fallen asleep, Jack took her hand gently.

"It's okay, sweet Helen, everything will be okay," he whispered to her quietly.

Chapter 20

A month later, on a Saturday night, after Helen had fallen asleep next to Jack in their bedroom at Helen's house, Jack got out of bed once he was sure she was in a deep sleep. He walked into the garage, sat down on a workbench, and closed his eyes. He sat there concentrating for several minutes, not sure if he could find what he was searching for, but then the feelings entered his abdomen and he winced in pain.

"Oh man, I wasn't expecting that much pain. This isn't natural; I can't hold this type of feeling," he said out loud as he grabbed his lower pelvis and fell to the floor. He lay there shaking, trying to grasp the feelings and hold them there with the power of his thought. The pain was a sharp, stabbing pain at first, but then dissipated into more of an aching, throbbing, dull pain in his lower torso. He lay there still for five minutes until he was confident he could hold it within him for a little while longer.

"I can't stay here; I can't be this close to her," he said as he got up slowly. He walked gingerly into the kitchen and scribbled a note, then stuck it on the refrigerator door.

"Helen, emergency came up, had to fly to Fairbanks, back in a few days, Jack."

Helen usually slept in Sunday morning, so Jack was hoping she wouldn't know when he left. He climbed in his truck and drove to Birchwood airport, where he kept his plane. He had to focus his mind without distraction, and flying was the best way to do it. Flying for him was second nature and only took up a portion of his concentration, allowing him to focus the rest of his attention on the pain in his lower pelvis.

"Where's he going?" the night watchman asked as he saw Jack's plane take off and climb into the night sky. "What the heck? It's eleven thirty at night. Why would anyone be flying out of here at eleven thirty at night?"

★★★★★

It took Jack just under an hour and a half to reach Fairbanks at full throttle. As he flew farther from Anchorage, he could contain the pain more easily, but he still had to concentrate to keep it within him. He made sure his cell phone was turned off in case Helen tried to call the next morning. He landed at a quarter till two, parked his plane outside the small hangar, and made the walk to his house, which was only a quarter mile away. By the time he made it to bed, he was exhausted and fell asleep quickly. He slept in late, not waking until noon the next day.

When he regained consciousness, he was startled, not sure where he was for a brief moment, but the dull pain in his lower abdomen was still there, and he quickly remembered the events of the previous night. He took a deep breath and exhaled in relief. His subconscious mind had taken over as he slept, maintaining the tender grip he had on that debilitating ailment. He got out of bed, brushed his teeth, and showered. As he showered, he rubbed his hands across his lower pelvis on either side of his belly button. Where he pressed, the pain became sharper and more intense. The area was tender but the pain was bearable, and he didn't see any bruising or blood.

He got out of the shower, dressed, and made himself some coffee. He needed to remain calm and sedentary to keep hold of it as long as he could. It was pleasant and calm outside, so he took his coffee and laptop computer outside onto the back porch. As he stepped onto the porch, the eagle was there waiting for him. He was perched on top of the feeder with his eyes fixed on Jack.

"My old friend, thank you for coming," Jack said as he set his coffee down on the long, rectangular patio table and opened up his laptop.

A few minutes later, once Jack was settled in, the eagle lifted off silently and flew over to Jack. He landed delicately on the edge of the old wooden table just a few feet from Jack, squawking lightly as he landed.

"Don't worry, old boy," Jack said as he reached out and stroked the eagle's head and back. "I'm okay, I'm okay but I do appreciate the concern. So wonderful to see you as well. After you left us at the wedding, I didn't think I'd see you again for a while."

The eagle tilted his head and squawked pleasantly, then ruffled his feathers and stood up straight.

Jack went inside and grabbed a wicker laundry basket from the washroom. His next-door neighbor had two horses in the backyard, and Jack took a few handfuls of hay from the yard and laid it in the basket.

"There you go, old boy. I stole a little hay from John, my neighbor, but he's a good friend; he won't mind. It's not the prettiest nest in the world, but it will do," he said as he put the basket down on the other side of the table opposite his coffee.

The eagle lifted his wings and settled down into the makeshift nest, making himself comfortable.

Jack sat back down and sipped his coffee, then logged onto his computer's Internet and did some more research on Helen's condition.

★★★★★

It had started happening when Helen was only thirty-three. As her menstrual cycle approached, she would experience painful cramping, headaches, and even muscle aches so severe that she couldn't function normally at times. For the first year, the pain was cyclical. Some months it was tolerable, but others it was painful and intense. At first she thought it was just a normal part of her menstrual cycle, that she was just experiencing excessive cramping and the symptoms that went with it. She talked to her sisters about it, and they all said they had experienced cramping off and on during their periods.

"Try some Ibuprofen, Helen," her younger sister Margery had told her. "Aleve works well, but Advil or Motrin will do also—they're all made of basically the same stuff. Don't worry, Helen, it's not uncommon to have bad cramping. I'm just surprised you've never had cramping like that before."

Helen tried the Aleve, then the Advil and Motrin, then any other over-the-counter drug that she could get her hands on to relieve the pain. At first they worked, but progressively over the following year, the cramping and pain got worse.

At first the pain began just a few days before her period started in earnest, but over that two-year period, the pain started earlier and earlier, to the point where she would experience pain for almost two weeks leading up to her period. She knew it wasn't normal, that she needed to talk to her gynecologist about it, but she dreaded what he might tell her and kept putting it off.

During her yearly checkup, she told the doctor that she was cramping during her periods and that she was taking over-the-counter medication.

"Is that working for you, Helen?" her gynecologist asked.

"Yeah, pretty much. It's not much fun, but I think I can manage," Helen replied.

"Well, okay," the old doctor replied, "but if it gets worse, you let me know, okay?"

Helen nodded her head yes in reply.

Then one day at the hospital, one month before her thirty-fifth birthday, the pain became so unbearable she had to leave work. As she made her way out of the elevator, the pain became so intense she stopped at the water fountain to get a drink and gather herself; but when she bent down to sip the water, she collapsed and lost consciousness.

"Helen! Oh my god!" the receptionist in the lobby screamed out when she saw Helen's body lying motionless on the floor. "Call a doctor, someone, please call a doctor! Helen's collapsed—please help us!"

They took Helen to the emergency room, put her on an IV, and gave her a heavy pain medication. When she awoke that evening, her sister Margery was by her side, as was one of the emergency-room doctors. The doctor asked her to describe what had happened. As Helen recounted the painful cramping she had been experiencing off and on for almost two years, the doctor nodded her head, listening quietly.

"All right, Helen," the doctor replied, "we're going to move you to the women's ward and then take you in for some tests. I'm going to talk to your gynecologist; he needs to be involved. Just rest now; we'll be with you in a little while."

"Oh, Helen, I'm so frightened," Margery said once the doctor left the room. "I'm so sorry, Helen. I should have told you to see your doctor when you told me all about this—I had no idea. I'm so sorry."

Helen simply took her hand and smiled. "Thank you for coming, Margery, thanks so much."

★★★★★

The next morning Helen was moved to the women's ward, and her gynecologist, Dr. Borrows, was there an hour later.

"Well, Helen, you had quite a day yesterday. How are you feeling?" he asked with a pleasant smile.

"I'm pretty doped up, Doctor, but I still feel quite queasy in my pelvis. What's happened to me?"

"Well, Helen, it's hard to say at this point, but the tests will tell us a lot. They should be here to pick you up any moment now, and I'll be with you the whole time. Don't worry; we'll know more shortly."

They used pelvic ultrasound to examine Helen, playing close attention to the areas where she felt the most pain, and then moved her to a special room with a more sophisticated scanning system.

"This is called a magnetic resonance imaging machine. To get a better image, we're going to inject some dye into your bloodstream," the medical technician told her. "You'll feel a warm sensation in your arm and abdomen as the dye enters, and then we'll put you under the scanner. It will only take a few minutes."

After that, they took her back to her room.

"We'll take a look at these images," Dr. Borrows told her. "They will give us a good idea of what's going on and what further tests we need to run. We'll get back with you in a little while."

★★★★★

A few hours later, the doctor returned. "Well, Helen, we've taken a look at the images, and we've found some abnormalities."

"Abnormalities? What does that mean?" Helen asked.

"I'm sorry, Helen, but it appears you are suffering from a severe case of endometriosis. I don't know if you have heard of this disease, but it is a chronic disease that affects your menstrual cycle. Endometriosis causes tissue to grow outside of your uterus, tissue very similar to the tissue you grow inside your uterus during a normal menstrual cycle. Unfortunately, this unwanted tissue can grow on your ovaries, fallopian tubes, and uterine wall. This tissue builds up during menstruation and begins to shed—only the blood has no way of exiting the body, as opposed to your normal menstrual tissue, which sheds through the uterus. As a result, this discarded blood and tissue remains in the body, causing pain, scar tissue, and organ adhesions. This is what you have been experiencing."

Helen lay there for a moment gathering her thoughts and then asked, "Is it curable, Doctor? What's going to happen next?"

"Well, Helen, it is a chronic disease, so hopefully we can treat it, but it depends on its severity. I'd like to do another procedure called a laparoscopy. The procedure involves making a small incision near your navel and inserting a laparoscope, a long, thin, lighted instrument, into your abdomen. We'll fill your abdomen with carbon dioxide to make it easier to see your reproductive organs. With this procedure, we should be able to see the extent of the endometriosis clearly. We will also remove part of the endometriotic lesions and examine them under a microscope to confirm the disease and see if there are any additional concerns as well."

A hundred thoughts were running through Helen's mind, but all she could say was, "Oh my god, Doctor, it sounds quite serious. Do I have to do this? Can't you just treat it now?"

"Without more information, I don't know how it should be treated,"

Dr. Borrows replied. "I would strongly recommend it. I believe your disease is limited to the endometriosis, but it could be a part of an even more serious condition."

"Such as?" Helen asked.

"I would prefer not to speculate, but instead would recommend we do the laparoscopy right away."

"Well, okay, Doctor, when do we get started?"

"We'll set up to do it tomorrow morning. Just rest now, Helen. With the painkillers you're on, you should be fine until then. Is your sister coming back this evening for a visit?"

"Yes, she said she'd drop by after work, along with Jennifer, one of my other sisters. Thanks for asking. We'll see you tomorrow then?"

"See you in the morning, Helen," Dr. Borrows replied.

★★★★★

The next morning they performed the laparoscopy after Helen was given anesthesia and went to sleep. Dr. Borrows came into her room that afternoon.

"Well, Helen, we've confirmed the endometriosis, and as I suspected, it is widespread. I'm going to put you on some Gn-RH agonists. They are a synthetic form of ganadatropin-releasing hormone. This hormone helps to control estrogen production in the body, which contributes to the growth of endometrial tissue. We'll see how you do with that treatment and do a follow-on checkup in three weeks. By then I will have the report back on the lesions we removed this morning. If anything comes up before then, I will let you know. We'll start you on the Gn-RH today, so you should be able to leave the hospital tomorrow. How are you feeling, by the way?"

"I'm a little frightened, Doctor, but the painkillers seem to be working, and my period started just a few hours ago," Helen replied.

"Good, Helen, very good. I'll get the nurses set up with the Gn-RH, and they'll tell you what to do and precautions you need to be aware of when taking the drug. I'll see you in a few weeks. Just take it easy between now and then and get lots of rest."

★★★★★

Three weeks later, Helen went in for her checkup.

"Helen, how have you been feeling?" Dr. Borrows asked when he came into the exam room where Helen was waiting.

"I feel tired and drowsy," Helen replied. "The pain in my pelvis isn't as severe as it was, but it's still noticeable. How did the tests turn out, Doctor?"

"Well, the good news is we didn't discover any other disease, cancers and the like, in your uterus or appendages. After further study, though, your endometriosis is more severe than we originally thought. It's widespread and covers your ovaries and uterus and is especially pronounced in and around your fallopian tubes."

"Well, I guess you could have given me worse news, Doctor, but that doesn't sound very comforting," Helen replied.

"Helen, I'm sorry, but it looks like your fallopian tubes have been permanently damaged. I'm actually quite concerned about your health, because that damage could lead to excessive internal bleeding, which can be quite dangerous, especially coupled with any infections the endometriosis may produce."

"Wouldn't the Gn-RH drug take care of that, Doctor?" Helen asked. "I've only been on it for three weeks now."

"It is possible, Helen, but with these severe cases, sometimes it has only a minor effect. It does lessen the pain you feel, but does little more beyond that. It is hard to say at this point. I suggest we meet again in six weeks, and I'd like to perform another laparoscopy at that time and compare the findings to those we did three weeks ago. That will give us a good indication as to the effectiveness of the Gn-RH, and we can see if the discomfort in your pelvis has diminished."

★★★★★

Six weeks later, Helen had her second laparoscopy, and the following day she met with Dr. Borrows.

"Well, Helen, how have you been feeling? Is the medication decreasing the pain you have been experiencing?" Dr. Borrows asked.

"To some extent, yes, Doctor, but it's still there. Before, the pain was intense sometimes, but I haven't experienced any of that. It is more of a dull pain that stays with me for a week leading up to my period. It is tolerable, I suppose. So how did the results of the tests come out, Doctor?"

"Well, Helen, we don't see much difference. I believe the drug dulls the pain for you, but for these severe and intractable cases, it does very little to stop these unwanted growths."

"Well, there must be some other options, Doctor," Helen replied. "What else can we do?"

"Well, we can continue on with this treatment, but there is some risk there, as I mentioned before. The treatment you are on is the most promising from a pharmaceutical standpoint. The next option beyond that would require surgery, but that route can be quite difficult. Many times when you attempt to remove these growths, it can damage the organs you are trying to protect and can lead to unwanted internal complications. Another option, which I believe is the safest route, is a hysterectomy."

"A hysterectomy, my god!" Helen replied in a surprised tone. She then closed her eyes and took a deep breath before asking, "You mean, you just remove my entire uterus, including the fallopian tubes and ovaries?"

"That's correct, Helen. I know it sounds like a drastic step, but endometriosis can lead to more serious conditions if the pharmaceutical treatments are ineffective. With a hysterectomy, we remove all the growths, along with your reproductive organs. We would then put you on hormone medication since the surgery does change your hormone levels considerably."

"I couldn't have any children, isn't that right, Doctor?" Helen asked, looking directly at him.

"No, Helen, you would no longer be capable of having children, and I know that makes it a very difficult decision. I need to tell you, though, as I mentioned before, the endometriosis has damaged and scarred your fallopian tubes and covers both ovaries. In order to become pregnant, an egg is released from your ovaries, and using a set of fingerlike projections, one of your fallopian tubes grabs hold of the egg. Once the egg has been pushed inside the tube, tiny hairs help to sweep the egg along the three- to four-inch length of the tube, until it reaches the uterus. Once in the uterus, the egg is then available to be fertilized."

Dr. Borrows paused and looked down briefly before continuing, "The problem, Helen, is both of your fallopian tubes have been clogged and severely damaged by the endometriosis. Thus the egg has no way of traveling to the uterus, rendering you infertile. I'm not sure what to say concerning your ovaries, but the endometriosis could well interfere with your ability to ovulate and produce a healthy egg. Given these two conditions, in your current state, you are not capable of having children, I'm very sorry. Modern fertility procedures offer other options that could be explored, but natural fertilization is not possible."

Helen stared down at the floor, trying to suppress the depression she was feeling now as her condition became clearer.

"I need to think about this," she said finally. "Can I just stay on the medication for now and see if it gets any better? I'd really like to get some other opinions on this before I think about a hysterectomy."

"Yes, I think that will be okay for now, Helen, but we need to have another follow-up in six weeks. I don't want your health to deteriorate, so if you start having more severe symptoms again, you need to contact me right away."

"I understand," Helen replied.

★★★★★

"A hysterectomy, oh my god!" Helen's mother exclaimed when Helen told her about the diagnosis. "Oh, these damn doctors, they just want to go to the extreme solution without even a second thought. It may be the safest thing to do, but my word! You need to get a second and probably a third opinion before going there, Helen. I'm so sorry, sweetheart, but don't do anything drastic like that. Just stay on that medication and see how it goes, give it a little time and see how things work. You're going to be okay, darling—just relax and don't worry too much. We love you so much, sweetheart."

"I love you too, Momma," Helen replied.

★★★★★

Helen got a second and a third opinion, and both doctors told her the same thing. She was at risk and a hysterectomy was the safest solution, but if she didn't want to go to that extreme, then the current medication was the next best alternative. They both confirmed as well Dr. Borrows's diagnosis that her fallopian tubes were grossly damaged and clogged, rendering her infertile.

Per Dr. Borrows's orders, Helen stayed on the Gn-RH medication for four months and then transitioned to another medication called Provera, which was less effective but could be used continuously; the Gn-RH was only allowed for a maximum of six months due to its potency. Her pain had diminished, and the new drug allowed her to have a normal menstrual cycle again.

"I would expect your pelvic pain will get worse once you stop the Gn-RH, but the FDA will only allow its use for a maximum of six months due to the risk of osteoporosis. You can use the Provera as long as you want. Expect some side effects, including breast tenderness, moodiness, headaches, and water retention, but these may be minimal, depending on how your body takes to the medication," Dr. Borrows said. "But, Helen, if you start to experience severe pain again, similar to what you experienced before you collapsed, you'll need to seriously consider a hysterectomy; your health could be in danger. In any case, I suggest we have a checkup every three months, and we'll see how you're doing."

"I understand, Dr. Borrows," Helen replied. "Thank you for all the effort you've put into this on my behalf, and thank you for your concern. I'll let you know how things are going."

★★★★★

Over the next six months, Helen's pain did get worse, but the pain only occurred during the two or three days leading up to her period, unlike before, when the pain could last for several weeks. At one point, the pain became so intense that she was seriously considering calling Dr. Borrows to inquire about a hysterectomy, but she couldn't get herself to do it. Luckily, the following month the pain was less severe. A few months after that, she met Jack at the astronomy club outing, and she noticed that the pain lessened a bit more once she and Jack started dating.

★★★★★

Before Jack and Helen were married, Helen told Jack about her endometriosis and the treatment she had been following over the last several years. Jack sat and listened silently, nodding his head and holding Helen's hand when she found it too difficult to tell her story, even though he already knew all the details of her illness, having experienced it when he entangled his mind with hers as she lay sleeping over a year before at his house in Fairbanks.

"I'm so sorry, Helen," he said once she had finished, and then he put his arms around her as she put her head on his shoulder and cried.

"Don't cry, Helen, there's still hope. We can still try, can't we? I know it's so important to you. We can still try."

Helen didn't say anything, but just kept crying on Jack's shoulder.

★★★★★

These thoughts and memories were running through Jack's mind as he sat on the back porch of his house in Fairbanks, with the eagle nestled in his makeshift nest beside him. It had been almost seventeen hours now since he had fallen on the floor next to the workbench in Helen's garage, and he was starting to lose his grip on the pain in his lower abdomen. "I need to hold it as long as possible," he told himself. He closed his eyes slowly and concentrated, but his mind was having trouble containing it any longer. Then suddenly, in a split second, the pain was gone. Jack opened his eyes and looked around, searching his thoughts and memories, trying to find it again, but it was futile; there was nothing there he could latch onto anymore.

"I hope that was enough time, I just don't know," he said out loud. He felt exhausted, both in body and mind, and he closed his eyes and sat still for ten minutes, letting his mind and body relax and rejuvenate after the experiences he had been through over those seventeen hours. A few minutes later, the eagle lifted his head, squawked loudly, fluttered his wings, and lifted himself out of the nest, resting his claws again on the edge of the wooden table, waiting. Jack sensed the eagle wanted to leave now, and he stood up and put his hand gently on the eagle's back.

"Thank you so much for coming here, my dear friend. I can't thank you enough for your company," Jack said to him. "You've been such a wonderful friend to me."

The eagle lowered his head as if to say thank you in return, then let out a loud screech and lifted off, spreading his majestic wings in the air, and flew briskly up into the afternoon sky.

"Good-bye, dear friend!" Jack yelled, waving as the eagle flew away. Jack waited until the eagle was out of sight and then he went inside and picked up the phone.

★★★★★

"Henry, how you been? It's Jack. I'm up here for a few days, so I thought I'd check in and see how the repair's coming along."

"Jack, great to hear from you," Henry replied in his deep, gravelly voice. "Oh man, you know, it's a real struggle. It's just time-consuming, but I need to get her back in shape so I can start back on my supply runs to those little towns north of here. It's my main source of dough this time of year, and I can't wait too long—they'll start looking for someone else soon."

"Can I lend you a hand, Henry? I'm going to be leaving probably midday tomorrow, but I'd be happy to help until then."

"Sure, Jack, of course, that would be great, thanks much."

"See you in twenty minutes," Jack replied.

Henry was a friend and fellow pilot and made his living taking tourists to remote parts of northern Alaska and delivering supplies to the small towns dotted here and there in the Alaskan tundra that weren't accessible by road. He rarely traveled south of Fairbanks, so he and Jack weren't really competing for the same business. When Henry got too busy with his deliveries, he'd call Jack up, and they would work together to keep the supplies coming. Two weeks earlier, Henry was trying to make a difficult landing in a nighttime snowstorm after delivering supplies all that day and lost control of his plane during landing. His left wing dipped too low and dug into the snow, spinning his plane wildly around, causing the landing gear to collapse and the belly of the plane to smack into the snow-covered runway. His plane was repairable, but being a solo operator, Henry did most of the work on his plane himself, including major repairs. Jack knew that Henry—at sixty-seven years old—could use some help fixing his damaged craft. Henry had crashed his plane at a small commercial airport where he kept it hangared, located ten miles east of Jack's house.

Jack made the short flight over to help Henry. They worked together until almost midnight repairing Henry's plane. Henry had ordered all the parts he needed, and he and Jack spent a good portion of the time removing the crumpled belly skin and stringers on the underside of the plane and fitting new ones in their place.

"Once I get this all done, I'll fit the new landing gear," Henry remarked as they worked in his hangar with the plane elevated on blocks. "I've already repaired the wing. I'll need to get one of those FAA inspectors up here, and I'm sure they'll want me to make some changes, but if all goes well, she'll be flying again in a week or so—that is if I can keep my eyes open. I've been working twenty hours a day on this puppy."

"Good for you, Henry," Jack replied. "You're a bulldog, and a determined one at that. You'll get her going soon enough. What do you say we get some rest now?"

Henry had set up a couple of makeshift hammocks in his hangar, so they both slept in them that night. Jack was still in a deep sleep the next morning when Henry got up and started working on the plane again. An hour later, Jack opened his eyes and stretched out his arms and legs.

"Hey, sleepy boy, you finally made it up," Henry said lightheartedly. "Hope you slept okay last night. It takes a while to get used to these hammocks."

Henry was sitting on a stool right by his plane with a drill in his hand and had just finished drilling a series of holes in the center section of the fuselage.

"Why don't you get washed up? Then I could really use a hand drilling these skins and stringers. This area isn't so bad, but it's tight access in there where the fuselage narrows down. I could use a second set of eyes, and a mirror might come in handy as well. I don't want to mess up and drill the holes off-center."

"Sure thing, Henry. I'll be with you in a few minutes."

They worked that morning fitting the new stringers and getting them drilled before taking them back off and deburring all the holes, then reinstalling them and fastening them to the fuselage skin. By noon, they had the majority of the work done on the stringer and skin repair, and what was left Henry could finish himself.

"Henry, I think I'm going to take off. My wife, Helen, is probably starting to worry about me, and I got a tourist trip planned for tomorrow afternoon. I better head out," Jack said.

"Sure thing, Jack. By the way, congratulations on the marriage. I've heard she's quite a gal. Sorry I didn't make it down for the vows, but you know how hectic things can get working this tundra. Listen, Jack, can I ask you to do me one more favor?"

"What's that, Henry?"

"I got a room full of supplies in the back I'm late on delivering. There's a small town northeast of here—I'm sure you've heard of it. It's called Allakaket, and it's about thirty minutes north of the Yukon River. The guy's been hounding me every day to get them to him, runs a grocery store up there. He started complaining to me that they're going to run out of toilet paper any day now, and he wasn't too interested in using pine needles after that—quite a kick, that old man. Can you run those supplies up to him for me?"

Jack shrugged, "Well, I don't know, Henry. I …"

"He'll pay you for it, Jack. Two hundred fifty dollars firm. Just tell him you're filling in for me. I don't want to lose his business, and it's less than an hour away."

"Well, sure, Henry, why not? A little extra cash wouldn't hurt," Jack replied.

"Yeah, you know, it's better than a kick in the face, ain't it, Jack? That's an old Texas saying my dad used to say when I was growing up."

Jack laughed and then walked up the runway to where his plane was parked, started her up, and taxied over to Henry's hangar. They loaded Jack's plane up with the supplies Henry had stored in the back. There were one hundred containers of canned food, sugar, salt, several big boxes of toilet paper, paper towels, toothpaste, soap, and shampoo, and ten large boxes of bagged potato chips and pretzels.

"Well, there you go, Jack, thanks for the help. When you get to Allakaket, you'll land on a dirt runway on the east side of town—it's on the map. It's a bit bumpy, so take her in gingerly. There's a big white building less than a stone's throw away, and that's where the store is located. I'll give him a call and let him know you're coming. He'll be out there waiting for you. He goes by the name of White Fish."

"Sure thing, Henry. Keep plugging away on that plane; you'll have her back in the air in no time."

"You bet ya," Henry said, winking. Then he turned and walked back into the hangar.

★★★★★

Jack landed on the bumpy runway an hour later.

"Easy does it," he said as his plane hopped several times before he could apply the brakes and slow down. He then turned the plane around and taxied back up the runway to the parking area. A big man with Eskimo-like features was waiting there for him as he shut the plane down and opened the door.

"You must be Jack," he said, stretching out his hand. "Well, you sure are a lot prettier and younger than that old codger Henry. My name's White Fish. What happened to that old boy of mine anyway?"

"Oh, he just bent up his airplane a tad trying to land at night in a snowstorm. You know Henry—a little snowstorm wouldn't slow him down. The plane's in the hangar now, and he's working on it as we speak. I've got a plane full of supplies for you. Mind giving me a hand unloading them?"

"Sure thing," White Fish replied.

Twenty minutes later, Jack was climbing back in his plane. He taxied down to the end of the runway, applied his brakes, and revved the engine to full throttle. He then released the brakes and went hopping down the runway, pulling back on the control yoke to keep his front wheel light as he accelerated over the rough terrain. Once he got to takeoff speed, he brought the control yoke back in earnest, ascending into the air, clearing the large evergreen trees at the end of the runway by no more than twenty feet. Three hours later, at five in the evening, he descended into Birchwood airport and landed. By the time he made it back to the house, it was close to six o'clock. Helen was in the kitchen cleaning up when he arrived.

"Jack, oh gosh, I'm so glad to see you. I was getting worried. I tried to call a few times, but just got your voice mail. So what happened? Where have you been all this time?"

"Oh, Helen darling, I'm sorry. I must have left my phone off. My old friend Henry—you know Henry—he's sixty-seven but still at it. He crashed his plane on landing in Fairbanks during a nighttime snowstorm. As you can imagine, he needed some help getting his plane back together, so I helped him with some of the repairs. I also delivered some supplies to Allakaket, a tiny town north of the Yukon River. Henry delivers supplies there every so often, and a guy by the name of White Fish was hounding him to make a run up there. I'm a little worried about the old codger trying to do it all himself. His two sons moved to Oregon a few years back and opened up a charter service so they're not available, and his wife really knows nothing about the business. I was going to call, but it got a bit crazy if you know what I mean."

"Well gosh, how's he doing? Is he going to be all right?" Helen replied.

"Luckily he just got a few bruises during the crash, nothing else, so he's fine in that respect. I think he'll get his plane back together—that is, if he doesn't collapse in the process. He told me he's been working at it twenty hours a day, but knowing him, he'll be back in the air in no time."

"Well, that's awfully nice of you to help him, Jack," Helen said. "Now why don't you give me a hand in the back garden? I could use a hand trimming the bushes and weeding, and then we can plant some summer flowers together. Come on, let's get going before it gets too dark out there."

"Well, all right, darling, of course," Jack replied, following Helen into the backyard.

Chapter 21

Ten days later, as Jack was saying good-bye to a group of tourists he had taken up on a sightseeing trip, Helen called him from the hospital.

"Jack, I need to talk to you," she said over the phone.

"Well, sure, Helen, what is it?" Jack replied.

"Can we talk at the house? I've leaving now and will be home in twenty minutes," Helen said.

"Well, I was going to do some routine maintenance on the plane, but it can wait until tomorrow, I suppose. Is something wrong, Helen?"

"Oh, not exactly," Helen replied. "I'll see you in twenty minutes, then?"

"Sure, darling, twenty minutes," Jack said as he waved to a couple who had been on the tour as they got into their car to leave.

★★★★★

When Jack got home, Helen was waiting for him in the living room. Her face was flush, and she had a curious, almost surprised demeanor about her.

"Helen, sweetheart, how are you doing?" Jack said as he walked into the room and sat down next to her on the couch. "What is it, Helen? What's going on?"

"Well, Jack, I didn't want to say anything at first, but it's been five days now. I thought it was time to tell you."

288

"Five days since what, Helen? What do you mean?"

"Jack, I missed my period. It hasn't started, and that aching abdominal pain I usually get a few days before my period hasn't begun either."

"Have you been nauseated, Helen? Fatigued? Are your boobs a bit tender?" Jack asked, half smiling.

"Well, let me think. In the mornings lately, I have been feeling a bit queasy, but once I eat something, I feel better. You know, my boobs—well, I mean breasts—have been tender. I've been going to bed a bit earlier the last few days, but really thought nothing of it."

Jack smiled a broad, full smile, and his eyes danced across Helen's face. Helen was looking down at her hands, not certain she should believe what her symptoms were telling her.

"Oh, Helen, sweetheart," Jack said, taking her hand in his. Helen raised her head and looked at Jack with a gentle, curious expression, but she couldn't help but show a certain pride in her face.

"Can you wait here for a few minutes, darling?" Jack asked. "I'm going to run down to the store. I think the next step is a pregnancy test."

★★★★★

Jack was back ten minutes later.

Helen opened up the package but then stopped. "Jack, I'm scared. After all the things the doctors have told me, I didn't think this was possible. Maybe something else is going on."

"Go on, Helen, everything's fine. All the right symptoms are there. It all makes sense, but there's really only one way to find out for certain."

Helen got up, went to the bathroom, and returned a few minutes later. They sat together on the couch waiting, with Helen tightly holding the pregnancy stick in one hand as Jack gently held her other hand. After a minute, a "+" sign appeared at the base of the stick.

"Oh, Helen, you're pregnant, sweetheart, how wonderful! We're going to be parents," Jack said as he gave her a warm hug.

Helen wrapped her arms around Jack in return and started crying, but this time she was crying out of joy.

"I can't believe it, I just can't believe it, I didn't think I could ever be a mother," she finally said. "I'm so happy, Jack. I'm just so wonderfully happy."

★★★★★

The next morning Jack took Helen to Dr. Borrows's office, and the nurse confirmed that she was almost two weeks pregnant. After the nurse told Dr. Borrows the results, he came into the room where Helen and Jack were waiting.

"Well, Helen, congratulations. I wasn't expecting this, I wasn't expecting this at all, but how wonderful. Yes, you're about two weeks pregnant. I just don't know what to say, but I'm so happy for you," he said, giving Helen a warm hug.

"Well, thank you, Doctor," Helen replied. "We're both so excited about being parents, aren't we, Jack?"

Jack was looking out the window, a sanguine smile on his face. "What? Well, yes, of course, we're very excited. It will open up a whole new chapter in our lives. I'm really looking forward to it."

"Well, wonderful," Dr. Borrows said, "but let's not get too far ahead of ourselves, you two. You've got a whole nine months to get through, well, really eight and a half now, and it can be difficult at times. At your age of thirty-eight, Helen, there are higher risks involved, so you need to be careful and listen to your body and follow all of our instructions."

"Of course, Doctor," Helen replied.

"I'd like to do some tests in three weeks, in fact. They're noninvasive and safe, but given your prior condition, I would recommend them."

★★★★★

Three weeks later, Dr. Borrows confirmed the embryo was well placed along Helen's left uterus wall and growing rapidly.

"As far as we can tell, everything looks great, Helen. You're on schedule, and the embryo is healthy and growing." Dr. Borrows then hesitated, looking down at the floor.

"What is it, Doctor? Is something wrong?" Helen asked, seeing the expression on his face.

"No, nothing's wrong, Helen, but I did get a chance to survey your fallopian tubes as we had done before, and they are still as damaged and clogged as they were when you were here three months ago. It's quite unusual, given your current condition. I don't quite see how you were able to conceive, but nonetheless, here we are."

"Could that cause any risk to the pregnancy, Doctor?" Helen asked.

"Well, I don't think so. The embryo is planted in your uterus now. The fallopian tubes just act as a delivery system to get the egg there. Each month when you ovulate, an egg is released from one of your ovaries, and for a healthy individual, the egg is simply swept along down one of the fallopian tubes until it is close to the uterus. The egg then sits in this part of the fallopian tube for twelve to twenty-four hours waiting for fertilization, and the lower parts of your fallopian tubes are actually quite normal. The damaged areas are closer to your ovaries. Somehow that egg was able to travel through the clogged and damaged areas and plant itself close to your uterus, where it was fertilized. Quite remarkable."

★★★★★

When Helen got home, she told Jack what the doctor said.

He looked down at the floor, nodding his head in agreement. "Yes, I can see that, yes I know, of course, that's what happened. Remember, Helen, the night before I left for Fairbanks, when we made love? It was just a few weeks before we found out you were pregnant."

"Of course I remember making love that night, Jack—it was wonderful—but that doesn't explain anything. All the doctors I've seen have told me the same thing Dr. Borrows told me in his office today. He was quite mystified that we conceived."

Jack looked at Helen, and then a solemn but peaceful look spread over his face.

"Helen, when I went to Fairbanks that night in a rush, it wasn't really to help Henry. I'm sorry I didn't tell you the whole story."

"What are you talking about?" Helen said, frowning as she put one hand in the air. "Henry called the other day to thank you; he was so happy to have his plane back in the air."

"Well, yes, I did help Henry, but that was afterward."

"After what, Jack?"

"I couldn't stay near you once I took that pain, Helen. My body couldn't contain it being that close to you. I mean, it's unnatural enough, the anatomy between a woman and a man are so different, especially there, but to then try and hold on to it was excruciating. It was like sand slipping through my fingers, but being farther away allowed me to grasp it and hold it. I had no idea if it would work or not, but I held on as long as I could."

Helen looked at Jack with a perplexed look on her face, but as she started to realize what Jack had done, a certain calm came over her face.

"My fallopian tubes, you healed them?" Helen asked.

"Well, I wouldn't say I healed them; my telepathic power is not that capable. But I repaired them temporarily, long enough for …"

"Long enough for that one precious, delicate egg to travel from my ovary down my fallopian tube until it was there, ready to be fertilized at the entrance to my uterus," Helen said, finishing his sentence.

"Yes, that's it, Helen."

"Oh god, Jack, you did that for me," Helen said joyfully. "The one thing I thought I would never be able to do but wanted so much. You're so amazing and such a wonderful husband. I love you so much. I don't know what else to say, but thank you, sweetheart. Thank you for allowing me to start this wonderful journey called motherhood."

Helen put her arms around Jack and hugged him warmly, then kissed him on the lips.

As they stood there in a warm embrace, Jack said, "I did it for both of us, sweetheart. I knew you always wanted to be a mother, but I wanted to be a father as well."

"Oh, darling, yes, of course, I understand. You're so wonderful to have taken that risk for both of us, and the baby as well," Helen replied. "How are you doing now, Jack? Is everything back to normal down there?"

"I'm fine, Helen, I'm fine. How about yourself?"

"I'm pregnant, Jack. Wonderfully pregnant," she replied, smiling.

★★★★★

Eight months later, after a relatively normal pregnancy, Helen gave birth to a healthy seven pound twelve ounce baby boy. He had sandy-colored hair and large, light brown eyes, and smiled easily when Helen rocked him back and forth in her arms.

Helen's mother was ecstatic when the baby was born. She and Helen's father came and visited the hospital a few days after the birth.

"My baby girl gave birth to her own little baby boy. Oh, Helen, I'm so happy for you. I can't believe I'm a grandmother now."

"You sure are, Momma," Helen said, lying in the hospital bed with her newborn son in her arms. "Want to hold him for a little while?" Helen asked as she gently laid the boy in her mother's arms. "There you go, Grandma, isn't he cute?"

Helen's mother smiled as she took him in her arms, then gently rocked him back and forth. "Can you say Grandmomma? It's not Momma, it's Grandmomma."

Jack and Helen smiled and held hands as Helen's mother enjoyed the moment with their son.

Helen's father put his hand on Jack's shoulder, congratulating him. To the child, he said, "Do you have a name, my good fella? What's your name, little buddy?"

"We named him Shane," Helen replied. "It goes well with his sandy-colored hair, doesn't it?"

"Hi, my sweet Shaney, Shane, Shane. Such a cute boy, you are," Helen's mother said as she rocked him in her arms.

★★★★★

Helen's three sisters came and visited later that afternoon.

"Congratulations, Helen, and you too, Jack, I'm so happy for you,"

Margery said when she came into the room. "After all the trouble you've had these last five years, well, this is such a wonderful turn of events. He's such a cute boy, isn't he?"

She reached out her hand and stroked the boy's cheek and gave him a big, exaggerated smile.

"Thanks for coming, girls. Momma and Daddy left just a little while ago, but Momma told me to tell you one of you is next. She doesn't want little Shane to be her only grandchild," Helen said, laughing.

Her sisters giggled.

"Well, I'm working on it," her youngest sister Gina said. "I'll try my best. I guess I'll need to find a boyfriend first, though."

They all laughed, and then they took turns holding and cuddling Shane.

"Did you enjoy being pregnant, Helen?" her other sister Jennifer asked as she cuddled Shane in her arms. "It must have been pretty tough."

"I loved it," Helen replied. "Well, maybe everything other than the labor, but no, I loved it all. It was a wonderful experience, and look what we have as a result."

She took Shane back from Jennifer and rocked him back and forth. "How you doing, my little cutie? Don't you love all this attention?"

Shane opened his eyes, smiled, and let out a little giggle. They all giggled back.

Chapter 22

O ver the next few years Jack, Helen, and their son lived a comfortable, stable life. Helen worked only part-time as a physical therapist in order to raise and care for Shane. They both loved being parents, but Helen especially took a liking to the task.

"I didn't think I'd love it quite this much," she told Jack one night after Shane had drifted off to sleep in the cot they had set up next to their bed. "It's really a beautiful thing, you know, to bring someone else into this world and to help them on their way."

"Even the diaper changing, Helen?" Jack asked jokingly. "I mean, when I'm cleaning up the mess, I'm not exactly thinking this is a wonderful experience."

"Oh, Jack, you silly goof," Helen replied playfully, hitting his head with a pillow, "it just goes with the territory. It's all part of the whole experience, taking care of someone. I wouldn't trade it for the world. I love it."

"I love it too, Helen, and what I love the most is being with you through all of it," Jack replied, smiling. Then he leaned over and kissed her.

★★★★★

During those years, Jack's telepathic abilities never waned. They were as powerful as they had ever been, but he found himself using his unique gifts less and less. He didn't really have the desire to exercise them, and unless he felt there was a specific need he could help address, he tended to leave his telepathic powers on the shelf. He found it too probing, too obtrusive, and to some extent, almost too painful to deal with. His ability was completely engulfing and took so much out of him that he was drained afterward, both physically and emotionally. Unless he could do something to improve a situation, he tended to steer away from telepathy and instead tried to deal with the task at hand like any other human being would.

There was the time, though, during the following Christmas when Jack and Helen visited the town square in a place called the North Pole, a small town situated just fifteen miles south of Fairbanks. Helen's parents each year took time to help decorate the square, and there was a beautiful, large white spruce tree that had been decorated with Christmas lights ever since Helen could remember. She took great pleasure in telling her friends how, when she was six years old, she helped her parents decorate that large white spruce for the first time. It was over eighty feet tall and stood in the corner of the square, its roots extending hundreds of feet under the square and into the grassy pasture next to it. The whole town would get involved in decorating the tree, and even the firemen would lend a helping hand. The lights at the top of the tree were installed with the use of the large extendable ladder that sat on the top of the fire truck.

That year when Helen and Jack came up to Fairbanks to visit her parents for Christmas, Helen insisted they visit the North Pole town square to see the Christmas lights. When they arrived, Helen gasped.

"Oh my god, what's going on here?" she said, as she looked at the white spruce tree. There were no Christmas lights installed, and the tree looked as if it were almost dead. The needles had turned a pale brown over large portions of the tree, and many of the limbs were sagging under their own weight, lifeless. "What's happened to our beautiful white spruce?"

"We don't know, Helen," her father replied. "Just over a year ago, it started to take a turn for the worse, and it's just been deteriorating progressively ever since. We don't dare try to decorate the old tree now in case of fire. Quite sad, isn't it? It must be diseased or something of that sort. The fire marshal said he'd probably have to take it down in a few months since it's becoming a fire hazard."

"That's horrible, how sad," Helen replied. "This tree brings back such wonderful memories of growing up here. I can't believe it."

Jack stood still, staring at the white spruce, examining its state to get a better idea of what was happening to the tree. It was definitely dying, that was evident, but even then, to deteriorate so rapidly over just one year seemed odd to Jack. Helen's parents lived only a few miles away, and a few minutes later, they got back in their car and drove back to the house.

"Do you think your momma is enjoyed babysitting Shane?" Jack asked as they drove down the winding single-lane country road.

"I'm sure she's loving it," Helen replied. "Isn't that right, Daddy?"

"Sure she is, darling. I'm sure she is."

★★★★★

When they arrived, Helen's mother had Shane cuddled in her arms and was quietly singing him a lullaby. When they opened the door, she raised her finger to her lips, telling them to be quiet. "He just dozed off to sleep," she whispered. She then got up and went into the next room and placed Shane in the cot Helen and Jack had set up in the guest bedroom.

Helen's mother had fixed dinner as well, so they all sat down to eat, but afterward, once everyone was settled in for the evening, Jack said he was heading out to the grocery store to pick up some cream for coffee the next morning. He drove back to the town square in North Pole, got out of the car, and walked over to the white spruce. He reached his hand out to one of the healthy limbs of the tree and closed his eyes concentrating, searching for a connection. He didn't experience anything at first, but slowly over the next minute, the images started to appear in his mind. He hadn't experienced anything quite like it before.

The tree was alive, yes, but living for a large, old tree was quite different than living for a human being, or an eagle for that matter. He felt himself morphing into the tree, experiencing its life. The tree had stood in this same spot now for over two hundred years, long before they had built a town square around it. Jack felt so planted now, feeling the great tree's roots extending into the ground for hundreds of feet. *Yes, the ultimate homebody, these wonderful trees,* Jack thought to himself. *Even if this wonderful creation wanted to move, it couldn't; it's planted here for as long as it lives.* The world revolved around the tree; there was nothing that the tree knew otherwise. At first the tree didn't understand the coming of humans and all that they brought, but over time, it took a liking to it. The tree liked the attention and the joy it appeared to give to the people who tended to it, and with the humans came an abundance of birds, since it was common for the townsfolk to leave food on the grounds of the town square for feeding. The tree especially enjoyed being the home for the wonderful feathered creatures that nested in its limbs.

Jack concentrated further, trying to understand why that great white spruce was finding it so difficult to live now; he could sense it wasn't any sort of disease. He suddenly felt it: one of the major roots of the tree that extended out into the pasture was practically dead. The gas company had laid a gas line there just above that major root several years earlier. They had dug a four-foot-deep ditch and then laid the piping down less than an inch above the tree root, unaware of the proximity of the root. There was a weld line there as well, where two sections of pipe had been joined before it had been laid down in the ditch. During the next few days, the pipe shifted as the construction vehicles drove back and forth over the site until the pipe was sitting flush against the tree root. Over the next year, as the pipe continued to settle into the dirt and the tree's root grew and shifted slightly over the course of the seasons, the pipe and root began to press against one another until finally the pipe ruptured at the weld line and a slow continuous underground gas leak began to poison the tree.

That's dangerous, Jack thought to himself, *not to just the tree but to the town as well.*

"Such a beautiful, grand tree, no wonder you're having such a difficult time. That gas is like putting poison in your veins," Jack said, trying to console the white spruce. Jack let go of the tree limb then, aware of the problem.

He drove over to a small grocery store not far from there and picked up some cream for the morning coffee and then headed back home. Helen's parents were already asleep when Jack got back, but Helen was awake, reading a book in the guest bedroom waiting for him.

"Well, you were gone for a long time," Helen said. "That must be some kind of amazing cream you picked up. I was starting to get worried."

"Oh, I headed back to North Pole to check on that white spruce—sorry I didn't tell you. I know why that tree is on its last leg, but if we move fast, we still may be able to save it."

"Really? What did you find out, Jack?" Helen asked curiously as she looked up from her book.

"They laid a gas line down in that pasture next to the town square a few years back, and that gas line has been pressed right up against one of the tree's main roots from the beginning, until finally the gas line sprang a leak. The heat and gas from that seeping line has been killing the tree ever since. The gas needs to be turned off, and the line needs to be moved."

"How do you know all this, Jack? I mean …"

Jack looked at Helen then, a blank stare in his expression.

"Oh yes, I see, well, why didn't you tell me, Jack?" Helen responded, understanding now. "Daddy worked in the gas industry for years, and he still does some consulting work part-time. Let's talk to him in the morning about it. Maybe he can round up a crew."

★★★★★

Over coffee the next morning, Manie, Helen's father, nodded his head as he heard the story of why the white spruce was dying. "Well, I know the foreman who runs the gas network for the town. Let's go over and explain the situation. If you can pinpoint the location of the leak, Jack, it shouldn't be too difficult to dig down and see what's going on. I'm sure they'd like to save that tree as well, and no one wants a leaking line either."

★★★★★

"It's right here," Jack said later that afternoon standing in the pasture that bordered the town square. "The leak is right here."

"You sure?" the foreman replied. "I mean, how could you know exactly where we need to dig?"

"I'm sure. Come on, let's get started," Jack replied.

Nicki the foreman, Jack, Manie, and another crewman spent the next half hour digging down until they reached the pipe. Once there, the crewman pulled out a gas detector and turned it on, but the smell was quite evident as well.

"I'm picking up a big signal, boss," he said to Nicki. "This isn't normal; something's wrong."

They dug all the way around the pipe, clearing out a four-foot-wide section. They dug around and underneath the pipe until they uncovered the tree root and the ruptured pipe line pressed up next to it.

"Well, I'll be darned," Nicki said. "You nailed it on the head, Jack. Man, it's a good thing we found this. With a little ignition source, we could have had an explosion on our hands. I'm calling the main plant this very second. They need to shut off this line now."

Fifteen minutes later, the line was shut off, and the gas levels seeping from the pipe dropped significantly.

"So what's going to happen now?" Jack asked Nicki.

"Well, we'll replace the pipe and have it moved a bit so it's not up against the root. That should be it," he replied.

"But the heat and proximity to the gas line is what's killing this white spruce," Jack said. "A cracked line didn't help the situation, but the line needs to be rerouted away from the tree root. Just moving the line enough to clear the root won't be enough. It needs to be rerouted. The tree won't survive otherwise."

"Well, I don't know what to say, but that's a big job," Nicki said hesitantly as he looked down. "I'd have to run it by my management, see if they'd be willing to foot the bill. I don't know."

"The white spruce is dying," Manie continued. "It's been the town's landmark for years. We've been decorating it for Christmas ever since I can remember. I agree with Jack; the gas line needs to be rerouted."

Nicki shrugged his shoulders, not knowing what to say.

★★★★★

That evening, Jack and Helen put a flyer together, and the next day they distributed it to the townsfolk of North Pole. It read:

> Come out and Help Save the White Spruce Tree in Town Square. It misses being decorated for Christmas. We need to dig a ditch so a Natural Gas Line can be rerouted that's been killing that Beautiful White Spruce. Please come out and Help. We'll be meeting in the Town Square at 9:00 a.m., Saturday, December 28. Please come out and lend a helping hand so we can decorate that Beautiful White Spruce come next Christmas. Bring a shovel if you have one. If you have any questions, please contact Manie or Jesse Thompson at (907) 352-7767.

★★★★★

Over the next two days, Helen fielded quite a few phone calls regarding the flyer, and the response looked promising. Manie discussed it with the gas company's director in North Pole, and they agreed that the line would be rerouted if the townsfolk were willing to lend a hand and expedite the job. The gas line supplied heat to most of the homes in town and could not be shut off for very long, and there was a short supply of earth-moving equipment and operators, especially over the holidays. That Saturday, with the outside air temperature at 10° F, Jack, Helen, and Manie drove over to North Pole, while Helen's mother stayed at home with Shane.

"Do you think anyone's going to show up, Manie?" Jack asked. "It sure is cold out here."

"Cold? Come on, Jack. It's like a spring day. It was 30 below the day before you two arrived. We've got some rugged folks out here. Don't worry; they'll come. Even Nicki, the foreman, said he's coming and he's going to bring a crew."

When they drove up to the town square at a quarter till nine, with the sun just coming up, there were already twenty folks standing out there with shovels in hand, and by nine o'clock they were thirty strong. Manie knew most of the people in town, so he got up and gave a speech, thanking them and telling them what needed to be done. Nicki had already laid out the rerouting plan, so by nine thirty that morning, the people were hard at work digging a four-foot-deep ditch to reroute the gas line. By three o'clock that afternoon, the ditch was finished, just as it was starting to turn dusk.

"No excuses now," Manie said, smiling to Nicki once they were done. "All you've got to do now is lay the pipe down."

"You got it, Manie," he replied. "We're coming out tomorrow to lay the pipe, and we'll have the gas back on by tomorrow night."

"Thanks for coming out, Nicki," Manie said. "And thanks for bringing out the crew."

"Thank you, Manie, and you too, Jack. You saved us from a potential disaster, and it sure would be nice if that spruce makes it. I bring my little girl out here every year to show her the Christmas lights, and that white spruce with all those decorations was the highlight."

Manie, Jack, and Helen thanked everyone else for coming, shaking everyone's hands as they left.

"You two did a good thing," Manie said as Jack and Helen climbed into his car at the end of the day. "I must have raised my little girl right, what do you think, Jack?"

"You sure did, Manie, and thank you," Jack replied as Helen gave her father a hug.

★★★★★

A few months later, Jack checked in with Manie to see how the white spruce was doing.

"Well, she's getting there, Jack," he replied. "There's still quite a lot of brown needles, but not nearly as many as before. She's coming back slowly, but looks a thousand times better than what she looked like over Christmas. The city hired a horticulture specialist; he knows every detail about these white spruces. He manages many of the tree reseeding projects around here after the loggers come in. If there's anyone who can bring that white spruce back to life, he's the man. I think that white spruce will make it, but it will be this summer when we really see her turn around. I'd put my money on seeing her all decorated up at year's end for Christmas."

"Well, glad to hear it," Jack replied. "You were amazing getting that dig organized so quickly with the gas company and all. Thanks, Manie. Next time we're up there, let's pay the white spruce a visit."

"Sounds good, Jack, let's plan on it."

Chapter 23

That year Jack and Helen became involved with the Iditarod Trail Sled Dog Race held each year in the spring. The Iditarod race involved a sled dog musher and teams of typically sixteen dogs who traveled 1150 miles over Alaskan terrain, starting in Anchorage and traveling to Nome, located in the western end of the state. The race began on the first Saturday in March, and the mushers and dogs took from eight to fifteen days to complete the course. The teams had to deal with the weather, whatever it was, so it was common that they raced through subzero temperatures, blizzards causing potential whiteout conditions, and gale-force winds that could cause the windchill to reach -100° F. The Iditarod course led the teams across harsh landscapes that included desolate tundra and forests, over rolling terrain and mountain passes, and across frozen rivers. It included treacherous climbs and side hills, long hours of darkness, and various hazards, such as water overflow from frozen lakes and rivers. Some called the Iditarod the "Last Great Race on Earth."

A ceremonial start took place in Anchorage and was then followed by the official restart in Willow, a city about fifty miles north. The trail proceeded from Willow up the Rainy Pass of the Alaska Range into the sparsely populated interior, then along the shore of the Bearing Sea, finally reaching Nome on the western coast. The typical race drew fifty to seventy mushing teams, who traveled through widely separated towns, villages, and Eskimo settlements along the route.

Henry, Jack's older pilot friend, had been involved with the Iditarod

Race since the early 1990s. He was a member of the Iditarod Air Force, a loose band of approximately thirty pilot volunteers who ferried equipment from Anchorage to various locations along the course. In Anchorage, mushers purchased supplies and equipment, which were then picked up by the Iditarod Air Force volunteers and delivered to the checkpoints. In addition, the pilots transported volunteers, judges, and veterinarians to the checkpoints, as well as moved injured or sick dogs who could not complete the race. In return, the Iditarod Race Committee paid the pilot volunteers for fuel, food, and lodging.

Over the twenty years he worked as a volunteer, Henry usually made three to four round-trip flights from Anchorage to the various checkpoints, but that year due to his age, he decided to scale back his participation and asked Jack if he would be interested in helping to pick up the slack. Jack gladly accepted the invitation. He had heard of the Iditarod race and the amazing dogs that ran the trails, but he had never actually gone out and witnessed the event. That first year, Jack made only one drop-off, to the town of McGrath, about halfway along the course, which contained a good airfield.

During the flight from Anchorage, Helen joined him, as well as a veterinarian, and the rest of the plane was stocked full of supplies. Helen and Jack stayed in McGrath for several days afterward while Helen's mother babysat Shane at their home in Anchorage. They both enjoyed it so much that Jack decided to participate again the following year.

★★★★★

The next year Jack, Henry, Helen, and little Shane were there at the ceremonial start line in Anchorage as the mushers and dogs headed out onto the course, separated by two-minute intervals. Since it was only the ceremonial start, the course ended only a few miles outside of the city, where the dogs and gear were packed up for the restart in Willow.

"Aren't these dogs just amazing?," Helen said as they watched the teams depart. "They're such beautiful animals."

"They sure are, aren't they?" Jack said. "I was told that the Siberian huskies are the most popular racing breed, but in reality, most of these dogs are mixed-breed huskies, bred for speed, tough feet, endurance, and of course, the desire to run. They must have some incredible stamina to compete in a race like this."

"Stamina, you don't know the meaning of the word," Henry said. "These dogs burn eleven thousand calories a day out on the course, and I heard the tidbit that's eight times higher than those sissy cyclists in the Tour de France. In fact, these dogs have an aerobic capacity three times greater than those Olympic marathon runners. We human beings don't hold a candle to these beasts."

"Pretty incredible," Jack replied as he watched another dog sled race on by.

Shane was sitting in a stroller next to Helen, and he raised his hand and pointed to the dogs. "Fast doggie, fast doggie!" he said with a thrill, and Helen, Jack, and Henry laughed.

"They sure are, little buddy," Henry replied. "They're screaming."

★★★★★

After the start, Jack and Henry headed over to the Anchorage convention center to pick up the supplies for the first drop along the checkpoints, while Helen headed back home to drop off Shane with her mother. Two hours later, Jack's and Henry's planes were full of supplies and ready to go. Helen showed up a few minutes later after Jack called and told her they were ready to head out.

"How's our little Shane doing?" Jack asked as Helen climbed into the passenger seat of his plane.

"Oh, he's doing fine. All the excitement at the start must have tired him out. He dozed right off to sleep on the way home. Momma's so sweet to take care of him."

Henry was heading to McGrath for his drop, but Jack and Helen headed to Skwentna, just a forty-minute hop by air. After Henry made his drop, he was planning to head back to his home base in Fairbanks since he had some commercial business booked out. Jack and Helen planned to stay in Skwentna one or two nights and watch the Iditarod competitors come in and out of the town.

When they arrived in Skwentna, it was starting to turn dusk. They landed on the airstrip next to the Skwentna River, and there was a team of race officials waiting there to help them unload the supplies. A good portion of the supplies were simply food, mainly for the dogs but for the mushers as well. They also carried extra paw booties for the dogs, headlamps for night travel, batteries, tools, and sled parts for repairs.

"Aren't these paw booties so cute?" Helen said as she helped unload the supplies. "Maybe I can sneak a pair as souvenirs. Little Shane would love to have a set, especially if he knew they are used to protect those beautiful doggies' feet."

"It's rough terrain out there, ma'am," one of the race officials replied to Helen. "How would you like to run 1100 miles barefoot? These dogs need some protection." He then smiled and gave Helen a wink. "Don't worry, ma'am, I'm sure we can find an extra pair you can give to your little one. We appreciate you two helping out."

They stayed out until eight o'clock and watched a few of the sled teams come in, but it was cold and windy so they decided to head back to the small lodge where they were staying for a good night's rest. The lodge was located right along the Skwentna River and was only a few minutes' walk from the Iditarod checkpoint.

★★★★★

The next morning, Jack got up early. He wanted to be part of the excitement as the mushers came in and out of town, but Helen wanted to sleep in and stay warm.

"Go ahead, darling," Helen said when Jack asked if she was coming. "I'm going to sleep in for a while. I'll be down there in a little bit, that is, after I get a nice, big, warm cup of coffee."

Jack headed over to the checkpoint, cup of coffee in hand, and it wasn't but a few minutes before one of the dog teams arrived. The dogs looked incredible, and if they were tired, Jack sure couldn't sense it. They just looked powerful and strong, and full of energy. The Skwentna checkpoint was only a tenth of the way along the course, so the dogs were still quite fresh, Jack suspected. There was a group of volunteers and spectators at the checkpoint close to thirty strong, and Jack watched as the mushers stopped their sleds and checked in. After checking in, they would find their delivered supplies and feed their dogs before checking out and heading on their way. Each team had a clearly marked number on the side of the sled and on the musher's chest, making it easier for the officials to keep track of the teams.

Jack walked up past the checkpoint along the Iditarod trail so he could watch the dogs run by at full speed. It was close to zero degrees Fahrenheit, so the mushers were covered head to toe with bandanas across their faces and their coats pulled tight around their heads and bodies. Jack waved as the teams came by, and most of the mushers waved back, but Jack's favorite part was watching those amazing dogs run on by. When they passed by him, there were running at full speed, and their gates were in unison. Every so often, one dog would bark, and almost simultaneously, the others would join in until there was a low roar of barking dogs, but it would only last for a few seconds as the dogs stopped to catch their breath and keep going.

Looking at those dogs, Jack thought back to one of his favorite novels growing up, *The Call of the Wild*. Jack could see any one of those dogs being Buck, the main protagonist in the novel—a dog who unwillingly leaves his comfortable life in California to live the life of a sled dog during the Yukon gold rush, living on the fringe between a sled dog and the wild that beckons him, until eventually he falls in with a pack of wolves and takes the wild as his own. Jack sensed now that wildness in these dogs as they came running by, almost as if the ropes that bound them to the sled were the only thing left to stop them from running wild forever.

There was a team approaching, and Jack could clearly see a red number 11 on the white bib worn over the musher's burly coat. Jack smiled and closed his eyes, thinking back to that novel, then he opened his eyes and focused on one of the lead dogs and concentrated. He wanted to run as part of the team and experience what it was really like to be a part of that fantastic pack of dogs. The musher came by, but Jack was so focused that this time he didn't wave as the sled passed.

As he became entangled with the body and mind of the lead dog, the first thing that caught his attention was the incredible power and strength the animal possessed. He was amazed that the animal had that much power concentrated into such an agile, nimble body. This dog was a world-class athlete trained to an incredible level of stamina and strength, like a marathon runner and a one-hundred-meter sprinter merged into one. It was wonderful to feel the power and grace of the animal as he sped forward along the trail, scanning the terrain ahead, yes, but also waiting and anticipating commands from his musher behind him.

The dog's name was Fang; he was a husky mutt, with a beautiful white and brown coat and deep blue penetrating eyes. Jack's mind was filled with the wildness of the dog and his immense joy of running, especially in this rugged Alaskan terrain. It was blistering cold, but when he ran, his body reached an equilibrium temperature that was pleasant and ideal for peak performance. The dog was working hard, but he felt comfortable.

That wildness was certainly a major part of Fang's psyche, but Jack was also feeling something else, something he hadn't anticipated. The dog possessed a deep loyalty to the other dogs on the team, and the sense of camaraderie was quite evident, as if they knew they had to work together as a team to succeed. But the loyalty wasn't just to the other dogs; Fang's loyalty extended to his musher as well. The musher had raised him since he was just a pup, and they had trained and raced for several years in preparation for the Iditarod competition. The dog had taken a real liking to his musher. The musher treated his dogs like extended family. He pushed them hard, yes, but he fed them well and took good care of them. It was clear that this was the first Iditarod for Fang, but it also appeared to be the first for the other dogs and the musher as well.

Jack loved that feeling of freedom and boundless energy he felt now as he ran with the dog. It was exhilarating and exciting, but for Fang, it was rewarding as well. Here he was finally competing in the event they had all trained so hard for. The sled team was speeding away quickly, and a few moments later, Jack was back in his own skin again, standing in the cold by the side of the trail. He looked to his right and saw Helen approaching with a huge cup of coffee in her hands.

"How's it going, Jack?" she asked. "You look a bit dazed. Are you having fun?"

"Well, that cup of coffee will keep you going for a while," he replied. "I'm just trying to take in the whole event, sweetie, but maybe I'm getting a little too carried away with it all."

Helen looked at him with a perplexed expression on her face, but then she took a big gulp of coffee and turned her head to watch another dog sled team pass by and didn't think much of it.

"Come here, sweetheart," Jack said, wrapping his arms around Helen. "I need someone to warm me up. It's cold out here."

★★★★★

They stayed until noon in Skwentna, but after grabbing lunch at the lodge, they climbed into Jack's plane and headed back to Anchorage. Jack had signed up to do three supply drops, and he needed to get the second round of supplies to the Rohn checkpoint before the lead dog sled teams arrived so he had to hurry.

En route back to Anchorage, Helen checked in with her mother to see how Shane was doing, and Jack saw her giggling on the phone as they talked.

"How's he doing?" Jack asked after she hung up.

"Oh, he's doing fine. He was asking where Momma and Daddy were. He was worried one of the fast doggies took us away, but he's quieted down. They're watching a movie together now."

Jack and Helen landed in Anchorage at 1:30 p.m. The checkpoint at Rohn was not much more than a log cabin stuck out in the middle of the forest and tundra, so Helen decided she would head back home and spend time with Shane and her mother. By four o'clock Jack was aloft again, heading for Rohn, three checkpoints out from Skwentna. Jack's third supply run to western Alaska wasn't scheduled until the following week, and for this second drop, Jack was only planning on staying until the next morning. He had several flights lined up to ferry a group of campers and whale watchers down to Kodiak Island, then to another island called

Chignik, and eventually back to Anchorage, so he was going to be quite busy over the next few days.

It was turning dark when he landed on the snow-covered runway in Rohn, and as he taxied to the end of it, he saw the log cabin with his taxi-light, located just a stone's throw from the end of the runway.

★★★★★

When he stopped his plane, the other race volunteers were waiting, and they quickly unloaded all the supplies.

"How's it going out there?" Jack asked one of them as he helped move the canned goods and dog food to the station.

"Oh, it's okay now, but it looks like a snowstorm's coming in from the west. I don't envy those mushers, especially if they get caught up in it coming through Rainy Pass."

Chapter 24

The musher was feeling more relaxed now. He had just taken his dog team through the mountainous portion of the Iditarod trail from Rainy Pass to Rohn, and so far things were working well. They were traveling at night, which wasn't recommended, but he had broken a runner on his sled early in the race and lost several hours having it repaired, so despite the risk, he decided to take Rainy Pass at night to make up for lost time.

Rainy Pass was known as one of the most treacherous trails in the race. The trail ran in the open tundra from Rainy Pass Lodge to the mouth of Pass Creek, and then it traveled northwest to the summit of Rainy Pass itself. The musher and his team of dogs had worked north and northwest up the narrow North Creek valley leading to Rainy Pass, weaving across the frozen creek and in and out of clumps of willow bushes as they steadily climbed.

It was almost ten o'clock when they reached the summit of the Rainy Pass trail, at an elevation of 3160 feet. From Rainy Pass, there were several miles of sometimes steep downhills and often tight, twisting trail through scrub willow bushes. The trail headed southwest along Pass Fork valley to another creek named Dalzell Creek. As they headed now through Pass Fork valley along a long snowfield, it began to snow. At first, it was light and easily manageable, but that didn't last for long. It started snowing harder and harder, and along with it, the wind picked up and the temperature dropped. Within twenty minutes, they were traveling in a blizzard.

The musher could barely see the dogs ahead of him and the ground was not visible, but he kept his eye on the side of the trail looking for Iditarod trail stakes, and more importantly, six-foot-high wooden tripods spaced every few hundred yards or so. The blizzard was coming down so hard now that he was even missing those, and the wind whipping in his face and sending chills down his back didn't help either. He wanted to stop, but stopping in those conditions would be more miserable than continuing and the dogs seemed to be handling it well. He knew he wasn't far from Dalzell Gorge now and the infamous "Watch Your Ass" sign, warning the mushers of an imminent two-hundred-foot steep hill down into the Dalzell Gorge, but at this point, the trail was flat, although there were quite a few curves to negotiate.

The musher only had four hours of sleep the night before so he was tired, but now he was also starting to get nervous. He was twisting his body and glancing backward looking for another trail stake when the Iditarod trail curved sharply to the right. Straight ahead, though, there was an old mining road, and the dogs, not knowing any better and without guidance from their musher, took it. As they passed the Y in the trails that separated the mining road from the Iditarod route, the musher caught a trail curving sharply to his right in his peripheral vision, but it didn't seem right so he proceeded straight ahead. Visibility was approaching total whiteout conditions, but he could still see the dogs' tails moving as they ran down the trail. It seemed to be easy running for the dogs; the trail was straight and wider than usual, so the musher kept going. He kept looking for the stakes, but several minutes and a quarter mile later, he still hadn't seen any. He wasn't sure if he was just missing them, or maybe now that the trail was straight, there were fewer markers placed along the trail.

He was still searching, telling himself it was time to stop, when the dogs came up on a sharp bend in the road. The two lead dogs pulled up, but it was too late; the other dogs kept running and accordioned into them, sending the team over the end of the bridge and into the dry riverbed below. The miners had built a wooden bridge over the riverbed years earlier, but now the only thing left of the bridge were the rotted wooden beams that extended only a small part of the way across the river; the rest of the bridge had collapsed years earlier. The dogs starting yelping as they fell down the steep drop, and the musher knew something was wrong, but the sled was already moving around the bend. He tried to stop, but it was too late. The musher was tossed violently to the left, and the sled fell on its side before being flung over the edge of the gully to the dry riverbed below.

The musher yelled out, "Holy crap!" as the sled tumbled down and he was thrown off of it. He stretched out his hands to try and break his fall, but as his hand hit the snow, he felt something snap in his left arm. He screamed in pain, but worse, he couldn't use his arm effectively to break his fall. His head hit the snow with a thud, knocking him unconscious. The dogs did their best to scramble down the fifteen-foot drop, barking and growling as they rolled on top of one another in a mangled mess of legs and snarling teeth. The lead dogs took the brunt of the fall. The dogs behind them fell on top of them and one another, cushioning the impact. One of the lead dogs took a hard hit as he smashed into the riverbed, breaking his left foot, but the dog to his right was thrown into him, cushioning the impact. The right-side lead dog hit the snow hard, but he rolled and scrambled, only sustaining some scratches and bruises.

For several seconds, the dogs snarled and barked at one another once they had stopped tumbling. They were angry and confused, not knowing what had just happened, but they settled down after a little while. Once they got beyond the initial shock of tumbling into the gully and were stationary, they started checking up on one another. One dog would whine and rub his nose into the dog next to him, and the other would respond in kind. In this way, the nine dogs there were accounted for, and they all appeared to be okay, except the lead dog who broke his foot. He lay in the snow flat on his stomach, groaning and licking his foot, unable to move.

The snow was still falling hard, but the gully protected them from the whipping wind. They were all still tied into the sled, and the other lead dog walked slowly over to the musher, who lay still a few feet from them. He whined and moaned and rubbed his nose into the musher's side, but there was no response. A few of the other dogs gathered round and did the same, but the musher did not move. One dog even grabbed the musher's arm with his teeth and pulled, but the musher was stone-cold out. They all looked up and stared at one another confused, not sure what to do next. They had mushed all day and were tired, and the temperature was twenty below zero and they were starting to get cold. They gathered between the dog with the broken foot and the musher and snuggled up to each other as best they could to stay warm. There was a dog on either side of the injured dog curled up next to him, and the rest lay side by side curled up against one another, with the last two resting up against the musher's side.

★★★★★

After all the supplies had been unloaded from his plane, Jack walked over to the checkpoint station in Rohn and watched a few of the dog teams come in after introducing himself to the race officials and volunteers there. They were out in the middle of nowhere. It was a heavily wooded area, and there was just the single log cabin sitting there in a small cleared area. The teams were visible for only a minute before they arrived, as they rounded a curve in the woods before a short straight run leading up to the station.

Jack had only been there for thirty minutes when the storm came in from the west, and it came quickly. The night sky was clear and the stars were brilliant, and then ten minutes later, Jack was standing in a heavy snowstorm, with winds approaching forty miles an hour. Jack walked up to the small group of race officials, who were now huddled up next to the log cabin door trying to stay warm.

"Well, it looks like I'll be staying here tonight. Don't mind if I crash here, do you?" Jack asked one of them.

"Of course not," one of the men who had helped him unload replied. "They aren't the most beautiful accommodations, but what do you expect being out here in the wilderness? There's some hammocks strung up in the back, but if you prefer, the floor works pretty well."

"Mind giving me a hand getting my plane tied down?" Jack replied. "This wind's getting pretty strong."

"Sure thing."

Jack stayed up late helping the other volunteers as the mushers came in. When the sleds came in, the mushers would check in at the station first, then find their dog food and start feeding the dogs. The mushers were tired, that was obvious, but per the Iditarod rules, they were not allowed to receive help feeding the dogs. Jack did help to clean up the area after feedings. The dogs were exhausted and swallowed the food as quickly as the mushers could pour it out of the bag. They were tremendous animals, wild yes, but well trained as well, and after they got their stomachs full, they laid down for as long as their musher would let them to get some rest. Jack counted eight teams who came in that night, and because of the conditions, most of the teams stopped for the night to get some rest; a few braved the conditions and continued. The next leg was mainly flat terrain and easy running, at least at the beginning, so a few took the risk, expecting to run out of the storm as they headed farther west. Jack stayed up until almost eleven o'clock, but it had been almost an hour since he had seen a dog team, so he decided to get some sleep.

"I doubt we'll see any more teams tonight," one of the race officials told him as he walked inside the log cabin. "These teams have to take three mandatory stops during the course of the race, one twenty-four-hour layover, one eight-hour layover to be taken along the Yukon River, and one eight-hour layover at White Mountain. If the mushers behind these lead folks have any sense, they'll be taking their Yukon River stop before Rainy Pass; it would be a nightmare trying to travel in these conditions between Rainy Pass and here."

The log cabin was larger inside than Jack expected and was kept warm with a wood fire. He picked out one of the hammocks and tried to get some sleep. He tossed and turned for half an hour before finally dozing off, but he didn't sleep well. His mind was anxious, and he woke up several times in a cold sweat. At one point, he woke up frightened, and after that, all he could do was lie in the hammock and stare at the wooden ceiling for what seemed like hours. He finally fell asleep, but was awakened again abruptly with the image of a howling wolf screaming in his brain. It was impossible to sleep now, so he got up, put on his coat, and walked outside.

There were a few race officials gathered at the door in conversation, and the seriousness on their faces showed their concern. One man was on the phone as the snow continued to fall.

"You sure they checked out of Rainy Pass? We haven't seen them yet," he said to the person on the other end of the line. "Seven o'clock last night, well, okay, and you're sure of that?"

Jack could hear the raised voice coming through the receiver.

"Well, okay, okay," the man replied. "You don't need to get upset. We just need to get all our facts straight. That was over nine hours ago. They should have been here by now. Just be sure to let us know if you find out anything, and we'll do the same. There's not much we can do about it now; we're just going to have to sit tight until this storm blows over."

"What's going on?" Jack asked the woman standing closest to him.

"One of the sled teams appears to have gone missing," she replied. "They left Rainy Pass before the storm hit, but no one has seen or heard from them since. Rainy Pass to here can be done in usually three to five hours, maybe six at a leisurely pace—it's been too long."

"Well, that's not good," Jack replied. "Do you think the musher stopped on purpose?"

"Possible, but doubtful. To stop in this would be horrible on the dogs, and the musher as well, being this cold and windy. These guys who get caught in a storm usually just slow it down but keep going and bear it out to the next checkpoint, but who knows? Maybe they got attached by a pack of wolves—we just don't know."

Once the man hung up the phone, the woman asked him, "What was the number again, Doug, the number of the race team?"

"It's race team 11," Doug replied. "God, I hope they're all right. Some of these high-dollar teams carry a GPS tracker nowadays, but this guy was a family operation on a shoestring budget. He doesn't have anything like that. If he doesn't show up by daybreak, we're going to send out a search party, but it's fifty miles between here and Rainy Pass. That's a lot of ground to cover. Sometimes the other mushers will pick these guys up and call for help, but if he went off route, well, then he's screwed."

Jack stepped back next to the door. *Race team 11,* he thought to himself, *isn't that the team I saw leaving Skwentna, the one with that wonderfully beautiful lead dog? Yes, they were the ones, race team 11; I remember seeing the musher's number on his chest as he approached.*

Jack closed his eyes and concentrated, whispering, "Where are you?" under his breath. He stood there, focusing his thoughts for several minutes, hoping to make a connection. Nothing appeared in his mind, and he opened his eyes. When he did, he saw one of the sled dogs from another team lying on the hay-covered snow outside the cabin, his eyes riveted on Jack.

"Not you, my friend," Jack whispered. Then he closed his eyes again and focused. "Where are you, Fang?" he said out loud.

After several seconds, his mind cleared, and he was there. Fang was scared and confused, not sure what to do. He was scratched and bruised but was thankful he hadn't broken his foot, unlike the other lead dog next to him, who was now unable to walk. The team had slept uneasily in the river gully, trying to stay out of the wind, but the howling wolves nearby disturbed their sleep. They didn't want to leave their musher, and they were waiting there, hoping he would come alive and lead them out of the riverbed and back to the safety of the trail. *The musher must have taken a hard hit to his head,* Jack thought. *Fang hasn't seen him move since the accident.*

Jack held on to Fang's mind as long as he could to try and get a better understanding of their location, but the storm was so strong, Fang himself didn't have any idea where they were. The only thing Jack could make out was that they had been on the trail for quite some time before the storm hit.

There's no way I'm going to be able to locate them, Jack thought to himself. *But maybe there's another way, if I could just …*

Jack held his breath, put his fingers to his temples, and concentrated, trying to communicate with Fang. The dogs were still tied into the sled with heavy-duty nylon rope.

Not easy to chew through, Jack thought to himself, *but for a dog with razor-sharp teeth, it's definitely possible.*

He's not going to wake up, not for a while, Jack tried to tell Fang. *You need to chew through the rope tying you into the sled. Backtrack to the sled trail, then find your way here. I'll be waiting for you.*

Jack kept repeating these thoughts, hoping the dog would somehow make sense of them. As he started to lose hold of Fang's mind, he could see the dog beginning to chew through the rope.

It might just work, Jack thought as the images of those dogs and the musher faded from view. *I just hope he can find his way here.*

★★★★★

It took Fang the best part of thirty minutes to chew through the two ropes tying him in, and as he broke free and ran down the riverbed gully, the other dogs started barking and howling loudly. The ruckus didn't stop Fang; he knew what he needed to do. He ran down the gully for several hundred yards until he found a spot shallow enough to get out. He made a jump for the ledge and scrabbled his way up onto level ground. He backtracked through the deep snow and ran past the other dogs, who were still barking loudly, then headed back down the mining road until he got to the Y where the mining road and sled trail intersected. When he got there, he hesitated, but remnants of Jack's entanglement were still there in his mind: he turned left and headed down the trail in the direction of Rohn. A few minutes later, he picked up the scent of the previous sled teams, and he went into a full-fledged sprint.

★★★★★

It was just starting to turn light in Rohn an hour later, and even though the snow was still falling heavily, the race officials and volunteers were gathering to discuss how they would organize a search party. There was just one snowmobile, so it wasn't going to be easy. Jack stood there on the edge of the group, listening but also scanning the landscape where the mushers had appeared the previous night, hoping he would see Fang coming through the falling snow.

Doug, the man who had been on the phone the previous night, and the woman Jack had talked to were just getting on the snowmobile when Fang appeared.

"Wait, wait!" Jack yelled out just before they were about to leave. "Look, do you see him?"

The others turned to him and then shifted their gaze in the direction he was pointing. Fang was running at a full sprint, with his harness still attached, and he was dragging his two tie-in ropes behind him. As Fang got closer, Jack stepped out into the open clearing in front of the log cabin. Fang's eyes were fixed on Jack; he was totally oblivious to the other people there and the other dogs who were resting by the side of the cabin. He was approaching Jack at full speed, but once he got a few steps away, he slowed down. Then he jumped up on his hind legs and threw his front legs onto Jack's chest, barking and playfully jumping up and down as he did.

"Fang, my wonderful friend," Jack said as tried to keep his balance before wrapping his arms around Fang's wiry frame. "You made it, my dear friend, you made it. You're a champion; you're a king. I knew you'd find me."

Fang was excited to see Jack, and he kept his front legs on Jack's midsection and looked up at him, barking happily.

"My dear friend, we're so happy to see you!" Jack replied as he petted Fang's coat. "We're all so happy to see you!"

Eventually Fang jumped down and put his front paws back on the snow, but he kept barking and rubbing his fur against Jack's legs as Jack stroked his back.

"Well, Jack," Doug said, "it looks like you've made a new friend."

"That I have, that I have," Jack replied, smiling.

"You see," he said back to Fang, "it's not just me; we're all so happy to see you, you wonderful doggie."

"Well, it looks like we may have found someone who can lead us back to that sled team," Doug said, winking.

"Well, what are we waiting for?" Vicki, the woman sitting behind him, replied.

"Go on, Fang," Jack said to the dog. "Can you lead them back to your team? It sure was cold last night, and I'm sure they're in need of some help. Go on in front of the snowmobile. They're waiting for you."

Fang walked over to the snowmobile and then started to trot slowly in front of them, leading the way as the snowmobile followed. He went about thirty feet, but then he stopped and turned around. Jack was standing there looking at him, and he looked back at Jack, a sad and confused stare on his face.

"Go on, Fang," Jack yelled out. "Lead the way!" but Fang didn't go any farther. He turned around completely to face Jack, whining, barking, and jumping as he did.

"Do you mind, Vicki?" Doug said after a few moments. "I don't think this mutt is going anywhere without Jack in tow. Don't worry; I called for a couple of snowmobiles this morning. They should be here in thirty minutes or so. I'll let you know what we find out."

Vicki got off the sled, and Doug yelled out, "Come on, Jack, want to go for a ride? This Fang friend of yours isn't going to budge without you."

Jack ran up and jumped on the back of the snowmobile, and Fang started trotting quickly, looking back periodically to make sure they were close behind. The snow was steady, but luckily the windstorm had died down and they didn't have any problem staying up with Fang even as he quickened his pace. After an hour and a half, they were there at the Y in the trail where the mining road intersected the Iditarod trail.

As Fang turned to his right to head down the mining road, Doug said, "Well, this is odd. I sure hope this Fang of yours knows what he's doing, Jack."

"Just stay close," Jack replied, "I have faith he'll lead us there. There must be a reason he headed off course."

They headed down the mining road for a quarter mile until Fang stopped by the old abandoned bridge and looked down into the gully, barking as he did. They could both hear dogs barking back in reply.

"That must be them—let's take a look," Doug said.

They got off the snowmobile and walked to the edge of the bridge. The dogs were there barking up a storm. The sled lay several feet away on its side, and next to it lay the musher.

"That's them," Doug said. He was on his walkie-talkie immediately giving directions how to get there. "All right, when you get closer, let me know, and one of us will be waiting at the Y in the trail that takes you to this location. We're on an old mining road. There's an old collapsed bridge out here, and they've fallen into the riverbed below it."

Jack was scanning the scene, and he could see one of the dogs was injured and the musher wasn't moving. They made their way up the riverbed following Fang until they found a spot where they could slide down into the gully. Luckily the other dogs were well behaved and waited for them until they were there standing by the sled. Doug tended to the dog with the broken foot, while Jack walked over to the musher. Jack took his hand and felt for a pulse.

"He's got a pulse," he yelled out to Doug, "but I see some blood in the snow by his head. He must have taken quite a blow."

"All right, Jack," Doug replied, "let me finish wrapping up this dog's leg as best I can, and then I'll take a look."

Jack got up and tended to the other dogs, trying to keep them calm; it was clear they were happy and relieved to see them there. He walked from dog to dog, making sure they were all right, and despite looking tired and cold, they appeared to be in reasonable shape.

Once Doug finished with the dog, he said, "Well, that should keep his leg set until we can get him to a vet. He busted it up pretty bad, but I don't think he's been trying to walk or run on it since the wreck, which is a good thing."

Doug rummaged through the backpack he had brought with him.

"Well, let me see, I know I have some smelling salts in here. Let's see if we can wake up this musher friend of ours. He's not going to like it, but it might do the trick."

He and Jack knelt next to the musher, and Doug gently felt the man's back, legs, and arms.

"I'm a bit of a doctor of sorts," Doug said. "Learned quite a lot during my medical emergency training. He's busted up his arm quite badly, but at least it doesn't appear he's hurt his back or legs. Let's see what these smelling salts will do."

He put the smelling salts under the man's nose, moving the salt back and forth. At first, the musher didn't respond, but after several tries, they could see his head move. The musher brought his good arm up toward his face and swatted at the salts, like he was swatting at a fly.

"Well, there you go, my friend," Doug said. "You've been asleep for quite some time now. You'll freeze to death out here if you don't get up."

The musher groaned and muttered something incomprehensible, but he did start moving his arms and legs.

"Be careful; you've busted up your arm quite badly. It's probably numb from the cold, but don't make it any worse," Doug said, putting his hand gently on the man's shoulder. "Are you okay to roll over? We can work on your arm better that way."

The musher groaned again and lifted his head, then set it back down, but he did take his good arm and tried to lift himself off the ground before collapsing back on the snow. He moved his body until he was in a curled position, with his head still facing down.

"You took a bad bump to your head, but we need for you to roll over so we can see how bad it is and dress it," Doug said. "Are you okay to turn over?"

The musher groaned again, but moved his head up and down in response.

Jack and Doug grabbed the musher's good arm and torso and gingerly turned him over. There was blood all over his face and a huge bruise and cut on his left forehead.

Doug took his broken arm and steadied it. "We're going to take your coat off so we can wrap up your arm, okay?" Doug said, and the musher moved his head up and down in response.

Jack gently removed the musher's thick coat and then laid it back down on top of the musher as Doug went to work on his arm.

Before they had left, Jack had grabbed an open bag of dog food one of the mushers had left, so he went back to the snowmobile and got it, then spread it in the snow for the dogs. They were amazingly well behaved, Jack noticed, as they ate up the little food that was there, each getting a mouthful but sharing what was there so every dog ate something. *This musher must have done a first-rate job of training these dogs,* Jack thought to himself.

Once they were done, Jack asked, "How's it going, Doug? Got everything set?"

"Well, as best as I can," Doug replied. "This cold doesn't make it any easier. Jack, I have some Handi Wipes in my backpack. Can you get them out and wipe some of the blood off this man's face and clean him up a bit? After that, can you head back up the mining road to where it intersects the trail? The other folks should be here in twenty minutes or so."

"Sure thing," Jack replied, and he went through the backpack until he found the Handi Wipes.

"You took a hard hit on your head," Jack said to the musher. "We're just going to clean up your face a bit."

"Can you tell me your name?" Doug asked the musher as Jack opened the bag of wipes.

"It's Joe," the young man said slowly, "Joe Lawson."

Jack hadn't looked at the young man's face in any detail, but he said under his breath, "Joe Lawson, that name sounds familiar. I remember a Joe Lawson from a few years back."

He looked at the man's face, now studying it in detail as he wiped the blood off his face and from his clothing. The man's face was more rugged and weather-beaten than Jack remembered from that day in Palmer, and he was sporting a full beard now, but the face was unmistakable. Before him sat Joe, the young man who had helped him with his glider and had driven him home after Jack's hang-gliding accident that had begun two thousand feet above that grassy field in Palmer.

"It is you, isn't it?" Jack said out loud now. "It's you, Joe. Well, isn't that amazing!"

Joe looked up at Jack and narrowed his eyes, then stammered out, "Jack, my god, it's you, Jack. I can't believe it. I didn't think I'd find you out in the middle of nowhere trying to save my ass. Pretty incredible, but how the heck did you find us?"

"Thank your dog Fang. He's the one who should take the credit. He found us; we didn't find him. Pretty resourceful dog you have there. He chewed through his sled ropes, made his way to the Rohn checkpoint, and then led us back here."

"That good dog Fang, he's a smart one, you know. How are the dogs faring in this cold? You mutts doing okay?" Joe asked, turning his head to the dogs lying several feet away.

The dogs whined and barked, and Fang got up and walked over to Joe.

Joe reached out his good hand and petted Fang as best he could, saying, "My fearless Fang, you brave old mutt. Thank you for saving our asses, you brute."

He then turned to Jack and asked, "How are the other dogs doing?"

"One of your dogs broke his front leg," Jack replied. "Doug's wrapped it up as best he could, but your dog will be out for quite some time it looks like. There should be several other snowmobiles showing up anytime now. We'll load him onto one of the snowmobiles and get him out of here."

"Where is he?" Joe replied. "My poor mutt, I'm so sorry."

Joe tried to get up on his knees, but Doug grabbed his shoulder to restrain him.

"Sit back down, Joe. You're in no state to be getting up and moving around. You took a bad hit to your head and probably have a serious concussion. Just sit tight. We'll be getting you out of here soon enough."

"Which one is he?" Joe asked Jack as he sat back down in the snow. "Which one broke his leg?"

"See him?" Jack said, pointing. "The one lying there with his head down in the snow between the other two. The one with the white fur."

"Oh my gosh," Joe replied. "That's my dear White Tail. He's not much older than a puppy, you know. I hope he's going to be okay."

"He's beat up and hurt," Doug replied, "but give him a few months to heal up, and I suspect he'll be good as new and ready to hit the dog trails again."

It was quite clear Joe was distraught and understandably so.

"Don't worry, Joe," Jack said. "I'll get him loaded into my airplane and get him back home right away. Your sled's a bit banged up, but surprisingly it doesn't look too bad. A few repairs, and it will be ready to go in no time."

"Well, okay. When I can get on the horn, I'll call my dad. He can pick him up out of Anchorage," Joe replied as he looked over his overturned sled lying just a few feet from his side.

"Well, Joe, I better get up to the trail and meet up with the others," Jack said. "We'll get you and your dogs out of here as quickly as possible. Well, what a strange coincidence to run into you, but despite the circumstances, it's great to see you again."

"Well, thanks, Jack, and you too, Doug. I can't thank you guys enough for coming out here and finding us. You guys are amazing," Joe said.

"I'm just returning the favor, Joe," Jack replied. "I'm just glad I could help."

Joe smiled back at Jack, and then lifted his hand to his head and touched his tender forehead. "Ouch, that hurts," he said. "That must have been quite a hit I took."

★★★★★

Jack took the snowmobile back up to the dog trail, and it was only fifteen minutes before the others showed up. One of the snowmobiles had a small stretcher that could be strapped to one side. Once they lifted Joe out of the ravine, he was put on the stretcher. He was suffering from frostbite in his hands and feet, and his head and arm needed a doctor's attention. Doug and Jack carefully carried White Tail out from the gully and loaded him onto the back of Doug's snowmobile. Jack sat on the back of the snowmobile steadying White Tail as Doug proceeded down the trail toward Rohn. The two riders on the third snowmobile hooked up the other dogs in front of their machine, and let the dogs lead the way behind Doug and Jack, keeping their speed matched to the pace of the dogs. They also towed Joe's sled back to the checkpoint in Rohn.

Once they arrived, a volunteer veterinarian looked over all the dogs, checked to see how they were faring, and then tended to White Tail to make sure his leg was set properly. Joe was carried inside into the log cabin and kept warm by the fire; he was told to wait there until one of the doctors stationed in McGrath arrived. Once White Tail was cleared for travel, Jack and the veterinarian loaded White Tail into Jack's plane, and all three flew back to Anchorage. When they got there, Joe's father was waiting for them at the airport.

"Well, hello, Jack, I'm Stuart, Joe's dad," he said, shaking Jack's hand. "It's so nice to meet you. Joe has talked often about you and your miraculous survival from that horrendous hang-gliding accident a few years back. You know, it wasn't until after that accident that Joe got really serious about competing in the Iditarod. I think that day inspired him somehow to take our dogs and turn them into a competitive sledding team."

"Well, I'm so happy to hear that. I'm glad some good came out of that episode, and Joe was a great help that morning, you know," Jack replied, smiling and a bit surprised Stuart knew of his accident. "It's nice to meet you as well, Stuart. This is Fred, the vet; we actually just met this morning."

Stuart and Fred shook hands, and then Jack said, "Well, shall we tend to your friend White Tail here? I think that was his first ride in a plane, and he's a little shell-shocked by it all."

They gently carried White Tail out from the back of the plane and loaded him into the flatbed of Stuart's pickup truck.

"I gave him a shot of painkillers to relieve the pain," Fred said. "If he stays off the leg for a month or so, it should heal up just fine. I'm sure it will be difficult for him to do that, but if he puts a lot of weight on it, it will break again. and then it's a crap shoot."

"I understand. They're a bit crazy, these dogs," Stuart replied, chuckling. "As soon as he sees the others hooking up, he'll go bonkers, but don't worry, I'm going to keep him penned up and away from the action until he's ready. Well, thank you two so much for helping, and don't worry, we'll take good care of him. Once he's healed up, we'll get him primed and ready for the Iditarod next year."

"Well, give our best regards to Joe when you talk to him again," Jack said. "He took quite a blow to his head, but when we left, he seemed to be doing just fine, and in fact, was pretty upbeat, all things considered."

"That's my boy Joe," Stuart replied, smiling. "He's not the type to be down for too long. He just pulls himself up by his bootstraps and gets on with business."

Chapter 25

Five days later, once Jack had made it back to Anchorage after picking up the whale-watching campers from Chignik, he gave Helen a call from the airport. They were planning to fly together to a place called White Mountain, the location of Jack's third supply run for the Iditarod, and then after a few days volunteering, they would head to Nome to watch some of the dog sled teams finish the race.

"Darling," Jack said standing next to his plane after he taxied up to the loading area, "are you ready to head to White Mountain? I'm going to get the plane loaded up and get some gas. I'm guessing I'll be ready to fly out in an hour or so. Better pack some warm gear, because it can get pretty cold up there. How's our little Shane doing?"

"Oh, he's fine. We were playing cards with Momma this morning, but he's taking a bath now. I'll tell Momma I'll be leaving in a little while. Just give me a call when you're getting close to heading out, and I'll be packed up and ready to go and be over in fifteen minutes."

They were in the air by four o'clock that afternoon, and it was just past seven when Jack set up for an approach into White Mountain, an area Helen had never visited. The atmosphere at White Mountain would be festive. The dog teams were required to have an eight-hour stop there, and it was only two checkpoints from the finish.

★★★★★

"Look at that sunset, Jack," Helen exclaimed as they came into White Mountain for a landing. "Isn't it beautiful? It's just amazing out here. I feel like a real frontierswoman, like the first settlers of this land."

"It is beautiful, especially with the way the sunlight reflects off the snow and ice. Pretty desolate, but spectacular nonetheless," Jack replied.

After dropping off the supplies at the checkpoint, they made their way to a motel, which wasn't much more than a big home converted to a guesthouse. The town was transformed from a small, remote Eskimo village along the Alaskan coastline to an Iditarod stomping ground, where dogs and mushers rested for the required eight hours before the final push into Nome. Helen and Jack stayed in White Mountain for three days volunteering. As the mushing teams came in, they helped with timing and scoring and team check-in and checkout times. The dogs were dragging now; they could see it in their eyes when they came in, so they helped to make their stay as comfortable as possible. They helped lay down fresh hay for the teams, kept the hay well stacked on the snow to give the dogs as much warmth as possible, and helped the mushers find their supplies. They also helped prepare the meals for the other volunteers and with cleanup.

On the third day, Helen and Jack did some sightseeing as well. They made it down to Golovnin Lagoon on a borrowed snowmobile for some bird-watching in the morning, and then midday headed inland to the White Mountain Recreational Area for a short hike to see the mountainous landscape north of town in an area aptly called part of the Alaskan interior.

"This place is nice," Jack said to Helen as they looked out across a river valley captured by mountains on either side. "But, you know, after being out in the wilderness for quite a few days now, I wouldn't mind just heading over to a tavern to get a nice microbrewed beer."

"I know what you mean, Jack," Helen replied. "Well, during the Iditarod, they call Nome the Mardi Gras of the North. Supposedly, the town's population grows by over a thousand people during the race, and with a population less than four thousand normally, well, I'd say it's got to be hopping. Most of the mushing teams have come through this town by now anyway; I'm looking forward to seeing what Nome is like."

*****

The next morning they flew to Nome, located on the shores of the Bering Sea, and checked into the Aurora Inn and Suites.

"Catchy name, isn't it, Helen?" Jack said, winking. "It's a good thing Henry reserved this place after the Iditarod last year; these places get filled up pretty quickly."

There were quite a few volunteers in Nome, but they checked in with the Iditarod office anyway.

"You all just have some fun," the bearded old man who organized the volunteers said to them when they showed up. "We're pretty well staffed here, it being the finish and all. It's at the checkpoints along the way we have the hardest time finding people. You two have done your part, and we can't thank you enough; just go on and have some fun in town, and don't forget the volunteer T-shirts we've made up for you all. They're stacked up in a pile on the table there. Just pick out the size you want," he said, gesturing toward a table behind them.

"The only thing we ask is if you hear the town siren hollering, come on out to the finish line and cheer the musher and dogs in. Whenever we see a team approaching town, we'll get that siren humming, so come on out. You two be sure to show up for the finisher's dinner banquet as well. It will commence once all the mushers have made it in. You don't want to miss that, and it's free for all the volunteers. We'd love to have ya. Oh, and by the way, ma'am, someone told me you wanted a pair of these—well, here you go," he said as he handed her a pair of dog booties.

"Oh my, yes, thank you. My son, Shane, would love to have a pair of these cute little booties," Helen replied, smiling. "Well, hopefully we'll see you by the finish line, and thanks again."

"Until then, I think I'm going to grab myself some nice lukewarm beer," Jack said. "What do you say, Helen?"

"Sounds like a plan to me," she replied. "I've heard the Polaris Bar is the place to be."

*****

Once at the Polaris Bar, Jack ordered some Cream Stout, while Helen had Chablis. The Polaris Bar wasn't a big place, but it was rustic and the people there were friendly and easygoing.

"In town for the Iditarod, are you?" the bartender asked as he gave them their drinks. "And you volunteered as well," he continued, seeing the volunteer T-shirts they were now wearing. "Well, good for you. The race wouldn't be here today if not for folks like you. Just splendid. Aren't those dogs just amazing beasts? We love this time of year, the beginning of spring, and what a way to get it started."

"We're having a great time," Helen replied as she sipped her wine. "The atmosphere is just so wonderful here."

They were in the bar for less than hour when they heard the siren hollering, but they both were only halfway through their second round of drinks. Jack got up and started to walk outside but realized he had a pint in his hand. He turned around to ask the bartender if he could take it with him.

"Go on, you two!" the bartender exclaimed before Jack even got a word out. "Go on and cheer those beautiful beasts in. Just come back when you're done and tell us some stories."

Several other people got up and walked outside as well, drinks in hand. It was a short walk to the finish line, and over the next ten minutes a festive crowd gathered. Jack and Helen stood a few yards from the finish line by the snow-covered road. As the dogs and a musher approached, one man yelled out, "Cheers to the mutts!" The people nearby laughed, and then those with drinks raised their glasses as most of the others gathered waved to the musher as he approached.

Once the team crossed the line, the crowd gathered around them as the race officials checked the musher in and corralled the dogs. There was also a short photograph session for the musher and his dogs. People were cheering and hollering, and the musher took great joy in waving to friends he saw and telling them a few war stories about his race. Once things calmed down and the crowd began to dissipate, the musher and dogs were led off to the holding area for the teams. There were several large shipping crates lying in the snow, with chain hung between the crates. The dogs were clipped to the chain with leashes, and then several volunteers brought out some open dog kennels with hay in the bottom for the dogs to lie down in and stay warm. As Helen and Jack walked back to the bar, Jack counted at least fifty dogs waiting there ready to be shipped out.

"They'll load the dogs into those big shipping crates," Jack told Helen. "Then they'll load those big crates on an Alaska Air 737 and fly them all back to Anchorage. Neat operation—they've got it down pretty well, don't they?"

At the bar again, Jack and Helen ordered some dinner and then took up a game of darts after ordering another round of drinks. The bar was quite crowded now as the Iditarod visitors made their way out on the town. It was after their meal of Bering Sea salmon with a side order of hush puppies that the horn rang out again. The sun had set, and it was starting to turn colder now. Jack and Helen had had their fill of food and drinks, so they decided they would head back to the hotel after seeing the musher and dog team come in. They both threw on their coats and made their way to the finish line. As they walked, more and more people gathered until there was quite a crowd waiting for the musher to arrive.

"This musher is going to receive the red lantern," Jack heard one of the race officials say.

Jack was curious and asked Helen, "The red lantern, what's that all about?"

"I really don't know, Jack. Why don't you ask him yourself? He looks like a friendly old chap," Helen replied.

"Excuse me," Jack said, walking up to the race official, "what's that all about, the red lantern?"

"Well, this must be your first Iditarod," the old man chuckled. "The red lantern is given to the last musher who crosses the finish line, so the lantern officially marks the end of the race. All the other sled teams have been accounted for, including all those who have dropped out and those who have already crossed the line. Many take it as quite the honor to officially close out this grand event each year."

"I see, well, neat," Jack replied. "Good for them. We'll find out who it is in a few moments, won't we?"

Jack and Helen stood there at the finish line waiting for the sled team to approach. Jack counted seven dogs pulling the musher, just one more than the minimum needed to finish the race. People were clapping and waving as the musher made it over the line, but oddly all the musher could do was move his head up and down in response. One hand remained on the rail of the sled, and it looked like the musher's other arm was against his side inside his coat as the empty arm of the coat dangled aimlessly. Once the musher crossed the line, one of the race officials helped corral the dogs as the musher stopped his sled and pulled his parka off his head.

"Look, Jack, do you see him? Is that your friend?" Helen said, surprised.

The musher had a bandage wrapped around his head, and as he turned around, Jack recognized his face immediately—it was Joe. He looked tired and flustered, but there was a bright smile on his face as someone helped him take off his heavy coat. Underneath, his other arm was tied in a sling. Joe's father, Stuart, was there as well, and when Joe saw him, his smile turned even brighter. He took his good arm and wrapped it around his dad as Stuart gave him a big hug.

"You did it, Joe, you did it, nine hundred miles with a broken arm and a concussion, but you did it—that was quite an amazing feat," Stuart said, proud of his son.

"I couldn't have done it without you, Dad—you're fantastic," Joe replied as Stuart helped him put on a finisher's jacket.

Jack and Helen walked up to the crowd gathered around Joe, and Jack tried to catch his attention.

Joe caught Jack waving at him, and he stretched out his good arm and they shook hands.

"Jack, my man, great to see you!" he said, smiling. "Glad you're here to see us in."

"We wouldn't have missed it for the world. We thought you'd be lying in a hospital bed about this time, but here you are. Well, fantastic. Congratulations, Joe!" Jack said, smiling.

★★★★★

The next evening at the awards banquet, Jack caught up with Joe.

"Joe, how are you doing? You been getting your fill of the prime rib? The halibut and king crab are quite tasty as well."

"Jack, great to see you again! Yeah, man, that Iditarod really took it out of me. I'm on my third helping of the halibut, and that's after a full serving of prime rib and crab. You can say I'm a bit famished."

"So how are you feeling, how's your head and your arm?" Jack asked.

"Well, you know, my arm is pretty stiff, and the cast isn't exactly comfortable, but it's okay. It actually aches a little more now that I'm off the trail. Out there, I think the cold numbs the pain, but it will heal up. My head, well, I had a bad headache for about four days after the fall, but it's finally subsiding. It was a loud roar in my head there for a while, but now it's just a cat's meow."

"If you don't mind me asking, Joe, how were you able to finish the race without being disqualified? And by the way, after seeing you after that fall, well, what you did was amazing."

"Thanks for the good words, Jack. Well, after my dad picked up White Tail in Anchorage, he flew out to Rohn to see me, and he took care of the dogs there. He also repaired my sled; he was so great. It gave me some time to heal up without having to take the dogs off the trail, but I made sure to still feed the dogs. If they had taken me to a hospital, I would have been DQ'd for sure, but I insisted I stay in Rohn. I wasn't going to budge one foot.

"I knew I had a concussion, but what's a doctor going to do to me in a hospital other than give me some painkillers and tell me to get some rest? When the doctor showed up there, he set my arm in a cast first off, and then he took a look at my head. He cleaned me up, but luckily I didn't need any stitches. I just had some bad bruising, and a few cuts and scrapes. He then had me follow his fingers and look this way and that, you know, the old cop with a drunk routine, and after that, he told me I had a bad concussion. He wanted me to go to a hospital, but I insisted I wanted to finish the race and I wouldn't go. After some hemming and hawing, he said it would probably be okay, but the race officials wouldn't release me until I had his approval. He said he would check back in a few days and see how I was faring before he would sign a release form. Well, you can imagine I was a bit upset, but at least there was a chance.

"Three days later, he comes back and checks me out and signs the release. Dad knows many of the race officials—he competed in the race himself fifteen years ago—so after some serious negotiating, they agreed I could continue on, but I had to backtrack from where I went off the trail in Rainy Pass, and my time started from there."

"How did the dogs fare through all this?" Jack asked. "Did they hold up pretty well?"

"Oh, the dogs were fantastic, especially Fang. I wouldn't have been able to finish the race without him especially. You can imagine it isn't easy guiding a pack of dogs with one arm in a cast, but he and I just connected almost like we were reading each other's thoughts. He led the dogs when I couldn't provide the guidance quickly enough, and the other dogs just followed in kind. He had an awareness I'd never quite seen in him before, and it made all the difference in the world. It was rough going in parts, especially from Unalakleet to Nome along the Bering Sea with that wind, but we finished! I'm glad it's over, but what an adventure! I just can't wait until next year."

"Well, with your spirit and positive attitude, Joe, you'll be on the podium next time around," Jack replied. "You're doing a wonderful job training those dogs. Just seeing the way they react to you and the way you all work together, well, it's quite impressive. There's a lot of love there, and I know they appreciate your care."

"Well, you know, they're not just my dogs, they're my friends, and I spend so much time with them, they're like a second family. They're great animals, just fantastic," Joe replied enthusiastically. Then he smiled and said, "Oh, we'll be back in full force next year, aiming for a victory. Do you think you and Helen will be back volunteering next time around?"

"Yeah, we'd love to come back. We've really enjoyed it. Our son, Shane, will have just turned six by then, so we might even bring him along, expose him to the wilder side of Alaska, as if it isn't wild enough. We'll see how things are going but we're planning on it."

"Well, Jack, I can't thank you enough for all your help and support, and that thank you isn't just from me, it's from all the mushers and the dogs as well. I wish there was something I could do to show my appreciation."

"No worries, Joe. We're all here enjoying ourselves and having fun. It's an adventure for all of us."

Joe didn't know what to say, but then he glanced down at Jack's quarter-full pint of beer.

"Come on, Jack, let me at least buy you a beer. Even for the volunteers, I know the bar isn't free."

"A beer, well, now you're talking," Jack replied. "I'm really quite fond of that home-brewed Nome Pale Ale. Have you tried it?"

"No, not yet, at least. Come on, I'm buying the next round," Joe said as he made his way to the bar.

Chapter 26

When Jack and Helen made it back to their home in Anchorage, Shane was waiting for them at the door.

"Mommy! Daddy!" he screamed out as Helen picked him up and wrapped her arms around him.

"Shane, my darling Shane, I missed you so much! We love you so much, so wonderful to see you!" Helen said as she warmly rocked him back and forth.

"We brought you some gifts from our trip, Shane," Jack said, patting him on the back. "So great to see you, little guy, we missed you so much."

"I missed you too," Shane said. "Did the doggies go home now?"

"Yes, they've gone home now," Jack replied, smiling. "They'll be back out next year. Look, did you see what your momma brought you? See, some dog booties. The dogs put these on their feet so they don't get too cold running through the snow."

"Like shoes people wear?" Shane asked.

"Yes, that's right. You're such a smart boy. Like shoes us humans wear to keep our feet warm," Helen replied, rocking him again.

Helen's mother was in the kitchen fixing dinner when they arrived.

"Well, hello, you two. You've finally made it back. We've been waiting for you. I'm almost finished fixing some sweet roasted chicken. Why don't you sit down and relax? Dinner will be ready in just a few minutes."

"Oh, Momma, I feel bad now. Why don't you let me help you? You must be worn out from babysitting Shane this whole time. What can I do to help?" Helen replied.

"Oh, Shane's been wonderful. We've had a great time together. I was hoping actually I could take him back to Fairbanks with me. I'm available anytime to do this again, Helen—he's a wonderful boy," Jesse replied. "Well, let me see, Helen, why don't you put out the plates and silverware, and Jack, can you get the drinks on the table?"

A few minutes later, they all sat down for a warm meal, with Shane at the head of the table in his raised child's chair.

"Well, Nome was fun, but there's nothing like some good home cooking with the family. What a wonderful way to greet us, Jesse, thanks so much," Jack said as he bit into his roasted chicken.

"How did the doggies go home?" Shane asked. "Nome is far away."

"That's right, Shane," Jack replied. "Well, what they do is load them on a big plane and fly them back here, where their owners pick them up."

"A big plane, bigger than your plane, Daddy?" Shane asked.

"Oh yes, Shaney, much bigger than my plane. That plane is so big, two hundred doggies can all ride together at the same time."

"Two hundred doggies!" Shane yelled out. "Wow, that's a lot of doggies to play with!"

They all giggled.

"That's right, Shaney, you'd be tired out trying to play with all those doggies," Jack replied.

★★★★★

After dinner, Jack and Helen gave Shane some more souvenirs from their trip.

"Here's a pair of socks," Helen said, handing him some child socks with two dogs imprinted on their side. "These are doggies Kiska and Kobuk. Aren't they cute?"

"Kiska and Kobuk," Shane repeated. "Are they brother and sister?"

"Well yes, yes, of course," Helen replied. "That's Kiska on the top, and her big brother Kobuk is below her."

"Look, Shaney, we brought you a stuffed doggie with a red harness, just like what the real dogs wear when they're pulling a sled," Jack said, handing him the stuffed animal.

"And here's a neat T-shirt," Helen said, taking the T-shirt out of its bag.

"Stand up, Shaney. Let's try this on and see if it fits you."

Shane stood up, and Helen pulled the T-shirt over his head. Shane was so excited, he ran to the hall mirror, stuffed animal in hand, to see how the T-shirt looked.

"Look, Mommy, three doggies and stars overhead!"

"That looks great on you, Shaney," Helen said, following him.

"Very nice," Jack continued. "Now you just have to name your three new friends."

Jesse was smiling in the living room watching Shane run around, so excited about his presents.

"Isn't that so neat, Helen?" she said as they walked back into the living room. "What do you say, Shaney, when someone brings you presents?"

"Thank you, Mommy and Daddy," Shane said as he gave them each a hug.

"Okay, Momma, we didn't want to leave you out," Helen finally said, grabbing something out of the closet. "I brought you some Iditarod red wine. I've been told it's quite strong and tart. I love the colorful label, and isn't that a funny saying on the bottom?"

"Goes Great With Mush," Jesse said, reading the label. "That is funny."

"And here's an Iditarod jacket and blanket," Jack said, handing them to her.

"Oh, you two, thanks so much," Jesse replied. "That's so sweet of you."

★★★★★

That evening as they got ready for bed, Jack pulled out one more present for Shane. It was a children's book, with a dog on the front cover sitting on his hind legs in the snow, being petted by a musher. A sled sat in the background, and two children were standing behind the dog smiling.

"Look, Shaney, we brought a book to read to you," Jack said as he and Helen lay in bed with Shane in between them.

"The book is called *Can Dogs Talk?*" Jack said as Helen smiled at him cutely.

"That's so thoughtful of you, Jack," Helen said, taking the book in her hands and reading the back cover. "Let's see, it says two children discover that dogs have their own way of communicating."

"Can doggies really talk, Daddy?" Shane asked. "I've never heard a doggy say hi to me."

"Well, Shaney, they can't talk like you and I talk, but they do communicate with us. When they want our attention or are mad, they bark. When they're sad, they whine. When they're happy to see you, they'll jump up on your leg and pant. When they want to sing, they'll howl."

"Yes, and when they want a doggie bone, they'll give you that sad, needy look and stare at you with big, wide-open eyes," Helen added as she handed the book back to Jack.

"Yes, that's right," Jack continued. "Do you see, Shaney, they can't talk to us the way I talk to you, but they can communicate with us in their own special way."

"But do they talk to each other, Daddy?" Shane asked. "Maybe they have a doggie talk we don't understand."

"Well, that's a very good point, Shaney," Jack replied as Helen nodded her head in agreement. "That's a very good point. Well, why don't we read the book, and hopefully we'll find out. What do you say, Shaney?"

"Yes, Daddy, let's read the book," Shaney replied, excited. "Maybe we can learn the doggie talk."

"Well, let's see," Jack said, turning to the first page of the book. "One bright, crisp spring day, two children, Mary and Bella, were playing in the snow in their front yard with their dog Bakila. They were having so much fun playing in the snow …"

Chapter 27

J ack, Helen, and Shane really enjoyed the spring and summer of that year. Shane was reaching the age now where he was beginning to think independently, but at the same time had that youthful exuberance that made it so fun for Jack and Helen. Being an only boy, he found real pleasure playing with his parents in place of siblings, and Jack and Helen did their best to keep up with him.

During that spring and summer, Jack never exercised his telepathic abilities. They were there, no doubt, but Jack was finding it more difficult to use them. It wasn't so much that he didn't want to explore what was out there; it was more that he didn't want to deal with the complexities of the human brain. There were so many depths to the human mind that Jack found it difficult to handle all those depths, and this was part of the reason he limited his entanglement. That complexity stayed with him like a thousand voices speaking in his ear. It was especially intense at night, when he found himself alone and unoccupied. He would lie there, and hundreds of emotions, thoughts, and images would flash through his mind, like a running picture of peoples' lives traveling through his brain. He couldn't handle it, or at least he didn't want to.

He had an exceptionally intense episode one summer night when Helen and Shane had left for the weekend to visit Helen's parents. Jack stayed behind since he had a charter flight scheduled for that Sunday. He couldn't sleep, the images were so vivid, and try as he might, he couldn't force them out of his mind. It was like he was at a party, but people kept interrupting and stumbling over each other vying for his attention, until the only thing he wanted to do was leave them all. That night he got up and sat on the back porch looking at the stars and the greenish haze of a dim aurora on the edge of the night sky. He realized then as he sat on the porch that the most enjoyable thoughts and actions he had shared were with the eagle and the dog and even the tree. Their lives were simpler, less complicated than humans', and as a result, their behavior was more direct and understandable, making it more fun and enjoyable to entangle with them. With humans, Jack always felt like he had to help solve a problem, help give direction in someone else's life. That happy-go-lucky, carefree mentality, so evident with the eagle, was buried so far down in the human psyche that he found it unreachable. He loved the people whom he surrounded himself with, no doubt about that, but he couldn't live their lives any longer, and he didn't want to deal with all the complex layers of the human brain that they carried with them.

★★★★★

There was that time, though, in the early fall of that year. It was a beautiful Saturday afternoon, and Jack, Helen, and Shane spent the day outside enjoying the lovely weather. They had gone to a local park and packed a lunch. While Helen and Jack enjoyed their lunch sitting on a blanket in the grass, Shane played on the park swing and jungle gym with the other children.

"Come on, Shaney," Helen yelled out to him when he was starting to slow down, "come and have some lunch. We've got turkey sandwiches and chips, and I even brought some cupcakes."

After a few minutes, Shane came running over, and they all enjoyed their lunch together as a family.

"Well, you sure have lots of energy, don't you?" Jack said to Shane as he woofed down his cupcake.

They stayed at the park until three o'clock and then headed home, but Shane still wanted to play.

"Come on, Momma, can we play tag? Or hide-and-seek? I want to play some more," Shane said to his mother as she and Jack relaxed on the back patio.

"Oh, Shaney, you're not tired yet?" Helen replied. "You've been playing all day."

"Come on, Momma," Shane said, grabbing her hand. "Let's play!"

"Well, okay," Helen finally said, getting up slowly, but then she stuck out her hand, tagged Shane on the shoulder, and yelled, "You're it!"

Helen scurried away as fast as she could, luckily catching Shane off guard. She ran into the grassy field behind the house as Shane chased after her.

"I'm gonna get you, Momma!" he screamed, giggling as the words flowed out of his mouth.

Jack sat in his chair watching the two play, smiling, thinking they were so cute together.

Helen turned this way and that, but when she slipped and fell to one knee, Shane got her.

"You're it, Momma!" Shane said, laughing as he tagged her, and then he ran away quickly.

Helen stayed there for a few moments, still on one knee, and when Shane realized she wasn't chasing him, he stopped and turned around.

Just at that moment, Helen popped up and yelled, "I'm gonna get you, Shaney!" Then she ran after him.

Shane let out a big scream and smiled as he ran around the backyard with Helen on his tail. He was quickly dodging this way and that, and Helen couldn't keep up.

Helen yelled back to Jack, "Jack! Come on, I need some help!"

Jack laughed and yelled back, "You're doing great, Helen. You just need to pick it up. Shaney's a fast one!"

Shane made a loop in the backyard and came running back by Jack, a giddy smile on his face, and it made Jack smile as well. Helen came by a few seconds later, but Shane had pulled out a bit of lead. As Shane turned and made his way back into the field behind the house, Jack's smile became even broader, and then he closed his eyes and concentrated. A moment later, there was Jack running with Shaney, with all the joy and innocence and giddy exuberance of a five-year-old boy as his mother chased after him.

THE END

CPSIA information can be obtained
at www.ICGtesting.com
Printed in the USA
BVHW072321071021
618414BV00003B/12